Madness. In the lonely passage of time between shifts, he sometimes wondered. There might be a tinge of madness to his actions. Then again, madness is what those with limited imaginations called inspiration, imagination, and even revelation.

He knew first hand of places where doctrine had taken firm hold, where free thinkers and visionaries were abhorred. But without revelation, civilization's zenith would yet hunker in caves, drawing stick figures by firelight.

True, some prophets walked too close to the line separating inspiration from crazed imprecation. But the ones remembered as paradigm-changers and world-savers far after the fact were derided by their contemporaries. And though they sometimes faltered and fell, others in their wake benefited from the sacrifice.

And it is horrifying.

FORGOTTEN REALMS®

THE DUNGEONS

DEPTHS OF MADNESS
Erik Scott de Bie

THE HOWLING DELVE
Jaleigh Johnson

STARDEEP
Bruce R. Cordell

CRYPT OF THE MOANING DIAMOND
Rosemary Jones

December 2007

FORGOTTEN REALMS®

THE DUNGEONS

STARDEEP

Bruce R. Cordell

Wizards of the Coast®

The Dungeons
STARDEEP

Printed in the U.S.A.

Cover art by E.M. Gist
First Printing: November 2007

9 8 7 6 5 4 3 2 1

ISBN: 978-0-7869-4338-8
620-95984740-001-EN

U.S., CANADA,
ASIA, PACIFIC, & LATIN AMERICA
Wizards of the Coast, Inc.
P.O. Box 707
Renton, WA 98057-0707
+1-800-324-6496

EUROPEAN HEADQUARTERS
Hasbro UK Ltd
Caswell Way
Newport, Gwent NP9 0YH
GREAT BRITAIN
Save this address for your records.

Visit our web site at www.wizards.com

Dedication

For Dee

Acknowledgments

Thank you Rob Heinsoo, Susan Morris, and John Staab for your superb advice, exemplary direction, and martial instruction.

Chapter One

Stardeep, Throat
Midwinter, 1375 DR

The Traitor lunged against his millennial bonds. Ethereal fires burned him, esoteric wards caught him, and synaptic blights stung him. His struggles availed him nothing but pain—but never enough pain to stop his heart. No, he transcended mortal weaknesses, including vulnerability to simple wounds, and even the need for food and water. His inability to perish due to neglect worked against him now.

Eldritch shackles allowed the prisoner to gesticulate, scream, and curse the black heart out of a demon, but only once during his long confinement had they failed to hold his physical form. He had nearly accomplished his life's goal in that instant. He had almost roused the old ones who slept away the ages.

But his wardens corralled him soon enough to thwart his catastrophic intention. His breakout was too short-lived for him to fulfill the ghastly deed that consumed his every thought. The Sovereignty. . . .

After his near success, the Traitor's chains were replaced with manacles of magic guaranteed unbreakable. He was sealed away once more in the hollow Well beneath a shimmering layer of warding sorcery.

For all the prisoner's frenzied writhing and threats of apocalypse, only light escaped the containment, harsh and exuberant with hate. It danced up the sheer sides of the Well. Colors bloomed into elaborate designs on the Well's circular interior. Now and then, violent prominences escaped the translucent, fiery barrier, illuminating the shaft for moments of stark clarity. The crash as of breakers on the beach murmured constantly up and down the shaft.

The boundary layer at the bottom of the Well, for all its agitation and turbulence, remained inviolate.

Which meant the Traitor remained secure, reflected Delphe.

"All's well in the Well," she said aloud, her daily litany. Since she'd initiated the verbal routine, the prisoner had made no credible escape attempts.

She shook her head at such foolishness. Speaking aloud those few syllables each and every day was fallacy, she recognized, yet she indulged in it all the same. What of it? Of course, she'd never admit the silly ritual to her fellow Keepers, Telarian or Cynosure. They wouldn't grasp the humor in her few mumbled words, but instead would see them as a waste of mindspace, each for their own reasons. Telarian was too humorless, Cynosure too unimaginative.

Then again, you couldn't argue with success. She smiled. The few words she daily spoke were a comfort, a comfort built by habit.

From her crystalline chair poised over the Well's lip, Delphe saw at least three, but perhaps as many as seven different protective wards and guardian impulses sleeting through the ectoplasmic barrier layer at the Well's bottommost depth. The intensity and color of the images varied from day to day, and even from moment to moment, but all were within parameters she was trained to recognize.

Two vertical lines creased Delphe's brow. On closer examination of the barrier, she noticed that a particular orange hue of the prominences spiking up from below was . . . unfamiliar.

Thankfully, Delphe had tools more potent than even her own arcane competency.

"Cynosure," she said, "what am I looking at right now? Is it new?"

A thin, cultured voice answered Delphe. "Not new, but perhaps a mixture novel to your experience."

The voice emerged from a ten-foot-tall humanoid forged of stone, iron, and crystal. The figure's stiff back was sealed to the ceiling above the Well, allowing it to stare unblinking into the containment fires. In all the years Delphe had served as Keeper, this particular homunculus of the many that composed Cynosure had never moved.

"Explain," said Delphe.

"Of course," Cynosure replied.

In truth, Cynosure's voice emanated from a circular crimson disc in the ceiling from which the figure hung. It was merely easier for Delphe to imagine the voice issuing from the stone figure instead of the ceiling. The voice continued. "Notice the glyphs at the edges?"

"All the time."

"They signify the containment layer is in good balance. They are potent restraining strictures, residue of the first delving," described the voice.

"Yes, of course. I was referring to the orange prominences."

"Certainly. I am providing background, so you'll understand what I say next."

Delphe smiled. Hard to take offense with the simulated entity. Cynosure's mind wasn't confined only to the figure above, like a construct or golem. In fact, Delphe doubted Cynosure wasted any but a fraction of its precious sentience occupying the statue. After all, its arcane awareness stretched insubstantially between dozens of other effigies and red circular nodes scattered throughout the halls, tunnels, and galleries of Stardeep. Cynosure, a sentient construct with multiple awarenesses, was the perfect warden of the dungeon stronghold where the Traitor served his eternal sentence.

Cynosure continued. "What you probably can't perceive, though I can, are wards swarming up from below the barrier interface. My wider, psi-assisted perception reveals these wards as yellowish sigils, teeming like fish. Simple mixing with the red—"

"Creates an orange hue? Are you serious?"

The shapes and colors visible upon and within the barrier were merely visual representations of a protective magical weave. Previous generations of Keepers had laid down disparate layers of security, all of them potent, though not all necessarily compatible. Still, instability of the barrier or activity on the Traitor's part would be visually detectable. So was it feasible for Cynosure to describe the activity in terms of mixing colors from the color wheel? She was a wizard of no little repute, and one trained specially in understanding the intricacies of the Well. If the . . .

She paused.

The runic entity had a ponderous, but definite sense of humor, Delphe knew from past experience. A few years earlier it had insisted a singing chicken was assaulting the Causeway Gate humming the ballad *King of Stars*, and seemed to draw immense glee with each pronouncement of the patently ridiculous statement. Was it joking now? The mental construct forged when Stardeep was first delved had evolved many personality-like traits since its creation, if the oldest records in the annals could be trusted.

"Are you having me on?"

"Sorry, Delphe." The voice relayed mischievousness.

"Do you think the Well is something that can safely be joked about?" Heat flushed her cheeks. Truth to tell, she was still slightly miffed by the chicken-on-the-Causeway incident.

"No, no! I merely implied the activity is not worth worrying about," insisted the construct. "Were it a true problem, making light of it would be my very last strategy."

She rubbed her chin, the lights thrown up from the Well giving her face a pumpkin glow. "Very well. Please keep an eye on it, will you?"

"What else would occupy me?"

Delphe sighed then finally chuckled. She shifted back in her seat. In some ways, her presence in the Well's Throat, or the presence of any living Keeper, seemed silly when compared to the resources Cynosure could bring to bear, both for watchful perception and raw physical power. Cynosure's mind and abilities were magnified—it was more than the sum of several constructs and nodes that shared the same consciousness, despite each being in a separate location around the stronghold. But the flexibility of a living Keeper had proven necessary, too. Elf Keepers were able to stem problems that a construct, no matter how advanced, was simply too constrained to deal with, even one as sophisticated and evolved as Cynosure.

Take the incident a little over a decade ago. Delphe frowned at the memory. It had happened before her service. Stardeep had been staffed by different Sildëyuiren elves, each a Keeper of the Cerulean Sign, just like she and Telarian who served in their place. The Traitor had made a particularly ingenious bid for escape, and partially bypassed the barrier layer! The imprints of the Traitor's hands on the lower portion of the smooth cylinder yet remained. Only early detection of the bid, hard planning by those earliest Keepers, and the ultimate sacrifice of one of them maintained the integrity of the Well.

In this age, Stardeep was optimally staffed with at least two Keepers, plus a contingent of Empyrean Knights who guarded Stardeep's Outer Bastion. But the life of a Keeper, or a Knight for that matter, was a life of lonely compromise. Especially in isolated Stardeep, separated from the greater Sildëyuiren realm by miles of perilous tunnels, and even from the daylight world of Faerûn by a mystical Causeway that opened only at irregular intervals. And then, only if Cynosure wasn't commanded to close it altogether.

She sighed.

"Do you require something?"

"No, Cynosure, thank you." As she spoke, she fingered the amulet on her chest, on which was emblazoned the Sign itself—a white, drooping, leafless tree on a background of sky blue. It was a potent symbol against the elder aberrations the Traitor served. The Sign's very lines, in their geometric perfection that extended beyond the mere physical, was anathema to aberrations. Or so the traditions of her order decreed.

The lore of the Keepers was nearly extinct in the outer world, and even in Sildëyuir, a realm hidden from other races, most star elves would be hard pressed to describe the hidden order's charter. And that only if they knew of the Keepers of the Cerulean Sign at all.

How many even in Sildëyuir recalled their own history, the rise of the Traitor, and the delving of Stardeep? How many understood that killing the Traitor for his attempted crime, or allowing him to kill himself, was tantamount to letting him complete his mad ritual of summoning? Few indeed. And those elf lore-keepers who bothered to study the Keepers of the Cerulean Sign often dismissed the group as an outdated and tired organization, its day long over, its relevance to the destinies of Sildëyuir and Faerûn concluded.

Delphe did not hold that view. She was one of a small group drawn to the promise and duty of the Cerulean Sign.

She was a member of the order and had achieved its highest rank: Keeper. She was one of only a handful.

Delphe wished it were otherwise. Merely because safety had been preserved for generations didn't mean the cause was any less important, or that the need for competent members trained to vigilance was any less critical. Thus, one of the secondary functions of membership in the order was the dissemination of knowledge. She and her followers were charged to preserve the knowledge of the Cerulean Sign and keep it alive.

And beyond that, she and Telarian were chosen for a specific mission in defense of the Sign. Delphe and Telarian resided within and held command over the dungeon complex of Stardeep.

Delphe's responsibility was the Inner Bastion, which included the Well itself. The Empyrean Knights answered to her fellow Keeper, Telarian, who oversaw the defenses of the Outer Bastion and lesser subterranean dungeon tunnels, where criminals of ancient days potentially lingered. Between them and accepted as one of them was Cynosure, whose awareness bridged the Inner and Outer Bastions of Stardeep. Cynosure commanded a fantastic library of knowledge, could provide communication between far-reaching parts of the dungeon stronghold, and was able to personally animate various homunculi staged around the complex in expedient locations, should physical aid be required.

Delphe cupped her amulet of the Sign and raised it before her face. With her opposite hand she traced the simple yet potent outlines of the symbol. Only a few amulets like this remained. They were strong talismans, and their diminishing numbers were a blow to the order. Over the years they'd been lost, scattered across Sildëyuir and who knew where else. Unfortunate. She couldn't help but see each amulet's loss as a dereliction of duty on the part of some previous era's

Keeper. They had tried tracing the symbol anew to form new Signs. They'd attempted to stamp the symbol directly from extant talismans in an attempt to transfer potency. Research in far-flung libraries continued to the very day. All to no end. The secret of making them was lost to antiquity. The exact nature of the influence each individual Sign exerted against aberrations remained a mystery. As did the secret of the Traitor's fascination with the ancient horrors.

Thank the stars she yet retained the amulet given her when she'd assumed her duties. It was solid and familiar in her hand. It shone blue and dependable, a bane to creatures born to atrocity. That the last known Amulet of the Sign was given to her and not Telarian caused some friction between the two Keepers a few years back. Thankfully, Stardeep's mortal wardens eventually mended their relationship.

Speaking of her fellow Keeper . . .

"Any word from Telarian?"

A pause, then, "No, Delphe. Telarian has not yet returned from across the Causeway. Shall I inform you when he returns?"

"No, no, it's just that I haven't talked to . . ." she stuttered, realizing what she was saying. "Actually, yes, please let me know." She'd just about told the construct she was lonely for not talking to anybody—anybody living, that is. She talked to Cynosure all the time.

"Of course," replied Cynosure, the very voice of civility.

"It just seems," continued Delphe, trying to hide her false step by talking past it, "he should have returned by now, by my estimation. How long does it take to procure reagents?"

"Telarian indicated the city of Laothkund was his destination, on the coast of Aglarond. A trip of several days each way. I calculate he is not yet overdue."

"Aglarond? Why didn't he fetch his ingredients in Sildëyuir?" At the shifting of every season, Delphe herself traveled down the Causeway into the sunlit Yuirwood, and from there to a nearby road into the star elf realm. Seeing the glittering stars and great glass citadels of her people calmed her and recharged her sense of purpose.

"He claimed the requirements of his latest divinations were straining the capacity of Sildëyuir. He believed the wider world could supply him with the crucial components."

"His projects have kept him very busy lately."

"He is a Keeper."

Delphe shrugged. As if that was a guarantee of anything. In fact, Telarian's overpowering belief in the Cerulean Sign's charter sometimes pushed him along personally dangerous paths. His recent obsession with expanding his divinatory skills, already exceptional, into the deep future, was a symptom of his fierce dedication. But if he pressed himself too hard, Delphe feared Telarian would burn out his mind. Despite her own specialty in the art of abjuration, she couldn't stop her friend from overreaching.

Her gaze swept the deepest chamber of the Inner Bastion, officially called the Chamber of Surveillance, though Delphe and Telarian always called it the Throat. And what would a Throat be without a Well? Her gaze dropped to the room's nadir.

The Well was a circular shaft, wide enough to swallow two of Cynosure's largest homunculi without difficulty. The Well's reflective sides were impeccably smooth, but dozens of glass slabs protruded from the concave wall, spiraling down from the top, forming a precarious stair. The slabs were enchanted to extend or withdraw into inset sleeves at her or Cynosure's command. Her observation seat was forged of similarly ensorcelled glass so it, too, could extend over the lip of the Well or pull back for a less precarious view, as it suited her.

Sheets of polished iron tiled the chamber's periphery, so smooth they acted as mirrors. Delphe saw herself reflected many times, slightly distorted in a different way in each image. No obvious doorway allowed entrance or egress. Access was controlled by Cynosure, who could open direct paths for Keepers anywhere within Stardeep. Traversing these paths always made Delphe vaguely nauseated, so she called on Cynosure's aid for getting around Stardeep only when absolutely necessary. She preferred taking the long way whenever possible. Unfortunately, no "long way" existed in or out of the Throat. That was one more measure meant to keep the Traitor secure.

She was halfway through her observation shift. Delphe leaned forward once again. The prominences below continued their unfamiliar cycle, strobing through the gelatinous barrier like thrusting, bloody spikes. If anything, they were brighter, though their hue had graduated from merely orange to a hideous tangerine-tinted scarlet.

She waited for the construct's voice to comment on the activity and act on its observation.

Cynosure uttered no sound and initiated no activity.

Worrisome. The idol should autonomously dampen irregular cycles that threatened to break into chaotic, unmodulated activity. The Well was displaying a classic pattern of stochastic feedback in the boundary layer.

She glanced at her amulet. Its emblazoned blue symbol was deepening, becoming dark as a starless night.

"Cynosure! Barrier layer modulation!"

Delphe leaned forward. She couldn't risk waiting for the disconcertingly silent construct. She shouted syllables of sealing and calming. More than merely audible, her words poured forth like a stream of blue smoke. Energy crystallized from her enunciation and strictures. The secret of the Keeper's wizardry relied on a lingua arcana older than contemporary wizardry, a language whose roots lay beyond the creation of the world itself. Her benediction became a sheen of silver-blue light that fell down the hollow Well. It fell upon the barrier layer like rain upon water, dotting the shining margin with hundreds of expanding circular ripples.

The bubbling, sunlike frenzy beneath the ectoplasmic film sizzled and spit in the silver mist, spiking in sudden frenzy as if in realization that if it didn't succeed now, its chance was spent.

The fury at the interface was inexorably smothered in Delphe's chant of silver-blue assuagement.

A few moments later, the prominences were completely gone.

The abjurer blew out a breath of relief.

"Cynosure—"

"Delphe!" the construct's voice suddenly blared out. "Instability detected at the boundary . . . hold . . . hold . . ."

Pain tweaked her jaw. She had involuntarily clenched it at the sudden reemergence of the construct's voice. She consciously relaxed her muscles. Was something wrong with the idol?

"I've managed the surge, Cynosure," she said. Was the construct seeing something new, or was its attention somehow delayed? Had it just now noticed the breach attempt she'd had to damp out? She glanced down. Yes, the instability was absent. The boundary layer was again as placid as she had ever seen it.

"But what about you, Cynosure? Why didn't you respond when I called? More importantly, why didn't you notice the disequilibrium before it grew into a problem?"

If the warden construct upon which all of Stardeep relied was becoming erratic . . . she didn't want to imagine it. The construct was too intimately wound through the structure, the fail-safes, and the Well itself. She waited, hoping for an answer she could believe.

After a pause, it replied. "Delphe, please accept my most heartfelt apologies. You were correct. The prominences you observed earlier were not merely an unusual mixture of incompatible protective wards. The light heralded an escape attempt. The Traitor does not sleep."

Dread blossomed in her stomach. What evil must live in the Traitor's heart, what power, that even a thousand years after his internment he still plotted novel escape tactics? Tactics so devious they were able to surprise captors well-schooled in the art of safekeeping?

If only he could be killed instead of kept. But with all his other options and original grandiose plans closed to him, death was exactly what the Traitor most desired. His personal martyrdom, he believed, would propel his spirit into the depths of Faerûn. His essence would become a necromantic signal burrowing through the rock of ages until it discovered an ancient cyst—a cyst where aboleths of the most ancient lineage slept away the eras in a city sealed outside time. They waited only for the proper signal to once more attempt to establish a realm of madness across all Faerûn as they had tried in the dawn era.

"I did not initially answer," explained Cynosure, "because I engaged the layer moments before you noticed the cascade. My counter-attack required the concentration of my entire sensorium—I could not reply verbally. I am happy to report that below the boundary layer, I deployed a protective enchantment that dazed the Traitor and concluded his bid for freedom."

"Thank the stars! When you didn't answer I wondered . . ."

"Again, I ask your pardon. But take heart—the ruse just attempted by the Traitor is now known to me. I have journaled the elements of this strategy and will recognize its tell-tales going forward."

"You had the situation in hand, then?"

"Yes, but your response was also required. Your ward kept the Traitor's attention the vital few moments necessary for me to finish my abjurative task."

Delphe chose to believe the construct.

After all, Cynosure was old. Who wouldn't expect a few hiccups after a few thousand years of constant awareness?

But, on second thought . . . hiccups in the mind of the warden idol could lead to disaster.

She probed further. "Cynosure, you did finally reply to my query—after the threat was past. Your response appeared out of sync with events."

The voice paused a heartbeat, then, "True. You noticed a side effect of my total concentration. You know that my 'mind,' such as it is, is widely distributed around Stardeep. The concentration of all my faculties in the Well led to some disarray in the weave that holds 'me' together. But I assure you my consciousness is functioning at peak performance."

"You would tell me if you noticed a change in yourself? I mean, you would warn me if you suspected your ability to watch over the dungeon and the Well were in any way compromised, correct?"

"You would be first to know if any of those parameters were even close to being met. They are not. Do not worry yourself over this, Delphe."

Delphe frowned, looking at her amulet.

The field around the tree remained coal black. The blue faded whenever the Traitor stirred, but she had quelled his latest activity.

Why, then, did it remain dark?

Chapter Two

Stardeep, Epoch Chamber

Telarian saw what protruded from the thunderhead's belly.

It was not alive—not quite. A glyph-scribed obelisk wrapped in eternal storm soared above the world. A writhing frieze was carved on the age-worn exterior depicting thousands of interconnected pictures. The inscriptions constantly shifted and changed, as if unseen carvers swarmed across the stone face, engraving atrocities to the beat of a mad drummer. The full meaning of the evolving image invoked a concept too ghastly for a mortal mind to comprehend and remain sane. Telarian jerked his gaze away, but felt understanding bridge the gap anyway.

Slime-crusted creatures crept within the obelisk's hollow interior. The vast object was inhabited, a primeval city regurgitated into the world that had forgotten its existence.

A squalid miasma altered reality in its vicinity, unfettering vast creatures of the deeps, giving them mastery of the sky as they before hunted the sunless seas. Tentacles slithered and crawled in cold rookeries encrusting the vast object's sheer sides.

But these were mere servitors, children compared to the sinful, gelatinous carapaces of those creatures within. Their minds churned with philosophies inimical to all beasts not part of their ancient Sovereignty. They waited for the call of mortal priests who perverted their souls and hollowed their minds to serve abominations.

Roused from the drowned depths, the fabled city was fable no more.

Telarian screamed and opened his eyes.

He lay on the floor in the center of a divinatory circle. The circle's periphery was decorated with skulls, hourglasses, butterfly wings, and unidentifiable sigils. A twelve-pointed star was inscribed inside the curved pattern. Smudgy lines of burning incense rose from each of the twelve corners . . .

. . . which meant the circle hadn't been broken. Telarian wished he could sigh in relief; instead, he wanted to scream again. If the pattern had been breached, he might have been able to convince himself he'd experienced a false foretelling. But his view into the far future, as chancy and unreliable as such arts were, remained accurate, unchanging, and too awful for Telarian to accept. The same scene had blistered his mind each time he looked so far forward.

He rolled to his stomach and pushed himself to his feet. Muscles in his legs shook from having clenched too long without ease. The scabbard of his new blade knocked awkwardly against his thigh. He wasn't used to carrying such a thing. But desperate times were the mother of desperate strategies.

Telarian walked the circle's exterior and carefully pinched off each burning stick of incense. With each glowing ember doused, he spoke a mental syllable designed to calm the mind and moor the spirit. When it came to the art of divination, ritual was important. Not so much for its own sake, but as a way to condition the mind against the rigors of peeling away the present to reveal the future. Most diviners could see heartbeats or moments ahead with relatively little effort, but days and years . . . few could match Telarian's skill. He'd pushed the art forward by centuries during his time in Stardeep. But he wasn't vain about his accomplishments.

As a Keeper of the Cerulean Sign in the heart of the dungeon constructed to hold the Traitor, unmatched resources were available to Telarian for his research. He had tapped those resources, especially the singularly potent construct Cynosure. His interactions with Delphe, his co-Keeper, were few and far between. Her duties monitoring the Well were substantial, and thus her relative absence granted Telarian free reign in the Outer Bastion. Not that she had any direct authority over him, nor could he command her. Still, best to keep Delphe mollified. Delphe's problem was she didn't quite know what to make of his ability for prophecy, and thus often failed to appreciate the personal costs true visions of the future demanded. In the end, when he labored to pierce the veil of the far future, he kindly refrained from telling her, and she did not complain.

Of course, his lapse in telling Delphe of his construction of the Epoch Chamber, the chamber wherein he stood at that moment, might one day make her doubt him. Nor would she look kindly upon him should she discover that he often directed Cynosure to lie about his location. It was a risk he was willing to take.

The Epoch Chamber was smoothly spherical. Its lower portion sloshed with mystical fluid he'd distilled from years of dream-wandering. A disk, scribed with a twelve-pointed star, floated immovably on the surface of the fluid, and when Telarian reclined in its center, his divinatory ability was enhanced by orders of magnitude. He'd predicted fires, earthquakes, the deaths of kings, and the initiation of wars years prior to their occurrences. He'd never been wrong.

Was there anything he couldn't foresee?

Perhaps, but he cared to preview only a single event. He obsessed over it, and each time the vision thundered through his mind's eye, his despair grew.

Despair wasn't an emotion a Keeper could afford, so he converted melancholy to a desperate plan. He disavowed the future he saw. He would prevent it from occurring. If he did less, could he honestly claim to be a guardian of the Cerulean Sign?

And so, his arrangements proceeded—daring, appalling arrangements that, if successful, might prevent the horrid soaring city of his vision from ascending.

The city he had seen in the thundercloud was Xxiphu, and it was inhabited by aberrations of the ancient world, creatures known as aboleths that were old when the sun was yet young. While aboleth splinter populations persisted in the world, Xxiphu was the seat of the Abolethic Sovereignty, possessed of a malignancy inconceivable. If it rose from Faerûn's core, shorn of its supposed dependency on the depths . . . could an age of terror and slavery be far behind?

Chapter Three

City of Laothkund, Shadow Tongue Lair

A man in soot-blackened clothes balanced on a ledge three stories above the winter-chilled street. A gaggle of sentries on its way to Sal's Tavern for warm buttered rum passed beneath him. The lamplight from their shuttered lanterns receded, once again plunging the shivering seaside district into night's full embrace. He loosed his held breath, wending steam into the icy air.

The man faced the wall, the pitch-soaked toes of his boots gripping the frigid mortar hardly at all. As if in supplication, he rested the side of his face against the tomb-cold stone, his arms splayed to either side. He hadn't counted on the freakishly chill weather. Gusts off the Sea of Fallen Stars usually kept the city of Laothkund bearably temperate, even in midwinter. Not tonight.

He eased his left foot forward. His supple, calfhide boots were ordinarily like extensions of his feet. But he was so cold he couldn't feel his toes, and instead of providing extra grip when he needed it, the pitch seemed determined to trip him. The wind, muttering with winter's chill, threatened to pull him from the precipice, with or without help from the pitch on his boots, and dash him to the street.

A particularly stiff gust nearly turned his speculation into reality. He hadn't had such a rude introduction to the hard cobble streets since childhood. Fear was not an option; he simply required a better hold. Immediately.

He inched his left hand along the too-smooth wall, feeling for irregularities between the bricks, his fingers searching for a grip. He'd removed his black gauntlets, as thin and fine as they were. Despite their demonic talents, an unimpeded sense of touch was too precious to hamper when taking the street less traveled. But his fingers were quickly losing sensation in the heat-thieving zephyr.

The man, known in the city of Laothkund as Gage, was no stranger to heights. He'd plied his trade too long and too successfully to hesitate over leaping an alleyway chasm, or to shy from ascending a tower in utter darkness. He was so familiar with the lofty, tight places of the city he actually preferred them to the wide streets. Normally.

His fingertips eased over a gap, deep enough for good purchase. "Thank the Queen of Air," he muttered. With the new handhold, he levered himself around to the east side of the building, out of the wind.

Gage was a slender man, so much so that most assumed he was a wood elf mix. Many in Laothkund were, after all. But his birth hadn't followed a moon date. No, his wiry shape was forged from years spent running through Laothkund's twisting neighborhoods. Few could match his knowledge of the city or his ability to quickly navigate the congested lanes. No one was better at jumps, vaults, wall runs, slides, or lucky tumbles. No one knew better which of the many laundry lines would hold a man's weight, and which would instantly snap if tested.

Serendipitously, the same skills were perfect for a

housebreaker. Or, as they called it in the narrow streets of the Tannery, thieving.

Ahead was the high shuttered window that had first drawn Gage's attention from the neighboring roof. He sidled along the ledge, moving with increasing confidence.

No light escaped from between the shutter slats. He pried a wooden strip away from the sill and saw the reason—behind the shutters, the window was completely sealed with brick and mortar.

He rubbed his nose, considering. The thief had reconnoitered the warehouse yesterday. This window was the only entrance not under constant scrutiny. Sure, he could probably engineer a ruse that would allow him to slip in the front door. But the time necessary to design and implement a plan subtle enough to penetrate the lair of Sathra of the Shadow Tongue would be onerous. And boring.

Actually, the bricked-up window might work in his favor. How could any of Sathra's stooges predict the resources Gage could bring to bear against simple mortar? He doubted whatever lay beyond the sealed window was guarded. Gage cautiously pried a few more slats away from the shutter.

He pulled his gauntlets from his belt and slipped them onto his hands, clenching his right hand as if squeezing something lest it wriggle from his grasp. The gloves were warm, almost hot to the touch, and his chilled fingers tingled. The eye on the back of the left glove opened and blinked up at him. A muffled voice groaned. Gage brought his right fist up to his face and whispered, "Quiet. We're on a job."

He unclenched his fist, revealing a disturbingly realistic mouth in the palm, complete with lips bordering a dark cavity where none should be, in which a too-sinuous tongue squirmed, dripping venom. The glove whispered, "I will eat your soul."

It always said that.

"Eat rock instead." Gage responded.

He turned the muttering palm toward the mortared wall and pressed, achieving complete contact. The eye on the other glove blinked stupidly, but the demon physically bound in the fabric of the thin gauntlets knew what he wanted.

The wall seemed to shrink away from his touch. A moment later, every brick in the sealed window shivered and pulsed, each pushing away from the other in defiance of the mortar that held them. Gage pushed forward and the bricks dimpled, parted around his silhouette, then closed over after him. He was inside. Behind him, the bricked window settled back into perfect solidity, hardly any worse for wear. Not a trick he could pull very often.

Gage carried many hidden advantages—a half-dozen throwing knives secreted about his body; a broad leather belt stitched with pockets containing a spool of stiff wire, a petite oil tin, several miniature abrading files, a flask of pitch, and an assortment of alchemical mixtures; and of course, his catlike grace and exceptional mind.

All these tools and talents paled in comparison to his gloves, despite their penchant for sneaking out in the middle of the night and getting up to mischief. Not for the first time Gage thanked the Queen of Air, Akadi, on his good fortune in acquiring the gloves. A year ago, he'd taken a commission to pilfer a tome called *Glyphs and Griffons* from the library of the mage Tenambulum. Once he'd secured the book, he'd been unable to resist looking around Tenambulum's sanctum. The absent mage had a reputation as a demon catcher. Most of a day later, shivering and bleeding, Gage had emerged wearing the Hands of Paymon. Almost all the days since then had proved his choice a good one. Though he'd learned it was dangerous to rely on the gauntlets too entirely . . .

He stood in the cluttered interior of a small, nearly pitch black room. A storage closet of some sort? He produced one of his alchemical oddities—a clear glass vessel that produced light nearly equal to a candle when shaken. He shook. Crates, barrels, and boxes jumped into visibility, jammed and jumbled together. A fine layer of dust covered everything. No one had opened the door into this room for some time.

He sidled up to the door, under which wan light peeked. He pressed an ear to the wood and held his breath. He heard nothing save the beat of his own heart.

Unless the silence heralded an ambush, he'd penetrated the lair without alerting the occupants. Although "penetrated" was perhaps too optimistic a spin on the depth of his entry into Sathra's domain. Metaphorically, the closet was more like a ledge to which he clung by his fingers.

He sincerely doubted the prize he'd come to claim resided in the jumble of crates and barrels.

Nonetheless, he examined the contents of a wooden container; old habits were hard to break. He found dried fish—and it had gone bad. He crinkled his nose and replaced the barrel-head, careful not to touch the rancid contents. A foul smell could betray him as easily as too much noise or straying into a sentinel's peripheral vision.

Back to the door. The hinges were chancy. He pulled the oil tin from his belt and dripped the lubricious fluid onto the two brass fittings. He stowed the canister, waited a moment for the oil to penetrate, then eased the door open a finger's breadth.

A hallway. Not very wide. Stairwell at the far end. Two other doors stood in view besides the one he peered from, one of which was ajar. A hanging lantern, its wick turned low, burned from the hallway's center. Both ends of the passage were thick with night shadows. Good.

Gage stowed his light and emerged from the storage closet. He eased the door shut and merged with the darkness. He crept down the hallway, approaching the glimmering lantern and the doors that stood across from each other. Brighter light danced from the slightly open door.

A raucous laugh told him the room was occupied. The laugh was followed by a hoarse shout, several jeers, and a draft redolent with stale pipeweed and vinegary wine.

He stepped up to the partially open door and squinted into much brighter light. Caps, overcoats, gloves, and cloaks lay in disarray on the floor around a large table. Six or seven hard-bitten figures sat under a crude chandelier of lanterns. They were absorbed by a game of cards. Probably Sathra's low-brow muscle, off duty from their tasks of intimidation and loan collection. He studied the amounts being wagered. A lot of copper, some silver, and a gold or two proudly glinting from a few players' stakes. Not worth making a play for.

He glided across the hall to the other door. It was unlocked. He risked opening it a sliver. The room served as a billet, currently empty, but with enough cots for ten or so men. He closed the door, considering.

Gage had options. He could flit past the card game and down the stairs, leaving the players none the wiser. But if he met trouble he couldn't deal with quietly at the bottom of the stairs, the card players would come running.

He could launch a surprise attack into the chamber and try to take out as many players as possible before they subdued him. Gage was certain he could knife a couple, and the blinking eye of his left gauntlet could probably put the fear of hell into one or two more—leaving the remaining few to beat Gage into the floorboards. He was at his best when his foes were not aware of his presence. Inviting a pitched battle was a risk he wasn't stupid enough to take.

He could try the special alchemical concoction he'd been saving—a nasty fluid that vaporized into a gas on contact with air, and brought sudden sleep to those who inhaled it. But the game room might be too large. The gas might not reach the farthest players before they raised the alarm.

Gage decided on a trick he'd employed on a couple other occasions with moderate success. He ran his finger down the pockets he'd sewn in his wide belt, and stopped at the one etched with two lines side by side. He pulled out a narrow tube filled with the gooey pitch he normally reserved for high climbs. Pitch had so many uses.

He rolled the tube from the end, forcing out a line of black paste he applied in a stripe up the door frame. He used half the remaining pitch in the tube, perhaps more than necessary. It was expensive, but he shrugged. Better to expend resources than wish he hadn't skimped later. Gage recapped the tube and returned it to his belt. Taking a breath, he slowly swung the door closed. Door and frame squeezed the sticky pitch between them.

No sounds of surprise or alarm followed. If no one opened the door for another few moments, they'd find themselves held inside. Not for more than a moment, at most. But a moment could spell the difference between Gage getting in and getting out with a minimum of punctures.

He nodded at his handiwork and made for the stairs.

Five steps and he stood on a landing with a switchback. He continued down.

Gage peered into another passage like the one above. More doors, though; two on each side and one at the far end.

He suspected the door at the end was his ultimate destination. Still, prudence dictated he check the other four on the way.

The first door on his left smelled like a chamber pot. Sure enough, a privy, and none too clean. He doubted Sathra used this one.

Across the hall from the privy he found an office. A man sitting at a desk strewn with parchment and quills looked up as Gage peered in. "Yes?" said the man.

Startled, Gage slammed the door closed. Nice. If he sat thinking for an eternity, he doubted he could imagine a more suspicious response.

He jerked the door open again. The man was rising, his open mouth wide with alarm. "Hey!"

Quicker than thought, Gage flicked a knife from the concealed scabbard below his left arm, flinging it across the room with the same graceful motion. The knife plunged into the man's mounting yell, silencing him.

The thief dashed forward and caught the body before it crashed onto the desk. He lowered the still-twitching form to mud-smeared floorboards. He retrieved his dagger and cleaned it on the man's pants. Poor bastard. He told the glazing eyes, "You asked for it, working for Sathra. I'm sure you've done far worse in your time."

He stood, sheathing his knife. Gage checked the hallway to see if he'd roused any activity, then pulled back, closing the door. Returning to the desk, he skimmed through the papers scattered across it. He discovered the man he'd just knifed was a mid-level functionary, captain of the muscle upstairs and another group on this floor. Not part of Sathra's personal force, then; the captain apparently didn't measure up enough to be counted among the so-called "Shadow Cadre." Gage hated that name. According to a rough floor plan he found, the cadre was housed on the ground floor. He kept reading.

He found documents describing traffic in hellborn drugs, a protection racket broader than he'd imagined the Shadow Tongue could engineer, the outline of a scheme to blackmail the ruling council of Laothkund by implicating them in a made-up alliance with Thay, illicit slave trade in children . . . things that would curdle the stomachs of any moral person.

But Gage wasn't here to right wrongs. He looked for a clue, any clue to the singular article he sought.

Was this it? A note about a detachment of Sathra's cadre deployed to retrieve an item, unnamed. Whatever it was, Sathra had issued specific instructions—the item was not to be fenced under pain of death to her underlings. She wanted it returned directly to her, in this building, as her prize.

That had to be it! For Sathra to name something as a trophy instead of merely selling it, an item had to be particularly special. As he knew it to be. Gage had never seen anything quite so beautiful, and no trinket had before awoken his acquisitive nature so surely. If he could, he'd keep it for a prize, too . . .

Gage shook his head. He couldn't let his covetousness overmaster him—the object wasn't for himself.

When Sathra's people stole it from under his nose, Gage was furious. He was here to steal it back.

He quit the chamber. Back in the empty hall, he didn't bother to check the remaining two doors. He made directly for the door at the end of the hallway. No more distractions. He glanced at a document he'd snatched from the desk: a map of Sathra's base.

He was close to retrieving his prize.

He was close to claiming Angul, the Blade Cerulean.

The door at the hall's end opened on a wide warehouse. Wooden crates of various sizes were piled everywhere in haphazard stacks. Dangling lanterns from above provided weak light. The smell of wet stone was strong in the chamber. Gage crept along the outer wall, ready to fight or flee should he be discovered. Voices in the central portion of the room bantered back and forth. Were they members of Sathra's Shadow Cadre, or merely brute laborers?

A man's rough voice echoed, "Didn't listen, did ye? Didn't listen when old Bendar told ye not to take that snake charmer's coin. Oh, no! And now look what ye got!" A laugh.

A different voice answered, this one slurred with drink or

disfigurement. "Damned hedge wizard. How'd I know he could make good on his promise to curse me? I had to slit his throat, though. Passing phantom coin just ain't good business. He had it coming. I don't deserve what I got in return, I'll tell ye that."

"Snakes keep finding ye, eh? Even in winter's cold. Gotta watch where ye step, eh?"

A grunt in return.

"Ha! Old Bendar told ye!"

Gage left behind the bantering voices as he slipped into a side passage. He caught his breath—a huge form was propped on a stool too small for it, blocking most of the corridor. An ogre! Tattooed and pierced, Gage recognized it as one of Sathra's trained guardians. The figure shifted and loosed a hooting snore. Not trained well enough.

He eased past the creature and tiptoed to the passage's end. Another look at the map, a grin, and he found the secret catch in the floor. Down the narrow, steep stairs he disappeared, guided by the greenish glowing eye on his left gauntlet.

He came to the secret sliding panel the map promised, and paused to listen. All was quiet in the chamber beyond. He slid aside the panel and saw a wide vestibule. To one side, broad steps mounted upward. On the other side, a rounded door closed off Sathra's personal quarters.

Gage moved along to the iron valve that sealed Sathra's vault.

Sathra's name was inscribed on the rusted surface. Rumors suggested Sathra's personal quarters served double duty as the treasury vault of the Shadow Tongue criminal organization, but he hadn't believed them. His skepticism may have been misplaced. Either way, vault or personal quarters, it seemed likely he'd find the sword Angul within. A pitted metallic wheel protruded from the iron door, next to a keyhole. To the side was a pull chain. A few heartbeats examining the wheel and keyhole revealed expertly wired elements of a mechanical trap. Mechanical, probably riddled with spells to boot. Sathra could afford to be lavish with her security.

But Gage was no slouch. He pulled his packet of alchemically hardened, arcane-proofed tools from his belt. It was rare that a mechanism, trap or otherwise, got the better of him. He just needed to study it awhile, get a feel for it . . .

The wheel spun, squealing. Someone was behind the door, about to emerge!

He stood from his crouch, dropping his tools to the floor. The sound of the turning wheel covered the noise of his metallic files as they slipped loose from their case and clattered on the floor. He kicked the implements into a corner.

No place to hide in the vestibule. Up was the only way to go.

He jumped, right arm straight up. His palm slapped the ceiling. *Crunch*—the mouth on his gauntlet bit into the stone, as he'd hoped. The little beast would bite anything it could get its mouth on. Hard. The trick was making the glove let go. He'd once used it as a climbing aid, but feeding the demon something tastier than stone with every handhold proved too cumbersome.

With his gauntlet holding flat against the ceiling, he swung his legs back and forth, and with a stifled groan managed to swing them up flush to the ceiling, then thrust them into the corner where two walls met.

The wheel ceased spinning and the iron door below Gage slammed open. Sathra stormed out, screeching. She cradled one hand in the other. The cradled hand was red and blistered. It trailed smoke and the odor of burnt flesh. Had she just botched a spell or alchemical mixture?

The decorative metal spikes in her hair barely cleared the thief's suspended form. The description Gage paid good coin for was accurate. Sathra's infamous gluttony was visible in a full figure beneath folds of black silk. An overabundance of black metallic jewelry pierced her flesh.

The description he'd paid for failed to mention the shroud of shadows coiled around Sathra like mist. The darkness trailed in her wake, uttering a susurrus of whispers, ". . . find out where . . . lost the light . . . so hungry . . . cold . . ." He held his breath, clamping down on an urge to gasp with fear.

Gage waited only a moment after the sound of the last whisper faded up the stairs. He dropped, or tried to. As before, the glove wouldn't release the ceiling. He hung down in front of the door by one arm. He rifled his belt with his free arm, anxiously glancing up the stairs, then into the vault. Lucky she'd forgotten to close the door . . .

Damn it, she must know he was here! But why hadn't she attacked him when she opened the door? Because she burned herself, he answered. She was in obvious pain. Perhaps she had simply forgotten to close the door. Not everything was a trap.

Right. That's possible. The leader of the Shadow Tongue forgot to close the door to the vault containing all her most valuable loot. Sure.

It was a false hope. You didn't become the head of a criminal organization as powerful as Sathra's if you made mistakes when distracted. Which meant she probably went up the stairs seeking underlings to deal with the intruder in her lair. Him.

With his left hand, he found a niblet of jerky on his belt and held it up next to his gloved hand, still affixed to the ceiling. The mouth unclenched and he dropped, landing easily on his feet. He flipped the jerky into the waiting mouth. It gibbered and noisily chewed its bribe.

Time to run. He hadn't adequately investigated the nature of the vault. He should retreat, make a plan. But wasn't that a blue glow ahead? It reminded him of Angul's signature aura. By the frost giantess's icy kiss, the sword must be just inside.

He ran. Into the vault, not up the stairs. Stupid, stupid!

His pulse pounded and a flutter of reckless joy stuttered his breathing. He was in uncharted territory, and he liked it. Taking uncalculated risks meant he wasn't dead. He took them willingly—they weren't pressed on him by any sense of duty or because of a devotion to a higher power. He was his own man.

He was too close to retreat. He was about to lay hands on Angul. No doubt about it. He'd recognize that unearthly flame anywhere. The blade must be secreted just ahead. He wondered how Kiril, Angul's legitimate wielder, was reacting to the loss of the sword she complained about so vociferously.

Chapter Four

City of Telflamm, Shou Town

The blueness darkened in the stone, leaching away over several days until it was black as grave dirt.

The sky's glad hue that had silhouetted the symbol of a white tree conveyed hope. Against the black, the white tree seemed defenseless and fragile. Overlapping inscriptions nearly too small to recognize as anything other than texture cramped every other surface of the stone, in a language not spoken for thousands of years. A silver chain clasped the stone, making an amulet of it.

The amulet was the single forget-me-not given to Raidon Kane by his absent mother. It was Raidon's most treasured possession. Fearing its theft, he hid it away. And thus he failed to see the transformation.

The amulet lay unobserved in a delicate cedar box. The box was carefully packed in a travel bag hidden behind a bamboo panel in the room Raidon shared with a man named Huang.

Huang was heedless of the concealed box, which would have made the man an ideal lodge mate, except for Huang's arresting odor. At first, Raidon endeavored to ignore the smell. Eventually, he decided the best way to disregard the aroma was to avoid it. Raidon began spending more and more of his free time away from their room.

Thus Raidon chalked up his discovery of a fine tea house to serendipity. The tea house became, in just a few short tendays, his favorite place in all of Shou Town.

The server poured another cup from a porcelain pot, and Raidon tapped three fingers on the table in thanks. Long Jing, also called West Lake Dragon Well, was the best green tea in the city of Telflamm, and maybe all of Thesk. He sipped.

Perfection. Some of his tension evaporated in the wafting steam and delicate taste.

Long Jing was shipped from the east at great expense—Raidon indulged himself, though he could scarcely afford it. It was grown only in the mythical Zhejiang province in but a few tea gardens. Local teas couldn't match it. Raidon hoped rumors of trade disruptions along the Golden Way were merely merchants' talk, a bluff used as a bargaining tool to drive up prices. Raidon didn't mind high prices, as long as the tea remained available. West Lake Dragon Well was worth it.

But his cares could never be drowned, only momentarily assuaged. Raidon grunted and took another sip. Around him, gentlemen of leisure enjoyed similar moments of peace, savoring their favorite teas. One man had brought his pet bird. The red-feathered creature held tightly to its silver perch and twittered a pleasant song. Singing wasn't permitted in the tea house, though apparently the ban didn't apply to pets. Or perhaps, the ban didn't apply to this particular man of leisure.

His name was Chun. Who could have guessed that from all the tea houses in Shou Town to choose from, Raidon and Chun would find the same one?

Raidon considered serendipity again—if not for his lodge mate's disagreeable scent, Raidon wouldn't be present to contemplate violence. Raidon would still be worried about his petition to the Nine Golden Swords. As the elders of Xiang Temple taught, "The usefulness of a cup is its emptiness." In other words, he hadn't known Chun would be here, but now that he did, Raidon could adapt the moment to his ambition.

Chun had wronged Raidon, though the man of leisure didn't know it. Chun had taken a family heirloom from his father in payment for a debt never incurred. Chun had stolen Raidon's family legacy. His grandfather's sword, his daito, handed down from his own grandfather, who gained the sword from a dragon. In the normal course of things, Raidon's father would have passed the daito down to Raidon's firstborn child—but Raidon's father was dead, and the daito was gone.

Raidon stood and shook out the sleeves of his decorous silk jacket. They snapped, as if he were initiating the first moves of the Leaping Tiger. He paid his coins on the table, then his hands were empty, open, capable of anything. Like the empty cup.

To restore the honor of his dead father and absent mother, Raidon had pledged the legacy would be restored to the family. He would claim grandfather's daito, even if comity in the tea house had to be sacrificed.

He bowed to the server, then walked toward Chun's table. Chun sat with two other men and a dark-haired woman—Chun's girl of the day? The men were of the Nine Golden Swords, as was Chun. Raidon knew it by the small tattoo each displayed. He had petitioned to join the secret society of vicious criminals. He had petitioned in order to get close to Chun, a mid-level thug in the hierarchy. All those preparations had been unnecessary—chance had dropped into his lap an opportunity to confront Chun.

Raidon reached the table. He stared straight at Chun, ignoring the unspoken rules of civilized behavior among strangers. Chun was no stranger to him. Raidon flexed his empty hands, hidden as they were in his long sleeves.

Had he known he would one day wield the family sword, perhaps Raidon would have spent less of his life training in the Xiang monastery, achieving mastery of his mind and body. Of course, sword play was one aspect of the training he received in Xiang; no monk of the temple could leave its bounds until he or she demonstrated facility with traditional weapons. But Raidon's best talents did not require such mundane implements as sharpened steel. His body was weapon enough.

"Your presence upsets my bird," said Chun in a bored voice. A dangerous voice.

"And your presence sours tea across Thesk," replied Raidon, his voice as calm as if he'd commented on the chance for rain.

The two men on either side of Chun jumped to their feet. The bird screamed. So did the painted woman.

Raidon observed the scene as if he stood apart from it. From their sitting positions in relation to each other and the table, Chun and his thugs had only a limited number of actions they might effectively take. Raidon knew what they were, and was prepared.

One thug knocked the table as he rose, spilling tea. The other's hand went to his dirk. Raidon backhanded the second man with his right fist as the thug's hand cleared his scabbard, sending the dirk whirling. Raidon followed with a hook from his left elbow, perfectly sticking the side of the thug's head. As the thug slumped, the monk slipped around the table, taking the fallen man's vacated position. This put Raidon out of reach of the final thug and next to Chun.

Chun drew his sword and expertly grasped its deadly

length. His two-handed grip on the wrapped hilt, called the tsuka, bespoke training. The blade was an unwavering diagonal line.

"Raidon Kane," said Chun.

Raidon paused, nonplussed. Chun recognized him? Perhaps the murderer's presence wasn't the coincidence Raidon imagined.

"You have named me."

"Your petition to the Nine Golden Swords is approved," said Chun. "I've been dispatched to tell you." The remaining thug to Chun's right edged around the table so only empty space separated him from Raidon.

Chun continued. "Your first task is a simple one." He caught Raidon's eyes with his own. "You are to journey to the Temple of Yarom here in Telflamm, where blasphemers claim a soul's salvation lies beyond life, even beyond the gods we all revere. Raidon, you are to deliver them to that final day. Today. See to it these fools who deride the gods are pushed through death's door. Since they doubt the gods' divinity, let them pass into darkness. As they've lived in ignorance, so shall they die. By your hand."

Raidon had never heard of the Temple of Yarom before. He shook his head and said, "I will not kill strangers in cold blood in the very halls of their temple, no matter their dogma."

"No?" Chun still sounded bored. "I'm afraid you've come too far to back out now. You know us. We know you. You must be brought in all the way, or . . ." Chun shrugged.

"I must restore the honor of my family."

"Honor is what you seek? I give you this"—Chun swirled the tip of the daito—"and your family's honor is restored, is that it?"

Raidon's earlier guess was on the mark. Chun wasn't sipping tea in the monk's favored tea house by chance.

"Our honor is too besmirched for such easy mending."

"I don't know about your family, but all I see before me is a baying mongrel dog," Chun noted.

A strand of Raidon's carefully woven serenity slipped free, but he held his focus. Despite his control, heat flushed his cheeks.

Chun continued. "I saw your name as a petitioner. I've watched you since then. I wondered if you were merely a revenge-minded idiot. Prove me wrong, and you get to live. Prove me right, and join your father. He made excellent pig fodder, and I guess you will, too."

Fury bloomed and crowned Raidon, choking his reply to an inarticulate snarl. His viewpoint contracted; his anger expanded.

Chun kicked the table onto its side, simultaneously rushing Raidon, trying for a disemboweling strike. Raidon flipped backward, head over heels three times, rolling to his feet twenty paces away, out in the busy street.

Chun lost the advantage of his attack by stumbling on the overturned table. The thug rushed forward unhindered and tried to shove a dirk into the monk's face.

Raidon leaned forward and slightly to his left; the knife flashed past his right ear. Before his attacker could retract his arm, Raidon caught the man's wrist in a painful grip. He twisted the wrist, levered the man around, and flung the shrieking thug onto Chun's advancing blade.

Screams, yells, and a few whistles blared in Raidon's ears. He hadn't wanted a fight. He had simply intended to demand that Chun hand over the blade. He hadn't realized Chun was trained in sword play. But Raidon was committed to seeing through what he'd started, despite the foolhardiness of engaging in a fight. A tea house in the market district of Shou Town was too public for anything prolonged and bloody. Chun had expertly baited Raidon, made him forget himself; he'd lost his center. Raidon concentrated on walling off his anger, separating it from the skill and grace that marked him as a Xiang Temple graduate.

His enemy, finally clear of the table, charged. Chun's blade perfectly shielded the center line of his body, and was simultaneously set to deliver any number of killing strikes to Raidon's head, neck, stomach, or wrists—

Raidon dropped and swept Chun's legs with his own. Unprepared, Chun toppled, his sword out of alignment. As the man hit the ground, Raidon rolled onto Chun's chest, his knees painfully squeezing the man's sides. He trapped the hand that gripped the sword on the ground with his right hand, and smashed the man's temple with his left elbow.

Chun went limp and the sword fell from his grasp.

Raidon stood. He clutched his grandfather's daito in one hand, raised it in a salute. Raidon had never held it before, only admired it from afar when his father had shown it to him as a child. It was perfectly balanced, a wonder of craftsmanship. His anger relented. Honor was his once more, and his family's.

He allowed himself a nod of acceptance, then noticed several newcomers on the scene.

A gang of tattooed men pushed through the crowded street toward him. They'd been hiding all along, watching Chun, waiting to ambush Raidon should he prove intractable. His anger had blinded him to all the clues of their presence. There were too many to fight. And why should he? He had what he'd come for, and Chun had been shamed.

He fled.

Behind him, a call went up. Chun's voice, bleary but loud, followed. "You're dead! Dead! You've crossed the Nine Golden Swords, whelp! You can't hide from us! Nowhere in Thesk is safe for you!" The man's half-hysterical threat faded behind him. But his words rang with truth, Raidon knew. The Nine Golden Swords made examples of those who crossed them.

He was a marked man.

Raidon Kane dashed through the market throng, swatting a fat man from his path. The man fell, his arms windmilling, into a fruit seller's cart. One hand knocked out the bottom row of a perfectly stacked display of red fruit, causing an apple-lanche.

Shoppers clogged the streets, mostly locals, but also adventurous tourists from the surrounding city of Telflamm. It was a perfect day for Raidon to lose himself in the crowd. He darted through a shouting match over bok choy, past the live turtle vendor, and into the chicken seller's shop. He didn't pause, but hastened through the piled cages and acrid odors, ignored the owner's shout, and parted the heavy felt material of the shop's back wall with a swipe of the daito.

He emerged on an unfamiliar side street. Dark bars clustered here, small, dark, and smoky. Men diced away their salaries and drank through their sorrows. Above the slanted roofs, Raidon spied the top of the towering Shou Town Gate. Getting his bearings from the landmark, he ran north down the narrow avenue, the daito extended behind him so he wouldn't alarm onlookers. He received a few curious stares. The Nine Golden Swords would soon know he'd gone this way.

And where was he going? He hadn't thought about it, and without conscious direction, his body was directing him back to the odiferous room he rented. If he'd planned ahead, he would have headed toward Xiang Temple. He recalled it fondly: brightly painted on the outside, wreathed in incense smoke so strong it brought tears to the eyes of the uninitiated. The temple was a sanctuary for the common person. Especially a person who had graduated its exacting training.

But Xiang was in the opposite direction across Shou Town. Better to continue toward his lodging. In fact, the Nine

Golden Swords probably expected him to flee to the temple. They might have an ambush set up, anticipating that response. He would be wise to stay away. He'd collect his things from his apartment and leave. He had no future in Telflamm. His mother had departed, his father was dead, and he had no siblings. He'd completed his training at the Xiang Temple, discharged his duty to the master. He had no debts to keep him in the city. But where would he go?

Raidon arrived at the three-story tenement and climbed the outer stairs to the top floor room he shared. The door was open. Good. Perhaps the chamber would be aired out—

A man flew from the open door, a staff in his grip. His tattooed hand proclaimed his Golden Swords allegiance, though Raidon could hardly discern it through the blood that streaked the man's hands and forearms. What had he been up to?

The newcomer stabbed at Raidon's neck with the staff's sharp butt. Raidon deflected it with his left forearm, making a wide circle. He held the daito in his right hand—he could better defend himself if he dropped the blade, but he couldn't bring himself to dishonor the implement he'd spent so many months recovering. Instead, he grasped the wrapped tsuka and brought the blade up.

A daito wasn't the perfect weapon to defend against a staff wielder, who had longer reach. But Raidon's advantage was his ability to put his mind outside his body. When he could coolly observe a conflict, he could take in every variable, every possibility, and react in a way most likely to end the conflict quickly in his favor.

Raidon feinted and stepped back, then again. The staff wielder advanced, encouraged by Raidon's backpedaling, jabbing with the probing end of the long wooden rod. When the man tried to push him off the walkway's edge, Raidon wove the end of the daito around the advancing pole, allowing the end to push into his space, but avoiding its tip. He hooked the staff and pulled, stepping to the side. The staff and its wielder flew off the three-story walkway.

He couldn't afford the time to watch the result of his maneuver. He dashed into his lodge, on guard for other Golden Swords. But the only one present was Huang. What was left of him.

He had never liked Huang, but he regretted the man's end. His lodge mate was staked to the wall, his extremities removed by a hatchet, which lay on the floor amid the awful mess. Raidon pulled his focus even further from his body to avoid reacting. Time was too precious to mourn Huang, or lose the tea he'd consumed to nausea.

Everything was in shambles, but Raidon found the pack he'd secreted behind the wall panel undisturbed. He'd prepared it a few tendays ago, in case his petition was granted and he penetrated the Nine Golden Swords compound. That hadn't happened; fate had stepped in and delivered his target early. The pack contained some food, a small tea kettle and four cups, an expensive packet of loose Long Jing tea, a pouch of coins, a change of clothing. Next to the pack was a delicate cedar box. He stuffed that into the bag, too.

What lay inside the box was more precious to him than the daito.

He left the room, his feet leaving behind a few bloody prints.

Five men pounded up the stairway, heavy swords unsheathed. They reached the second floor as Raidon watched. The monk tightened the packs straps holding it to his back, held the daito straight out with one hand, then flipped off the edge of the walkway not far from where he'd pushed Huang's tormentor. Unlike the bloody-handed hatchet wielder, who still lay groaning, his limbs painfully askew, Raidon dropped in a series of graceful rolls, one hand free to catch, slow, and moderate his fall. He landed none the worse for wear and sprinted north, toward Waihun Road.

The men in the lead saw him, yelled, and turned to dash back the way they'd come, but the men below, who hadn't seen Raidon jump down, suddenly became obstacles to those higher up who reversed course.

Raidon left them all behind. He plunged into the cloaking anonymity of the crowd.

The monk passed into the gloriously decorated Shou Gate. The grand structure marked the most widely used route between the Shou community and the greater city of Telflamm that hosted the foreign district. Elaborate lamps sculpted to resemble golden dragons lit the way. Raidon had played near the gate, against the directives of his mother and father, as a child. Pretending to be some silk-draped trader arriving from mysterious eastern lands had been his favorite diversion.

As the gate fell behind his carefully measured steps, he wondered if he'd ever see it again.

The streets of greater Telflamm were different from Shou Town. Alien. He recognized many Shou walking the streets, but the smells, the markets, the structures, even the people, Shou and non-Shou alike—everything was atypical of the streets just blocks away. He wondered why the Shou Towners kept themselves apart from the natives of the lands they now called home. Afraid of losing their traditions? Unhappy with the culture of the indigents? Western traditions were somewhat known to Raidon. He suspected he was about to become intimately familiar with many things formerly unknown.

As he walked, he decided against the docks—it was the first place he'd thought of to flee Telflamm. The Nine Golden Swords would hit on the same strategy. So he hurried down the cobblestone streets in the opposite direction. His destination was the trade road that passed southeast out of the city. Perhaps he could sign onto a caravan heading to Two Stars. He'd always wanted to make that trip. It would be his coming-of-age journey, he decided.

Perhaps he eluded the Nine Golden Swords. Or maybe they gave up the chase of their own accord. Whatever the reason, Raidon was unmolested when he exited the city proper through high gates. As best he could determine, no Golden Sword marked his departure.

He questioned a few seedy-looking merchants whose wheeled stalls were set up just outside Telflamm's legal boundary. They pointed him down the road toward a rambling edifice surrounded by stables, carts, and several large warehouses—an eatery called the Leaping Ogre Taproom. According to one gap-toothed fellow, the place was a touchstone used by caravans departing and arriving in Telflamm down the Golden Way. Raidon learned he could get a job working a trade wagon if he was "good with that sword you got there—watch it! Put it away, why don't you?"

Raidon required a sheath for his daito—a saya, as they called it in Shou Town. Carrying a naked blade in one free hand was attracting unwelcome attention. And despite his joy at regaining the blade, it proved awkward for all activities not related to fighting. He asked among the vendors and found his way to an old chicken keeper. The suspicious looking woman sold him a ratty saya for an obscene price. Raidon didn't have time to haggle. He had enough coins in his pouch to cover the price, barely, and besides, he'd soon find work on the road.

The Leaping Ogre Taproom was a bustle of activity. Raidon quickly learned that all new work was assigned at dawn outside, in front of the tavern. In the meantime, would he like a tankard of mead?

Raidon demurred, and instead spent the remainder of his coin on a room for the evening, a private room. He didn't want to find any more lodge mates strung up and dismembered. Tomorrow, if he landed a position with an outgoing trader, he'd be sharing living space with other hired hands soon enough.

He pulled out the cedar box where he kept his mother's forget-me-not. He hadn't gazed at the shining blue stone for some tendays. He'd been too busy as his plans for infiltrating the Nine Golden Swords moved toward culmination.

Raidon considered. Was his attachment to the old amulet a childish behavior he should leave behind with his departure from his home? It looked valuable; he could probably sell it for a reasonable sum. But his sentimental attachment to the object was forged over a decade of ownership. Raidon believed that as long as the stone shone, his mother, wherever she had gone, kept him in her thoughts. Selling it was out of the question.

He opened the box—

—and saw in an instant that the blue field around the tree was obscured in darkness.

Raidon's eyes lost focus and he blinked rapidly. His stomach clenched. What was he seeing? He couldn't understand. He looked in the pack for the real cedar box—this couldn't be it . . .

But it was. The amulet had, before this moment, shown a white tree silhouetted in brilliant cerulean. Now the tree-like symbol seemed shrunken, as if the encroaching darkness clenched it with savage pressure.

He couldn't imagine what had caused the change—his actions? Had leaving Telflamm caused this?

Growing up, he often gazed into the stone after his mother's departure. He always imagined the treelike symbol was emblematic of an ancient grove of trees his mother sometimes described.

A place she had called "Yuirwood."

Conviction crystallized. He would seek this place, this Yuirwood. What other reason did the amulet have for changing color, if not a sign declaring his destination?

CHAPTER FIVE

City of Laothkund, Shadow Tongue Lair

Gage passed into an expansive, obsidian-tiled chamber. It was wide like a temple, similarly solemn, and equally quiet. Ahead, two broad stone pillars framed his path in the direction of the chamber's far wall. Each square column bore a blazing, smokeless torch, lending bright, if uneven light to the front of the room. The columns blocked the torchlight from finding the chamber's rear, which was lost in depthless shadow. Except for the blue glimmer that lured Gage.

He passed into the shadowed end of the chamber and moved to the rear wall. His eyes adjusted, and he saw a fortune to rival a dragon's horde.

Boxes of rare perfumes that never arrived at the Nobles' Quarter.

A wide gold vessel filled with depthless liquid whose smell hinted at an ocean without bounds.

Paintings of dead masters, bricks of gold, rings of platinum, casks of vintages a hundred years old—the vault held treasures so tempting Gage was nearly overwhelmed. But none compared with the value of the singular magical sword that was his objective. He gained the far side of the chamber; he found that which he sought.

The blade, still in its scabbard, leaned vertically on its tip within a glass cabinet. Blue fire flickered on the pommel and limned the entire scabbard. The blade wanted to be noticed.

He took the time to carefully search the floor around the cabinet, the seams between the glass panels, the wall behind the cabinet, and the ceiling above. He smiled—no dastardly traps waited to part life from body of an offending thief.

Gage flipped the case open with his right hand and grabbed the pommel of the blade with his left.

His demon-gloved left. The instant he gripped the pommel, the eye on the back of the glove popped open wider than Gage had ever seen it.

Abominations shall be purged, a voice pronounced in his head. Then his left hand disappeared in a nimbus of burning, searing fire.

Gage screamed, as did his glove. He danced back, leaving the sword in the cabinet, waving a fireball of blue agony up and down, back and forth, streaking the air with lines of pain. He tripped, rolled, came to his feet, knocked over the box of perfume. Glass shattered and a pungent mix of odors bloomed. Next to it . . . he plunged his burning hand into the vessel of depthless water. He thrust as far as he could reach, until his shoulder was submerged. His hand didn't touch the bottom, even though the vessel looked only a foot deep. Was it an interface between Faerûn and an oceanic elemental plane? Regardless, its chill liquid swaddled and doused the fire.

The glove was burned to nothingness. The gauntlet with the demonic eye, whose gaze put fear and awe into his enemies . . . was completely gone. Its destruction had at least served him, providing some protection from Angul's defense, though his hand was red and blistered, and lingering pain tested his composure.

"Didn't like me, or my glove?" Gage wondered aloud. The image of Sathra's burned hand flashed in his mind's eye. Now he knew what had caused it.

The mouth on his remaining gauntlet began to cry and gibber.

"Hello, thief."

Gage snatched his burnt hand from the vessel. He saw that the door was blocked by Sathra and at least eight, perhaps ten bloody-eyed men. Those in the front carried knives, clubs, swords. Those behind aimed steady crossbows his way. The shadows whirling about the woman continued their sad litanies unabated, ". . . cold . . . knife in my side . . . face in the window . . . lost . . ."

The woman's hand seemed perfectly whole. She'd apparently found magical healing before returning to deal with him.

"Sathra! I can explain!" Gage backed toward the glimmering blade, his hands out in front of him as if to ward off an attack. His lone gauntlet continued sobbing.

"Oh, you will explain," she chuckled. "As soon as I strap you into something I've got downstairs. The fellow who sold it to me called it a Sembian Cradle. Very simple little chair—the cushion's replaced with a point. We strap you with a belt and hoist you onto the point, and pretty soon you'll be explaining more than you can imagine."

Gage swallowed. Sathra's use of torture devices was legendary. He'd die before he'd allow himself to be taken to her famous "Red Room."

"It's not like that—I've come to warn you! I—"

One of Sathra's fingers idly pointed. A shadowy form dropped out of orbit around her and charged Gage.

Gage extended his raised hands to arms' length, and hoped.

The flickering shape, a silhouette of a bent, haggard man,

reached an astral claw toward the thief. Soul-numbing cold brushed Gage, but the mouth on his gauntlet bit down.

Despite the immaterial nature of the gray-black creature trying to embrace Gage, his demon glove gripped it—at least, the horrible little mouth did. It somehow found toothy purchase on the insubstantial body. The shadow jerked, shuddered, and attempted to pull away, but failed. The mouth held on, began to chew and swallow. The silhouette bucked and scrabbled, frantically thrashing back and forth.

Gage, Sathra, and her men watched with various degrees of horror as the glove quickly ate the trapped shadow creature, leaving nothing behind but a final, whispery cry of pain. The thief was aghast, but tried not to reveal his shock on his face.

"So you see, Sathra," said Gage, getting his voice under control, "send me all the lightless souls you want. I can defeat them. And my demon glove enjoys sucking down living flesh twice as much as unmoored souls."

The woman glared, her eyes narrowing as she considered. The confident, cruel expressions on her thugs' faces were gone. Mutters of uncertainty broke out behind Sathra. Good. But his display and bluff would only hold them, not defeat them. He knew his gauntlet had a hard limit on its daily wakefulness, and even then, it could eat only one man or shadow at a time. Gage had to use their moments of confusion to find a way out. He backed up another step until he stood next to Angul's open case.

"Angul!" whispered Gage. "I know you can hear me. Listen. Allow me to wield you, and I'll return you to Kiril! These before you are the enemy; they stole you, not me. Let me wield you against them, and we both can get home. Deal?"

Sathra finally said, "Impressive trick. Binding a shadow to my own is expensive. But I've got more than one. Can you eat all of them at once? And deal with all my men while fending me off, too? Shall we find out?" Sathra had hit upon his earlier conclusion, damn her guess.

The thugs at her back didn't look happy at their mistress's proposed experiment, especially those in the first rank. But Sathra's instincts weren't wrong.

The thief ignored the crime lord, focusing instead on his only hope for salvation. "Angul, be calm . . . don't burn me, all right?" he whispered urgently to the blade. Would the sword take his deal? Gage reached out his left hand, ungloved and raw. Deal or no, he didn't want to antagonize Angul with another demon-gloved grasp.

"Stop that!" yelled Sathra.

She raised her arms toward the ceiling, then brought them down in a sinuous movement, mimicking an ocean wave. Her halo of flickering darkness tore away, becoming a wave of whispering shadow that crested toward Gage. Her men yelled and followed in the shadow's wake.

Gage snatched Angul and thrust its point toward the ceiling. Blue fire bloomed, bright as day, driving back darkness. Gage suddenly felt the strength moral certainty lends—felt it as if he'd always owned it. Tears broke from his eyes as all the failings of his life were laid bare, revealed in the sword's unrelenting light. Did he have Angul in his grip, or did the sword grip him?

These weren't his thoughts! He lived his life according to a code all his own. The enchanted blade sought to pervert his self-image. He wouldn't allow it! Gage wrestled with the feelings of remorse and repentance seeded by the blade. As he struggled, Sathra's shadow-surge foundered in Angul's sun-bright flame. Foundered, wavered, and began to evaporate like mist.

Sathra growled and with a gesture, dispersed the dark flock. She screamed, "Kill the man and get the burning sword, gods damn you!"

The men in the front rank flinched at her curse but launched themselves toward Gage. Gage remained still, transfixed with unsought enlightenment.

Those in the rear rank leveled crossbows, already cocked. The volley of bolts broke Gage's deadlock. Angul ceased its brainwashing ambush to sweep the air of iron bolts, deflecting all but the one that plunged into Gage's thigh.

He tensed with expected pain, but none came.

Your pain does not serve me yet.

The thief gasped as his legs, as if of their own impetus, propelled him toward Laothkund's crime lord. The offending, evil, blasphemous female would be eradicated for the world to be cleansed—

Gage grimaced and scrabbled to bring order to the tumultuous flow of his thoughts. The damned blade was in his head, changing his perspective, his outlook, his very sense of self. The sword's violation was . . . wasn't right. Even with his mind muddled, he was pretty sure Angul's mental violation wasn't the sort of thing normally ascribed to a good-aligned sword.

I am the arbiter of what is right, *and that which is not.*

Sathra retreated from his advance, gesticulating, creating a tracery of dark lines in the air. A spell was being birthed, she its dark midwife. Her men moved to buy her the time she required to finish its weave. He hacked with Angul, hacked again. One man sat suddenly, missing an arm. Another was felled like a tree. Another's head he stove in with the blunt side of the Blade Cerulean.

He parried a fourth's knife thrust, but the fifth clubbed his head. Light flared, then dimmed. No pain followed, no blood. Gage plunged the sword into the club wielder's chest. The man cried out in surprise, but Gage was already withdrawing Angul and swinging for the last fellow, who raised a sword.

The crossbowmen were swearing and fumbling to reload in mortal terror. They released another volley of bolts, more or less in unison. A few bolts tagged him, but he didn't pause to assess the damage.

Sathra's chanting took on a desperate note. Only one defender remained between her and Gage. Or more accurately, between her and Angul.

But that final defender parried two of Gage's thrusts with a maul of gray stone. The man's beard was snarled with small stone trinkets and charms. His head was shaved, and the tattoos scribed there marked him as a barbarian from the plains of Rashemen. Gage had heard tales of the tribesmen of that wild borderland. This was no ordinary thug.

"You're *my* meat," cried the barbarian. "I am Stolsin, the Grinder of Tribes!" As he spoke, he brought the maul down with force enough to render Gage's flesh to jelly. It would have ended there had not Angul jerked him clear.

Stolsin lifted his heavy maul into the air with no visible strain. The muscles twining his forearm were as thick and corded as tree roots. He screamed, "I've destroyed walking dead on the outskirts of Thay!" He moved, catching even Angul off guard, and struck Gage's left shoulder. Pain flared before the burning sword could erase it.

"I've dared the cold drake's icy lair on the glacier of—"

Gage lunged and pushed the Blade Cerulean's point into the man's abdomen. The barbarian gasped and fell. Gage guessed Stolsin, Grinder of Tribes, wished he'd parried more and boasted less.

But the barbarian's braggadocio had bought time for his crimelord. Sathra ceased chanting and finger waving. The fruit of her spell took its final form: a black-scaled, obsidian-toothed, shadow-clawed thing. A demon of the inky void. Cold air blasted Gage and he took a step back despite Angul's grip on his mind.

"Meet Demoriel," crowed Sathra, brandishing a fist still steaming with shadowstuff. She looked to the crossbowmen and said, "Finish him. Help the demon!" She turned and dashed toward the exit.

Gage wanted to run, too. But like a dog distracted by the scent of fresh spoor, Angul focused all its attention on the newcomer demon.

If it couldn't sizzle away Gage's remaining glove, if it couldn't slice Sathra into thin twins, it could, by the Cerulean Sign, bite deeply into this denizen of the Abyss. The blade's surety of purpose threatened to completely drown Gage's awareness of himself.

With an unfamiliar part of his mind, the thief wondered what the Cerulean Sign might be.

The crossbowmen howled, whether in fear or triumph, Gage couldn't guess, but they followed Sathra's command and continued to harass him with a hail of iron. The Blade Cerulean twitched and danced in his hand, deflecting those bolts it deemed fatal. Despite its tightly focused mind, the blade was rational enough to keep its wielder alive. But a few bolts slipped through.

Then Demoriel pounced. A writhing atrocity, it croaked forth a verse in a language unknown to Gage, but whose consonants seemed to grind at his soul. Angul translated directly into his mind, *Come back with me to the Abyss, sweet-meat! You already wear one of my brothers on your hand, mauled though he is!*

The thief's mouth went dry and his heart hammered. He had to flee, had to get past the demon—

Demoriel bore Gage down to the hard floor. It began to tear at his flesh. The crossbowmen paused, their eyes wide with horror. One said, "What if it finishes eating before its summons lapses?"

Sathra's men turned tail.

The demon tore a chunk from his shoulder. He yowled in surprised pain. This was how he would end? Eaten by a damned demon?

Join with me, and this demon shall fall.

Gage struggled even as his skin ripped and peeled away. Fighting the blade hadn't helped him; it had left him vulnerable. And in another few moments, he would be dead anyway . . .

He surrendered himself to Angul's will.

A blue haze fell across his eyes. Through the filter of Angul's perceptions, everything was suddenly, gloriously, perfect.

Someone was screaming, but the noise was distant, unimportant, not significant to the task at hand—even though the screamer turned out to be himself. He coughed blood, but the many weaknesses of flesh were no longer his concern. Something far stronger girded his frame and held him steady.

Angul's flame flashed and new vigor flooded his limbs. Flayed skin sloughed, unsullied flesh burgeoned and sleeted across his gaping wounds. Gage stood, heaving the demon up, too. Overbalanced, man, sword, and fiend crashed into heaped treasures.

Demoriel's grasp slackened and Gage pulled away, slashing with Angul, knocking the demon backward. It rolled, sinuously as a snake might, onto two cloven feet. It screamed again in its unholy tongue, *You anger me. More than your soul is forfeit—have you parents? A wife? A suckling child you spawned? I will find them, and they—*

The Blade Cerulean seared the demon's sharklike skin, textured its flesh with vicious swipes, broke its teeth on the hard side of its invulnerable iron. Yet Demoriel withstood this punishment as if it enjoyed the pain. It never ceased its obscene banter, but screamed louder, abyssal curses that smote stone and liquefied metal. A portion of the ceiling collapsed and the demon grappled Gage once more.

But this time, it was a clinch of desperation—Angul's punishments had weakened it. Demoriel attempted to encompass Angul and Gage in a great hug, trapping the blade against its body and thus preventing Gage from swinging the enchanted sword. Gage danced away, ending the demon's best chance to turn the battle's tide. Demoriel's wounds burned with fire, its eyes glazed with pain, and its mouth dripped, a bloody mass of shattered fangs. Yet it fought on. A bound thing, it was compelled to struggle until it triumphed or failed, or until the words that yanked it forth from outside the world lost their force . . .

Angul staked the demon to the floor. The blade pulsed with purifying fire. Of Demoriel, only ash remained. The demon's time in the world had proven brief.

Gage released his grip. Strength rushed from him like water emptying from a holed aquifer.

His remaining glove whimpered a childlike gurgle of loss and misery.

Chapter Six

City of Laothkund, The Gutter

"G'way," mumbled Kiril. Daylight pried at her eyelids. Worse, something small and four-footed pattered around on her back. What the Hells?

Where in Mystra's starry hair was . . . the smell of garbage and bile brought with it her memory. She lay in an alley alcove.

A fuzzy image of her defeating a sweaty dwarf in an arm wrestling contest took shape in her mind's eye. Had she quit the Smokehouse Inn after that? Maybe. If not then, then later. Somehow, lost in a whisky haze, she'd found her way to the alcove. Her muddy, sodden clothes hinted she'd been there a while. The greasy yellow clay on her shoes, legs, and arms matched the hue of the muck between the cobbles. That must have been earlier, when it was still warm enough for mud. The winter night, now giving way to day, had stolen the previous day's heat. The mud was ridged with ice and a coating of snow hid treacherous ruts.

She was frankly surprised she hadn't frozen to death. And the creature sharing the alcove with her . . . a rat!?

She gave an involuntary jerk, spooking the creature resting on her back. Its squeal sounded like a bag of dropped bells. It flew up across the alley and landed on a ledge. Despite being opalescent and faceted, it moved uncannily like a live thing. It reminded her of earth magic exploits performed by an old friend . . .

"Xet!" she exclaimed. "I thought you'd left me for good!" She shook her head, jarring loose a headache waiting in ambush.

Kiril brought a hand to her forehead and dislodged a heavy fur covering her body. She didn't remember the fur when she'd passed out. Of course, her faculties had been much the worse for wear then.

The crystal dragonet tolled a happy note and flew down to her.

"Did . . . did you bring this fur?"

A tiny, drakelike head on the end of a sinuous crystalline neck nodded.

"You saved my life. Damn interfering beast!"

It rang a resentful tone.

She glared at it a moment or two, but the headache wasn't so fierce it was able to conquer her desire to pierce last night's gloom.

If history was any guide, she'd done something humiliating, if not downright dangerous. She hoped she hadn't hurt anybody. Killed anybody, she amended. She was sure she'd hurt someone. She couldn't truthfully call it a bender if she didn't get into a fight. Lately, her barroom brawls were much more entertaining. Because of Gage.

Since she'd come to Laothkund, her new acquaintance Gage had proved the perfect partner on the tavern circuit. He was funny, could almost match her drink for drink, and fought like a wildcat. A sneaky wildcat. His forte was disabling assailants quickly.

This was how it usually went down: Kiril's foul mouth, purposeful baiting, and derision were enough to launch a stiff-necked merc or a righteous priest off a bar stool into Kiril's business. She took the brunt, and Gage backed her up, if he was around. They would laugh about it later. A few bruises here and there, a few more for their foes—what was the harm in that? Though she one time saw Gage lighten the purse of a cleric who lay groaning beneath a mead-sopped bench. She wasn't one for robbery, but to her mind stealing from priests was merely putting already stolen gold back into circulation.

Her stomach intruded with a new question: When had she eaten last? An image of thick porridge crystallized in her bleary brain. Next to a rasher of bacon. And some thick ale, of course . . .

She swayed to her feet, bracing herself on a wall. "Come if you're coming, then, I don't care," she lied to Xet. Truth was, she was pleased to see the gemlike dragonet. Its absence had revealed her attachment to it. Who would have guessed? Its most accomplished trait was its ability to irritate her. But it reminded Kiril of the time immediately before she'd come to Laothkund. The only good memory of the last ten years . . .

She knew an innkeeper who owed her a favor. She began trudging in the direction of the man's establishment, unsteady at first, but gaining composure as she moved. Xet chimed, then flew over and lighted on her shoulder. Kiril resisted her initial urge to shrug the creature off.

As she walked, her right hand fell of its own accord to her empty scabbard.

Angul!

Gone.

Vertigo and defeat pushed a forlorn groan from her lips.

She remembered, again. He'd been gone for days.

She knew it already, of course. But the mind's knowing and the body's are not the same. If she ignored his absence long enough, perhaps the next time she checked, he'd magically be back, as if never gone.

"Yeah, right, you canker-ridden half-wit," she chided herself. Thank Shar's dead promises she still had her flask of all-forgiving whisky if nothing else.

The flask was forged of bronze, probably made by wood elves. Verdigris obfuscated the deranged face chiseled into the flask's side—some ancient god of the vine. She didn't care who it was. She cared only that in all the years she'd owned it, it had never failed to produce its potent drink. Once a bottomless flask to assuage her infinite shame, it was now a reservoir to fill the hole of Angul's absence.

After some food, she'd pull out the flask and continue the cycle, until death claimed her.

A crowd milled in front of the entrance of the Green Warrior Inn and Tavern. Her thirst had grown desperate as she'd walked, and she scowled when she considered there might be some kind of delay in quenching it.

A crash, and an unkempt but hearty dwarf came hurtling through the front door. He screamed some consonant-laden phrase as he regained his feet and charged back into the inn.

More yells, the sound of breaking crockery and splintering wood; she recognized the telltale signs. This early? The crowd must have carried over from a particularly hard-drinking night, but . . .

She sidled up to a swaying man at the edge of the gathering who stank of fish and grease. She doubted she smelled any better considering how she had spent the night. "Who's fighting?"

The man, his skin a pallid yellow, slurred, "Crazy man

come in this mornin' afore dawn. Talkin' to his blade the whole time. Arguing, like. Then he went after a couple women of the evening, like he wus' gon' cut them . . ."

A crash blotted out part of the man's stumbling story.

". . . so everyone tried stop 'im. He's in there, waving that blue sword around—"

"Angul?" she exclaimed. Kiril shoved the drunk aside. He fell, complaining loudly. She paid no mind as she pierced the mob and charged through the tavern's gaping entrance. Xet clamped painfully down on her shoulder, holding on through the bustle.

She saw Gage. And there . . . was Angul! Gage held the flaming sword in a scalded hand. The man whirled around like a marionette whose strings were snagged, brandishing the burning blade with jerky motions. The mob from outside spilled into the tavern, but only the most hardened and most drunk encircled Gage.

How had Gage managed to pick up her sword—why hadn't Angul fried him? By the look of Gage's naked hand, the blade had at least tried. And what lunacy was Gage up to now?

A bald man with a menacing tattoo branded on his scalp yelled, "We're tired of your performance, freak! Get out of here!" He hurled a wooden tankard. The sword twitched, but decided against deflecting the attack. The tankard struck Gage on his right shoulder. He grunted and yelled, obviously at the sword, "Defend me, or our deal is through!"

A moment later, he screeched as a flaming blue ember dripped from the blade, licking Gage's hand clutched on the hilt. But he didn't give up his grip. He probably couldn't. Kiril recognized Angul's methods—punishment was its first recourse against a balky wielder. Which had never before been anyone but her, from the moment Angul was first forged.

Kiril broke through the ring of people, said, "Gage!"

Her old acquaintance whirled. "Kiril! Thank the Queen of Air! Make it let go!"

"Make 'him,' " she corrected. She hated the blade, hated him . . . but hate couldn't blunt her dependence.

Kiril held out a hand. Gage presented the sword, hilt forward, trepidation on his face. Relief washed all else away when Gage easily relinquished his grip to her.

When her hands touched the hilt's leather wrappings, she began to cry and curse. "I missed you," she whispered. Angul's angry flames flickered out, and a sense of utter well-being descended over the elf swordswoman. She didn't fight it.

Gage stood rubbing his hands together, one gloved, the other bare, looking at woman and sword reunited. His brow creased with the weight of his conundrum.

In a private room at a different inn across town, Kiril and Gage shared a plate of olives and cheese. Xet perched near the door, annoying wait staff and customers in the outer chamber with its incessant tinkling. Or so Kiril assumed, though no one complained.

"And here's the strange thing," said Gage, continuing the story of finding her stolen blade and stealing it back.

"Yeah?"

"Sathra didn't crave the blade herself. She was in the employ of someone else who wanted it. Someone named 'Nangulis.' "

In mid-swallow, Kiril choked.

Shaking off her coughing fit, she demanded, "Who?" Her tone was incredulous and hoarse. "Did you say . . . ?"

"Nangulis. Do you know him?" Gage watched her coolly, appraising her response. Kiril was too astounded to notice.

"Yes. I do. I did—he's dead. It can't be Nangulis."

Now Gage was surprised. He shook his head and replied, "I'm . . . Sathra was certain it was someone named Nangulis. Could you be wrong?"

Shaking with barely restrained emotion, Kiril replied, "Impossible." She unstrapped her scabbard and put Angul, still in his sheath, on the table between them.

"I know it couldn't be who you name because all that remains of Nangulis is Angul."

Gage stared at her, uncomprehending. "I don't understand."

Kiril barely heard him—she replied, faintly, "Half of him, anyway. Half his soul, forged into this unbending, bastard blade."

Gage's eyes grew wide. "His soul?"

Kiril nodded. "It's what gives the blade such power—he is a living soul, trapped in steel forever."

"So, you knew Nangulis, before . . ."

"Nangulis and I were close. We would have been joined in marriage had our duty allowed. Those dreams are long dead. All I have left of him is Angul." She put her hand on the sheath, her eyes tight and shining with moisture.

"Which is why I can never give up this damned blade. He's not Nangulis, but he's the closest thing I'll ever find of my love. You've returned something I would have died without."

The thief looked startled, and somehow guilty. He began to speak, paused, began again. "Well, thank the Queen of Air I was able to bring back your most cherished possession."

Kiril nodded, but grimaced.

"You don't really seem that happy about it. Is it—"

"The story is not so tidy, sadly," interrupted Kiril. "I treasure Angul, but at the same time, the sword is killing my conscience; killed it, actually, soon after I came to wield him."

Gage started to speak, but stopped again, his head cocked. He fumbled out a few words then started over. "You're going to have to explain. I haven't the faintest conception what you're talking about."

Kiril sighed and rubbed her eyes. "Gage . . ."

"I'm listening."

"You deserve to hear about him, if you care to. I'll tell you how I came to wield Angul, what I once was . . . and the sins I've committed in the name of an unbending ideal." The moisture in her eyes broke into twin tracks down her cheeks.

"I'd like to hear about it," Gage responded, his voice soft. He moved his gloved hand from the table, out of view.

"Before Angul, before I wandered, fought, and drank so much, I was a different person. I was a dutiful servant of an ancient order—the Cerulean Sign. Heard of it?"

Gage shook his head.

"Would have surprised me if you had." Kiril scrubbed away the wetness on her cheeks. "The Cerulean Sign is a rune of power created when things were not as they are today. Before men, or even elves walked the world, when the continents were divided differently than now, entities strange and powerful fought. When the future was a toss-up between sanity and abomination."

"Sounds bad."

"You can't imagine. But the Cerulean Sign was forged to oppose creatures that oozed down from mad realms to colonize Abeir-Toril. To a large extent, those long-vanished defenders of the virgin world succeeded. Abominations, both godlike and inconsequential, were pushed back. Abeir was forgotten. Mortal races eventually inherited the earth."

"Like you and me?"

"Right," agreed Kiril. Her voice regained a little of its strength as she spoke.

"Who were these defenders?" wondered the thief.

"Unknown. Too much time since then. They were damn tough, though. Gods, probably, or whatever passed for gods before people were around to call them divine."

Gage let out his breath, shaking his head ever so slightly, as if in disbelief. Kiril's eyes narrowed.

"You want to hear this or not?" She tensed as if to stand.

"No, please—I apologize," said the thief, leaning forward, suddenly conciliatory. "I didn't realize your story was going to have such . . . cosmic . . . size to it."

Kiril said, "I need to say this. Believe it or don't."

"I do believe it, and I want you to go on—I saved your sword, didn't I? I have a big interest in this."

The elf nodded. She leaned back in her seat and continued. "So, these vanished defenders and their Sign, while mostly effective, weren't completely successful. Monstrosities slipped into the world, some openly, others less so. Most are hidden away, yet remain terrors to those who find them in the dark below the surface. You've heard of aboleths?"

"Aboleths are the abominations?"

"Yes—well, related to the originals. Far worse tried to openly colonize reality. They failed, yet they retain a foothold even after all these eons. There's always a chance they'll rise as one from their ancient strongholds. But that prospect is not unopposed. Once, I guarded against the possibility."

"You did?"

"Blood, yes! Don't sound so surprised. I told you I was not always as I seem now. Once I had a civil tongue." Kiril laughed.

"I was a Keeper of the Cerulean Sign—one of a small group of guardians loyal to the ancient knowledge. We nurtured comprehension of the Sign, so that primeval aberrations are opposed whenever they stir."

"And do they? Stir, I mean?"

"They do. Mostly by proxy—they send nightmares that insinuate dreams, hollow hearts, and madden minds. Sometimes, their influence finds particularly susceptible, but powerful mortals. If the seduction goes to completion, a priest of the old ones is born, a priest whose single self-proclaimed duty is to call the oldest abominations forth into the light of day. A priest pledged to call forth apocalypse. A twisted bastard who wants nothing more than to stand laughing amidst the ashes of reality."

"Akadi's tricky fingers!" exclaimed Gage.

Kiril nodded, agreeing with the man's sentiment. She cleared her throat. "In a hidden realm where elves dwell, within the Yuirwood, a man succumbed to this very seduction. He was branded the Traitor, and he was locked away in a dungeon forever. The name of that dungeon is Stardeep—"

Kiril paused, noting Gage's sharp intake of breath. "What is it?"

"I'll tell you when you've finished. Don't interrupt your story—the name sounded familiar, is all."

"All right . . . so anyhow, up until ten years ago, I was a warden there—in Stardeep. So was Nangulis. We served together for five years in that role, but knew each other even before that."

Gage cupped his chin in his hands, resting his elbows on the table. He asked, "What happened—did the Traitor get out? Is that why you're . . . so sad and disillusioned?"

"Yes, he escaped. When he got out, he assumed a mantle of abominable power, becoming seemingly invincible. Things seemed bleak but Cynosure told us of one last fail-safe . . ."

"Cynosure?"

She frowned at the interruption and said, "Cynosure is a sentient idol whose mind lives throughout Stardeep. The idol commands embedded sorceries throughout the dungeon. For instance, he can teleport willing Keepers from place to place."

"Really? That's incredible . . . uh, sorry, never mind. You found a fail-safe, you said?"

"Nangulis and I, along with the mind of the fortress, called upon ancient Cerulean lore to fashion a weapon potent against all evil, a weapon whose righteousness would be especially effective against aberrations, as well as the Traitor who wielded their abilities."

Kiril ran her hand down Angul's sheath. "But the creation of such an effective weapon was not possible without sacrifice. To create the weapon, we required the willing contribution of a living, purified soul. All the goodly, just, righteous aspects of a soul, which would be transformed and manifested as a physical object. Over this, Nangulis and I fought, but time was short, our plight desperate. I know not how he convinced me; it would happen differently now if I had it to do over. But in the end, the Blade Cerulean was forged, and Nangulis, what remained of him, emerged from the process as unyielding steel."

"Incredible."

"And so I took up this new weapon, untested, its essence vibrating with he who I couldn't yet believe was gone. I took up Nangulis, renamed Angul, and with him, battled the Traitor to a standstill, though his vile tricks nearly killed me. We beat him, battered him, schooled him in the ways of Righteousness . . . and returned the dung-eating bastard to the nadir of the Well, Stardeep's most secure prison."

"If you overcame the Traitor, why didn't you just kill him? Seems like a lot of trouble to keep him alive."

"If it were only that simple, Stardeep wouldn't have been built in the first place."

"Oh? Some sort of elf law against killing your own?"

Kiril snorted and shook her head. She said, "His death would be a clarion call to the very creatures we do not wish disturbed. Left to his own devices, he would have induced them to rise. Killed, his flaring, dissipating essence would signal the first day of a renewed colonization. The Traitor is more abomination than man; he's their highest high priest. So we keep him safe."

"He doesn't try to starve himself to death down there?"

"When he signed his soul over to the Abolethic Sovereignty, his mortal needs were erased. He cannot die merely through neglect."

Gage blinked. "I need a drink." He stood, walked to the door, and yelled into the hubbub of the common room, "Two ales!"

A drink sounded like a first-class idea to Kiril, too. She remained silent until the flagons were delivered, and Gage refrained from plying her with more questions until they'd both had a chance to sample the brew. Not especially good. She took another swallow. She needed it if she was going to tell Gage the whole story to its awful conclusion.

Gage said, "You must really miss him. Nangulis, as he was, I mean." He waved at the sword on the table.

"You still don't know it all," Kiril declared, then she fell silent again.

Gage waited her out.

Finally, the elf continued. "You've held Angul. So you know the overwhelming nature of his personality. When you wield the Blade Cerulean, remaining in possession of your own thoughts is difficult. Everything seems decided already, and Angul believes himself the final arbiter. Frankly, I can't believe you resisted running through everyone in that bar. Angul would see them all as dissolute wastrels crying out for his special loving attention."

"Only because I made a deal with it—him—before I picked him up. The second time, anyway. The first time, he ignited one of my gauntlets." Gage raised his left hand, red and blistered, and flexed it. Pain flitted across his face.

"He's that way, now," sighed Kiril. "Punishing. He doesn't like that I've discovered ways to temper his influence. He wants total control—he believes such is his right. But I wasn't always so resourceful. Nor did I see a need to be. Angul seduced me to his will by being in some ways identical to Nangulis."

Gage nodded. "I sensed he was trying to take over my mind."

"After the Traitor was remanded back to Stardeep's most secure dungeon cell, I stayed as the Keeper as I had been, now wielding Angul. I spent most days in constant contact with the blade, so I could mingle with his sense of certainty, what I thought was his glorious revealed knowledge. His absolute distinction between good and evil. While I was out on patrol one day, that distinction fell on the wrong side of the dividing line."

When Kiril's pause threatened to become a full stop, the thief asked, "What do you mean?"

"I mean Angul decided that a group of unruly children who had wandered too near Stardeep, when they should have known better, were no longer worth tolerating. Before that day was over, while wielding Angul, I . . ."

An oft-thumbed memory swept up from the abyss of Kiril's soul, as it sometimes did when her defenses were most fragile. In her mind's eye, she saw she was dressed as a Keeper of Stardeep; her mail was black, trimmed with silver thread. In her hands, Angul burned, shedding the warm certainty of the *truth*. A promise soon to be shattered forever. She began to tell Gage about the worst day of her life.

"I was patrolling beyond Stardeep, in the daylight world, looking for spies on the perimeter . . ."

The swordswoman walked beneath a dark pine canopy. The burning sword she held aloft illuminated her path, as if she were an avenging angel. And wasn't she? Her cause was *just* and *good*. Her blood was fired with Angul's conviction, her mind focused with his clarity, and her heart hardened with his faith. Nothing could stand in their way, and while she gripped the burning blade, fear was an emotion unknown to her, and more; an emotion reviled.

Prowlers camped near the Causeway Gate. Too near. If the Causeway emerged from the interstitial mists that cloaked it, the intruders would see Stardeep's main entrance. Considering the recent escape attempt by the prisoner, the encampment's sudden appearance was too suspicious to let pass. After the sacrifices made to ensure the Traitor's continued captivity, Kiril was determined not to take any chances. Angul, new to her hands, agreed emphatically.

Sneaks and cutpurses coddled fear, and used it to inform their bloodless deceits, retreats, and ambushes. Worry was fear's watchword, and it nudged and pushed the timid into the grave just as surely, if not as quickly, as a fearless attack that failed to win the day. At worst, the eulogy of the warrior who bravely fell in conflict would be remembered for centuries, whereas those whose fear preserved them would die unremembered in cold beds, alone.

Not that death was likely with a magical blade of Angul's strength in her keeping. Joined, hilt to hand, she and Angul would be together forever. After all, the blade's power made certain little could permanently harm her flesh.

Kiril spied the camp. Two hide tents, finely cured, with subtle sigils cut into the surface. The interlopers were apparently not orcs or the other coarse peoples. No, these must be wood elves who ranged yet in Aglarond. They should know better than to camp so close to the megaliths! It was part of the compact established when the Yuir elves first moved out of Aglarond and into their artificial realm. Had the remnant elves forgotten?

Ignorance is no excuse, Angul imparted to her conscious mind, *their presence is in violation of the compact of Yuireshanyaar.*

"Yes," she breathed, "of course." The intruders must be induced to leave. Immediately.

Kiril moved to within five or so paces of the tents. She saw no movement, despite the warning her blade's light provided.

"Come out and be judged!" she bawled in Elvish.

Whispers broke from the tents, and a moment later, four or five lithe forms emerged. As she'd guessed, wood elves, or half-elves most likely, members of the degraded fey race that remained behind after the Yuir departed. She hadn't guessed these would be children, or nearly so.

The oldest, a youth of no more than fourteen or fifteen suns, stepped forward. His hair was strung with garlands, his torso inked with patterns of leaves and acorns. He responded in the same language. "We are on a quest, and mean no harm. We—"

"You have broken the compact," interrupted Kiril. "Why?"

"We . . ." the youth's initial confidence began to collapse in the face of her asperity. ". . . We seek to discover a truth. Our seer spoke of a prophecy."

"What prophecy?"

"About the megaliths. She said the Yuirwood's 'salvation or destruction lies beyond stony bounds of the ancient rings.' "

Kiril frowned. She'd never liked prophets. The riddles they spoke were too easily decoded in a manner convenient to the interpreter. And true prophets irked her more; she had a visceral distaste for the concept of predestination.

"Who is this prophetess?" demanded Kiril. If some hoary old tribal shaman was able to determine which among the hundreds of stone circles in the Yuirwood opened onto Stardeep, well, that was a real security hazard.

Instead of answering directly, the boy said, "We came here to see if the words she spoke were true. Who are you?" The last was asked with a tremulous waver, as Kiril's stony expression hardened into a scowl.

"Your judge," she responded. "And I judge you've overstayed your welcome. Be gone."

They have disregarded the treaty upon which the realm of Sildëyuir was born, and on which the security of Stardeep depends.

Kiril's sword spoke the truth. It saw past all distractions to the heart of the matter, she was learning. She lowered the tip of the sword to point at the interlopers. The boy's companions shrank away.

Not the boy. He held his ground, screwed up his courage once more, and said, "You are not of the tribes, are you? I see you are a full-blood elf, but not of these woods, or even those far to the north. Have you come from behind the menhir circle? Is it true star elves roam there, in a realm apart?"

These children guess too much. Stardeep's defense is imperiled.

"Yes!" she agreed aloud with her blade, not the child. The sword lent her a focus completely new to her experience. It was almost like having Nangulis himself at her side. When he was alive, he had called her his Bright Star . . .

"You are? But that's wonderful!" exclaimed the boy, misunderstanding her response. He had no inkling of the death sentence silently handed down by the Blade Cerulean.

She closed the distance between them with five quick steps and brought the sword around. When the blade swept through the space beneath the boy's jaw, she hardly felt a tug on the hilt. The youth's head rolled into the underbrush. Fluids sprayed. She blinked blood from her eyes.

The murdered elf's companions stood frozen in soul-stopped horror. She continued moving, making one harvestlike motion after another, taking advantage of the interlopers' shock. Sword in hand, she moved to eliminate Stardeep's liability.

Her lips moved, too, but Angul's words were in her mouth. "We do not suffer abominations."

She learned that day that Angul impelled where dry reason faltered. Angul excited where debate and philosophy failed to motivate. With Angul in hand came purpose, exaltation, and the ultimate high of being part of a spectacular moment. A moment in which Angul delivered triumph in the face of insurmountable odds . . .

The screams of the children, as she cut them down, penetrated her blade-given conviction. She paused, wiping blood from her face with the back of one gauntleted hand, her eyes blinking. Abominations . . . ? What in the name of the Well was she doing? These were children! And she had . . . she was . . .

An arrow bloomed in her abdomen. She shrieked, went down on one knee. A girl had run when the others had remained within Kiril's fatal reach. She'd escaped the swordswoman's initial onslaught. But she stopped to loose an arrow, despite the fear trembling her limbs. The half-elf girl pulled another arrow to her bowstring.

Kiril struggled onto both feet, her breath ragged. Angul flared and the ache in her stomach melted. Like moral distractions, pain was a diversion to the glorious certitude Angul burned to dispense. With the pain, her moment of confusion, too, was swept away in cerulean light.

She raised the sword and his blue-white light doubled, then redoubled. Sunrise came early under the branches of Aglarond. Or was it sunset?

Kiril swatted the girl's second arrow out of the air with a twitch of her wrist. The half-elf turned to run. The swordswoman launched Angul through the air as if he were a spear.

Her aim was true.

When all was quiet again, she gathered the bodies and burned them on a pyre. To do so, she sheathed Angul.

Later, she retrieved from the heaped ashes the fire-cleaned skull of the girl, the elf archer, the only one who'd put up any kind of fight. She decided she would bring it back to Stardeep as a trophy, a sign of her vigilance in keeping the hidden dungeon stronghold safe.

As the fire burned down, she resisted drawing her blade again. Instead, she fingered the skull, looking at it, worrying it between her hands. Something was hideously significant about the object she held so tightly. It indicated something portentous, but like a puzzle box, she couldn't solve its significance. She stood, thinking to return down the Causeway before the access failed. But . . .

The longer she avoided contact with the blade, the more the blade's influence waned.

Finally, her captive conscience burst through the final, benumbed layers of Angul's influence.

Kiril screamed, long and loud. She collapsed to her knees, clutching the skull in front of her, her eyes bulging in disbelief. It couldn't be! She hadn't! But the warm, fire-blackened skull in her blood-stained grasp refused to retreat to the phantasmal state she needed it to be.

Then Kiril went insane.

Kiril's voice broke, but she managed to croak, "I slaughtered them."

The elf looked down, tears streaking her cheeks.

Gage whispered, "Damn."

"It broke me. I've been running since then, running from what I did. But I . . ."

". . . you kept the thing. Why?" interjected Gage.

Why hadn't she gotten rid of the sword? At first, she was crazed, incoherent; she couldn't quite recollect what she'd done in the year after she'd slain the children. One thing was certain; she had not returned to Stardeep. By fleeing, she renounced her position as Keeper and her identity as a star elf.

She'd thrown it all away. But Angul, she kept.

Even mad, she couldn't bring herself to cast him away. And now, ten more years, at least, had got behind her.

Aloud, she said, "I couldn't leave Angul behind! He's all I had left of Nangulis! But he's a curse, too, don't I flecking know? And now you tell me Sathra dealt with someone called Nangulis. Impossible! Isn't it? Where is she? I must talk to her." Kiril made to rise, determination firing her eyes.

"Hold on!" Gage reached across the table and put a restraining hand on her shoulder. "After I got hold of the sword and got clear of her vault, she attacked me again. With the blade in hand, I killed her. So, uh . . . sorry. She can't tell you anything because she's out of the picture. But . . ."

"But?"

"She indicated the fellow she was working for hailed from someplace called Stardeep."

Kiril shook her head, tears again tracing tracks on her face. She said, "Stardeep. After all these years, it reaches out to me."

Slowly mastering herself, the elf considered. The name, the theft, the possibility, however minute, that Nangulis might somehow be among the living again. She couldn't ignore that chance.

"Stardeep has called, and I must answer," she decreed, tears breaking around a sudden unexpected smile.

Chapter Seven

Stardeep, Epoch Chamber

"Cynosure?" Telarian asked the empty air of the Epoch Chamber.

"Yes?" said the disembodied golem's cultured voice.

"I'm done for now. Connect me to my quarters."

"Very well. Hold still . . ."

Telarian waited for the idol to set up the transfer. Cynosure always required a span of moments to process each new point-to-point teleportation in the Outer Bastion. Of course, such tricks were not allowed at all in the Inner Bastion, which contained the Well. That is, they were not normally allowed, but Telarian had been working on contingencies . . .

Just one more thing he'd failed to inform Delphe about. As with everything else, he justified keeping her in the dark on some of his activities because her role in Stardeep was so time consuming. Yet her dedication was futile. Her vigil at the edge of the Well was doomed to failure. He now understood, thanks to his visions, Xxiphu would one day rise whether or not the Traitor gained his freedom.

A blue flash and piercing odor, a moment of disorientation,

and Telarian was back in his private room, a few levels above where he'd secreted the doorless Epoch Chamber. His room opened off a common hall in the Inner Bastion.

His unsteady hands found the neck of a wine bottle, then a glass. Not even the finest vintage could withstand neglect, and the wine in the bottle had turned vinegary and rancid. He should have finished it sooner after opening it a few tendays past, but he drank alone these days, and in moderation. Hard to finish a bottle before it turned sour. But his own cussed fastidiousness wouldn't permit him to throw it out and uncork a new one. Waste not, want not.

His thoughts remained on Delphe. For the thousandth time he wondered if perhaps he shouldn't bring her up to date on his preparations. Would she understand the risk they must undertake to avoid the disastrous certainty he had foreseen?

No, he didn't think she would. In fact, she would likely declare him mad with one breath, and disown him with the next.

Madness. In the lonely passage of time between shifts, he sometimes wondered. There might be a tinge of madness to his actions. Then again, madness is what those with limited imaginations called inspiration, imagination, and even revelation.

He knew first hand of places where doctrine had taken firm hold, where free thinkers and visionaries were abhorred. But without revelation, civilization's zenith would yet hunker in caves, drawing stick figures by firelight.

True, some prophets walked too close to the line separating inspiration from crazed imprecation. But the ones remembered as paradigm-changers and world-savers far after the fact were derided by their contemporaries. And though they sometimes faltered and fell, others in their wake benefited from the sacrifice.

Telarian's problem was he couldn't wait for the historians of later ages to acclaim his actions as heroic and necessary. What he had to do in the present, without the context the future would bring, was hard to explain to someone who doubted the effectiveness of divination magic to begin with.

Like Delphe. If he told her the truth, her apprehension concerning the predictive arts would lead to questions, accusations. Action. He couldn't afford strife. It was the same conclusion as ever before: he would proceed as he had been.

Thankfully, convincing Cynosure to side with him relied less on the art of persuasion and more on technical wizardry. Telarian had a knack for golem and construct enchantment, despite his primary focus in oracular insight. He had surreptitiously applied that skill to the linked nodes making up Cynosure's mind. After a year of gradual tinkering, the sentient idol was now partially under Telarian's control.

Cynosure was free-willed no longer, though its greater mind didn't realize a lesser portion of itself was almost completely commandeered. Despite this success, Telarian remained stymied; none of the tactics he'd devised had proven capable of overriding Cynosure's control over the Inner Bastion. It was too fundamental to the construct's creation. He eventually realized he would never succeed in gaining complete control of the sentient idol. It had become necessary to pursue other options. Of course, even if he had complete control of the construct, another tool was also required.

He trailed a finger up the length of his sword scabbard. What would Delphe do if she found out about Nis?

He shuddered. He removed the scabbard from his belt, careful not to touch the pommel of the dark blade.

His conscience skittered across the surface of his resolve. Too late. He'd done it; he couldn't undo what he'd forged.

He had learned the secret of the armory's existence, a place created by the previous Keepers, with Cynosure's help. In the armory, he found the vessel containing the split soul.

It was a half-soul, separated from its lighter half. Before being split, all the soul's goodness, all its righteousness, and all its morality were strained and infused into an animate blade of virtuous light: Angul. With that singular blade, the Traitor's most successful bid for escape in a millennia was foiled. The success of that event was known to all Keepers, though none realized what had gone into making the Blade Cerulean. None now recalled the sacrifice of the man who made the blade's existence possible.

A soul split along philosophical lines has two parts, as there is no light without darkness. Sin would not exist without morality. What is certainty without doubt to measure it against? The half-soul Telarian found was the detritus left over from Angul's forging.

Why the half-sentient thing had been preserved, when it should have been destroyed, was a real question. Perhaps the Keeper who forged it with Cynosure's aid was too sentimental? Or had fate stepped in on Telarian's side? Either way, that lapse was Telarian's opportunity.

His elaborate plan took form in the ashes of dream-tossed nights, as so many of his divinatory visions had since he'd come to Stardeep and looked into the Well. Something had opened in him then, and now his best insights came unbidden. In fact, it was during just such a divinatory dream that he first learned of the armory, and the stored half-soul. The future had seized his eyes and shown him the way.

Upon waking, Telarian asked Cynosure to transfer him to the armory, despite the idol's protestations that no such place existed in Stardeep. But Telarian trusted his vision, and overruled the idol. Cynosure teleported him into a space that didn't exist on any map—and found himself where Stardeep's history had been fashioned.

A dark, decommissioned vault, it contained a furnace,

forge, magical fire, and masterwork tools capable of forging weaponry. And most importantly, in a darkened alcove resided a glass vessel where the fractured thing dwelled.

Soon thereafter, Telarian began his sword-forging project. He knew little of the craft, so his dreams began to instruct him.

He recalled how he carefully decanted the half-soul, inky and deceitful, into the cast already seething with molten steel. With Cynosure's halting aid, he mixed soul and metal into a singular bound thing.

He remembered beating the howling, screaming shaft of white-hot metal. It cried for release from torturous pain, as if alive. He could still smell the acrid salt and oil of the quenching.

When he removed the blade from the bath, its white-hot glow was gone. But it was only as Telarian tempered the blade over the ensuing tenday that all trace of hue slowly faded, until it was utterly colorless.

The naked blade was like a blind spot, a gap in perception. It took the name Nis, the Blade Umber. When Telarian grasped its hilt . . .

When he grasped the hilt, he forgot fear. His disordered thoughts cleared. The solutions to problems and difficulties he'd noted in other parts of Stardeep rushed upon his brain as clarity washed over him, and cold logic grasped his heart and squeezed. As he caught his breath, it seemed to him that nothing was really beyond him—no problem couldn't be overcome, nor challenge met, if only he was able to devise the appropriately reasoned plan. Lucidity wracked his frame, and his mind ran and leaped, but could not win free. Some part of him did escape, and darted out upon a dim plain of disquietude. But it was fragile, easily eviscerated.

Telarian gasped, allowing his reverie to lapse. He took another large gulp of the nearly rancid wine. He'd learned not to touch the hilt. The time for drawing Nis would come soon enough.

Already, his agent in the outer world reported success in locating the bright twin of his newly forged dark sword. He disliked dealing with liars, backstabbers, and spies. But in this particular circumstance, the ends justified the means, he wholly believed. Telarian would stymie the Sovereignty's appearance, but only if he pushed through all interference, all weakness. All foibles and regrets of conscience.

His success would be assured once his agent completed the assignment and delivered him the sword Angul.

With Angul in one hand and Nis in the other, he would combine the blades, merging the split souls into the unified whole they once were. Then he would see about the Traitor's release.

Chapter Eight

City of Telflamm, Gates

The caravan set out from Telflamm, making good time down the Golden Way. Grasslands and cleared farmlands soon gave way to forested boughs in the north—the Forest of Lethyr.

The saddle transmitted a jolt up Raidon's spine with each step of his steed. At first tolerable, he was fast approaching the point where he supposed the regular punishment would probably kill him. Where swords, enchantments, curses, and vengeful criminals had failed, a long journey by horseback would accomplish.

Raidon wondered if contracting as a caravan guard had been the best idea. Quent, the caravan chief, explained he would gain his saddle legs soon enough. In the meantime, Raidon required all his discipline to ignore the pain.

They stayed the night beyond the walls of Phent, where Quent received several wooden crates in trade for a few stained barrels. Raidon didn't inquire what was contained in either. It wasn't his business to know, but more significantly, extinguishing the least hint of saddle-soreness from his joints required the majority of his attention.

When Raidon's hauling and lifting duties for the evening were complete, he moved some distance from the encampment to practice his forms. Soon enough, he was stepping lightly over the frosted grass, slicing the air with his moon-sheened daito, his breath a cloud of white, the jolts of the day a mere memory.

The next morning they veered off the Golden Way, taking a lesser-traveled trade route south, toward the jagged spine of the Dragonjaw Mountains. Quent boasted of a secret pass he knew that would see them straight through to the edge of the Umber River, and then back to the city of Emmech in Aglarond. Raidon nodded, but thought about his darkened forget-me-not.

They camped in a slew of rugged, bare-topped hills bordered by sharp, razor-edged peaks. As darkness descended, bone-chilling winds stole down from the Dragonjaws to race each other through the maze of surrounding hills and valleys. The temperature dropped so precipitously the horses had to be gathered in the lee of the wagons for fear they would freeze.

Raidon supposed that he trusted Quent. The man was obviously a veteran of several trips. The caravan chief led a tight crew. From the discipline he instilled in the scouts who ranged ahead, keeping eyes out for trouble, to the concern he demonstrated for the welfare of the pack horses, to the punishment he doled out to the grub cook for failing to give Raidon equal portions the previous day, it was clear Quent wasn't one to leave things to chance.

The next morning broke with an out-of-season storm. The night's screaming wind had been the harbinger of a movement of warmer air out of the west, but the scourging rain that pelted them was worse than snow. Quent thought they could get clear by heading over the pass instead of waiting the storm out. So they broke camp and rode south, up the hills toward the razor peaks, huddled on the necks of their horses or within the shelter of the three wagons. Quent found the track and they ascended through lashing winds and a downpour of rain that turned to bitter sleet. They pushed forward through a slender ravine, while above them thunder followed closely on the heels of shrouded streaks of lightning. Raidon clung to his horse, its warmth a welcome aid in conserving his own heat.

The storm fizzled out after they left behind the highest point of the pass. Quent called a halt and passed around a celebratory flask of watered wine. Raidon sipped, despite normally abstaining from such things—this was a celebration of sorts, and he wouldn't insult his employer by refusing to partake.

With half a day's light left, the caravan chief called camp. His entire crew was exhausted. And one of the three scouts had yet to return from his foray down to the edge of the Umbar.

Raidon prepared a small fire only ten or so paces from the larger cook fire and, with supplies from his pack, boiled a kettle of water. He produced his precious package of loose Long Jing and brewed a fragrant kettle of tea. Raidon offered to share a cup with everyone who wished to sample it.

Quent, his black hair peppered with experience, gratefully accepted a cup. The man was worldly enough to properly thank Raidon for an excellent pour.

Quent's crew was less practiced. Hark and Sulvan, the two scouts who had returned on schedule, each accepted a cup and smiled. The wagon drivers, Ledroc, Corthandu, and Khuldam the dwarf, waved him off. They were happy sharing a flask among themselves. Raidon got a whiff from the flask; it was something harder than tea.

Three others who, like Raidon, had signed on to guard the caravan against brigands and move crates, all accepted a cup with silent nods. One was a dwarf who spent an inordinate amount of time braiding his beard. Raidon never did learn his name—the dwarf either couldn't or wouldn't speak in a tongue anyone could understand. The dwarf never strayed far from his pride and joy, a crossbow runed with faintly glowing lines.

The two brothers, Erik and Adrik Commorand, argued constantly. Raidon tried to follow their talk, but it concerned topics too esoteric for the monk's training: somatic, material, and verbal power components, mostly. The brothers were sorcerer-mercenaries. The two were Quent's concession to reports of increased Red Wizard activity in the area. The monk wondered at the brothers' abilities—either the Commorands were rank novices, or the caravan chief had deeper pockets than Raidon would have guessed. Either way, the brothers were gracious to Raidon.

In fact, everyone was friendly enough, or at least not unfriendly, except the grub cook Japhoca.

Japhoca was a blond-haired, hard-bitten tribal from the plains of Rashemen, and she disliked Raidon the moment she laid eyes on him. From the comments she'd let slip, she held his ancestry against him. Strange. He supposed the woman had tangled with the Nine Golden Swords. Those outside Shou Town didn't always know that the organization was reviled among honest Shou. But it was not his responsibility to bring the woman clarity. Her prejudice was her burden to bear, not his.

When he offered her a steaming cup, she grunted and said, "I don't treat with half-bloods." She spat and stalked off. Raidon paused a beat, then poured the cup of tea out on the ground. He hated seeing Long Jing wasted, but the cup had been poured and refused. Decorum insisted on its disposal.

His surmise concerning Japhoca's dislike had apparently been mistaken. What had she meant by half-blood? His mother's blood, of course. Something he never gave thought to. Her likeness manifested in him only faintly. His ears may have been slightly pointed, the shape of his skull was perhaps narrower than other Shou, and his bearing was straight, though no straighter than any other practitioner of Xiang Do. He thought of himself as Shou. The knowledge that others might see him as something different threatened to pull him out of his carefully constructed focus. He concentrated on rinsing out the cups and tea pot, imagining his mind a depthless pool of water. Insult, injury, and pain were as pebbles and rocks thrown into that pool—the water would absorb them all and show nothing but a placid, untroubled surface. Raidon returned his implements carefully to his pack.

A shout. Heads turned down the tree-lined path. The last scout appeared, riding hard.

His voice came harsh and panicked on the wind. "Thayan patrol! Red Wizards on the river!"

The camp exploded with hustling forms. Quent screamed for his caravan guards. The Commorand brothers and the dwarf crossbowman immediately heeded the chief's call. Raidon glanced at his pack with all its precious contents. No time to stow it—he slipped it onto his back as he joined Quent and the others.

Quent was pointing up . . . two figures hung red in the air over the trees, as if standing on an invisible tower. The hard-riding scout looked up and back, terror evident on his face. The hovering Red Wizard on the right, a woman, raised a ruby-tipped wand. From its tip burst a swarm of angry red pinpoints that descended unerringly upon the scout. The scarlet points burrowed into his flesh as he screamed and convulsed.

The scout's blood-spattered, wild-eyed horse returned to camp without its rider.

Quent pulled an arrow from his quiver, drew, and released. The shaft arced high into the air. Mere feet from its target, it bounced away, as if hitting a brick wall, though one without color or shape. Undeterred, the dwarf crossbowman cranked hard on his enruned weapon. An iron bolt screamed up and buried itself in her torso. She shrieked and her stance wavered in the air. A shimmering globe briefly sparked into visibility around her then faded.

The dwarf voiced something incomprehensible, though his tone was satisfied. He selected another metal bolt and began to crank again on his crossbow's mechanism.

High above, the male Red Wizard pointed a strangely irregular blue wand. Raidon, responding to cues he couldn't articulate, dived away from the dwarf an instant before a bolt of the storm's pure fury connected wand and dwarf. The blast still lifted and threw the monk against the side of a wagon, though he absorbed the impact with a midair roll. A dark, many-legged column lingered across his vision; he blinked away the after-image and saw the smoking remains of the dwarf, charred fingers yet clutching his beloved, red-hot crossbow.

Quent was across the clearing, staggering to his feet. One Commorand brother was on the ground, his staff blown to splinters. The other, Adrik, remained upright, the grass around his feet unburned.

Raidon gained control of his breathing and dashed toward Adrik. He gasped, "Can you bring them down?"

The sorcerer nodded briskly, his hands already essaying a complicated nulling pattern, his lips shaping words whose meanings slipped across Raidon's memory without leaving a mark. Adrik finished by throwing wide his arms. A pulse of mazing, twirling energy leaped up and around the suspended wizards. The woman, her footing in thin air already questionable, dropped like a stone. The man wavered, then rapidly dipped behind the tree line. The Red Wizard hadn't fallen; he'd merely descended under cover.

"By the coin!" yelled the sorcerer, "he's still alive! If he gets away, he'll call down a full Thayan patrol!"

Raidon bolted down the path, then into the trees where he expected the wizard would find the ground. If he could surprise the man . . .

Red fabric flashed ahead past intervening trunks, and a sinister chant floated on the air. The Red Wizard was casting. The Xiang monk summoned his training and became like the wind, flowing through the trees without slowing. He rushed the lone wizard like a zephyr—

A flash of green light, and the wizard was alone no more. A rubbery-skinned, olive-hued creature towered before the Thayan. The newcomer was thin, but wiry muscles sheathed its ungainly arms and legs. Its hair was thick and black, and seemed to writhe as if straining for a life of its own. From stories he'd heard and images he'd seen in books, Raidon guessed it was a troll.

The Red Wizard called out, "Devour the Shou peasant! Rip off his arms and save one as a trophy!" So much for surprise. The monk broke off his charge several yards from the troll.

Raidon shook out the sleeves of his travel-stained silk jacket. They snapped, and the troll's eyes flicked toward the distracting sound. Just long enough for Raidon to kick a nearby stone hard, launching it directly into the troll's left eye. The partial blindness distracted the creature, and Raidon vaulted up and over the troll and its too-long arms. He landed lightly in front of the wizard, the troll at his back. Better to deal with the spellcaster before all else; it was a certainty the Red Wizard was capable of other destructive spells.

A strangely luminescent scar disfigured the red-robed man's face. And he was already chanting. Raidon stepped forward and delivered a magnificent roundhouse kick. It was like hitting a stone pillar. His shin flared with pain, but despite the rocklike density of his adversary, Raidon also saw the man flinch. Something of his attack had penetrated the wizard's stony ward. He delivered a killing elbow strike to the scarred man's face. The wizard flinched again, but the ward absorbed most of the strike's lethal energy.

Ribbons of black fire streamed from the wizard's open hands. Raidon evaded, leaping sideways. His pack, an unfamiliar weight on his back, snagged on a low-hanging tree branch. The monk's trajectory skewed left, and he fell.

Raidon was already rolling to his feet when another volley of darkling fire found him.

Warmth streamed from Raidon's open mouth, from his nostrils, even from his eyes and the ends of his fingers. Numbness raced through his limbs. He tried to pull himself upright on the bole of the tree his pack had snagged, but failed.

Desolation beckoned.

Then something warm touched him on his back, high on his shoulder blades. Heat returned to his core, and tendrils of sensation stole back into his limbs as quickly as cold had numbed them. Raidon whispered, "From form to formless and from finite to infinite." It was a mantra of his temple about overcoming limits. He'd overcome a limitation, but not through his own efforts.

Accepting the gift of salvation without understanding, Raidon deflected a green-muscled claw with his forearm. The troll snarled—his left eye was bloody, but was already visibly regaining its normal hue and shape. A memory surfaced from stories he'd heard—few things could permanently hurt these hulking terrors. Raidon slipped below another claw's vicious thrust.

He couldn't be distracted! The Thayan was still the greater threat.

Raidon ducked beneath the troll's legs and charged the wizard, unsheathing his daito. The look of triumph on the Red Wizard's face crumbled, and he backpedaled. A root caught his heel, and he went over onto his back. The monk leaped forward, his knee coming down firmly on the wizard's neck.

"Yield," he instructed the scarred man.

The red-robed caster mumbled something unintelligible, then clearly stated, "You have made an understandable mistake—I am your friend, so I forgive you. Now, get up and help me to my feet." The words rang through Raidon's head like a gong, growing stronger and more reasonable the more he considered the new idea.

Then warmth touched his back once again, and the compulsion blew away like ash, leaving only powerless words, naked in their inanity.

The man's eyes narrowed as he exclaimed, "That's the second spell you've thrown off! What fell resistance guards your—*urk!*"

Raidon leaned, exerting slightly more pressure with his knee on the scarred man's carotid. With the blood flow to his head restricted, the man passed out heartbeats later. The monk jumped and spun, but the rush of wind signaling the troll's attack had warned Raidon too late. The troll grabbed him and raised him in the air.

Whatever guardian spirit had protected him from the Thayan's magic failed to respond when the troll beat the monk like a wet rug against a nearby tree. The initial impact nearly jarred loose Raidon's grip on the daito.

The troll raised him high once more, ready to dash him against another tree. Raidon cast away pain and bent his body forward, slicing at the brutal fingers squeezing his leg. The troll squealed and lost its hold plus a few fingers. The monk dived into a shock-absorbing roll. He grunted on impact but used the energy of the fall to propel himself several yards away from the green-skinned giant before coming out of the maneuver on his feet.

Raidon turned and assumed a thrusting stance with the sword before him. He preferred using his limbs as weapons, but the daito was Raidon's answer to the troll's enormous, clawed reach.

Its roar of challenge was the sound of a furious waterfall at snowmelt. Raidon held steady in the blaring noise, but faint nausea touched him when he noticed new fingers growing from the bloody stumps of the troll's hand, waving and reaching like worms. It was obscene, too much like watching the birth of tiny monstrosities.

Raidon charged. The troll waited, its arms apart, its mouth wide and hungry. The monk feinted left and chopped right. Off came the troll's entire right hand. The creature's lack of response to such an injurious loss was unnerving. Raidon had expected to press his attack, but the troll was already clawing at him with its remaining hand and biting at his shoulder. Its breath stank of spoiled meat.

A sparkle of green light washed across the troll. Where the light passed, the troll melted away, entirely disappearing in the span of an eye blink.

The monk's head swiveled. Had a Commorand brother tracked him down and banished the Red Wizard's guardian? No, he remained alone, save for the scarred man. Raidon shrugged. The creature, called by a spell, had probably returned whence it came. He hoped that was so. The less palatable alternative had the troll in some nether realm waiting to ambush him. Raidon decided to act as if his first surmise was true.

He studied the defeated Red Wizard. He bent and wiped the troll blood off his daito on the man's expensive garment. The Thayan was not breathing.

"Xiang forgive me," he mumbled. He'd pressed more forcibly on the man's neck with his knee than he'd intended.

Raidon sheathed his blade and quickly stripped the man of his belongings, including a tome and a jagged blue wand. Raidon blinked when he found a writ of marque authorizing raids up and down the Umber River, even unto the edges of Aglarond. The writ was signed by Ansuram of Nethentir, Warden of the Fifth Lore. Raidon shrugged. If the scarred man had survived and regained consciousness without equipment or outer clothing, he would have fled upriver toward Nethentir and probably returned with an overwhelming force.

Raidon threw the man's red robe into a ravine. He pulled off his own pack and stuffed the book and wand into it, amongst the splinters of his cedar box. He'd felt it collapse when the troll had bashed him against the tree. He reached in and pulled out his mother's forget-me-not. It was warm to the touch.

A familiar warmth. It was the same temperature as that light touch on his back when he'd thrown off the wizard's spells. He wore his pack high across his shoulders . . .

Raidon's eyes widened. He clutched the forget-me-not, hard. Could it be true? Had his mother left him more than a simple remembrance? It seemed clear the amulet was suffused with a potency he didn't understand. A potency that had twice saved him.

He reverently drew the chain over his head. He gazed down on the stone as it lay on his chest, then dropped it beneath his silk jacket. Against his skin, remnants of its original warmth seeped into his body. The years of storage in a dark box were done. Raidon vowed to wear his mother's forget-me-not from that moment until he found her.

She had left him an unexplained relic, something important. Why hadn't she told him its real nature? Why leave it with him in the first place? She must have been more than she seemed. After all, what was she doing with a relic of magic?

He would find her, as she must have anticipated. Then she would explain mysteries to him whose outlines he couldn't conceive.

CHAPTER NINE

Stardeep, Outer Bastion War Room

From the shadows, Telarian inquired, "Commander Brathtar, how stands the Causeway?"

An elf caparisoned in mithral greaves and hauberk started, then looked up to the unlighted balcony. Brathtar stood before a great oak table scattered with maps, miniature figures sculpted in lead, and quill pens. Several others around the table, similarly armored and armed, if not quite as grandly as Brathtar, broke off their discussion, which had grown heated.

The Empyrean Knights were pledged to Stardeep first and foremost, and their watchword was valor. A knight who joined the elite in Stardeep first learned that anyone, meek or brave, could wake to valor if the cause was true. Empyrean Knights held fire in their hearts, but were not unthinking brutes. Knights held tight to sword in one hand, and strategy in the other. That strategy was determined first and foremost by the Knights' commander, Brathtar.

Brathtar studied the shadowed gallery, squinting, and said, "Keeper Telarian, I didn't realize you were observing the War

Room. Please forgive my lapse." A questioning, attentive mask settled upon the Knight Commander's face. A mask, because Telarian knew the commander had come to view him with grave misgivings.

Telarian allowed one gloved hand to fall, as if by accident, upon the pommel of his darkly sheathed sword. With its touch, even through the barrier his glove offered, the confidence of his convictions reasserted itself. He said, "I couldn't help overhear the concerns you and your people were discussing regarding my orders. Did I hear correctly?"

Brathtar visibly steeled himself, then replied, "Keeper Telarian, I'm afraid I must admit to real tactical incomprehension regarding the foray you've ordered. I judge such an action will merely draw the attention of the wood elves. My intelligence gatherers assure me the Causeway's location, and perhaps even the existence of Stardeep itself, remains a well-kept secret in the Yuirwood. If we venture forth in force . . ."

Telarian nodded, saying, "My orders may seem counterintuitive, Commander. But, as I'm sure you appreciate, as a Keeper my sources of information reach farther than yours. I assure you, Brathtar, this foray is imperative. A physical patrol is warranted, lest sympathizers of the Traitor creep too close."

Rank disbelief battled across the face of Telarian's most trusted commander. The Keeper wondered from where his first reaction came—to bash sense into the man with the blunt side of his sword, and if that did not suffice . . .

Telarian shook away the impulse. Not the most diplomatic of responses. But the commander had been showing more and more disregard for Telarian's orders the last few years. His insolence was becoming tiresome.

As Keeper of the Outer Bastion, the Empyrean Knights answered ultimately to Telarian. He should not have to suffer Brathtar's second guesses and impudence. When had the trust between them evaporated? In the not too distant past, Telarian had occasionally joined Brathtar and his captains for their dice games. Other times Telarian had invited the Commander to his quarters for a glass of the sparkling white he imported once a year, at great cost, out of Sildëyuir. Once they'd even ventured into the first leg of the surrounding dungeon tunnels, tunnels whose existence hadn't been realized when Stardeep was initially sited and constructed. Apparently, Stardeep hadn't been the first prison to occupy this out-of-the-way locale. Brathtar had saved his life during that foray, when they'd disturbed a swarm of fossilized . . . undead? They were mindless but cruelly animate. Brathtar had ordered the tunnels closed after that, of course.

Telarian supposed things began to change between him and Brathtar after his Epoch-enhanced gaze first glimpsed the glyph-scribed blasphemy in the clouds. When he'd foreseen that the citadel of the Traitor's hope was fated to emerge from prehistory, Telarian immediately bent all his thought toward averting that fate. With his investment in saving the world from catastrophe, time to nurture friendships was difficult to schedule.

Altering a fated future was said to be impossible—all the classic divinatory texts warned against such attempts. It was a fundamental philosophy of his school. When one attempted to thread destiny's needle, unplanned consequences always followed. But it wasn't in Telarian to give up. Even when sacrifices were required.

The Keeper's gaze fell to the silent, brooding blade sheathed at his side.

The stakes were too high to back out now. Nis was a requirement of his plan, even if his dreams were sometimes tainted by the thing's dark influence. If his relationship to Brathtar was another requisite sacrifice to change the future, then so be it. Better a soured friendship than a world overturned.

He looked back to his commander, who was impatiently enduring Telarian's long silence. He could relieve the man of his office . . . but Brathtar's competence was unmatched. He needed Brathtar in his current role. Too bad force wouldn't secure him Brathtar's trust. Nor would truth—his plan spiraled too far from what any sane person would accept without the proof that only an Epoch Chamber vision could provide. And no one in Stardeep was properly trained to endure such a vision. Except himself. So secrecy was required. Yet his commands still met resistance.

So he'd tried diplomacy. It had always been one of his strengths. Had he completely lost the knack? No, it was Nis. The blade put everyone off, even if they didn't realize why. But Telarian couldn't bring himself to leave the blade unattended, even locked in his inaccessible quarters.

But beyond Nis, the falsehoods he daily mouthed were taking their toll. The justifications he provided for all his recent decisions were a tapestry of partial truths.

To be sure, the carefully constructed bed of untruth served as the necessary and moral foundation of his true effort to avert the final apocalypse. In the balance, he doubted a few truths twisted for sake of all Toril would stain his soul.

Yet he remained a poor liar.

"You have my orders. Your place is not to question, but to act as instructed. Please do not provide further reasons for me to wonder about my choice of Knight Commander."

Brathtar's eyes narrowed. But he said, "You are the Keeper. I am pledged to Stardeep and will do what is necessary to protect her. I've already prepared the foray. A handpicked troop will venture forth down the Causeway."

Telarian let the commander's dig pass unremarked, giving a curt nod. He called to the air, "Cynosure? Connect me to my quarters."

Moments later, only shadows inhabited the balcony above the War Room.

When Delphe opened the door from her chambers that led to the common area of the Inner Bastion, something fluttered to the floor. A vellum envelope. She bent, retrieved it, and examined its exterior. The red wax seal proclaimed the letter was from the desk of Stardeep's Empyrean Knight Commander.

What was the man's name . . . ? Brathtar, that was it. She recalled seeing him in the Inner Bastion from time to time, enjoying Telarian's patronage, though not recently.

"What have you found, Delphe?" inquired Cynosure, his voice issuing from a small statue standing in its niche at the center of the hallway.

"A memorandum from the Knight Commander. How odd. Why didn't Brathtar ask you to pass the message?"

While useful for communication sent beyond the confines of Stardeep, a hand-delivered letter was hardly a substitute for asking the idol's aid. Cynosure was everywhere in Stardeep. Perhaps the man enjoyed his formalities?

Silence greeted her question, so she broke the seal and shook out the parchment within. On it was scrawled:

Keeper Delphe,

Forgive this sudden request, but I humbly ask you to meet me at your earliest convenience. Please come in person.

Yours,

Commander Brathtar

"Odd . . . Cynosure—please relay to Commander Brathtar a question: Why do you want to meet me?"

Cynosure's voice remained silent a moment, then relayed, "I'm afraid that's impossible, Delphe—Commander Brathtar and a contingent of his Knights departed Stardeep via the Causeway just this morning."

The Keeper nearly dropped the letter. "Empyrean Knights rode forth from Stardeep? What's happened?"

"Telarian ordered the excursion. I believe he had some concerns regarding a nearby wood elf encampment. You'll have to inquire of Telarian directly. My purview doesn't extend beyond the Outer Bastion."

Delphe turned from her door and strode the curved length of Tardoun Hall, so named for one of the first Keepers to inhabit Stardeep after its delving. A frieze of carved figures ran along both sides of the hall, depicting elves involved in all manner of clerical and teleological pursuits—charting the courses of the stars figured prominently. She passed doors leading to the lounge, the baths, the archives, the repository, the noisy chamber housing Cynosure Prime, the dining hall, the steeply sloping stairs that led down to the Outer Bastion, and various lesser side halls. Finally, Telarian's personal chamber. The door was closed. She knocked.

No answer.

"Cynosure, please tell me where I can find my fellow Keeper."

"He is in the Epoch Chamber."

"The what?"

"Some months ago, Telarian completed construction, with my aid, of a chamber designed to focus his precognitive talent."

The abjurer blinked. "Why didn't I know about this?"

"The chamber lies just beyond the limits of Stardeep's Inner Bastion."

"So it is also outside my concern, is that what you're implying? Everything in Stardeep is my concern, Cynosure!" Her earlier worries about the sentient idol's faculties woke again.

"Would you like me to connect you?" Cynosure volunteered.

"You said this new chamber lies beyond the limits of the Inner Bastion. How—"

"It is close enough for me to transport you. It has no entrance or exit besides me."

Just like the Well, she realized.

"Yes, Cynosure. Warn Telarian I'm on my way, then connect me."

A parabola of blue light spun out of nothing, engulfing her. Her stomach lurched and darkness descended. She blinked, and her eyes readjusted. She stood within a small dome.

The floor was scribed with a star-in-circle configuration she recognized from old texts—a predictive tool prized by diviners. The floor gently rolled and pitched in an unsettling manner, as if floating on liquid. Telarian reclined at the star's center, staring at her, surprise evident on his face.

"Delphe!"

"Why, hello, Telarian. I see you've been delving new chambers within Stardeep?" She tried to keep her voice light, but was mostly unsuccessful.

Telarian raised himself to a sitting position then stood. His features resumed their normally placid countenance.

He said, "As you can see." He gestured around. "I find the Epoch Chamber helps concentrate my talents."

"Ah—so Cynosure informed me. And have you learned anything useful?" She gazed down at the smaller symbols scribed around the circle's periphery and at the slowly burning incense sticks.

He squinted at her, a yearning expression briefly inhabiting his face. Then he smiled ruefully. "Not yet. But if I can look forward far enough, I can foresee all potential escape attempts by the Traitor. Once I know of them, I can eradicate each and every possibility from the time stream."

Her eyes widened. "Is that possible?"

He shrugged. "So I hope."

"The Traitor tried today—I would have told you earlier, but I couldn't find you. Did you foresee that?"

"He tried today?"

"Yes—your new chamber didn't foresee it?"

Telarian considered, frowning. Then he said, "It did not. But then, it wouldn't, would it? You obviously foiled the effort."

"But he mounted a genuine, credible effort! If I hadn't stemmed the attempt . . . what good is your early warning chamber if—"

He put up a hand. "Why should I focus on escape attempts already destined to be foiled by our efforts? Interference in such events, already predetermined to proceed one way, could finish far differently. No, I'm looking for instances of probability where the Traitor successfully breaks free of all our containment efforts."

Delphe blinked. "Successfully?"

"Yes. If I can identify those instances, how ever far in the future, I can take steps right now in the present to make certain those circumstances fail to develop and materialize."

Delphe put a hand to the side of her head. Telarian's voice seemed so matter of fact, so rational. But the meanings behind the words he spoke seemed unbound by reason. She spoke out, "How far do you look?"

He smiled. A note of pride crept into his voice as he explained. "Before I crafted this chamber, I could see only moments, perhaps days at most. Now I can see years. The misty edges of a century ahead are becoming clear to me . . ."

Telarian broke off, frowning.

"And you've seen . . . what?"

He plied her with another gauging look. Finally he said, "I've seen worrying images . . ."

She grasped his shoulder, squeezing. "What? What did you see?"

He frowned again, said, "I'm too close to the edge of temporal resolution; I can't be sure. I'm working to increase the clarity of that vision so the details will firm up."

"You must have seen something—I can tell by your expression you hold something back. From your fellow Keeper!"

"Delphe, until I could be relatively certain, I didn't want to commit all of Stardeep to a plan that might be unnecessary. I—"

She squeezed harder. "Describe the images you saw."

He swallowed, then spoke. "Alliances. The Traitor retains alliances with those outside Stardeep, outside even the hidden realm of Sildëyuir. I've seen visions of wood elves unearthing old tomes, old journals, and becoming ensnared. But the seeds of corruption have already been cast, or soon will be. If we do not act in relatively short order, I fear that wood elves will find this cache."

Delphe released Telarian's arm and stepped back. She said, "You are certain?"

"No, not certain. But I am making preparations, gathering resources, sending out agents."

"Is that why you sent Empyrean Knights across the Causeway?"

His eyes narrowed but he nodded in agreement. "Yes, that's right. I sent them to reconnoiter a wood elf encampment established a fair distance from the Causeway. If the Knights reach the secret cache I saw in my vision first, the wood elves will never know the soul-corrupting danger they were saved from unearthing."

"Telarian, once more, explain why you've learned so much, taken so much upon yourself, without informing me."

Now it was his turn to grasp her shoulder, but she pushed him back. She considered asking Telarian to explain the significance of Brathtar's strange summons, but decided to keep that information in reserve.

Telarian paused, said, "If this all turns out to be a mad fancy, I wouldn't want to waste your time and thought on it. You're the Keeper of the Inner Bastion, the Watcher of the Well. Your duties are immediate and vital."

"But—"

"Trust me, Delphe. If this reconnaissance mission to the wood elf encampment confirms any of my visions, however slight, I shall instantly and immediately inform you. That was and remains my plan. Please don't make more of this than what it is—a foray to gather information, and perhaps to save a few elves from their own curiosity—nothing more."

A thought struck Delphe. "The appearance of strange elves in the armor of the Empyrean Knights could reveal the presence of Stardeep to the wood elf encampment."

The old twinkle returned to Telarian's eyes as he explained. "The Knights are not unskilled in woodcraft. They are abroad to observe only, not interact. Anyhow, Brathtar may not have to go anywhere near the village to find the cache."

Powdery snow accumulated across boughs, between pine needles, and across saplings and the dark ground under the great boles. Bit by bit through the night, it formed a curving white blanket covering the sleeping forest.

When Janesta Leafgrace emerged from her double-hide pavilion, she laughed as she shook the snow out of her hair that plopped down from above. She breathed in the crisp air that came with the newly laid covering. After snowfall, the woods took on the aspect of a fey wonderland that called her to explore a terrain transformed. Without disturbing anyone in her pavilion who reclined in remembering trances, she was away.

The snow was smooth and pristine, save for the elf-light tracks she left behind. The murmuring pines and hemlocks had fallen quiet under their newly made garments of white. Yes, even the sad, old voices of the so-called "elder druids" of the forest were speechless in the morning's wonder. Or so Janesta fancied.

And—

She spied a set of lone prints! Another early explorer, like her. Not a fellow from the encampment—it was a wildling of the forest.

She pursued the trail uphill, skirting an icy boulder field, staying beneath the canopy of oak branches. The prints were only partly familiar; certainly a big cat, but one new to the area, or at least new to her. The snowfall made following easy, but Janesta still practiced her forestcraft; she examined broken foliage, measured the length between prints, moved as quietly as she was able. When she saw a patch of disturbed snow, she dug up a shallowly buried cache of spoor.

It was a cougar after all, one from eastern Yuirwood. It had wandered close to the encampment. Janesta decided to stay on the trail to see if she could track it to its lair, if it had one. She suspected it might be a female, hungry to feed new cubs. If so, perhaps she would bring down a bird to help supplement its diet.

As she examined a spot where it had circled a stump, probably to mark its scent, she heard the first horns.

High, piercing, strangely thrilling . . . but ominous for their unfamiliarity. They sounded like something described in a shaman's tale, something that warlike humans beyond the Yuirwood might produce on their metallic instruments. She frowned and turned toward home.

The sudden cries and screams that broke under the calling horns jolted Janesta into a run.

When the huntress reached her village under the snow-bowed canopy, she couldn't understand what transpired before her eyes—the scene was too far outside her experience for comprehension.

Humans—no, elves . . . elves! Not wood elves like her tribe, or high elves she'd glimpsed on the Yuirwood's borders, nor even half-elves. Strange, steely eyed elves on mailed steeds. They were everywhere, surrounding the village, cantering through the center circle, sweeping down the side avenues. Resplendent in mail so fair it could only be mithral, the newcomer elves assailed her home without mercy.

Surprised and beset on all sides, wood elves died.

She saw friends taken in the back by scything swords. Others were pushed from high bowers by cruelly aimed arrows. A group that sought to flee beneath the boughs was ridden down by flashing hooves. Slender blades cut screaming throats. Dying children cried out to their parents, husbands to their wives. Janesta saw her friend Natal Peacethorn pulled from his home, shrieking. Her brother's wife Sarana was felled with two arrows. The monument stone that had stood three full tendays since the encampment's hopeful founding was toppled and smashed. Five hunters attempted to drag away wounded, but they were ridden down for their efforts.

Janesta was witnessing a heartless slaughter, nothing less. What courage she always assumed was hers failed; she shrank back into the undergrowth, all strength stolen from chilled, clammy limbs.

She turned, swearing, crying, hating herself, and ran blindly through the snowy woods, careful to keep her feet light and sliding, leaving as little sign as her snowcraft allowed. If she were to survive the annihilation of her home at the hands of these strange, steel-eyed elves, cowardice was her only option.

At first she ran without goal, holding no thought other than escape. As the heat of her exertion warmed her, a seed of fury blossomed, burning at the loss through which she labored. She adjusted her direction and set her course. She was bound for Relkath's Foot, one of the largest communities of wood elves in all the Yuirwood. There she would tell her story, pour out her anger, and gather a force. Only vengeance could sate her loss.

She would go to Relkath's Foot and alert the Masters of the Yuirwood.

The image of stern-faced elves in shining, blood-slicked mail maddened her. The kin-slaying elves hadn't dropped from the sky, nor were their horses lathered as if from a long ride. They had appeared from somewhere not far from the encampment. After she put a few miles of forest behind her, thinking all the while, Janesta was pretty sure from where.

On the edge of a pocket reality, a massive gate loomed, cold and gray, a lattice of strange script and tiny cracks bespeaking hundreds of years of weathering.

Telarian waited for Brathtar just inside the great stone gates that opened onto the mist-shrouded Causeway. Telarian often stood thus, year in and year out. The chiseled granite of the gate's face was as familiar as a friend. The Keeper knew every edge, every crack, every discoloration. Moreover, he was more than familiar with the inscriptions, sigils, and glyphs so prominently displayed. They warned of danger and death for any who entered uninvited, in a variety of tongues and alphabets:

This place is not a place of honor. No highly esteemed deed is commemorated here . . . nothing valued is here.

What is here is dangerous and repulsive. This message is a warning about danger.

The danger is present in your time, as it was in ours.

The danger is to the world, and it can erase all life, overwriting all with abomination.

The danger may be unleashed if this place is disturbed. Shun this place. Turn around.

The warnings were not endowed with magical force capable of steering away the curious, but danger would certainly befall any who ignored the warnings and ventured into the shadowed Grand Vestibule.

On more than one occasion in the long history of Stardeep, the gates had withstood attacks by fools loyal to the Traitor, who had discovered his prison despite all the effort of hiding his location. But neither those ancient attacks, nor all the time that had since elapsed had discernibly weakened the façade. Stardeep's entrance stood strong and patient, capable of repelling anything thrown its way.

Above the gate was scribed the massive symbol of a strangely curving tree: Stardeep's emblem. Around the white tree was a circular field that glowed and flickered with bluish fire. Though of late, to Telarian's eyes, the fire seemed darker, sootier perhaps.

Telarian watched as the commander and his men slowly filed back across the hazy land bridge, as if resolving from imagination into reality. The men didn't speak to each other, or look up to salute the Keeper, as was his due. Desolation hung in their slack postures and in their limp hold on their reins.

Telarian recognized they had followed his orders.

Commander Brathtar brought up the column's rear, his mail dimmed by a sheen of dried blood. Behind him, the

Causeway faded into the encroaching mist, hidden or truly dissolved, Telarian did not know. Either way, it would return when next bidden by Cynosure or him, and again provide a connection between Stardeep and the Yuirwood.

Brathtar reined up and fixed Telarian with a glassy stare. Some indefinable essence was missing in the man; he seemed anchorless. The Keeper regretted the change he saw, but neither pity nor concern were his to dispense. Brathtar's actions had been required, an important element of his delicate plan. Sacrifices were necessary if so much more was to be saved. What was the blood of dozens compared to the souls of all the world?

Brathtar said, "The encampment is cleansed, Keeper. The dissidents who planned the attack you described are . . . no more."

"Your service is greater than you can know, Commander. Well done."

The elf commander cleared his throat, dropped his eyes for a moment. He had more to say.

"What is it?"

"As we cleaned up, one of my Knights found a trail. Someone escaped the encampment. We gave chase, but lost the track."

Telarian sensed something fall away into the suddenly yawning void of his mind. He hadn't foreseen a survivor. Over the sudden roaring in his ears he asked, too loud, "Are you certain?"

Brathtar nodded.

The noise in his ears grew louder, not unlike the horns he tested on occasion in the Outer Bastion. How . . . ? Where . . . ? But . . . Telarian fumbled for reassurance as the floor of his certainty threatened to fall away. His gloved hand found the pommel of brooding Nis.

The horns ceased. Lucidity was restored, and with it, calm acceptance as wide as the untroubled Sea of Fallen Stars.

A fey thought danced across his mind; he would tighten his grip on Nis, pull forth the blade, and reward Brathtar for his failure.

Don't be a fool, Telarian, Nis whispered. *We yet have uses for our Commander. With the completion of this last task, he is now a tool broken to our hand.*

The Keeper let out his breath. He drowned his concerns in the unflappable serenity that oozed up from his fingers out of the unguessed depths of the black blade.

Chapter Ten

Aglarond, Yuirwood Forest

Magnificent yellow pines crowded the edge of the Yuirwood. Their short, forked branches drooped under a burden of snow, instead of turning up like drakes' tails as they did during the summer. The spirelike tops created a jagged canopy above, though from the understory, all that was visible were naked branches ending in tufts of green needles. The cones were savagely spiked, curved like a bee's stinger to catch the unwary.

At ground level, melting snow mixed with the fine detritus of the forest floor, absorbing most of the runoff, but creating occasional muddy sinkholes. Kiril discovered one by stepping directly into it. She muttered a clipped stream of invectives as cold water doused her foot. Not for the first time that day.

Her heavy furs had gone from cozy and comforting in the morning chill to heavy and stifling as the day advanced. Though direct sunlight rarely touched them beneath the pine ceiling, her reckless pace contributed to what seemed an unseasonably warm morning.

Ahead, the crystal dragonet flitted from branch to branch.

Shafts of sunlight sometimes transfixed the creature, making Xet's translucent carapace glow as if afire.

Kiril was suddenly reminded of the time she'd first met the creature. After fleeing Stardeep, she lost herself amid lonely mesas in the southeast. Too much a coward to end her own life, she eked out a living trapping dune rats, working as a bodyguard, and drinking herself into oblivion each night. Eventually, she found a dwarf hermit whose heart craved solitude as much as hers, though for different reasons. Xet had been his lone companion. The recluse, a geomancer named Thormud, recognized her as a potent warrior despite her wasted life. He hired her as his lone bodyguard.

Defending Thormud, she'd rarely drawn the Blade Cerulean. That was a good decade, or as good as she could have hoped for. Alcohol fully claimed her, but she found refuge in a surly attitude and foul language.

As it always did, the world intruded. Kiril accompanied the geomancer on his last escapade, into the Desert of Desolation. Thormud followed a trace of evil infecting the earth. She and the geomancer, and a few others met along the way, cleansed that infection; an Imaskaran war relic was kept safely inactive.

That triumph had awakened something in her. It was the first truly good thing she'd accomplished since her personal downfall. Her victory, the sense she'd achieved something noble, instilled in her a seed of hope.

Hope made people act funny.

She decided she would return to Aglarond, perhaps even to Stardeep, or at least to the hidden realm of Sildëyuir where her people dwelt. She said her good-byes to the geomancer. He gave her a gift—his tiny crystalline dragonet named Xet. Xet bore the shape of a dragon, but he lacked the size and courage to match.

Kiril accepted the gift with her typical lack of grace and

then departed, Xet flitting and chiming in her wake.

She headed northwest, toward Aglarond. The dragonet kept her company on the long trek, she had to admit. But as she approached her homeland, dread and shame reemerged, and the memory of her recent success faded.

Hope proved too hard to hold. Habits cultivated over a decade toppled hope's façade.

Almost at the border of the great Yuirwood, she paused in Laothkund. A few days became a few tendays, then a few months. She lost her conviction. She foundered.

Until now.

A ray of sunlight briefly flashed from one of Xet's facets directly into her eyes, startling her out of her reverie. She excoriated the brittle-brained creature. Not that the dragonet cared. Xet seemed determined to remain with her.

Like Gage.

Behind Kiril, the man doggedly brought up the rear. She'd discouraged him, called him terrible names, and even left without telling him. But the clinging bastard discovered her plan and joined her. Her protestations didn't move him except to produce a smile, which only infuriated her. He said he wanted to help.

Right, that's what motivated all thieves, and she knew Gage well enough to know his profession. Still . . . he had returned the sword—a selfless act accomplished at some personal cost. Gage didn't speak of it, but she sometimes caught him looking at his left hand—it had once borne a dark gauntlet nearly twin to the one on his right. Yet he stayed with her, even now. While she didn't want to dismiss Gage's offer of aid outright, Kiril guessed he merely craved excitement. Hadn't the thrill of danger been the lure and glue that so often drew them both together in the taverns of Laothkund?

Though a companion on the trail wasn't necessarily a bad thing.

Kiril snorted. After being so disagreeable when she first realized he followed, admitting she was glad to have his company was the last thing her ego would allow. But it was true. In a very real way, she doubted she would've made it as far as the edge of Laothkund, let alone to the border of the Yuirwood without him. Last night, as heavy clouds stole away the day's remaining light and snow began to fall, they pitched their tents beneath the outer eaves. This morning, they moved northwest through yellow pines, toward the Causeway.

The image of Nangulis, as he had been before his self-sacrifice, bloomed fully realized into her consciousness, instantly becoming the sole focus of her attention. Not for the first time.

Nangulis! Tall, silver haired, with dark eyes of mystery that never failed to enthrall Kiril even after the years they had spent together. Was he returned to life and body? Could any possibility explain such a resurrection? No, she knew it was impossible! Kiril carried a sliver of Nangulis's soul with her even now. But yet . . .

Gage had heard her dead lover's name from Sathra's lips. A name displaced in time and forgotten. It could not be active and involved in the theft of the sword imprinted with a life lost . . .

Each notion she entertained that might explain such a possibility seemed more ludicrous than the previous. Impossibility heaped upon ridiculousness, until she felt she would go mad.

She groped for her flask and took a drink that temporarily numbed her racing thoughts.

The answers to all her questions lay in Stardeep.

She didn't dare hope those answers might fall from the lips of Nangulis himself. As she pressed him in her arms. She didn't dare imagine that scene, but once entertained, she couldn't scrub away her soul's fondest wish.

Some time later, Kiril paused in her breakneck rush through the forest. Her furs were too damn hot for one moment longer, even in the canopy's shadow. She was tempted to fling off her cold-weather clothing and keep going. But she would need the furs again at night. Which meant she would have to carefully pack them. She growled. Repacking supplies was finicky work, just the sort she hated. But it was now or never, otherwise she would broil.

To her left, Kiril spied a fallen tree—broad, unrotted, and most importantly, free of snow. She removed the heavy pack and balanced it on the log, then shrugged out of her coat.

From behind, Gage called, "Splendid! I could use a break, too." He joined Kiril and threw himself down on the log next to her pack. She noticed with some irritation he had already removed his coat, hood, and single fur glove. Removed and stowed them in his bulky pack while walking behind her, without raising a sweat. She narrowed her eyes, but didn't give him the satisfaction of commenting on his feat.

As she undid the knots securing her pack, Xet lit suddenly on her shoulder, pinching her flesh with its crystal-hard claws.

"Damn it, I told you to warn me before you do that!"

Xet pealed a strangely familiar tone . . . when had she last heard it? An image of the dark halls of an Imaskaran ruin to the southeast came to her, with Xet's cry echoing on stone. In that dark tower she had wielded Angul against creatures that deserved the Blade Cerulean's righteous bite . . .

Xet was sounding a warning.

"Gage—"

He turned to regard her, and the black-fletched arrow only tagged his shoulder instead of finding his heart. He grimaced, flipping backward off the log. He landed on his back behind the fallen tree.

Xet flew up as Kiril spun around. She stared into the thickets of wavering daylight. The dark trunks of pines multiplied in all directions in numbers beyond counting. Where was the archer? There . . .

A pulse of dimness, like night's clasp when the sun dipped below the horizon, oozed from every shadow. But darker yet, a squirming ball of gloom bounded across the forest floor, ricocheting between the unmoving pine boles . . . aimed right at her. Kiril dropped and the shadowy missile struck the log. A burst of fire with flames the color of coal arced in all directions. Kiril cried out in relief, until she spied several more shadows racing toward her.

"Blood!" she swore, rolling to her feet.

From behind the log, she heard Gage mutter, "Sathra! Why would she . . . ?"

Her head jerked around. Too bad—no time to ask the thief how Sathra could be attacking if she were dead, as he had told her in Laothkund. If they both survived, she would skin the truth out of him.

The racing shadows resolved into humanoid silhouettes, each merely a dark outline cast on reality.

Kiril drew Angul.

Truth's clarity burned away the darkness all around her, searing her consciousness in the bargain. Doubts, worries, and pains of mind and body were cauterized in the absolute conviction of Angul's steel. The Blade Cerulean flamed triumphantly in her welcoming grip, its star blue fire belling out and banishing shadows in every direction.

The three silhouettes resolved into charging men wielding daggers and slender swords. She held back Angul's sure retributive strike; she retained hold of her mind by the barest of threads, enough to ask the sword, "Nangulis? Are you in there?"

The blade answered only by wrenching itself around in

her grip, shearing off the crown of the man who charged her. Certainty of purpose beat up from the blade through her skin as it always had, like heat. Whether or not Nangulis walked again, Angul remained as he always had been: judge, jury, and executioner of what he knew to be *right*.

A dagger sprouted in the throat of a second attacker. He burbled and fell at her feet. Gage was flinging daggers from behind the log. The last attacker was turning, an expression of uncertainty breaking to fear, even as she strode forward and swept Angul through him from neck to navel.

From nowhere, the air cracked, louder than anything she'd ever heard.

The breath was drawn from Kiril's lungs, and Gage fell to one knee, gasping. Halos of shadow spun around both of them, off kilter and wobbling like a swarm of ethereal wagon wheels. A voice, far-off and airy, was audible over the ringing in Kiril's ears. An arcane voice. A voice in the midst of calling down more destruction.

She leaped just as the air convulsed again, even louder. She landed face-first in muddy snow, but her legs churned for purchase and her left hand groped for Angul's hilt. The blade pulled her to her feet despite the absolute silence that had descended. Blood seeped from her ears. The sword did not comprehend failure. The weakness of her flesh was something he would not tolerate.

Ahead, a clearing in the woods surrounded a bare hillock, mostly free of the night's snow. Upon the bald hill's crown was a woman. She was sheathed in black fabric and obsidian jewelry that pierced ears, nose, and eyebrows. Even in the full light of day, shadows curled and scampered around her like negative flames in a stiff wind. The darkness whispered, but the words were too faint for Kiril to make out.

The woman gestured to Kiril, inviting her into the open. Kiril accepted the challenge.

Gage saw Sathra of the Shadow Tongue appear on the bald hill. "Queen of Air, why doesn't she give it up?"

The crime lord of Laothkund apparently valued a prize as potent as the Blade Cerulean too much to allow it to slip away. Gage could understand that. But he wouldn't have guessed the woman would track them into the wilderness.

"Bitch of Dark Corners!" he hissed when he saw Kiril charge toward the slope. He'd told Kiril he'd already dispatched the crime lord . . . now she'd know he'd lied.

A branch snapped, then two more. Something lacking grace lumbered through the trees, heading directly for him.

He was running low on blades! Gage pulled a throwing knife from the felled attacker lying across the log, simultaneously drawing a dagger. He tensed, seeing a dark figure moving closer through the trees.

It was . . . a man sustained by shadow. Not a man hiding in shadow, like the three who'd first attacked. No, this one was dead, but animated by tendrils of darkness that clawed and writhed across his body. It was someone he'd met before.

Stolsin, Grinder of Tribes. The Rashemi barbarian he'd killed in Sathra's lair. Back from the dead with a little push from Sathra's necromancy. The barbarian carried his maul, but dusk dripped from the gray stone cudgel as if it were dipped in ink. The tattoos scrawled across the man's flesh now writhed and twisted, as if ready to animate with tiny, nasty lives all their own.

Gage flipped the dagger, grasped it by the blade, and threw. His aim was true. The blade punched straight into Stolsin's left eye.

The beshadowed barbarian opened his mouth to yell or scream, but all that emerged was dripping night. He didn't cease his relentless march across the forest floor.

The thief jumped up onto the log, then ran along it to the

great root ball that had come free when the tree crashed over in whatever wind or rain had ended its days.

Stolsin the Reanimated altered his trajectory like a lodestone. He moved unerringly toward Gage. The thief grimaced with sudden realization; Sathra had used Stolsin's death to track him into the Yuirwood. When one person kills another, a terrible linkage forms—a linkage a skilled necromancer can follow. Finding him meant finding Kiril, and the sword Sathra apparently desired above all else.

On the other hand, all Stolsin sought was vengeance.

Gage transferred his dagger from gloved hand to bare.

"Today our linkage doubles, Stolsin, because I'm going to kill you again!" His demon gauntlet would win the day and defeat the walking corpse. He hoped. Although he did carry a few vials of alchemical acid particularly good at disrupting leather . . .

A dark pulse on the hill caught Gage's attention—black lightning from clear skies smote Kiril, once, twice, then again. The elf was hurled down the slope, a net of gibbering shadow entangling her thrashing limbs.

Stolsin swung his maul while Gage was distracted. Gage slipped back, but the blow caught him on the left shoulder. Agony seized his arm and the dagger dropped from his nerveless hand.

Gage lunged forward with his right hand, the demonic mouth on his gauntleted palm gaping. The revivified corpse backstepped, avoiding the slap. Gage overreached and stumbled to one knee. The maul whistled down, catching the thief on his left leg as he tried to roll clear.

Then he was back on his feet. He winced when he tried to put weight on the left leg. He had retrieved his short blade, this time firmly held in his gauntlet. The demon mumbled curses around the hilt. Gage ignored the vile suggestions.

His foe stood a good chance of flattening him with the

maul if Gage moved inside its reach. It would be less risky if his left hand could properly grasp the dagger, but until feeling returned to it, he had to hold the blade right-handed to stay outside Stolsin's sweep. To bring his gauntlet to bear against Stolsin, he'd have to do so from a distance.

The reanimated barbarian groaned something, its swollen and dry tongue rasping ineffectually within its gaping mouth. Indecipherable.

"You have seen better days, my friend," Gage observed, wondering if he could bait a creature whose brain was probably maggot food. More inscrutable groans and grunts followed, with a swipe from the maul that nearly removed the thief's head.

Gage leaped up onto the log, then off again before the maul splintered down. The log broke into two pieces under the mighty blow.

When he'd defeated Stolsin last time, he'd been wielding Angul.

A slender thread of worry burrowed up to pierce Gage's confidence. The thing had already tagged him twice unanswered, and was forcing him to flee with an unholy energy born beyond the grave.

Another shuddering of the light behind the walking corpse let him know Kiril remained in the fight. Whether succeeding or failing, he didn't divide his attention to ascertain. Stolsin battered the log a few times with its maul, but even its damped brain recognized that smashing through the obstruction, as satisfying as such destruction might be, paled before the opportunity to pulp the thief. The creature made an awkward jump onto the log, crudely aping Gage's agile leap.

Gage swung his dagger in a wide arc, encountering resistance mid-swing. Stolsin's foot and lower calf parted from the rest of its body. The undead crashed sidewise onto the log, groaning as it impacted. It rolled off the other side.

Gage grinned and looked over to see where the monster had landed. The maul caught him on the side of the head.

Whispered exhortations sheathed in gloom poured from Sathra's outstretched fingers and enveloped Kiril and her blade. Within the midnight embrace, cold prickled Kiril's skin from a hundred wraithlike hands, growing from merely unpleasant to life-sucking agony in moments. The elf screamed. Where in the Hells was Angul's balm? Didn't she yet hold the blade? His flame was hardly visible in this tumbling dark, but his presence yet touched her consciousness.

"Help me, damn your blunt edges!"

The blade, dulled and cold, trembled at her words. Strength continued to pour from her exposed skin into the murmuring clutch of dead shades. Why wasn't he helping her?

"I'm dying, you rusted reject from a halfling's smithy! I—"

The sword trembled again, as if straining . . . then ignited with cerulean incandescence. He pulled power from a source that had always seemed inexhaustible. Whether that strength had its origin within Angul himself, or in some external font of moral power, Kiril had never before wondered. The sword was always equal to every task, capable of keeping its wielder alive no matter the threat.

Was Sathra's power of shadow inimical to Angul, or was he, after all these years, drawing to the end of his enchanted lifespan?

Angul's certainty sought to whelm in her once more, becoming the balm she'd fought to hold herself aloof from during the last decade. Her newfound doubt about the weapon's longevity transformed her usual sentiment of dread to relief. The blade was still up to its old tricks. She wanted—

No, she *needed* to ask Sathra about Nangulis! But that

desire was washed away in Angul's all-encompassing belief that nothing he—and by extension his wielder—did required explanation.

The necromancer's shadowy influence burned away in blue celestial fire, revealing the light of day and a surprised-looking Sathra. Kiril stood up where the necromancer's last blast had flung her. She intoned Angul's words. "Suffer not abomination, nor she who gives up her soul to evil."

Kiril sprinted back up the slope, her sword's fire pumping her limbs with boundless energy.

Sathra spoke anew, her voice a series of unfathomable vocalizations that smoked into reality, her hands frantically waving in rhythm with the foul syllables. Kiril recognized enough spellcasting to identify the cadence of a magical escape.

Sathra wasn't quick enough.

The career of the most-feared crime lord of Laothkund ended in the snowy eaves of the Yuirwood.

An interminable sea of discomfort slowly focused, finally shrinking to the size of his skull. Dull throbs, the stings of scrapes and cuts, and three sharp pinches told him the position of his body; he lay in a splayed posture, facedown on a hard surface. He tasted dirt and bark in his mouth.

He yet lived! Gage throttled his first instinct to groan. Better not to reveal that life hadn't fully departed if enemies lurked nearby. He opened one eye the merest slit to reconnoiter the situation.

Stolsin lay not far from him, cut into three or four bloodless pieces. Closer stood Kiril, tending a small fire. Her pet construct perched on her shoulder. He sucked in his breath when he recalled his last few conscious moments. The elf's head turned. She gazed at him, one eyebrow going up in speculation. She said, "You awake?"

Gage considered. Better not to dissemble, just in case. He let out a loud groan and let his eyes flutter open. When the pain redoubled, he realized he wouldn't have to put up much of an act.

"What happened? That damn walking corpse clipped me with his hammer. Last thing I remember." He levered himself up so his back was supported by a log. A very familiar log. A log much the worse for wear. He'd be happy to see the last of it.

"I'll tell you what happened. A whore came out of nowhere and tried to kill me—which is pretty flecking odd since you told me *Sathra was dead!*" Kiril moved until she stood a foot from Gage, her eyes narrowed and wild. Xet flew up from her shoulder, chiming a rebuke at her sudden movement.

The thief held up his left hand. "Hold on! You think I lied to you? I *thought* Sathra was dead—I left her as good as. How could I know someone would pull her out of the sewer and fix her up?" It was as compelling a scenario as he could invent on the spot. He was good at it, but would the enraged elf buy his story? More importantly . . .

"Did you ask her the questions you wanted, Kiril?" Gage asked, anxiety straining his faked credulity. "Did you ask about Nangulis?"

The elf clenched both her fists, neither of which, luckily, was wrapped around her sword. She yelled, "Blood, no!" and slammed a fist down on the log next to Gage. He winced despite himself.

The swordswoman took a deep breath, visibly getting hold of herself. She continued. "No, she came upon me too strong. The only way I could stand against her was to kill her. That, and Angul got the better of me."

"Yeah," agreed Gage, "I know how that goes." He watched her clench her fists and eyes, her mouth a tight line, as she decided to believe his story. He relaxed fractionally.

The fact was, he was having second thoughts about his involvement. How could he have known, when he agreed to steal the blade, that Angul was far more than a simple piece of enchanted steel? How could he have known the sword was Kiril's entire reason for living?

Gage had committed petty larceny, and not-so-petty larceny, from the vaults of the fabulously rich and probably crooked. He had killed, but only those whose hands were stained with years of evil—he'd never knowingly cut the life from an innocent. By his own lights, he was a moral person, one whose skills allowed him to tread the edges of the law, but one whose actions, in the balance, wouldn't endanger his soul's final destination.

He didn't spend all his money on whores and hounds, as did some of his companions, nor did he use his strengths to take advantage of the weak and credulous.

In short, Gage didn't think of himself as a bad guy. Which was an image he found increasingly under siege as he continued supporting the façade he'd created to interact with Kiril . . .

He shivered and put the unpleasant topic from his mind. He'd deal with the ramifications of his actions soon enough. Not a strategy most people would recommend for success, but one that had served him well enough in the past. Him, but rarely those around him.

"So, what now?" he ventured.

"Now we get you fixed up and continue to Stardeep. We're not far from the Causeway. I'll have my answers soon."

Gage almost told her the truth then. Instead, he nodded and said, "First, let me collect my daggers. Wouldn't want to run low later."

Chapter Eleven

Aglarond, City of Emmech

The Umber River flowed down from the heart of Thay, splitting the Dragonjaw Mountains between its tall and rugged ranges to the north, and the bare-sloped griffon nesting peaks to the south. The river plunged into the wide Tannath gap, passing the great Aglarondan fortress at Emmech before emptying into the Sea of Fallen Stars.

Emmech was a large, ramshackle town with a military air, its rough stone buildings huddling around a far older castle, Fortress Emmech. The fortress bristled with towers and parapets, and its wide hollows housed a significant portion of Aglarond's Army of the Lion; the last Thayan invasion down the Umber River wasn't so long ago that fear of the Red Wizards had passed, despite recent trade agreements. The fortress's most important structures were the two strong towers on either side of the Umber, which could raise from the river floor an ensorcelled chain to bar the passage of watercraft.

Raidon first saw Fortress Emmech in hazy evening light, as the caravan cleared the last descending limb of the Tannaths, and the river valley opened into the distance. They traveled the so-called "Umber River Road," a pitted, crumbling ribbon of rarely level, often snow-packed ground bordered by unscalable cliffs on one side and a river-filled chasm on the other.

Quent told Raidon that morning that the river was an oft-traveled trade route of late, for those willing to pay the Thayan tax. On the other hand, the adjoining "river road" was too dangerous for regular business. Unless your name was Quent and you wanted to shortcut the competition and avoid said tax, the caravan chief boasted. Even if that meant potentially facing the wrath of Red Wizard patrols.

The monk was certain two lives lost to river raiders was too high a price to pay for avoiding the Thayan river levy, but he held his tongue.

The caravan wound its way down the slope to the river gates, such as they were. The real defense of the town obviously lay behind the towering fortress walls, not here at the periphery, though a few token guards stood to attention when the caravan moved to gain entry. The guards looked over the wagons, then asked for a perfunctory trade fee in return for being allowed inside. Quent paid and asked, "Does Lord Demelin still command the fortress?"

One guard spit and replied, "Sure." Another nodded, but the rest were already moving back to the guard house. Interest in the caravan lapsed once it was determined Quent wasn't sponsored by any concern out of Thay.

Inside, the caravan quickly found the bazaar. This late, traffic was sparse, and many trade carts and temporary shops had already shuttered their wares behind lengths of dark tarpaulin, sail cloth, or wooden planks. Some merchants swept up while others packed away goods. Here and there, wily Emmechers wrangled for day-end deals.

With the help of everyone but the scouts Hark and Sulvan, who took their pay and departed for the dock quarter, the three-wagon caravan was converted into a tidy but temporary shop. Raidon at last saw what Quent bought and sold—pears, persimmons, oranges, grapes, and other fruit. Though such was common in Shou Town and Telflamm, such variety was rarer the farther one traveled from The Golden Way. Especially this far out of season, explained Quent.

Raidon bid the caravan chief and his fellow laborers farewell. The wagon drivers, Ledroc, Corthandu, and Khuldam the dwarf, waved after him. Quent, after paying him, was already busy making a deal with a local shopkeeper. Japhoca scowled and flipped him a rude hand gesture. The monk chose not to take offense.

His contract fulfilled and gold heavy in his pouch, Raidon walked into city twilight. Chandlers, elderly men in soot-stained aprons, lit lamps along the main street that led down to the docks. The Commorand brothers Erik and Adrik caught up to him and walked along, talking about how they hoped to find a new patron in Emmech willing to employ their sorcerous talents. Maybe even one that would take them across the Sea of Fallen Stars, or perhaps deep into the heart of the Yuirwood, where stood stones scribed with arcane glyphs—

"The Yuirwood?" Mention of the forest drew Raidon from his walking reverie. "What do you know of it?"

Adrik grinned conspiratorially and said, "This I read once in a moldy book: 'Strange enchantments and old, strong magic are thick in the Yuirwood's tangles. The ancient elves of Yuireshanyaar were masters of powerful spells, and they left behind menhir circles, standing stone monuments carved in an ancient Elvish dialect. The magic of these circles has faded with the strength of the Yuirwood itself, but some power remains in them yet.' "

Raidon gauged the sorcerer's manner, then asked him, "You wish to enter the Yuirwood?"

Adrik, the younger brother, nodded earnestly. Erik, the

older, said, "We go wherever coin takes us." He shrugged.

"I travel into the Yuirwood. I need help, maybe a guide. I have this much to pay." Raidon poured out the contents of his pouch just filled with Quent's salary, the gold heavy in his palm.

Erik looked skeptical and said, "That's enough for one of us, not both."

"I'll go," said Adrik. He turned to his brother. "You stay here and find a wealthy sponsor with a ship, one who'll take us both across the Fallen Stars."

Erik considered. "Raidon, how much time do you intend to spend in the forest?"

"I seek my mother," replied the monk.

The older brother frowned. "Indeterminate, then. I don't know—"

"Erik, I'll be back within two tendays. The Shou's gold holds me only that long."

It was Raidon's turn to frown, but he could offer no rejoinder. A sorcerer's rate was high.

Erik said, "Then go, brother. You'll find me here when you return, seeking our glorious future in a smelly dock tavern." Erik Commorand smiled, waved, and walked away.

Adrik waved after his brother. "See you in two tendays, or less, if the Shou finds what he seeks!"

The sorcerer turned and clapped Raidon on the shoulder. "This will be a fantastic opportunity, I just know it! When do we leave?"

"Dawn. I need nothing in Emmech."

Adrik nodded. "Sure, sure . . . where are we going, specifically, within the forest? It is a wide, trackless place. Let's see the map."

"I have no map."

The sorcerer cocked his head. "No map? Well, what landmarks shall we steer by?"

"I only know that my vanished mother came from these woods."

"You only know . . ." Adrik's smile faltered. "That's all, nothing else? I'm not sure . . . but perhaps we can work with that. From what Yuir village did she hail?"

"I know not."

"What about her name? You must know that. We can ask around . . ."

Raidon was already shaking his head. "To me, she was Mother. One day, she told me her old home called her back—the Yuirwood. She gave me something to remember her by—a forget-me-not—and she departed, twelve or so years ago. That is the sum of what I know."

Adrik's smile wholly departed and became a frown. The sorcerer's gaze fell to the heap of gold Raidon still proffered. A ghost of the grin returned.

"Right," he said, scooping up half the coins. "Looks like we still need a guide. I don't know this forest from the Rawlinswood."

Daylight turned dull needles emerald and snow into heaps of glittering diamonds. In the chilly twilight beneath the sunlight canopy, three figures followed a narrow and faintly marked forest path.

Nécalama, an elf, walked at the head of the procession. Perhaps he was a half-elf—Raidon couldn't be sure. Regardless, he moved with an easy, certain stride, rarely looking behind to see whether the monk and sorcerer still followed. Nécalama had agreed to lead Raidon Kane and Adrik Commorand through the forest to the well-known if less well-traveled elf refuge of Relkath's Foot.

Raidon offered their guide payment, but Nécalama had shrugged and indicated he was going anyway; the two travelers might as well accompany him. Either way, he explained, it was an easy trek along a well-blazed path.

Raidon wasn't certain he agreed with the man's assessment of the road—the path they followed, when he could discern it, was nothing like the trade routes he'd traveled since leaving Telflamm. Half the time, it seemed they walked no path at all through the snow-sprinkled forest.

In fact, walking among the Yuirwood trees was an entirely novel experience to the Shou Town native. He was used to lanes bristling with fellow city dwellers, hurrying this way and that, intent on business or pleasure or both. Colorfully dressed citizens and dual-story buildings clogged perspective whichever way you looked, and the clamor of thousands living next to each other could never be drowned out.

Here, wind brushed through the trees, whispering green secrets Raidon couldn't decipher, though he suspected messages of tranquility. On more than one occasion, white-coated hares broke from hiding in a flurry of snow and bounded away, racing toward some private corner of the woods. A hawk's cry sounded above the canopy, and once, more distant and higher, a mighty roar stopped Raidon and Adrik in their tracks, though the noise barely drew an upward glance from Nécalama. When the elf in the lead showed no sign of pausing or providing any explanation about the origin of the great snarl, Shou and mercenary exchanged a shrug and continued.

Their guide explained that Relkath's Foot lay across almost the entire breadth of the Yuirwood from where they entered the forest south of Emmech. Such a trip might stretch to four or more long days of travel, or so Raidon initially expected. However, the elf claimed he knew secret paths through the Yuirwood deeps that would end up shaving a day or more off their trip. The sorcerer asked about the possibility of seeing some standing stones marked with ancient glyphs along the way. Nécalama had smiled and said they certainly would, else the savings in time would never come to pass.

On more than one occasion, Raidon found himself listening to the ever-talkative Adrik, who seemed compelled to speak of his many pursuits, a few of which the monk was surprised to find vaguely compelling.

For instance, Adrik told of how he once emerged from a moldy tomb clutching a spell-twined parchment containing an epic spell of true prophecy . . . and then an interesting tree had Adrik off the path and exclaiming over its silver leaves, leaving Raidon wondering about the oracular magic. Another time Adrik was describing a competition he'd entered in a distant city—something called the Duel Arcane, where wizards, sorcerers, warlocks, geomancers, and others with any claim at all to magic congregated to show their art . . . and then a bird-cry interrupted the tale. So much for the Duel Arcane; Adrik sidetracked into a long diatribe about a pet hawk he owned as a child.

Raidon held firm to his focus.

On day two, Adrik was telling Raidon about something he referred to as chaomancy, which involved all manner of unfamiliar terms such as strange attractors, resonance islands, and words so foreign they failed to find even a fleeting hold in Raidon's mind. Nécalama raised a hand, cutting Adrik off in mid-explanation, and pointed, first to the left then to the right.

The monk scanned for threats, but saw only two stone obelisks, one on either side of the faint trail. The obelisks were weathered and provided a home to many shades of green moss, though intricate inscriptions were clearly visible under the living veneer.

Adrik broke off his story, clapped his hands together, and ran to the obelisk on the right. "A Yuirwood rune stone!"

Raidon strangled a sigh before it could shake his focus.

Nécalama smiled. He said, "Such things are scattered all through these lands. The work of an elven civilization long gone, but magic yet remains in some of them."

Adrik reached out and gingerly traced an angular inscribed symbol. He said, "Yes—I sense something slumbering. I can't quite make out its purpose . . ."

Their guide said, "No need for you to trouble yourself—I know their power. These obelisks are bound with enchantments that bend distance, making shortcuts of what would otherwise be long roads."

"A portal?" Adrik stepped back.

The elf waggled his hand, tilting his head to one side. He said, "Close, but not precisely correct. So yes, you might describe it as a portal. Follow me through and you can decide for yourself what you want to call it."

So saying, Nécalama strode down the trail. Raidon tensed, waiting for the half-elf to disappear in a flash of smoke or in a sparkle of strange lights.

Nécalama passed the invisible line between the two standing stones. And nothing; Nécalama walked unconcernedly forward, the stones behind him. The guide remained stubbornly, fully visible. After he moved ten or so feet, he paused and gazed back. "Coming?" he asked, amusement curling his lips.

"It did not work?" inquired the monk.

"*Something* happened," said Adrik, one hand held forward, palm out. "I sense a discharge of magic, even now."

"Come along—follow me between the stones."

Adrik and Raidon exchanged glances and followed.

Passing through the stones failed to disturb Raidon's equilibrium in the least. He sensed no change in the environment as he walked. The faint trail ahead remained steady, and looking back, he could still see the route they had traveled prior to passing between the stones, without any discontinuity.

The monk decided their guide was having a little fun at their expense. Weren't elves known for such foolishness?

Which meant they still had a few days of travel ahead of them, if their goal was on the western side of the Yuirwood as Nécalama earlier indicated. Adrik was mumbling about probability and sliding four-space projections; in other words, gibberish.

Ahead, the trail broadened into a real, easily discernable path, almost a road. They passed through a copse of rustling aspens. A breath of sweet air moved through the murmuring aspen leaves, refreshing Raidon's mind and body with an insubstantial touch.

When they emerged from the tiny grove, they found themselves walking down a sun-dappled, leaf-strewn street in a half-elven forest enclave.

"Welcome to Relkath's Foot!" proclaimed Nécalama, his arm sweeping across the panorama.

Four majestic conifers towered hundreds of feet from their broad bases, thrusting high above the forest canopy. These four splendid specimens, old beyond the years of humans, were the heart of Relkath's Foot. From this central landmark radiated hundreds of elevated wooden platforms resting in the boughs of the surrounding forest, strung together by a network of leaf-twined ropes and suspension bridges built of hardy pine. Green-clad half-elves, made tiny by their height above the forest floor, moved here and there across them, intent on personal tasks.

Elaborately carved and adorned platforms hung in the four largest trees—amazing structures of living wood that served as floors, walls, and lofty ceilings. Leafy doors studded these tree homes, and everblooming flowers grew around all. Warm lamplight flickered from the many open-air windows.

Though the air was wintry and Raidon's breath steamed, the layer of snow covering the ground in eastern Aglarond was absent.

Nécalama pointed at the top of the tallest of the four conifers, at the largest and most impressive structure. "The Royal Hall," he said. "Princess Blindelsyn Olóssyne resides there. The only thing higher near here is an aerie of song dragons allied with the city."

"Can we go up there?" exclaimed the sorcerer.

Their guide looked doubtful. He said, "Outsiders are rarely permitted in the boughs. But travelers are welcome in the merchants' square, which includes a pair of inns."

The elf gestured toward dozens of quaint wooden structures built around a massively wide square on the ground bracketed by the four towering trees. Dozens of figures, mostly elves and half-elves, milled through the area. Raidon recognized some humans, a few halflings, and even a dwarf. The scents of grilled food and the tinkle of music washed across them.

The mouth-watering aromas enticed the monk, but . . .

"I have questions," Raidon said, turning to face their half-elf guide, "about my mother. Where can I ask—who should I ask?" When Raidon had shown Nécalama his mother's forget-me-not during their trip, the elf failed to recognize it, though he said someone in Relkath's Foot was sure to know the meaning of the smoothly regular tree symbol.

"Inns are good places for questions and, as I said, we have two," replied Nécalama. "The Green Man"—the elf pointed to an ordinary wooden house on the north side of the square—"and the Taproot"—he pointed at a lower building that sprawled back into the undergrowth—"are both fine places. Outsiders are more common at the Taproot, which boasts a first-class alehouse and private rooms. The Green Man has only a single common room in which visitors can bed down. The locals prefer it."

Adrik enthused, "Alehouse! I say—"

"Best we try the Green Man, then," said Raidon. "The locals are more likely to be able to help me."

The sorcerer frowned and nodded.

Nécalama said, "You'll find that its spirits are just as fine as the Taproot, Adrik. In fact, if you don't mind my suggestion, ask for a glass of rootweal wine—you'll never find better."

"I will!"

They bid their guide good-bye. At the last, Raidon convinced the half-elf to take a couple gold coins for his aid. Then they made directly for the Green Man. The savory smells intensified with every step.

Perhaps a little food before questions wouldn't hurt.

The Green Man's common room shimmered with tiny gleaming lanterns that hung as if strung from a garland along the rafters and walls, then twined down the living wooden supports. The light picked out long-legged figures attired in golds, greens, and browns. Most held long-stemmed goblets in one or both hands, others held instruments, and at least a few grasped graven pipes from which fragrant smoke emerged.

A forest beast turned on a spit in the fire; it was the source of the mouth-watering odor. A woman, a half-elf no doubt, stood in the center of the common room, surrounded on three sides by a sturdy bar of living wood. Dozens of long-stemmed goblets hung bowl-down above her. She smiled a welcome at Raidon when he entered. Adrik received a puzzled nod. "Is he with you?" she called to Raidon.

The monk blinked, nodded. Again he was struck with surprise—to the residents of Relkath's Foot, he was of elf blood. Of course, he *was* a half-elf; his heritage was twined with the blood of his mother. But growing up in Telflamm, he considered himself to be Shou first and last, nothing else.

"Then welcome to the Green Man, travelers," said the barkeep, her smile returned. "What is your pleasure?"

They crossed the room to stand before the bar.

"We'd like to try the rootweal?" said Adrik, his voice uncertain as he looked around the room. He was the only human in the Green Man's common room.

"You have heard about our specialty, I see. Are you sure you are up to it? The draught is potent for one not of . . . someone not used to it."

The sorcerer ducked his head and said, "If it's all right, I'd like to try it."

"Of course! And the same for you, traveler?" She looked at Raidon.

"None for me—please, could you prepare a pot of tea?" he responded.

The woman cocked her head and a few nearby patrons glanced quizzically at Raidon.

"I am most sorry, but we do not serve 'T' in the Green Man. I have a few wines, including the rootweal of which you speak. I can offer you a pipe, packed with any of a variety of leaf harvested and dried with an eye toward quality. We also have boiled mushrooms, a multitude of fresh berries, baked biscuits, and roasted venison."

"Venison sounds perfect, with a few mushrooms? And, very well, I would like to try the wine, too. Rootweal."

"You shall find none better, traveler."

In short order, Raidon and Adrik sat opposite each other at a high table. Steaming platters were set before them, heaped with all manner of food, hardly any of which Raidon recognized. But it was all delicious.

The rootweal was oddly compelling. Raidon expected it to be too sweet, too sour, or too much like drinking vinegar—such was the extent of his experience with wine. The rootweal, a wine the color of red silk, was smooth and full, and tasted . . . of something for which he had no name. If pressed, he would have to say that it tasted like a forest meadow alive in the glad light of the sun.

As they ate and drank, listening to the musicians, Adrik's face grew redder and redder. His smile widened and his laughter grew more frequent and louder. Raidon found a smile on his own lips as he listened to the musical anecdotes.

A bard strumming a lyre launched into a song describing the founding of the city. The four central trees, he sang, sprouted from the buried foot of the ancient god Relkath of the Numberless Branches. This god, claimed the lyrics, walked the woods primeval along with several other mysterious powers who predated the elves. Several stanzas described unlikely adventures featuring Relkath, and the song ended with the god deciding to rest.

The bard wrapped up the song with a flourish of twanging strings and announced, "Relkath yet sleeps beneath the forest's soil, someday to awaken when the people of the Yuirwood need their ancient gods once again."

Everyone in the Green Man raised a goblet, pipe, or whatever was handy high in the air, cheered, and drank.

Raidon followed suit. Adrik sighed, "Tha' wa' nice," and toppled from his chair.

Several half-elves nearby laughed, their eyes glinting with festive glee. One said, "Your friend sleeps well tonight, if a bit early." More chuckles. Raidon looked beneath the table. His sorcerous traveling companion was curled beneath the empty chair, already snoring the sleep of the over-intoxicated.

The monk, familiar with similar antics from Shou not pledged to Xiang Temple, nodded. If the truth were told, he was surprised he hadn't followed the Commorand sorcerer to the floor. Never before had he consumed wine in such quantity.

It occurred to Raidon that his relative clarity of thought was more evidence of his mother's blood.

The monk set down his wine and pulled forth his forget-me-not from beneath his clothing. The white, treelike symbol in the center was haloed in night's darkness. Night, where sky blue once winked.

Raidon stood and held the stone on its silver chain high above his head. He called out, "Who knows the meaning of the symbol on this amulet, an amulet given me by an elf who hailed from these woods?"

Those nearby laughed, perhaps thinking he posed a riddle. But riddle or no, they were game, and all wanted to take a look. He allowed the amulet to be passed around to those interested in handling it directly, though he kept an anxious eye on it.

While the treelike symbol drew most of the interest but no recognition, an elder wood elf named Yármarion seemed more interested in the cramped, overlapping inscriptions that crusted the sides and rear of the stone. He sat alone, smoke curling up from the pipe clamped in one corner of his mouth. He turned the amulet over and over, squinting hard at the miniature text. Yármarion said, "These writings are in an ancient tongue, one no longer spoken in the world."

"What, the language used by sleeping Relkath?" called the bard who'd sung about the resting god.

Another chimed in, "Would that make it the language of sleep? Sleep that is denied us, which others enjoy so much?" He pointed to the sorcerer's snoring, smiling figure beneath the table. Merriment erupted, but the wood elf holding the amulet slowly nodded, his face a study in consideration.

"Perhaps," Yármarion replied. He leaned back in his seat and glanced toward the rafters. "The inscriptions remind me of the text I saw once in an old book. Where was I? Oh yes, a library of Mystra near Calimport, right before the agents of Old Night burned it to the ground. What was it about? Something to do with the theft of sleep, ensuring the first mortals would never discover the truth in their dreams."

Several patrons laughed and toasted, "To the first mortals, whoever they are!"

Raidon broke in. "Will dreams show the way to my mother?"

Yármarion squinted at the amulet and shrugged, "How could elves like us ever know?" He tossed it across the room to the monk. "Sorry, traveler, I have never before seen the primary symbol. But I can tell you this—a potency lies within that stone, slumbering."

"A potency?"

"Powerful magic is wound deep within your amulet. I am not so old that I can't sense sorcery, especially of such strength."

"What kind of sorcery?" Raidon whispered, suddenly wondering if he were channeling Adrik's relentless manner.

Whatever explanation Yármarion might have provided was lost in clear, shrill cries of clarions. The clamor sounded from outside.

The bard exclaimed, "The Masters' summons!" The elves and half-elves in the Green Man immediately set down their instruments, their pipes, and their goblets; they moved as one to the exit. Raidon followed, asking, "Who are the Masters?" Someone yelled, "The Masters of the Yuirwood, of course!" The explanation did nothing to lessen Raidon's confusion.

Thin, elegant figures streamed into the square from all sides, and on the boughs above, hundreds of elves looked down into the tumult, pointing and gesturing, trying to make sense of the chaos. A shining white figure emerged from the Royal Hall high above. The princess, presumably, though Raidon didn't spare her a glance. He gracefully navigated the congestion and push of bodies, judging and using its tumult to unerringly propel himself, first widdershins and then the other way, to the square's center, where the horns yet sounded.

Yármarion followed in Raidon's wake. The elderly elf was more spry than he looked. Raidon worried briefly about Adrik, then shrugged. Nothing was likely to befall a man sleeping on a tavern floor worse than burglary.

A half-elf woman in ragged, blood-stained clothing stood at the square's center, accompanied by elves clad in militaristic outfits of green, gold, and dun. Their clothing was resplendent. From the way the patterns on their clothes shifted and changed, Raidon guessed the colors would blend perfectly into forestlike hues and textures should one of them step into the pathless wild.

Raidon touched Yármarion on the sleeve. "Are those the Masters of the Yuirwood?"

"Yes. But not the woman. I've never seen her before."

Three of the Masters continued to blow long, shrill notes on brass horns.

"Masters—are they called that because they rule this forest?"

Yármarion replied, "They do not rule. But their order is elite. They are afforded great respect because they keep the ancient Yuirwood free of evil influence. Without their efforts, the forest's slow retreat would proceed all the faster. The Yuirwood once covered all the peninsula."

"They must know many things."

"They lay claim to ancient lores, and know all the secrets of the menhir circles that dot the Yuirwood deeps."

The Masters gave one last long tone, then stowed the instruments at their belts. One of the regally accoutered half-elves stepped forward. A great yew bow was strapped on his back. He projected, "Invaders threaten our forest borders! This wood elf, called Janesta, witnessed their terrible attack, and is the lone survivor of her tribe!"

The assembled audience, which hadn't completely quieted when the Master had started speaking, now hushed as one.

The speaker continued. "The attack was launched from *within* the eaves of the Yuirwood. The attack was carried out by strange, kin-slaying elves. And no, I do not mean our long-sundered brethren, the drow."

The silence was broken by gasps, protestations, and cries of surprise. The man spoke over the turmoil. "It is true—Janesta describes her attackers as steely eyed elves more noble and terrible even than gray elves, mail-clad, and astride mailed steeds. Her description matches the likeness of the long-vanished Yuir elves who ranged these woods when the trees ruled all. Whatever nobility they once possessed, it is clear some surviving splinter of that race lives still, old, corrupt, and senile with age!"

A voice rang out from above—the princess. She asked, "Where have these stagnant Yuir resided all these centuries without our knowledge, we who now claim the wide woods?"

"They linger behind the wood, we guess, in a veiled space to which the menhir paths lead for those who know the route."

The princess called down, "This is possible? Do the Masters not know all the routes?"

The speaker shook his head. "We know many—not all. We've long suspected that deeper, more tangled paths lay outside our lore. Now we know it is true."

"Let Janesta speak," said the princess, from where she stood as if on a mighty branch, not empty space. "From whence came these awful destroyers? Tell us, for we are kin of your kin. We will avenge your tribe's memory and defend the sanctity of the forest."

The wood elf, disoriented and pale, looked up into the sky and said in a weak voice, "They came from across a causeway—a causeway fronted by two soaring obelisks. We set our encampment nearby to study the stones, and the strange mist that so often obscured the causeway from sight and even touch."

"Tell us more of this causeway," commanded the princess when the woman faltered.

"The day prior to the attack, my friend Natal Peacethorn and I . . ." Janesta choked, wiped at her eyes, then continued. "Natal and I found the causeway clear for the first time. We crossed it. On the other side we found a massive granite gate sealed against all entry. And above . . . stars wheeled in the sky, though Natal and I crossed the causeway in full daylight."

The assembled Masters looked at her with consternation, though a few nodded, as if her words confirmed a long-held conjecture.

"The gates were closed, thick with glyphs we couldn't decipher. Above the gate was scribed a single massive symbol—a white, treelike symbol surrounded by a field of flickering blue-tinged darkness."

Raidon's eyes did their best to leap from their sockets just as his jaw threatened to detach from his skull and clatter to the ground.

Yármarion turned and fixed Raidon Kane with a measuring glance. He said, "It would seem your arrival today is not accidental, traveler."

Chapter Twelve

Stardeep, The Causeway

Elven war-horses cantered down the narrow Causeway, their hooves striking thunder through the glade. Empyrean Knights sat astride them, a rush of silvery mail, righteous fury alive in their eyes. On they raced, across the narrow lane, three dozen star elves draped in pleated mithral hauberks worn over silk. Their swift steeds were sheathed in plate that glinted in the morning sun. Those in the vanguard drew down the tips of their lances, those in the rear unsheathed great swords.

Arrows burst from the boughs of the encircling forest, a rain of flint-tipped death, falling among the Knights, dealing death or mercy at random. The screams of horses and Knights marked a sudden and growing knot at the Causeway's middle—horses went down, breaking Knights beneath them, but worse, clogging the charge line.

Figures clad in green, gold, and dun broke from the eaves, light and silent, drawing bowstrings for another flight even as they ran. Astonished shouts greeted the attack, followed closely by the ring of sword on steel, axe on bow. The narrow line of the Causeway became choked at its head with grappling, hacking figures. The blood of wood elf, half-elf, and star elf mingled in the dark waters of the hidden Chabala Mere.

The Empyrean Knights were outnumbered, but despite the bloody toll exacted by their foes, and regardless of the fair-featured nature of their enemy, the defenders slashed the wood elves, split chests protected only by stitched leather, cracked wooden shields, and finally slew the Yuirwood elves to the last man and woman.

Silence descended for a beat, followed by a victory shout. The Empyrean Knights had again defended Stardeep's entrance from the latest infiltrating attack by the suddenly, unaccountably warlike wild and mixed elves of Aglarond.

Kiril topped a wooded rise and saw the great boulder beneath which she had once so often rested, though now it was tufted with patches of snow. A little farther, there was the old birch tree, still standing tall and regal among the conifers after so many years. Here was the narrow ravine that sheltered a small, trickling tributary to the Chabala River, which fed into the Mere—on which sat the Causeway.

"We're close," she threw back over her shoulder—her right shoulder; Xet perched on the left. Gage stiffened, as if hearing difficult news, then showed her his impish smile. Her self-proclaimed friend seemed oddly shaken since their encounter with Sathra. His jokes were few and far between, and forced. A strange melancholia gripped him. Of course, she didn't have time to worry about him now. She could be moments from finding Nangulis!

If she allowed herself, she could project herself back into the memories of her life before the events of the last decade, before she'd become merely a "swordswoman." When she had been a Keeper of the Cerulean Sign. When she had performed an important duty, one she had executed for years. She and Nangulis both—he in the Inner Bastion, she in the Outer, though no day passed that didn't allow time for them to be together, either within the guarded bulk of Stardeep, or beyond its dimensional veil in the sunlit groves of the Yuirwood.

When off duty, she and Nangulis spent more time in Faerûn than in Sildëyuir, for that realm, their home, required a longer trek than a mere stroll down the Causeway. If the Traitor were ever to escape, Stardeep's remote location would prove a buffer between the Traitor's curses and the home realm. The elders sited the dungeon in a tenuous pocket of Sildëyuir, one they further splintered in order to make it its own discrete space. To penetrate the starry realm, if he escaped, the Traitor would have to emerge, when open, on the tightly controlled Causeway, then travel overland through the Yuirwood to find the closest active menhir gate.

Either that, or travel the ancient dungeon tunnels beneath Stardeep, where the mazelike passages, dug by no star elf, were black mystery. A mystery, except that if one traveled their labyrinthine twistings all the way through, one might find a way back to the realm from which Stardeep was calved. When she'd first come to Stardeep, Kiril thought the connection was myth. But upon becoming a Keeper, she'd learned such a path indeed existed, but it was a path possible only for those possessed of great power. Dire threats menaced all who attempted that dim path. In any event, a trip to Sildëyuir was not a simple process, whether you were a Stardeep escapee or a Stardeep Keeper.

Ahead, the trees thinned, revealing the edge of a broad pond. A thin sheen of ice coated its surface. The far side was lost in a low mist that clung thick, heavy, and impenetrable to the water's surface. Kiril walked to the edge and squinted into the edgeless white.

"I don't see the land bridge you described," Gage groused. The man was uncommonly out of sorts. Moody, quiet at turns, then accusatory.

Kiril said, "Like"—she decided not to tell Gage about Sildëyuir and cleared her throat—"other realms beyond this world, Stardeep can be reached only when a way is opened. When the portal is not open, only a mist-drenched marsh is apparent. When open, a causeway—*the* Causeway—is visible."

"All right, let's . . . hold up. There's been a fight," said Gage, standing back among the trees, his gaze low and intent on something in the brush.

The swordswoman scanned the edges of the Mere, recognizing disturbances in the ice and the telltale sign of erased tracks in the newly disturbed soil. "I see signs of recent activity, but a fight? That seems unlikely."

"Come over here," replied the thief in a subdued voice.

Kiril turned and joined Gage among the trees. He used a dagger to scrape away a recently piled mound of earth. More digging revealed a shallow grave in which lay an ashen wood elf, wearing a uniform of green, gold, and dun.

"Blood!" exclaimed Kiril. The wood elf had been hewed nearly in two.

"The ground's been disturbed all through here. It was a big fight, with many deaths."

"Many deaths?"

The thief held out his gauntleted hand, the one with the disturbingly toothed cavity. He said, "My gauntlet can smell many more corpses buried all through the area, though this one was the most lightly covered."

They dug up a few more—each was an elf or half-elf, and all wore the same colors. None of the elves were star elves, Kiril was relieved to discover. "These colors indicate some sort of uniform, I think," said Kiril. "I'm not familiar with the rangers of Yuirwood. Why did they attack Stardeep?"

Gage shrugged.

Kiril shook her head, looked down at the blade sheathed at her side. No more idling. She returned to the Mere's edge and tried to recall the access keys. Only one Stardeep function extended from the dungeon's core to the edge of the Mere, and Keepers were trained in accessing it. She mentally probed across the water, calling on skills she'd forsaken a decade earlier. Contact! Though Stardeep lay across a planar veil, she could trigger a connection . . .

The mist churned and rolled away from the Mere's center. A narrow land bridge slowly resolved, as if always there beneath the mist. Perhaps it always was. The blue sky above slowly darkened, and stars came out, strange to the sky of Yuirwood forest, but familiar to Kiril. She'd memorized those constellations as a child.

A horn sounded, pure and glorious. Xet chimed, dug his crystal claws painfully into her shoulder, then launched himself straight up. Kiril jerked her gaze down from the darkening sky to see chargers plunging across the Causeway—Empyrean Knights! The defenders of Stardeep. Not a danger, despite Xet's swift departure—merely a welcoming committee.

She raised both hands and waved, yelling. The Knights were a doughty crew, if formal. Their training demanded no less—theirs was a duty every bit as demanding as a Keeper's. Despite her anxiety over Nangulis, her spirits rose at seeing the Knights in their flashing hauberks and military poise. The Knights in the lead, halfway across the narrow bridge, lowered their lances to point. Their speed did not slacken.

The swordswoman frowned and called, "It is me, Kiril Duskmourn, a Keeper. Slow your steeds!"

The full-throated braying of horns split the air. The forest boughs rang with the echo. Arrows burst from the rear of the charging column. Most clattered harmlessly from Kiril's mail, their force spent and tips blunted or shattered. A few, however, bit flesh. The swordswoman let out a wounded howl, as much in pain as disbelief.

The Knights didn't recognize her, didn't believe her, or didn't care. Kiril dodged left, just avoiding the barb-tipped lance of a scowling Knight.

She scrambled to avoid falling backward into the Mere, spewing obscenity. "Pox-faced rats on a bender! What the Hells are you doing? Look at me! I'm a Keeper, gods roast your blood-flecked souls!"

Five elves on horseback charged off the end of the narrow causeway, wrenching their mounts around in a tight arc to face her. The two in the lead, who'd nearly skewered her, dropped their lances as they wheeled their mounts. Kiril's back was to the dark, wintry Mere.

"Where's Commander Brathtar? By your rutting gods, bring me the Commander, he'll know who—"

One of the Knights raised his long sword and spoke. "The Commander is indisposed—we take our orders from the Keeper of the Outer Bastion, who commands that imposters and liars be slain." The man spurred his mount, which reared, its steel-shod hooves flashing. Kiril ducked beneath the hooves. The man's sword flashed down and she dropped flat into the frozen mud.

Stamping hooves and sword tips harried her into the water's cold grasp. The near-freezing chill shocked her as she dipped into the Chabala, but even half-submerged, she heard the sudden high-pitched scream of a horse and the clatter of metal on metal. It sounded like a mounted Knight being brought low—had Gage revealed himself?

Kiril didn't know to what depths the Mere plunged, nor did she wish to personally plumb it. She got her feet beneath her and stood up off the soft bottom. The water reached only to her waist, but the slope dropped steeply away. Water streamed from her hair and face. The cold shock of the biting liquid sought to freeze her muscles, reminding her of a creature she'd once fought whose breath was winter itself.

Blinking water from her eyes, Kiril saw that a Knight was down and still, a dagger butt protruding from his neck, his horse rearing. Five Knights wheeled away from her, bringing their weapons to bear on the threat materializing on their flank. Gage. The crazy thief stood just within the soft cover offered by a copse of trees tufting a small rise, his hand with the disturbing gauntlet raised high. The gauntlet's demon mouth screamed forth a terrible, mind-punishing keening. The Knights advanced, bringing their barbed lances low, deadly tips toward the thief.

One Knight remained intent on Kiril. His horse stood at the water's edge as he regarded her, denying her access to dry land.

The Knight's attack made no sense! She tried diplomacy as her aggressor stood silently. "You've made a terrible mistake! I was once a Keeper here—I'm no threat! If you force me to draw my weapon, your life will end here, in the sun! You'll never see Sildëyuir's stars again!"

The Knight hesitated, looking back to his brethren who now occluded her view of Gage, then back to her. She saw by the insignia on his shoulder the Knight was a captain.

The captain explained. "Telarian foresaw you to say exactly that. He said if you give up your sword without a fight here and now, you'll be allowed to enter Stardeep, where we can discern friend from foe, imposter from the genuine. Hand it across to me." He extended one palm, open and waiting.

Kiril sought to gather her wits to understand the captain's request, but the hellish screaming of the thief's demonic gauntlet rattled her. Despite wondering if she would regret it, she replied, "I give up my sword to no one!"

The Knight looked surprised. He said, "Are you sure?

Keeper Telarian was certain you'd give up the blade to gain entry. He sees all futures . . ."

Over the yowl of his hellmouth, Gage called, "Kiril! They want the sword, that's all! They want Angul—this is a trap!"

"What?"

A gap in the crowding Knights briefly revealed the thief. He extended his gauntleted hand higher above his head, and the hellmouth's scream redoubled in volume, a soul-grating shriek promising insanity.

Stardeep's defenders, closer than she to the hellish sound, shuddered and cringed, their eyes suddenly wild with supernatural dread. Some moaned, others dropped their weapons, but most importantly, they allowed their discipline to fail. Kiril bolted from the water, boldly ducking past the one who'd offered parley, then through the mounted, milling Knights nearer Gage.

One Knight, perhaps harder of hearing than the rest, lowered his lance and charged the thief. Gage ducked to the side, but howled as the horseman thundered past and down the other side of the rise. A moment later, Kiril reached Gage's side.

The thief had taken a lance strike to his right shoulder. His gauntleted hand hung limply, and the hellmouth was silent. Blood flowed down the front of his creased leather armor. His eyes were full of amazement. He mumbled, "I think he landed a good one . . ."

Kiril put off questioning the bleeding thief about the "trap." She said, "They'll flank us, but we can hold them. I'll take your right."

Gage nodded and drew a long knife into his left hand.

She unsheathed her weapon. A spark of well-being stole through her, but Angul failed to burst into blue flame. What?

"Angul, aid me!" she ordered.

These Knights Empyrean are aligned with the cause of righteousness, the sword imparted into her mind, *and I will not destroy them.*

"You bloodstained monster, help me or these brainwashed Knights will slay your wielder!" The sword remained adamantly unlit. Nor did it attempt to overpower her sense of reality . . .

The Knights most affected by the hellscream were shaking off its effects. They began to separate, intent on spreading out around Kiril and Gage.

Before they could implement their strategy, a pebble of flame skipped into the midst of the Empyrean Knights and exploded, briefly silhouetting them against a field of boiling red light before enveloping elf and horse alike.

Someone was throwing fireballs! And that someone had attacked the Knights, not herself and Gage, thank the Sign.

Kiril scanned the perimeter of the clearing. She spied two figures. One figure . . . a human male, she saw, was gesticulating as if preparing to cast another spell.

Gage cried a new warning. She whirled to see the same Knight who'd skewered the thief retracing his path, this time his lance aimed at her.

She dropped into a crouch as she raised Angul in a vertical line, pointed at the earth. Her blade clashed along the lance shaft, deflecting the tip sideways then into the ground. The Knight held his seat despite the terrible jolt, but his lance remained behind. The impact nearly caused her to drop Angul; the blade was staying true to its promise, and provided her not one drop of supernatural strength, speed, or solidity of frame. At least it wasn't actively inhibiting her from using it as an ordinary weapon.

Gage flipped his grip from hilt to blade in a blink, then threw the knife after the Knight. His aim was off, and his target cantered forward, undeterred.

"What's wrong with your sword?" he asked, his voice weak. Blood continued to run from his wound.

Before she could answer, two of the Knights upslope launched their lances as if they were javelins. Gage stepped left and avoided the one aimed at him. Kiril stumbled, and the sharp pole plunged into her right leg, driving right through flesh and into the ground. An unfamiliar tug pulled through her entire body and she gasped in surprise.

One of the newcomers broke from the encircling eaves, moving from a standstill to full sprint instantly. The fire thrower remained partially hidden, his hands aflame with another spell.

The sprinter was a human—no, a half-elf in a black, tattered silk jacket. A slender sword was strapped to his back. He charged the closest Knight. A full ten feet before reaching his target, who failed to realize he was under attack, the newcomer leaped into the air, spinning as he did so, and delivered a flying kick straight into the mounted Knight's chest. As the newcomer landed gracefully, the Knight tumbled from his saddle and smashed limply to the ground.

Another Knight spurred his mount forward and slashed at the stranger, missing completely—the half-elf rolled beneath the mount's prancing legs, came up on the other side, and jerked the man off his horse. The unseated Knight crashed to the ground, and the half-elf followed him down with a brutal elbow to his windpipe.

With her left hand, Kiril pulled the lance from the earth, freeing her right leg. The shaft of wood still protruded from her flesh, and she could barely walk. Even with the unexpected aid from the strangers, she wondered if she would survive the day. She advanced, stiff-legged, down the slope, Angul held high but still nothing more than dumb metal in her weakening grasp.

Chapter Thirteen

Stardeep, Throat

Delphe stood on the Well's lip. Unsettling reflections played on her face. A stagnant wind blew up the shaft, tousling her hair and cooling her skin. A wind where none should be.

Something stirred below.

"Cynosure, initiate primary containment!" She glanced up at the idol of stone, iron, and crystal. The figure stared unblinking into the containment fires, as always. But from it, no answer came.

"Cynosure?" Delphe's stomach fell away as sweat broke on her brow. The wind up the shaft turned colder.

A crash, as of crystals breaking, or perhaps reality tearing, echoed through the Well. If Cynosure were somehow disabled, a full-scale containment breach could be moments away!

Delphe shrugged away the panic prowling her mind. Time to work. She extended her arms over her head, calling on her connection to the Cerulean Sign. An arc of silvery blue fire spanned her reach, then dropped into the Well, broadening as it fell toward the interface. She watched her magical quelling fold into the sun-bright chaos of the containment layer.

A green-gray burst of energy bounced back, flaring brightly before resolving into a ropy loop of phantom matter. The object gyrated and spun, almost like something alive, as gravity grabbed and pulled it back toward the scalding boundary layer.

One end of the spiraling phantasm flailed wildly and managed to touch the smooth side of the Well, and stuck.

Delphe gasped. Whatever had just emerged, or been projected from the Well, wasn't mere illusion, as sometimes happened when the Traitor dreamed. Whatever its origin, this sluglike entity had to be sterilized. Immediately.

Like an obscenely thick snail, the grayish thing began to inch up the concave wall of the Well. The light of the boundary layer failed to fully illuminate its sickly gray flesh.

"Cynosure, burn it!"

Nothing. The mind of Stardeep was focused elsewhere, if not worse. "Stars guide me," she murmured. Cynosure's wardenship had failed again.

The thing on the wall crept higher.

Delphe channeled the Sign. Blue fire warmed her chest, then burst out upon her arms, hair, and palms. Her eyes blazed, and she saw deeper into the slowly rising aberration.

Beneath its gray skin, the creature continued to modify itself, trading possibility for strength, raw energy for tissue, and dreadful desire for fell ability. It pulled mass from tiny particles in the air, and magical energy from the very spells meant to contain that which lay below it. It was fortifying itself, empowering itself . . .

The longer it was allowed to persist, the more difficult it would ultimately become to defeat! She couldn't wait for Cynosure to wake from its somnolence.

Delphe pointed down, recalled the proper key phrase,

and spoke the awkward syllables. The dozens of glass slabs protruding from the Well's concave wall, spiraling down the sides, swiftly and silently retracted. The tentacle-like head of the creature, which had been reaching for the bottommost step, now found only a slippery, smooth surface, like the rest of the Well. At least Stardeep's manual functions remained accessible, despite Cynosure's absence. If that obscenity wanted to escape, it would have to inch the entire way.

Which should provide her with more than enough time to incinerate it, Cynosure be damned. Only one way to test her hypothesis.

Ragged words burned her throat. Arcs of energy trailed her gesturing hands as she wove an arcane discontinuity, a discontinuity shaped like a scythe. It burned with cerulean fire. The spellscythe neared the height of her magical arsenal, and cost her a large part of her strength.

For its part, the slender monstrosity continued to heave its way up the vertical shaft. As it moved, it shed streamers of gray flesh, like dead scales, revealing a larger, appalling bulk beneath. Silvered now, and sleek rather than stringy, the entity bounded an entire body length upward with a single leap, slapping onto the wall only fifteen or so paces beneath Delphe's protruding toes.

As it gathered itself for another, stronger jump, Delphe hurtled the spellscythe down the Well shaft, directing her weapon's motions with an outstretched hand. The aberration scuttled sideways. The spellscythe just missed the fleeing creature, and smashed instead into the Well's glossy side. Oh, shards!

An explosion hurtled up the Well's shaft, expanding as it breached the lip. The abjurer was battered, but kept her feet. Her ears rang in the aftermath, but through the cacophony she heard snuffling and growling down in the well. A terrible, hacking cough, chillingly similar to how a man might clear his throat of phlegm. Something was straining to speak, perhaps, or more likely seeking to sing forth dark sorceries all its own.

She rushed back to the edge, gazed down through the explosion's residual haze, and saw the remnants of her spellscythe unraveling. Near it was the entity, rent and smoking from the near miss, but already scabbing over with nacreous flesh even tougher and more spell-resistant than that which had burned off.

One of the rents remained, a gap which protruded greenish fangs even as Delphe watched. The flesh around the opening flexed, elongating to become an obscene organ. From this orifice echoed the coughing. Soon it would be capable of uttering terrible words of power, if it could evolve the capacity before Delphe eliminated it.

The abjurer desperately clutched at the threads of the dissipating spellscythe. Quicker to salvage its energy than attempt to summon a new tool.

Words floated up from below, stinging the elf's flesh with their magical import. "I . . . call . . . call upon the Final Pact of—"

Delphe jerked her spellscythe to the left, despite her lack of complete control. It sliced into the creature's roiling skin. Where it touched, the entity hazed away like mist, and its words collapsed into a basso scream of transcendent pain.

Three pseudopods burst from the creature's sides, each tipped with an ebony spike. Two of these scrabbled for a better hold on the Well's side. From the last emerged a cloudy green beam aimed at the spellscythe. Where it struck, portions of the abjurer's weapon boiled and failed, as if touched by the putridity of rot.

Delphe palmed her amulet with her right hand. Lifting it high, she chanted hoary words older than some races that now walked Toril. Her amulet took on the hue of the limitless sky. In its glow, the spellscythe was fortified.

The creature was only moments from cresting the lip.

"Delphe! Delphe!" Cynosure's voice, strident with alarm, blared suddenly from overhead. "Category two breach in effect, on the cusp of category one!"

The idol, attached horizontally to the ceiling, took on the hue of Delphe's amulet. The idol's eyes snapped open, revealing a vista of shining sapphire. As if windows to a world apart where storms raged, a blast of howling wind poured forth.

A spindle of madly spinning air extended, its tip reaching down the shaft, growling with pure, elemental fury. A heartbeat later, the lengthening funnel stabbed the creature, even as Delphe's spellscythe cut at it with waning strength. Cynosure's vortex caught the aberration, snapping its tendrils away from the walls. It screamed, a booming moan that caused ice to crystallize from the air throughout the Inner Bastion. Then it plummeted, spinning and flailing, back through the boundary layer.

The ensuing splash of boundary fire rose high in the shaft, burning so fiercely Delphe's eyelashes were singed. She didn't care. She continued to gaze down the Well, anxiety clutching at her lungs. When the disturbance subsided, she saw that the boundary layer was still intact. Thank the Cerulean Sign.

The abjurer studied the Well's lowest reaches a while longer, suspiciously eyeing each new swirl and pattern.

"Delphe!" said Cynosure again. "We are under attack!"

The abjurer balled her fists, considering whether to utter the words that would shut down the sentient artifact immediately, or to query it first. While its aid had been ultimately necessary to defeat that which had leaped from containment, its inability to stay connected with real time events had become a liability she could no longer overlook.

But years of history required she give the construct fair warning.

"Cynosure," she began, "the attack is quelled. Recall to mind the previous instance? You and I thwarted the Traitor's—"

"Yes, yes. Do you think my mind broken?" interrupted Cynosure. "I meant what I said—at this very moment, the Empyrean Knights have ridden forth to repel an invasion occurring at the end of the open Causeway!"

Surprise made Delphe catch her breath. "Show me!" she commanded.

CHAPTER FOURTEEN

Stardeep, The Causeway

Telarian watched the fight unfold at the Causeway's end.

He stood just within Stardeep's open Causeway Gate. Nearby loitered Commander Brathtar, also watching, though the Commander frowned and scowled by turns. A small cavalry unit of mounted Empyrean Knights waited in the gate tunnel, ready to ride out and again defend Stardeep from what they believed to be another foray of violent wood elf invaders.

Anxiety tightened Telarian's throat. Something was wrong. No, that word wasn't weighted with enough soul-churning dread; something was terribly, horrendously off beam. He'd foreseen the addled, alcoholic Keeper would give up her sword to avoid a fight. Yes, he'd prophesied a struggle to convince her what must be done, but in her need to see Nangulis reborn, she gave up her one remaining connection to Stardeep: Angul. He'd seen the future!

But reality unreeled right in front of him far differently. Knights lay dead, and a former Keeper was imperiled by orders he'd given those same Knights. How had it come to this? How could his divination be so much in error?

Just yesterday, a wood, wild, and half-elf force of considerable size approached Chabala Mere and attempted to lay siege. Three Knights had perished in that attack, plus a host of wood elves that hadn't understood what they assailed. A few of their bodies lay in scattered graves, while the bulk of that defeated force lay at the bottom, if it had a bottom, of Chabala Mere.

He hadn't foreseen that, either.

Events were tumbling out of control, and worse, beyond his sphere of foreknowledge.

The thought assailed him, not for the first time: if his ability to see the future was careening wildly away from reality, should he not entertain the possibility his most terrifying vision of the far future, the rise of the city Xxiphu, might also—

Divination is muddied if one relies on those hiding betrayer's thoughts, intruded the simple, irrefutable voice of Nis.

Betrayers? Which were they? The two survivors of the devastated wood elf force who'd reappeared to save the day? A crazed half-elf monk and a wounded human sorcerer. They should be dead, like the other elf attackers—hadn't he instructed Brathtar to sweep the area beyond the Causeway and eliminate all signs of conflict? Yes. Brathtar . . .

Perhaps the Commander was the betrayer Nis described. The appearance of these last two, unlooked for, was just one more failure the Commander had laid at Telarian's feet. Now that he thought on it, it was Brathtar's failure to completely purge the tribe of wood elves that had summoned the mixed-blood elves of the Yuirwood to Stardeep's very porch.

Was it possible loyal Brathtar worked against him? The fight beyond the Causeway was undeniable proof of *something,* after all. Perhaps Brathtar truly was to blame. Because of the Commander's list of failures, Kiril's return hadn't followed the script his vision had foretold. She'd fought instead of sued for peace against those who once served under her, the Empyrean Knights.

He tightened his grip on his belt, a mere inch from Nis's beckoning pommel. Strange. He'd failed to don his protective gloves today. Such lapses were not like him. The first chance he got, he'd retrieve them.

Despite everything, his new turn of thoughts brought clarity. He was emboldened, heartened even, now that he had pieced together Brathtar's lies, failures, and misrepresentations. He'd found the flaw at the center of all his plans: Brathtar.

If only the Keeper, returning to the fold after these long years of her absence, would surrender and enter Stardeep peaceably . . .

As he watched Kiril fight, bloodied but unbowed, a fury growing in her eyes—if not her weapon—he recognized the possibility of parley with the swordswoman was past. If she survived the initial foray, she'd never give up Angul to him.

She must, Nis insisted. Telarian nodded, knowing his dark blade spoke truth.

He raised his right hand and waved the cavalry unit forward, down the Causeway. "Attack!"

The Knights failed to advance.

He looked behind him, "I ordered an attack!"

"Keeper Telarian," said Brathtar, "I recognize that woman, and believe she is who she claims: Kiril Duskmourn, once a Keeper here, a Keeper of the Outer Bastion. She held the same position you now hold. She successfully defeated the Traitor's attempt to escape. Surely you don't mean for us to slay her?"

"What I mean . . ." said Telarian, then he paused. He paused because his ungloved hand had just unconsciously slipped along his belt loop and onto Nis's protruding hilt.

It occurred to him in that instant that convincing Brathtar to return to obedience was not something he had the time or patience to accomplish. Nor could he trust Brathtar not to return to his questioning ways with the very next order Telarian issued. Questioning the Keeper in front of the Knights he commanded—Brathtar knew such a breach of protocol could only seed discipline problems. Thus, he obviously questioned Telarian for just that purpose. A demonstration was required.

Telarian swiveled his head to regard the Commander. With an air that seemed like lazy curiosity to the onlooking Knights, he pulled Nis from his sheath and plunged it into Brathtar's stomach, burying the blade to the hilt.

"Keeper! What . . ." were Brathtar's last words. The slumping body of the Commander of the Empyrean Knights slid off Nis's bleak, life-ending edge and clattered to the stone.

Telarian turned to face the mounted Knights who yet queued up behind the gate, Nis free of its scabbard and idly clutched in his left hand. The blade seemed to pull the very light from the air, creating a zone of shadowless gloom, dim at the edges, but blackening to utter night around the sword blade.

"Congratulations, Dharvanum," said Telarian, addressing the closest Knight, who stared back at him with eyes wide. "I confer upon you the title and rank of Commander. Now—ride out and bring back that ex-Keeper's sword, or I'll gut you, too."

Telarian was surprised how the sight of Brathtar lying in his own entrails failed to faze him. He gave the body a tentative nudge with his toe. Yes, stone dead. With Nis in hand, cool logic bracketed him and defined him. Emotion served only to conceal the shortest paths to achieving desired ends. Brathtar had proved himself too much an obstacle. With the Commander now punished so utterly for discipline's lapse, the remaining Knights would fall in line. They were pledged to obey the Keeper first, and their Commander second.

The Knight named Dharvanum lowered the face-plate on his helm and drew his sword. He spurred his mount toward the Gate.

They have turned against you, warned Nis, an instant before Dharvanum turned back his mount, swinging his sword in a vicious arc at Telarian's neck.

The Keeper calmly parried with his drawn weapon. Where Nis met the lesser steel of the Knight's blade, black phantoms momentarily capered.

Dharvanum screamed at the remaining mounted Knights. "The Keeper's reason has deserted him. For Stardeep, cut him down. For Brathtar!"

Telarian backpedaled, holding Nis in guard before him. He ducked into the open door at his back, the Causeway Gate's guardroom. He slammed the metal door and threw the bolt before any Knight could dismount and follow him through the entrance.

The woman on duty, a Knight-in-training named Deobra, said, "Keeper? I heard a yell and the sound of sword on sword. Have the attackers—"

Deobra died before she realized danger threatened.

The seven Knights out there must also be eliminated, lest they carry their poisonous thoughts to all the legion, counseled Nis, still clutched in Telarian's white-knuckled hand.

The diviner nodded. The soulbound blade saw the truth. A wastrel thought squirmed around the back of his mind—he'd killed Brathtar and the apprentice Knight, and now he was actually considering killing all these men, too?

Yes, answered Nis.

Reason required all who'd witnessed Brathtar's end and who turned against him be eliminated in turn. When the Traitor's ultimate scheme was finally countered by Telarian, all those who died along the way would be remembered. And perhaps Telarian would be brought to just account for his actions. Tomorrow's children would judge such things. For now . . .

The Keeper stepped over Deobra's body and grasped in his left hand a great lever protruding from the guardroom floor; in his right hand, he retained his grasp on Nis. Telarian knew the five-foot-long iron lever was connected to a great mechanism of wheels, pulleys, counterweights, and braces.

He pulled. The lever shifted, then caught, its mechanisms rusty from decades of disuse. Cool energy trickled from Nis's hilt into his blood, heart, and thews. Telarian pulled. The lever shot home.

A clang thudded up from the floor, followed by a louder one from outside. A moment later, the sounds of screaming men and horses burst into the chamber, but faded quickly before ceasing altogether, as if plucked up and away by some passing giant.

Or, as if they'd fallen into the gaping cavity beneath the suddenly withdrawn floor in the tunnel between the outer Causeway Gate and the Inner Bastion Gate. The lever and the deep pit were a last-gasp defensive measure designed to drop an invading force into the underdungeon. In that subterranean tunnel-strewn region beneath Stardeep, lesser felons lived out squalid lives in windowless dungeon cells, and older tunnels squirmed away into darkness.

Telarian knew that neither the Knights nor their horses could hope to survive such a drop.

He let go of the lever and grabbed Deobra's hair. He pulled the body to the trap door and tossed it, too, into the lightless pit beyond. The form dropped limply away, a rag doll into the refuse heap.

Best to dispose of all evidence of the slaughter.

CHAPTER FIFTEEN

Stardeep, Throat

Delphe saw the Knights fighting invaders on the Causeway's edge, if fight was the right word; mostly, the doughty Knights fell beneath swords, fists, and the flashing magic of the mysterious attackers. The clarity of Cynosure's scrying was erratic, but she clearly identified at least three foes: a sword wielder, a martial artist, and a spellcaster. She also spied the shadow of a humanoid lurking about the periphery, throwing knives. The Knights seemed outmatched—where was the full company? And why did they fight with the Causeway wide open at their backs? Was Telarian even now readying to send forth another unit or two? Perhaps, but if the Knights she saw now fell in the next few moments, the invaders would penetrate Stardeep's open front gate.

She gasped, understanding the invaders must have timed their attack to coincide with the Traitor's escape attempt she'd just quelled.

"Cynosure, close the Causeway Gate!"

"Yes, Delphe," responded the construct, in a voice as steady and calm as if she'd asked Cynosure to confirm the dining menu for tomorrow.

Mist swirled up from Chabala Mere, pulling the land-bridge into a nether realm of nonexistence. The scrying relayed by Cynosure onto a mirrored wall panel of the Throat jittered, scrambled, and vanished.

"Causeway Gate is closed, Delphe."

The Keeper drew in a long breath, then darted an anxious glance into the Well, at the boundary layer. She no longer trusted its integrity. A terrifying thought.

The construct noted her glance and said, "Delphe, please allow me to apologize for my earlier lapse. Because of the attack on Stardeep's gate, I committed the bulk of my attention there. I recognize that this behavior violates protocol, and I am frankly at a loss to explain myself."

"Do you . . . do you suspect a breakdown of some sort?" Delphe swallowed, knowing the answer to the question was a definitive "yes," whether or not the sentient idol would admit it.

Cynosure responded, "Delphe, I am forced to confess—something is indeed interfering with my decision-making. I am unable to determine what. I recommend you take me out of the command and control loop. Doing so will eradicate the possibility that my next lapse will imperil the Well. I can use the time to trace the source of the difficulty, and if possible, remedy it."

The construct wasn't wrong, though she could hardly believe she would follow its recommendation . . .

Delphe's voice quavered as she responded, "I agree. I hereby command you to extricate yourself from Stardeep. Disengage all higher order functions, both in the Inner Bastion and the Outer. Please leave those functions available for Telarian and I to use manually."

"Yes, Delphe. I am retreating into my original form. I wonder what it will feel like to be singular again . . ."

Silence stretched. The Keeper looked up at the sculpted stone on the ceiling, knowing it was empty. Cynosure was disengaged. Had that ever happened before in Stardeep's history? Not that she could recall.

She poured her attention into the Well and anxiously studied the patterns of sigil and flame. Had the Traitor exhausted himself? A dimensional veil separated Stardeep from the invaders Cynosure had shown her. She was not planning on permitting the Causeway to be opened again anytime soon.

The most pressing question was whether the idol's leave of absence in monitoring the Well was more risky than allowing it to remain active. Cynosure had eventually perceived the escape attempt, and provided the impetus necessary to reenergize the boundary horizon. But if the construct were functioning properly, would the Traitor have been able to launch his probe in the first place? It chilled her to think the latter might be a possibility. The heart of Stardeep's defenses may have become corrupted.

Where was Telarian? Cynosure couldn't help—perhaps could only hinder her. She and the other Keeper had to confer immediately.

She mentally extended her senses, searching for the magical ley lines that threaded Stardeep. When asked, Cynosure quickly and easily manipulated those functions on her behalf. In some ways, those functions were one and the same as Cynosure . . . better not to worry about that right now.

Delphe closed her eyes and began to search the stronghold.

Telarian grabbed the sweat-slicked guardroom lever and pulled. The mechanism yielded slowly, with a drawn-out screech resembling a banshee's scream. The gate tunnel's iron-reinforced floor ratcheted into place, sealing the Knights—their corpses, at least—in their final resting places.

The Keeper rushed into the tunnel to gaze across the Causeway. He estimated the Knights who remained outside were unlikely to succeed. It was time for him to directly intervene. His grip tightened on Nis's pommel. He stepped . . .

The landbridge faded into pale mists.

Several blinking Knights appeared in the gateway tunnel, turned around and nauseated from their sudden recall. What—

The Causeway had closed!

"Cynosure! Open the Causeway! Immediately!"

No answer. He sheathed Nis to wipe his brow. The instant he lost contact with the hilt of his darkling sword, Telarian's composure collapsed.

With a voice now breaking with sudden fear, he called again, "Cynosure? Answer me! Cynosure, open the Gate!"

Telarian looked left, right, up, down as his mind whirled with confusion. His eyes finally settled on the two niches in the gate tunnel, one on either side. Each was filled with a hulking stone shape. Either or both could serve as a temporary nexus for Stardeep's construct sentience, even physically animating to defend the entrance. At the very least, speaking if spoken to.

The diviner ran to stand between the two shapes. Both stared vacantly down at him. Cynosure was resident in neither.

A crackle of light and the sudden scent of ozone pulled his gaze around. Striding from a rough discontinuity was Delphe.

"Telarian!" she yelled, her eyes wild, her face flushed as she approached him. Did she know what had just occurred? Were all his secrets laid bare to his fellow Keeper? A guilty conscience grabbed him roughly, draining blood from his face and putting a shake in his hands. To salvage his scheme, and thereby save future generations unborn, must he now cut down Delphe, too, in cold blood?

As he reached for Nis, Delphe said, "Cynosure is corrupted, and the Traitor stirs! Thank the Twelve Stars I've found you—we must prepare our strategy!"

Telarian's wavering hand dropped away from his weapon's hilt.

"Tell me, Delphe, what has happened?" he asked, his voice hoarse. He gripped one hand with the other to hide a telltale quaver.

She began, "An entity . . ."

Her eyes looked past him down the tunnel. Telarian turned and saw the bloody streak smeared from the open guardroom door, as well as the gore splash from where Brathtar and Dharvanum had gasped out their last. He'd disposed of the bodies in the deeps, but there'd been no time to scrub away the incriminating blood. The recalled Knights yet milled at the far end, still pale and confused to Telarian's eyes.

"The invaders breached the Causeway?" she gasped. "I closed the Causeway not a moment too soon!" She turned to look at him. "Why didn't you close the Causeway Gate after you sent forth the Knights to defend Stardeep?"

Telarian replied without missing a beat. "Of course I tried, but Cynosure failed to answer me. By the time I realized a manual seal was necessary, I and a reserve unit of Knights already fought to hold the tunnel. If you hadn't closed the Causeway Gate when you did, I'm not sure what would have happened." Internally, he cursed her for an interfering fool. If she hadn't closed the Causeway, even now he'd have Angul and Nis, together.

"What kind of force—"

He interrupted, "Hold!" The diviner knew where Delphe's questions led. A distraction was required lest she too closely examine the gate tunnel. If she queried the Knights now visible in the tunnel, she'd learn they hadn't been part of any tunnel defense—they'd been fighting a Keeper! If she began unraveling that knot, he'd have to spin his web of lies all the wider.

Telarian continued, "You claim Cynosure is corrupt and the Traitor's dreams are uneasy? I would hear more of that!"

Delphe nodded, her eyes again focusing on Telarian. She said, "Some sort of . . . probe entity burst from the boundary layer and ascended the Well."

Telarian didn't have to act surprised. Delphe continued, "A powerful working, not a phantom. It was a qualified escape attempt."

"What shape did it take?" Telarian's voice was hoarser.

She replied, "A self-improving tissue mass. It resembled an eyeless snake, or a questing tentacle. It improved and expanded every moment it remained free of the Well. What a time for Cynosure to fail!"

Delphe raised a conciliatory hand as she noted his eyes growing huge. "Breathe easy. I quelled the escape. Cynosure woke up at the last, and between his working and my abjurations, the Traitor's sending, if that's what it was, failed to emerge into the Throat."

Telarian shook his head. "I am sorry I was not there to aid you." The Keeper of the Outer Bastion's faith in his prognostication was fast approaching zero; he hadn't foreseen such a potent emergence so soon. Still . . .

"But Cynosure *did* acknowledge the danger and helped you, if not as quickly as you desired. Are you certain he is corrupt?"

"I'm not certain of anything. I know this, though; he has suffered too many lapses of late. Have you noticed? Too many silences during critical moments in the Well. I was forced to turn off some functions."

Telarian hissed with surprise.

She nodded, misunderstanding his response. "Yes, it was necessary, despite the danger."

"But, Delphe—"

"Telarian, listen! Add up the Traitor's sudden flurry of activity with Cynosure's glitches and the attack on the Causeway, and the result is trouble. It could imply an external force seeks the Traitor's release, and worse, has managed to infiltrate Stardeep so thoroughly that Cynosure, our first and best defense, is compromised. Then again, you already knew something of this, didn't you?"

Telarian cocked his head, guilt once again rising like gorge in his mouth.

"You knew an external force might move against us. You told me yourself you had the Knights investigate a suspicious wood elf encampment in the Yuirwood. What did they find?"

He breathed easier. She didn't know anything. "Delphe, in all truth, the Knights found no evidence the wood elves knew anything of the Traitor or about Stardeep." He spoke no untruths, he reflected. He wiped his brow with the back of his hand. Of course, to safeguard the presence of the Knights, the encampment had been eradicated.

"What of these that attacked recently? Were they wood elves?"

"Some were. I'm not sure from whence they came. Certainly not from the encampment, which disbanded not long after the Knights investigated."

Delphe nodded, considering, her eyes narrow in thought.

Telarian continued. "How do you suppose the attackers managed to corrupt Cynosure, when they've yet to enter Stardeep? Are you sure Cynosure's problems are part of this conspiracy you've outlined?"

Delphe rocked back, shook her head. "Of course I'm not sure. But the timing is too awful to be a coincidence. Isn't it?" Telarian saw she was willing to be argued away from her theory.

Relief continued to cool his feverish mind like a spring rain. He knew with certainty Cynosure was not corrupted by outsiders.

No, he himself was responsible for Cynosure's odd habits. He'd sought to gain control over the sentient idol's abilities and knowledge. It appalled him to think his efforts might have prematurely compromised Cynosure's ability to restrain the Traitor. If the Traitor emerged too early . . .

It wasn't his plan to release the Traitor until all the ingredients of his scheme were in place.

Before then, his first priority must be to bring Cynosure back to full functions. For that, he required Delphe's cooperation and willing aid. Though any single Keeper could decommission the construct's consciousness, only two or more could reinstate him. Telarian's hand brushed Nis's hilt. It occurred to him that once Cynosure was restored, it would prove best to remove Delphe's unpredictable actions from the equation, lest she complicate his divinations. As Brathtar's betrayals proved, even the most powerful vision of the future could be altered by too many variables.

Telarian smiled and began to speak. It wouldn't be difficult to allay Delphe's suspicions about the construct, the timing of the Traitor's escape attempt, and the utter improbability of a conspiracy. She wanted everything to be all right, and would be amenable to being led to that conclusion.

Once Cynosure was back, he'd order the construct to throw wide the Causeway Gate. Telarian wouldn't send a force out to greet Kiril; that had been a terrible mistake, one born of ego, not reason. Nis castigated him on his foolish plan. No, he'd allow Kiril to stroll of her own volition across the dimensional veil to find her destiny. He and Nis would be waiting.

CHAPTER SIXTEEN

Stardeep, The Causeway

A fey wind came up, blowing obscuring mist across the Causeway. Streamers of fog advanced, fused, and blotted the landbridge into a cloud of billowing gray-white. The Empyrean Knights and their mounts were leached of their color and faded, too, called back to their commanderies and stables beneath Stardeep.

"Come back!" screamed Kiril at the empty air. She dashed forward, cutting ineffectually at the ice-clogged water with Angul. "Blood!" she coughed, realizing she was too late. Stardeep had pulled back its drawbridge, leaving only the unassailable moat of misted water for her to curse. She obliged.

Stabbing pain in her wounded leg cut short her stream of invectives. Damn Angul for refusing to provide healing. Usually, it was all she could do to fight off his influence. Now that she most needed his balm, he remained dull, unconcerned metal. She savagely shoved the blade in his sheath, a bitter oath in her mouth. She groped for her flask.

The pain in her leg redoubled, pounding as if a spike were being inserted. Blood slicked her calf and clouded the icy water with a scarlet plume. A wave of dizziness pulled at her and she stumbled.

Gage appeared at her side with a supportive arm.

"How is your wound?" he asked, concern turning down the corners of his mouth. The thief's own injury no longer seemed to bother him . . . Then she saw the glint of a discarded glass vial lying unstoppered and empty along his path.

"Are you blind? What do you think? You could have saved me some of your healing draught," she mumbled. "Help me sit."

The thief lowered her to the ground and said, "Sorry Kiril, I was in a bad way. I didn't think to save any." As Gage's gauntleted right hand guided her to the ground, her sheathed weapon finally sparked and glimmered.

She gave up scrabbling for her flask. Instead, she grasped Angul's hilt. It was just like him. Despite himself, the willful blade couldn't remain quiescent in such close proximity to the hellbred glove. As her fingers slipped around the hilt, warmth suffused her. It suddenly occurred to her that amputating the thief's hand then and there was probably a reasonable course of action.

Above and beyond his fraternization with tools born in hellish dimensions, Gage knew more about the Knights' emergence than he should. What had he said during the heat of the fight? Her eyes narrowed in suspicion as she looked up at him. She gripped her sheathed sword tighter. Angul stanched her blood and fused severed flaps of skin and muscle, knitting them together as if never parted.

When she stood, her strength was renewed, and more. Her eyes burned as she roughly threw off the thief's hand, turning to face him. He realized his peril and backstepped.

Kiril groaned with the mental effort of relinquishing her grip on Angul's hilt. An arc of blue-bright fire persisted a moment, a connection between her hand and the blade, before spitting and snapping into oblivion, burning her palm with petulant fury.

"Not today, Angul," she told the blade, which quivered and audibly groaned, impotent in its leather scabbard.

"Kiril, I—" began Gage.

"Quiet! I need to think," she interrupted. But did she have time for that luxury? Doubtful. Something was terribly wrong within the bastions of her old home. How could she come to any other conclusion when the bodies of wood elves lay in shallow graves before the Causeway, and its once doughty defenders attacked former Keepers?

She mentally reached out, feeling for the planar veil and the access points that would flip the Causeway open once more—and found nothing. The Causeway Gate had been sealed from within, and no external force, not even a Keeper, could access it until those inside decided otherwise.

The half-elf martial warrior and his sorcerous companion approached. Where had they come from, and what would they demand of her? Too many thoughts competed for her attention. She didn't need any more complications. She was close to breaking. Maybe a sip from her flask would do the trick. She grabbed the enchanted container, easily unclipping it now that Angul had mended her . . .

No.

No! She shook her head, so violently she saw flashes of light.

No. If Nangulis had somehow, beyond all reason, returned to Stardeep, dulled wits wouldn't pave the road to that reunion. Quite the opposite. Better just to run herself through here and now than allow her decade-old habit to sabotage her, on the cusp of comprehension. Kiril returned her flask to her belt.

The strangers bowed their heads in greeting. Their unforeseen aid had turned the tables, or at least preserved her life long enough until someone within Stardeep pulled back the Knights. Perhaps the newcomers had answers, if Gage didn't. The half-elf, the one who'd fought with only his hands—his skin and hair were dark for an elf, and his features possessed a cast and shape unfamiliar to her. Yet his likeness reminded her somehow of the Sildëyuir realm.

She addressed the newcomers. "What do you know of this debacle?"

Gage held up a gauntleted hand to point. "Be easy, strangers. But answer the question."

The half-elf spoke. "I am Raidon Kane. My companion is Adrik Commorand. Who are you?"

Kiril shook her head. "All in good time. I have a legitimate reason to stand here. I acknowledge the aid you provided and am in your debt, but I would know how you came to be here, and why?"

Raidon nodded. He said, "Mounted elves of stern visage, like those we just faced, rode from across the misted water to attack an expedition of some dozens of elves we accompanied, including a sizeable contingent known as the Masters of the Yuirwood. Adrik and I numbered among the survivors. When the defeated remnants of that force departed, Adrik and I lingered."

"Why did these so-called masters approach Stardeep?"

Raidon responded, "Stardeep? Is that the realm beyond the water?"

Kiril said, "Yes, though calling Stardeep a 'realm' is inaccurate—it is much smaller." To speak so to strangers broke rules she'd sworn as a Keeper. Too bad—if these were agents of the Traitor, she would end their days soon enough.

The half-elf, his voice serene and strangely composed, said, "Some tendays now past, mail-clad elves of unfamiliar demeanor rode forth from this location and exterminated a nearby wood elf encampment. The Masters sent a retaliatory force, thinking to extract vengeance, and perhaps seal the portal from whatever realm of discord the murderers originated."

Kiril swore, "Bastard sons of whores!" Raidon cocked his head at her outburst. Adrik took an involuntary step back.

The Empyrean Knights were now striking out into the sun-warmed world to commit genocide? She couldn't grasp the man's story; she didn't want to believe it. If he spoke the truth, then the worst may have already happened. The Traitor must have escaped his bonds and taken control of Stardeep's forces. But if that were true, wouldn't she know? Though a Keeper in exile, she retained sensitivities born in her years of service to the Cerulean Sign. Somehow, she thought she'd know if the Traitor ever completely slipped his bonds.

She controlled her voice enough to ask, "And you are one of these Masters of the Yuirwood?"

Raidon shook his head. "Neither I nor my companion are native. I've been on the road for some time, a road that has led me here, where I hope to find answers concerning the whereabouts of my absent mother."

So saying, the half-elf drew an amulet from beneath his shirt and brandished it for Kiril to see.

She gasped, "Where did you get that?"

Kiril could scarcely credit what flashed before her in the afternoon light: a Seal of the Cerulean Sign. Thirty-six Seals once were known, or perhaps double that; Keeper histories were confused and incomplete. But the knowledge of their making was certainly lost, and as the centuries blurred forward, more and more Seals went missing, were stolen, or were consumed in use. In recent times only a single one remained to Stardeep, the one Nangulis had worn in his vigil over the Well. When Nangulis was transformed and Kiril left Stardeep, she'd left the amulet with Commander Brathtar to pass to the next Keeper of the Inner Bastion.

Raidon said, "This was given to me by my absent mother, before she returned to her people, who she claimed lived in the Yuirwood. I have followed signs and clues that led here, where I hope to match the symbol on the amulet with that said to be scribed on the gates of what you call Stardeep."

Kiril reached out her hand for the amulet. After a moment of consideration, Raidon relinquished the stone. She peered at its convoluted textures, the Sign displayed so prominently, and along both sides, looking for the telltale marks that would identify it. No. It was not the same Seal Nangulis had carried; it must be one of the earlier Seals, returned from history's obscuring grasp.

And it was dark. The amulet Nangulis had carried had been sky blue. She wondered if the color was a mute warning of the Traitor's activity. Too late in coming, if so.

Kiril looked up and met Raidon's anxious eyes. "You carry an extraordinary relic. She who gave this to you—who was she?"

The man shook his head. "I know not. I called her Mother. She left me when I was a child. Now that I'm grown, I've sworn to find her."

"She was an elf," Kiril stated. "Your father, a human?"

Raidon nodded. "He was an honorable man. I had not realized prior to a few tendays ago my mother was a wood elf of the Yuirwood."

Kiril raised a single eyebrow. "Your looks argue against that, not to mention you carry a Seal unlikely to have originated in the Yuirwood. I doubt she was a wood elf of the wood. No, she came from somewhere else."

The half-elf squinted at her, his face framing a question.

She continued, "She came from a realm behind the Yuirwood, a place called Sildëyuir."

"Another name for Stardeep? She is one of these murdering elves?"

"No. Stardeep is a splinter of Sildëyuir, long disconnected from it. Elves dwell in that starry land—I am one. And they are not a murdering people. Normally." Kiril glanced at the blood still staining her leg.

She allowed, "Something awful has happened, I fear . . ."

Kiril swung to face Gage. "Tell me what you know about Stardeep."

Gage swallowed, turned pale. But he nodded.

"Kiril, Sathra did steal your sword, as I explained. And only because of my efforts was it returned to you. Please remember that while you listen to the rest of my tale."

She gave a fractional nod of her head. "Time is not on our side—out with it, thief."

He swallowed, a blush heating his checks. "Sathra took your sword, but it wasn't she who worked for Stardeep—it was me. I was the spy . . ."

Kiril backhanded Gage so hard he spun and fell. Adrik the sorcerer took another step back, concern growing on his face. A high-pitched bell tolled from a nearby treetop; Xet was concerned about what might follow the slap.

Gage lay where he fell for a moment, rubbing his jaw. He coughed and spit out a bloody tooth. Kiril didn't much care. She said, "I knew you lied when you said you'd killed Sathra, you bastard."

The thief slowly sat up, but didn't stand. Anger threaded his voice, but he replied, "You were justified in doing that. Now, are you planning on hitting me again, or do you want to hear my story?"

"I thought you were my friend!" Gage's betrayal was the oil that fueled her fury.

He looked down. "I made a terrible mistake, Kiril. I *am* your friend, or would like to be, if you can forgive me."

She wanted to strike him again, oh yes. Pick him up and throw him, kick him. Eradicate him from her memory. Instead she said, "What about Nangulis? Was that a lie, too?"

Gage levered himself to his feet and backed off a pace before replying. "My contact from Stardeep was someone named Telarian. A male elf. In Laothkund he offered me a contract to steal a meaningless sword from a drunken swordswoman. That was before we ever met. If I had known—"

"I asked you about Nangulis, thief!" yelled Kiril. Rage burned her stomach; acid gave an unpleasant tang to the back of her mouth.

Gage rubbed his reddening jaw, said, "After we met, I realized I couldn't carry the blade myself, due to Angul's unique nature. So I sent word to Telarian—"

"How?"

"Telarian had a drop box set up in Laothkund. After I reported my failure, I was contacted again, and told to let slip the name Nangulis. I was to implicate Nangulis as the person who wanted the blade. Telarian said that would draw you to Stardeep without need for Angul's theft."

"Nangulis didn't contact you at all?"

"No, Kiril. I'm sorry."

The ex-Keeper put a hand to her brow. Was hope dead anew? She couldn't trust the thief, that was obvious. But Nangulis's name was in play. Who was this Telarian? Wait, she recalled someone named Telarian . . . a diviner among the Knights. Toward the end, he had taken vows to learn the duties of the Outer Bastion. Now that she thought about it, Cynosure itself had indicated the diviner possessed exceptional talent and a strategic mind.

"This Telarian—did he call himself a Keeper?"

"Not in my hearing, Kiril."

"He must have become one, in my absence."

Gage shrugged apologetically.

Kiril said, "A Keeper corrupted, though, by the Traitor! Why does he want Angul? Or is it that the Traitor stirs in the

Well and Telarian requires the Blade Cerulean to quench the effort? Why then, did he not simply tell me? I would have come."

Well, then again, perhaps she wouldn't have responded. She had washed her hands pretty thoroughly of Stardeep when she'd fled. Washed them in the blood of innocents.

What if the new Keepers of Stardeep feared her, and didn't want her homicidal help, only her blade? The last anyone in the hidden fortress had seen her, she'd been crazed and murderous. Perhaps they had sent the Knights against her to protect themselves.

No. Regardless of how her guilt attempted to fix her with all the blame, earned or unearned, the Knights' slaughter of the wood elf encampment and the subsequent murderous rebuff of the Masters of the Yuirwood happened before she ever returned to the Causeway. That argued for the Traitor's influence, if not his actual presence, loose in Stardeep. The vows forsaken when she'd fled struggled now in her breast, fluttering long unused wings.

And what if Nangulis truly had returned?

Kiril muttered, "I must gain entry! But the gates are closed, and I can't reopen them. I'll have to go the long way 'round . . ."

She turned to address the barehand fighter, Raidon Kane. "You are welcome to accompany me, half-elf. I don't know if we can find your mother, but it seems clear she was of the starry realm, and I must journey through Sildëyuir in order to enter Stardeep from beneath. I saw how you fought. Few I know could stand against you, and you didn't even draw your blade. I could use your help."

Raidon responded, "I shall not rest until I find my mother, or what became of her. Can Stardeep provide what I seek?"

Kiril said, "Your mother's possession of a Seal of the Cerulean Sign indicates a connection with the dungeon stronghold. Within Stardeep is an archive that names each of the original Seals, their owners, and when and where they were lost, if known. Perhaps those texts will provide the lead you require. Help me gain entry, and you can peruse them in full."

"My path seems destined to lead to Stardeep. I accept your invitation," replied the monk.

So saying, Raidon turned to his companion. "Adrik, your commission concluded some time ago. Thank you for remaining when the others retreated. Return to Relkath's Foot, and from there, seek your brother in Emmech. He must wonder what has become of you. Go with my thanks."

The sorcerer shook his head. "As you say, I've already outstayed the service for the coin you paid. Since my contract is concluded, I can do as I please. I'm coming with you, if you'll have me."

Adrik glanced at Kiril and continued. "Dip me in honey and set me to run through the Great Wild Wood if I pass up an opportunity to find the ancient realm hidden behind the menhirs of Yuirwood! My brother'd boil me in formalin if he found out I turned my back on such a chance. I—"

Kiril raised an arm. "You're welcome to join me as well. I saw you hurl fire like a warmage. If the Traitor's minions stand in our way, we'll have use of such talent."

Adrik beamed.

"Very well," interjected Gage, "I'll get our packs. How do we get to Sil—"

"No. You are not coming with us." Kiril pointed south. "Leave the forest—the closest border is that way. No way I'd let a blood-flecking backstabber accompany me into the starry realm, and into Stardeep itself."

"I've come clean with you, Kiril. I've told you the truth!"

"Which is the only reason you're not dead, despite Angul's

wishes to the contrary. Get out of my sight before I change my mind, you damned liar."

"You need me! I've talked to Telarian, and he'll recognize me. We could trick him into—"

"I said no, thief. You dealt with Telarian, and perhaps you still have a deal. Just how gullible do you think I am? For all I know, you're playing a deeper game than I can pierce, even now. I'm done talking about this."

So saying, she walked forward, her left shoulder roughly shoving Gage to the side as she swept past him.

"You two, follow me. We can't waste any more time than we already have."

Kiril led Raidon Kane and Adrik Commorand away from the shore of the misted Chabala. The three figures melted into a line of short pines. The high-flying crystal dragonet darted a glance at the thief, who stood alone on the icy shore, unmoving, then flew after its mistress.

Gage picked up his pack and turned away from the Mere. Shoulders stooped, head down, he stumbled through the leafless glades of the Yuirwood, alone. His long strides ate the distance, but without companionship, the way ahead seemed long. Time spent in conversation passes more swiftly than the same span spent in self-loathing doubt and second-guessing.

And when his journey was concluded, it would be at Laothkund's gate. Back to the cold city walls and slick rooftops. Quick thefts, quicker escapes, and finding a fence trustworthy enough to unload his take. Repeat. Only another fabulous heist away from a month-long party with fifty of his closest friends . . .

Friends who'd lose interest when the money ran out.

The only one who'd never cared who was buying had been Kiril. And he'd rewarded her by trying to steal the only remaining thing in her life about which she cared.

"By the Queen of Air!" he swore. Gage paused beneath the bole of a hoary old evergreen.

It came down to the kind of man he wanted to be. He looked at his gauntleted hand. The demonic mouth drooled, its teeth working. It whispered, "One day I'll have your soul, you know." He frowned, shook his head.

"Don't put off what you've already decided," he muttered to himself. He turned and traced his own trail back to the edge of the Mere. There, plain as day, was the trail in the snow left by those who'd cast him aside.

"I'll show her who she can trust, and who she can't!" he promised.

His gauntlet growled, maybe in protest, perhaps in agreement, or possibly because it had not supped on blood in over a tenday.

Chapter Seventeen

Stardeep, Telarian's Quarters

Shivers coursed through Telarian as if he stood in an icy waterfall. He considered his predicament; were his machinations ill-conceived? Cracks of failure on every front threatened to erode and crumble his endeavor, potentially causing the very catastrophe he sought to avoid. Incompetence, betrayal, and perhaps insinuations of the Traitor's growing influence outside the Well worked against him.

He just prayed none of the incompetence was his own.

The Keeper of the Outer Bastion grabbed the edges of his cot and held tightly, as if it threatened to suddenly launch him toward the high ceiling of his personal chamber. His breath shuddered, his mind skittered for any answer, any assurance.

Maybe Nis . . . ? He allowed his head to roll to the left. Nis nestled in its sheath, leaning against a stone scroll shelf on the far wall. He'd decided he needed to distance himself from the black blade, physically and mentally, if only for a little while. Now, after candle-spans of separation, a strange anxiety mounted, an anxiety born of more than the shambles of his designs. It was an anxiety born of his desire to once again hold the blade.

Was he becoming addicted to Nis's calming presence? No! A crazy thought! He wrenched his gaze back toward the ceiling. He was the master of his own destiny, by the Sign!

He concentrated on easing his breathing. As he did so, he slowly opened and closed his eyes. The glittering points of light sprinkled across the ceiling blinked into nonexistence, then back, over and over. A minor decorative illusion meant to convey the homey feeling of Sildëyuir, a realm he'd not walked in years, despite it being his place of birth, and despite it being relatively close. Duty prevented him. Duty not just to Stardeep, but to Sildëyuir, and the wider world behind which the starry realm rested: Faerûn.

Faerûn . . . and the monstrosities that yet hungered to consume it! He rose, so quickly his lower back twinged in protest. Just a minor distraction, like all the distractions, minor and major, that sought to deter him. How sad it would be if he allowed mere distractions to cloud his vision of what he had to do. How pitiful. He wouldn't!

Telarian strode across the chamber, grabbed up Nis's sheath, and tied it securely to his belt. This was the tool he'd created. It was his own true work, not something to be denied by fear-fed whispers. Weakling doubts might assail him, but he did not have to heed their traitorous suggestions, or even listen. He would fight to the end, using every weapon in his arsenal to its maximum.

The room darkened as he paced; the blade Nis streaked gloom behind him, briefly marking his path, despite residing snugly in its scabbard. Telarian failed to notice.

Besides Nis, his other tools included his own intellect and the special knowledge his divinatory craft revealed in the Epoch Chamber. That and his partially successful efforts to bring Cynosure under his direct control. But then Delphe had taken the sentient construct out of the control loop that interwove all Stardeep. Without the capacities of that mighty magical idol, Telarian's scheme would certainly fail!

He hadn't guessed or foreseen his fellow Keeper would take such direct and effective action. Nor had he counted on her refusing to listen to his many justifications for why Cynosure should be returned to active cognizance immediately. He'd finally been forced to give up his arguments for a time, lest she become suspicious over his zealousness.

Telarian always thought her a passive player, concerned chiefly with staring into the Well. His divinations had failed to reveal the depths of character Delphe would bring to bear when true danger threatened.

Damn her, though, for removing Cynosure from the equation! Without the construct's pinpoint ability to grant passage around Stardeep, he couldn't access the Epoch Chamber. It was too dangerous for him to attempt the connection manually.

After all these years of dissembling, perhaps he should simply blurt the truth to Delphe, appeal to her reason. He imagined her working with him, instead of blindly countering his moves by chance and accident.

No, the auguries had been clear about what would happen if he succumbed to that temptation. She'd turn on him. Then he'd be forced to cut her down with Nis. She didn't have the breadth of imagination to understand he did what he did for a reason. All the atrocities he would commit, all the lies he would tell, all the lives that had to be expended were required if apocalypse were to be prevented. If his vision of the future containing the awful soaring city was to be foiled, he could do nothing else.

Telarian closed his eyes and briefly saw the glyph-scribed obelisk wrapped in eternal storm, hollowed and inhabited by slime encrusted creatures whose hunger could never be sated, the city that heralded a change so extreme nothing would be the same ever again.

He shook the tendrils of the vision clear of his mind's eye. Not now.

"Cynosure?" Silence followed. Just checking.

Without Stardeep's mind to guide him, he didn't know which functions to manually access to locate Delphe. Even if he guessed properly, he wasn't particularly adept at manually managing instant transfers. He hoped she wasn't in the Throat overlooking the Well; then he'd have no choice but to trust his skill—

Or you could allow me to manage the transfer, offered Nis. Telarian looked down and saw his hand absentmindedly draped on Nis's pommel. Where were his gloves? No matter.

"Perhaps I shall," muttered Telarian. Time was of the essence. Who knew what the swordswoman was doing beyond the Causeway? With the Causeway Gate sealed and Cynosure unavailable to relay external events, he was blind. Time to return control of the situation to his own hand. Like Nis, Angul was indispensable to his world-saving plan.

Telarian left his room. Tardoun Hall curved into dimness to the left and right, the friezes intricately carved onto the facing walls blurring into obscurity. He'd always hated the carvings.

As he walked, the unusual quiet cloaking the hall seeped into his awareness. Normally a constant susurrus of bangs, clicks, and whistles bled from the chamber where Cynosure Prime was housed. Not now.

Silence reigned because the idol was asleep, of course. It was pulled back into its original self, alone with its thoughts.

He paused. Now that he thought of it, perhaps it would be prudent to confer with the disconnected construct before he talked with Delphe. He was sure all traces of his interference with the sentient object were hidden, most of all from Cynosure itself, but it wouldn't hurt to check.

He started forward down the curving corridor, but stopped short of his destination at double doors that opened onto Cynosure Prime's chamber. Each was carved with a great white tree bordered in cerulean.

He threw wide the doors and entered.

The chamber was a great vault filled with hulking, dimly glowing rectangular objects. Most protruded from the floor, but some stuck out from the walls and several hung from the ceiling. Ancient magical script glimmered across the face of each shape; the source of each object's glow was this script-born light. Cords extended from each stone shape, some bulky and metallic, others thin, fleshy, and moist. The cords trailed away from the blocks and were gathered in thick bundles, suspended from the high ceiling.

Telarian walked to the center of the chamber, following the fattest cord bundle to its nexus: a great humanoid shape standing in darkness. The cords plunged onto the shape on every side, as if catching the figure in a great web. But it was not caught—quite the opposite. The many connections offered transcendence. For this shape was Cynosure Prime, the artificial entity that served as Stardeep's sleepless warden. Normally, the cords pulsed with light, indicating the distribution of the construct's mind across the citadel. Their dullness revealed the idol's mind was, after centuries, reduced to the single node before him.

Cynosure Prime was the shape the construct had used upon first entering Stardeep, before the incorporation of its mind into the very fabric of the dungeon stronghold. Despite the construct's diminishment, Prime remained an immense humanoid forged of crystal, stone, iron, and more exotic components, now rusted, pitted, streaked, and stained. Standing nearly thirty feet tall, its dimly shining scarlet eyes calmly observed the approaching Keeper. A design was fused onto its metallic chest, unblemished by time—The Cerulean Sign.

Delphe stood at the construct's feet.

The diviner caught his breath as she turned and saw him. He smoothed his features—quickly enough, he hoped, to hide his consternation.

She said, "Telarian. Just the man I wanted to see."

"Ah, um . . . Delphe! You surprised me!"

"My apologies." She continued looking at him, her head cocked to one side.

Telarian's face grew warm. He spoke, "After our talk, this is the last place I expected to find you."

She nodded and said, "I thought more about your arguments. Perhaps you had the right of it."

"My argument?" The diviner's mind swirled, his surprise muddling his ability to concentrate. He resisted the urge to grasp Nis's hilt.

"You argued Cynosure's reconnection was vital. I'm afraid I put you off. But the more time I spend in the Well, the more I realize the task of sole wardenship is beyond me—no spell I erect in my absence can hold a candle to Cynosure's constant surveillance."

"Of course," exclaimed Telarian. In fact, he'd argued from that point of view, though his hidden goal was to reconnect Cynosure so he could open the Causeway Gate without alerting Delphe. Without Cynosure, revealing the Causeway required a mutual effort from both Keepers. He'd prefer not to answer her pointed questions if he made such a request.

"So," he continued, "shall we reintroduce Cynosure to Stardeep?"

"First," she said, turning her gaze back to the stony figure, "I must satisfy myself that its mind is not touched by corruption."

"Right, right. And what have you found?"

The massive form of Cynosure Prime shifted its weight, ever so slightly, as it fixed its granite visage on Telarian. The construct spoke, its voice resonant and sure. "Delphe has riddled me with questions, and we've discovered I remain inviolate."

"That's a relief—"

"However," continued the smooth voice of the construct, "we suspect some of the outlying nodes have been partly compromised."

They knew! He managed to avoid flinching. Were they waiting for him to bolt, confess, or attack?

"Compromised?" Telarian inquired. Grab the blade and end this—no. He didn't know if Nis could stand before Cynosure's original avatar.

Delphe said, "It is the only conclusion that fits all the criteria. Thankfully, the avatar poised above the Well seems to be untouched."

True enough, thought Telarian guiltily. Most of Cynosure's homunculi scattered about the dungeon were too visible, too open to scrutiny by Cynosure itself. He recalled his covert interactions with Cynosure's most vulnerable node: a miniature statue carved of jade currently hidden at the bottom of a silver chest in his quarters.

Without so much as the ability to articulate its limbs, the jade sculpture was merely a handspan in length. The ancient statuette was a prototype created to test the possibility of adopting Cynosure as Stardeep's warden mind. When perusing the oldest documents in the archive, Telarian had stumbled across the reference. Sure enough, he'd found a proto-node in the dusty, cryptlike recesses of the repository. With his divinatory craft, he had soon determined how to inject the sculpture back into Cynosure's mental loop as a fully functioning node. Functioning save for a lack of wards against magical manipulations. Through this tiny flawed foothold, Telarian had begun to subvert the entire distributed intelligence of Stardeep, node by node.

"You have no idea what a weight is lifted from my mind to hear the avatar in the Throat is clean. Have you found the vulnerable node?"

Delphe shook her head. "Without bringing Cynosure back into the loop, no method exists to trace the corruption back to its origin."

It dawned on Telarian they didn't suspect he was the culprit. Yet. His mind whirled. Could he completely throw them off the trail of his culpability?

Telarian took a deep breath, said, "You should have come to me right away, the moment you suspected node corruption. I have an idea. What if we selectively activate Cynosure's nodes? We don't have to distribute Cynosure's cognizance across Stardeep all at once. Let us begin with nodes we know to be safe, as is the one in the Throat, and work from there, one by one, carefully checking each node for distortion. Bring Cynosure back into the loop in controlled steps."

Cynosure's voice rang out. "A reasonable approach."

Delphe's frown finally broke. She said, "So simple and obvious. You may have just saved us, Telarian."

He spread his hands. "Keep me apprised of your progress—I must return to the Outer Bastion and review the disposition of the Knights."

"Certainly. Convey my thanks for their bravery as well."

Telarian waved at Prime's massive figure and took his leave. Through his own words, he'd guaranteed Cynosure's higher functions would remain unavailable. He would not be able to command the idol to open the Causeway Gate. But he'd had no choice. If he hadn't produced such a reasonable plan with aplomb, how long would he have been able to sidestep Delphe's suspicions? This way, he put himself beyond all questions.

Of course, it didn't hurt that he could inject his prototype node into a fledgling network as easily as into the complete Stardeep-spanning mind Cynosure earlier possessed. In a day, perhaps two, he'd do just that. Unless the sentient idol managed to discover the recollections he'd blocked its higher mind from incorporating . . . a possibility.

Either way, by then Kiril and her blade Angul would be long gone. His spy, the roguish Gage, would likely be dead in the bargain, too. He'd frankly been surprised the man had flown so long beneath the former Keeper's notice. But his foreteller's sense told him that ruse had now run its course.

Regardless, the hook had been set. She couldn't open the Causeway, but she would not give up entering Stardeep. So what would she do? What could she?

It was obvious.

She would attempt the "long way around," a path open only to natives of Sildëyuir. She would attempt to slip in through the underdungeon!

Telarian hurried past the doors open to the dining room, ignoring the fabulous smells emanating from within. When was his last real meal? Later. He turned onto the marble dressed stairs and took them two at a time down to the thick iron doors that opened onto the Outer Bastion.

He'd promoted someone to the position of Knight Commander with Brathtar's . . . departure. Dharvanum. Of course, he'd had to kill Dharvanum moments later. After that, he'd walked down to the War Room and promoted the first Knight he'd seen. An elf named Thindhul? No matter. Telarian smiled. He had a task for the new Knight Commander. A force of Knights must be prepared to enter the subterranean dungeon tunnels in which lesser criminals were housed. Those tunnels were widely known to connect, in their meandering, dangerous fashion, directly onto Sildëyuir.

And it must be an overwhelming force of Knights! Not because Angul represented a threat—the blade had already shown himself uninterested in turning his energies against pledged Cerulean Knights.

No, the force must be overwhelming because nothing less would survive that which stalked those long-abandoned passages and crawlways beneath ancient Stardeep.

Chapter Eighteen

Aglarond, Yuirwood Forest

Raidon Kane followed the elf Kiril Duskmourn as she stalked through shallow snow drifts. She was of the same fey race to which he was kin, if he could believe her claims. She was a harsh woman, a lodestone of reluctant authority, a comet trailing foul language, threats of bodily harm, and the smell of strong drink. Nothing like his memory of his mother—were they truly of the same race?

Yet during their walk, she had relented and spoken more of the strange realm Sildëyuir. She told Raidon and Adrik the star elves had created the hidden land as a refuge, a place to which they could retreat from the cruel and ambitious human empires of old. More than a thousand years before the raising of the Standing Stone in the Dales, the human kingdoms of Narfell and Raumauthar, as well as Unther and Mulhorand, had fought furiously for dominion in the region. In western Faerûn many elves had retreated to Evermeet to avoid human ambitions, but the star elves had decided to move their entire realm rather than abandon it. All Sildëyuir was a construction of high magic, an echo of the Yuirwood itself spun into starshine and dusk through mighty craft of old.

Since the creation of Sildëyuir, the star elves had slowly slipped farther and farther from Faerûn, leaving the daylight world to its own devices. Some still traveled through the old elfgates and roamed Aglarond or the Inner Sea, but they passed themselves off as elves of other regions, and did not speak of their homeland to strangers. And of the star elves that remained in Sildëyuir, only a fraction cared enough for the Cerulean Sign to take up its practice. Had his mother been one?

The monk considered the moment, tendays past, when he'd fought Chun, a member of the Nine Golden Swords, in the Shou Town streets. His mental discipline allowed him to perfectly picture the moment he'd retrieved the daito from Chun's limp grasp. He'd clutched his grandfather's blade, raising it in a salute. On that day the honor of his family had been restored. And on that day he quit his old life, lest Nine Golden Swords vengeance find him.

If he hadn't retrieved the daito but instead turned his back on family honor, as would have been the far easier road, Shou Town would yet be his home. Perhaps he would even now be called master by fledgling students in Xiang Temple, and by old Shou merchants in the colonnaded bazaar he walked past each day. A safe life, if honorless. A familiar life, if without meaning or purpose.

Looking back, he couldn't find a time when he'd pondered the two possibilities, then decided between them. He'd never considered *not* reclaiming the daito. And once free of Shou Town, on what course other than finding his vanished mother could he have embarked?

From Raidon's perspective, he rode a narrow river of fate. On it he rushed, sometimes through rapids, other times on calm water, but always too swiftly for him to pause. While it was his grandfather's daito that seemed to precipitate his exit from Telflamm, he suspected the origin of his current circumstance was his mother's forget-me-not. He'd learned it possessed a mysterious power. Perhaps that power had reached out and guided the threads of his destiny.

Now fate was drawing him toward a realm few knew existed, a realm Kiril claimed was synonymous with eldritch beauty, a land of perpetual twilight illuminated only by glittering stars. She said the star elves dwelled there in glass citadels. He looked forward to seeing that.

Then there was his forget-me-not. Not merely a reminder of maternal affection, but apparently an object whose power could prove useful against monsters. Was it fate, serendipity, or cruel chance that pulled him into an age-old conflict? A conflict in which the enemy was shrouded in an evil so cruel it eclipsed the Nine Golden Swords as a mountain overwhelms a pebble.

They'd spent a bitterly cold night sheltering from another snowfall beneath the downward branches of a mighty conifer. Adrik had gathered several cones and exclaimed over their novelty. Only Xet seemed to care.

Today they'd walked only a few miles when Kiril said something in a language he didn't know.

The swordswoman stood at the base of a snowy slope crowned with evergreens and massive boulders. The confluence of boulders and boles created, from a particular perspective, an inviting cavity.

"This is an entrance to Sildëyuir," said Kiril.

"I thought all the gates were magically scribed menhirs," pondered Adrik.

The woman shrugged, "Stab me if I know. This one isn't." Raidon and Adrik followed as she headed up the slope. She paused when she stood between two of the veined, snow-dusted boulders.

"How does this damn thing function again?" Kiril muttered. With uncertainty writ plainly across her features, she traced a series of geometrical signs in the air as she spoke several words unfamiliar to Raidon.

"Something's happening," reported Adrik, his hands out before him. "A magical charge comes into alignment . . ."

Kiril finished speaking and a silvery light flared in the cavity between the boulders. "The gate is open. Welcome to the realm of the star elves." She walked into the gap, Xet sitting quietly on her shoulder. As she moved, whirling shadows leaped and spun from the boulders. As the shadows proliferated, she became harder to discern, while her tracks in the snow became shallower by the step. When Kiril reached the center of the hollow, she was nothing but a fading shadow, and a moment later, completely absent.

Raidon and Adrik looked at each other. Adrik yelled, in fear or exultation, Raidon could not determine, and plunged into the hollow. Gone.

The monk, surprised to note a faint tinge of nausea, walked forward.

A handful of heartbeats passed in silence. Of those who had walked ahead and disappeared from the Yuirwood, no sign remained. A two-legged shadow slid from behind a boulder and dashed into the hollow, one hand bare, the other gloved with a bound demon.

To Raidon, it seemed day plunged into night's darkling gates. In the extravagant sky revealed, cloudless and crystal clear, all the stars of the cosmos seemed crowded. Heaven's span glittered with a million points of sparkling light, diamond white, ruby red, emerald, sapphire, and citrine. He saw circular clusters and bands of light that, when he focused on them, revealed themselves as millions of yet tinier brilliant points. Streamers of glowing nebulae poured and frothed across the firmament, mingling within them all the colors of existence.

The monk gasped, realizing he hadn't drawn breath for many heartbeats as he stood transfixed, staring upward.

The dragonet darted above them, diving and soaring, chirping bell-like tones of wonder. When it occluded a star, its crystalline body flashed sapphire, green, or red. Xet's antics broke the spell, and Raidon dropped his gaze from the entrancing heights.

Raidon stood in a half-forested valley whose opposing ridges spread away from each other as if the land itself had thrown wide arms to embrace the glorious sky. A pearl gray glow clung to the horizons, as if promising the first hints of dawn. A promise that would never be met, according to Kiril. The valley, glimmering and dreamy in the brilliant starlight, had left winter behind, or perhaps had never known it. A stream burbled through the valley, sparkling.

He breathed and smelled an odor not unlike dawn's promise, rich with growing things. It was cool, but not cold.

"Incredible!" repeated Adrik every few heartbeats. The sorcerer was turning in a slow circle, his head bobbing up and down as he sought to absorb it all.

Kiril said, "Enough sightseeing. Take it all in as we walk. We have a fair march ahead of us."

The sorcerer asked, "Will we see a glass castle? And meet any star elves? I mean, besides you?"

The swordswoman merely grunted, "Could be. There're fewer of us than there used to be." She walked toward a far ridge, paralleling the stream.

The monk yearned to demand an answer to Adrik's question. Instead he concentrated on finding his focus. The shock of bodily traveling to this alien place, coupled with the thought that his mother might be close . . . well, truth to tell he was too much in the grip of the moment, not apart from it. He wrapped the lessons of Xiang around himself and followed. Adrik skipped along behind, stopping every ten heartbeats to marvel at some newly revealed celestial phenomena, then running to catch up, jabbering with a child's unrestrained wonder.

As he walked, Raidon was mostly successful in keeping his gaze below the trees' crowns, away from the captivating sky. The otherworldly landscape was somehow bound to the Yuirwood; he could see the connection in the way the starry realm's forests and hills matched the landscape he recalled from the snow-speckled forest they'd left behind. The congruence was not perfect. Here the trees were taller and wider, and more majestic, silver-trunked with little undergrowth. Their smooth boles stretched in elegant lines, supporting a silvery green canopy.

Adrik's voice rang out, calling more questions after the swordswoman who stalked ahead. "How wide a realm is Sildëyuir?" The sorcerer seemed oblivious of the dangerous mood that enveloped their new-met companion since they'd arrived.

Raidon saw the woman's hands clench, then loosen. She threw back over her shoulder, "As large as the Yuirwood, no bigger."

The sorcerer's brows knitted as he muttered something under his breath. Then, "Nearly three hundred miles?"

Kiril made no reply. Instead she raised her hand and pointed at a stone bridge silvered with moss, and a partly paved path. Here and there, silver-green grass burst up through the loose paving stones, indicating the road's infrequent use, Raidon supposed.

"Ah ha!" Adrik exclaimed, gazing raptly at the bridge and path.

Kiril walked across the bridge; monk and sorcerer followed. When he reached the top of the span, Raidon gazed down into water. It reflected the stars above, rippling and shimmering with the moving water. Of the bridge, or himself and his companions, he saw no reflection.

They walked the broad path into the forest depths, passing fully beneath the canopy. It was cooler beneath the eaves, and darker without the direct radiance of the starlight. Despite the relative gloom, the dearth of undergrowth provided Raidon long, open views to either side. As they walked, he heard the rustlings of forest creatures, and the occasional cry of a night owl, the lonely howl of a distant wolf. A few times he saw silver-gray deer flashing in the distance. Another time he saw a wheeling, darting flight of gemlike dragonflies whose slender forms burned emerald and sapphire. Because he couldn't accurately judge their distance, he was unable to measure their size, but he guessed they were large. Once, a dark, furred beast shuffled parallel to their track for a mile or more. Raidon strained his eyes to discover the creature's shape, but soon enough it turned and was gone.

"What was that?" inquired the sorcerer.

Raidon replied, "A bear, perhaps?"

"No, something bigger," said Adrik, looking forward for some confirmation from the elf.

Kiril paused and frowned back to where the sorcerer pointed. She squinted and shook her head.

"It ran off, I guess," Adrik explained, peering into the gloom.

"Sildëyuir is not entirely free of threat. You can die here from a wild creature's attack as easily as you could in the sunlit world."

"I don't think it was a bear," maintained the sorcerer.

"Did I say bear? Far worse than bears hunt my homeland, especially of late." The elf began walking. The ridge was only dozens of yards ahead, clear of trees and promising a wide view beyond.

"What? What's worse?" persisted the sorcerer, running to keep up. Raidon continued to quietly stride as the rear guard.

"Before I took up my post in Stardeep, a couple of communities went dark—a glass citadel here, a tower there—and they were found vacant. The inhabitants were gone with no explanation or sign of violence. Later it was learned that invaders were responsible, awful creatures called nilshai."

Adrik interrupted, "Invaders from where? I haven't heard that name before."

"Nilshai invade from outside Sildëyuir—not Faerûn, but from the gray misty expanse that borders all worlds."

"Does this 'gray misty expanse' have a name?"

Kiril shrugged. "Who cares? Our time in Sildëyuir is short. We go to the closest edge, and from there, we'll bridge the distance to Stardeep's underdungeon via little-used paths."

Kiril topped the rise and stopped, her head swiveling to the left, then to the right. She muttered, "What the Hells? That isn't right . . ."

Adrik and Raidon joined her and looked across a wide, fey plain beneath an even broader and more breathtaking swath of sky than was visible back in the valley.

Below them, a slumping glass citadel burned.

Gage moved from shadow to shadow in the gloom beneath the canopy. The great silver trees were wider than any in his experience and offered an ideal breadth from which to hide along the whitestone path. However, he was exposed to anything that hunted the deeper forest lanes behind him. His back itched at the thought.

When he'd seen Kiril and the strangers disappear without a trace between two massive boulders, he'd dashed forward hoping to take advantage of the portal before it slammed shut. His gamble paid off. A moment of sickness, and he'd opened his eyes elsewhere.

The splendid stars! How long had he stood rapt? He shook his head. It seemed like moments, but could have been longer. It was difficult to measure time in this realm that seemed always and forever a summer night. Once his wits returned, his quarry was gone.

Gage followed, or so he hoped. At least two figures had gone by foot from where he'd appeared, through the grass and trees until they found a path of overgrown stones. He was fairly certain he'd chosen the same direction as Kiril, though doubts pestered him.

Wait. Did the branch on the tree ahead just move? He stopped dead, squinting into the gloom.

It wasn't a branch, it was . . .

A monster.

Its shape was like a large worm with glistening, blue-black flesh. Small tendrils or limbs branched from its body. It dropped from the tree, but stopped before striking the earth. Buzzing insectile wings beat at the dusky gloom, sickeningly small but large enough to hold the creature aloft. Three golden orbs projected from a blunt, bulbous thickening that served as the creature's body, or perhaps its head.

Another appeared, and Gage caught his breath. This one squirmed along the forest floor, with a rolling corkscrew gait reminiscent of a serpent. This one was closer, and Gage perceived its alien body in all its awful asymmetry. The horrid creature possessed three clawed legs, a ropy body, and three long whiplike tentacles, each divided at the end into stubby, strong fingers. Its head was a bulbous case atop its trunk, crowned by three stalked eyes. This one's three membranous wings folded tightly into its torso as it ambled along the ground. Its hide was slick and slimy, and mottled blue and black in color.

The monster slithered straight toward Gage.

The thief drew a dagger and hurled it. The blade plunged into the creature's flesh right between the stalked eyeballs. It screamed and reversed direction.

Gage drew another dagger, holding it ready. The hovering monster's tentacles writhed, and a searing blast of lightning leaped from its stubby fingers to ground itself in the space where the thief had stood a heartbeat earlier. How many more daggers did he have ready? Only three, he realized.

As Gage ducked out of his instinctual evasive leap, his brain realized what his body already knew; the damned things could wield sorcery! He raced around the wide bole of the closest silvery tree, eluding another blast of electricity that scattered wood chips in a dozen trajectories, followed by smoking trails.

He stood, his back to the trunk, breathing hard. He yelled, "Any chance you've made a mistake? I'm no threat. What say you go your way, I go mine. No harm—"

A blast of electricity shuddered into the tree, this time penetrating all the way through. Agony seared his upper back and shoulders.

Gage darted away from the thing, to duck behind the next tree he reached. He placed a dagger in his mouth and rummaged through the pockets on his belt. Lucky his maneuvers hadn't broken any of the vials. With practiced fingers he undid a clasp and pulled forth a glass vial labeled *Inhalant.* Dark yellow liquid sloshed within. He whispered a prayer to Akadi, crouched, and tossed the vial onto the path he'd taken.

He heard the vial smash and the hiss of the contents as they volatilized in the air. He waited a moment then leaned to peer back.

A yellow haze hung in the forest, and at its edge lay one of the creatures. As monstrously odd as it was, it still required breath. Its inert bulk showed it was as susceptible to alchemical poisons as he was. But where was the flying one?

Perhaps it fled when its companion succumbed to the gas. Or did it merely hide, lying in wait to ambush him should he reveal himself? No way to predict the psychology of a creature so alien; it only barely possessed something resembling a body.

He had to risk it. The longer he huddled unmoving, the colder the trail of his quarry. He glanced around the tree.

He looked again at the body of the fallen creature and shuddered. The elf hadn't mentioned such dangerous predators roamed her homeland—the creature was unlike anything he'd ever seen. He sniffed. At least it didn't have the stench of the Abyss.

Nothing swooped from the canopy; nothing rose from the forest floor.

He continued on, setting a comfortable pace—not so quick as to miss the trail, nor so slow that his quarry eluded him.

Nor did Gage forget about the monster that had peppered him with sorcerous bolts. As he advanced, a conviction grew that the creature hadn't fled. No, it had merely hidden, perhaps by magic. Perhaps it followed him, waiting for him to grow tired or drop his guard.

Something creaked above him and he rolled to the left as if evading another bolt of lightning. As he pulled out of his roll he drew daggers and glared upward. Nothing but a break in the canopy, through which a scattering of stars gleamed and winked.

His gauntlet chuckled.

He resisted the urge to smash it against a nearby tree. Instead, he sheathed his dagger and curled his hand into a fist, squeezing the foul-breathed mouth as tightly as he could. "Quiet, while I try to find all my blades," he told his gauntlet.

The demonic titter was muffled, but the unholy mirth could not be stilled.

Chapter Nineteen

Stardeep, Cynosure Prime's Chamber

Delphe rested, her back against a wide stone slab written with cramped, writhing script that glowed as if by starlight. A moment earlier, she'd been in the Throat staring anxiously down into the Well. All was well in the Well . . .

She grimaced. So much for silly little superstitions. Activity in the boundary layer had seemed within normal tolerances, but how long would that last? How long could she continue to personally monitor the Well without Cynosure's never-sleeping cognizance? Cynosure was designed to be the first line of defense against the Traitor's escape; mortal Keepers were merely meant as fail-safes.

She had only spent a short time in reverie in the last couple days, and her brain fizzed with fatigue. Manually triggering Stardeep's useful but complex transfer function was exhausting. Add to that the stress of worrying about the Traitor while at the same time attempting to evaluate Cynosure's nodes for possible contamination, and the result was a Keeper a hand's span away from collapse.

Delphe mentally tallied her success. She'd checked twenty of the thirty-some partial and complete nodes through which Cynosure's mind normally resonated while he was in Stardeep's command loop. All seemed clean, with no sign of decay, corruption, or tampering. Likewise, Prime itself was a paragon of health. Good progress, but . . .

It would take at least another day to finish checking the rest of the nodes.

She dropped her head into her hands.

"Are you well, Delphe?" Cynosure Prime's deep voice boomed from the darkness.

She lifted her head, tracking slowly up the immense, streaked, and stained form of the sentient idol, and looked into its dimly shining scarlet eyes.

"I fear I'm about to discover the limits of my competence," she admitted.

"Have you finished your trace?"

"No, I am two-thirds complete," she replied.

"Then our progress is positive—why so forlorn?"

"I don't have the strength to finish," said Delphe, slumping further.

"I have been monitoring your progress, and I agree," rumbled the idol. "I have a solution, if you wish to hear it."

She blinked. "Please, share."

"It is not necessary to bring me completely back into the loop in order for me to gain access to a majority of my previous functions. Many of my nodes are redundant. You could drop from the loop the nodes you are uncertain about, then reroute and reintroduce my consciousness to what remains."

Delphe blinked again.

"That . . . is not a bad idea." She considered Cynosure's words. It was true, now that she allowed her tired mind a moment's contemplation—every one of the focus points serving as nodes were not strictly necessary. She had checked out and passed more than enough nodes to do exactly what the idol suggested. Enough nodes were clean.

At least, clean as far as her abilities could trace. Which was the real worry—what if some insidious error or malign influence lay hidden from her yet, like a cyst in a piece of meat about to be eaten? What if she brought Cynosure back into the loop only to trigger that influence once again?

"Dark the stars, what choice do I have? Cynosure, prepare yourself to be reinvested into Stardeep's control functions."

Delphe pushed herself up and walked to stand directly beneath the towering figure. She grasped her amulet containing the Cerulean Sign and invoked one of its abilities, one of the few still recalled. The same symbol on Cynosure Prime's chest blazed the color of heaven, and the red glow in its eyes flashed once, then faded.

She asked, "Am I speaking to Cynosure Prime, or Cynosure?"

A moment of silence, then, "I am back in the loop, Delphe. Thank you." The voice emerged from the air next to her as if to prove the point.

"And how are you . . . finding the landscape now that you've returned?" The abjurer clutched her amulet, ready to sever the idol's connection with Stardeep at the very first sign of anything untoward.

"I find everything a bit . . . cramped, I suppose is the best way to explain it. But other than some awkwardness, it seems that my access to Stardeep's functions is reestablished. For instance, I note all conditions are ideal in the Well."

Delphe nodded, allowed herself a shard of hope. She said, "Cynosure, please transfer me to the Throat now."

A shiver of discontinuity, and she stood in the mirrored chamber. The glow from up the Well cast her features in flickering orange hues. As usual.

"By the Sign, I'm happy to leave those transfers to you!"

"It is my pleasure, Delphe."

She walked to her glassy command chair and sat.

"Delphe, I have something I'd like to ask you about."

Her heart caught in her throat. Apprehension pitched her voice higher than normal as she said, "Ask away, Cynosure. Is something wrong?"

"Perhaps. As we speak, I am reacquainting myself with the nodes that have returned to my control, including the statue in the Throat, and those in the Inner Bastion and the Outer, as well as all those in between and underneath. However, I find myself unable to access certain memories stored in the loop."

"Memories?"

"I am unable to access records for specific places and times within Stardeep, beginning some two years ago."

A chill crawled across Delphe's neck. "Is it a corruption?" Did she need to flush Cynosure from Stardeep's control functions once more?

"I am unable to access specific memories because of a command lock. A command lock I wasn't even aware of until you reintroduced me moments ago. Prior to taking me out of the loop, one of the nodes, now inactive, must have been preventing me from noticing. But now the missing records are obvious, and I must admit, unsettling."

"What is the authorization on the command lock?" she asked. Unless the idol itself had experienced some sort of schizophrenic error localized to one of the nodes she'd dropped from the network—

"Keeper Telarian ordered the lock."

It seemed that the entire world dropped a foot.

She started breathing again and said, "Cynosure, listen. I am giving you a counter command. As a Keeper of the Cerulean Sign, I command you to erase those locks and integrate those memories. Now."

Just in case, she keyed her mind, ready to flush Cynosure.

Clicking issued from the large statue on the ceiling, then the idol said, "All records are integrated."

"And?"

"Delphe, we have a problem with Telarian."

Delphe sat in her chair, watching a landslide of events unfold that she could scarcely acknowledge. She saw Telarian unearthing an ancient test node from the repository with Cynosure's unsuspecting help, a node that the diviner then used to infiltrate Stardeep's command functions. One of his first actions was ordering Cynosure to keep part of itself private and secret from its larger cognizance, and what's more, from her.

"How . . . why . . . why would he do that?" she murmured as she watched.

She saw Telarian leaving and returning to Stardeep via the Causeway far more often than she'd ever realized. Creeping dread tingled up her spine.

And Delphe witnessed Telarian accessing an ancient space known to the previous Keepers but which appeared on no map she'd ever seen: the fabled armory.

In that dark space, Telarian found a glass vessel containing a wraithlike essence—a soul, or part of one. In that container was the detritus of a spirit left behind after every hint of nobility was extracted to forge the Blade Cerulean.

Delphe was familiar with the history of Stardeep, especially the momentous events of ten years ago. No one connected to the Cerulean Sign didn't know Keeper Nangulis's personal sacrifice, though because it had occurred a decade ago, few recalled the event with any regularity. Nangulis's body had died, and his fellow Keeper had wielded his soulforged blade to quell the Traitor. The Traitor's foiled effort severely weakened him, and he had not stirred again within the Well until just recently. The remaining Keeper, unfortunately, had then fled Stardeep with the Blade Cerulean in hand, robbing the Keepers of the Cerulean Sign of a potent weapon.

She watched as Telarian moved around the darkened vault, slowly refurbishing its furnace, reconditioning its forge, and relighting its magical flame. He spent months studying the masterwork tools. He spent an equal amount of time staring into the carved alcove at the chamber's rear where a crystal vessel was stored. Where the half-soul writhed in anticipation.

Until then, Delphe had never considered the fate of Nangulis's soul-residue not used in the creation of Angul—she'd assumed it had simply . . . dissipated. It had been stored in Stardeep all this time. Waiting, half-alive but alone. Wrathful, but impotent. Until Telarian found the armory. How had her fellow Keeper even known where to look? His divinatory talent, most likely—a talent, she now hypothesized, that perhaps left him too open to manipulation.

She watched Telarian decant the inky, deceitful spirit into a cast of molten steel.

She asked Cynosure to compress time. Days of Telarian's activity flew by in moments. Finally, she saw the diviner grasp the hilt and hold the darkling blade high. But who grasped whom? When his naked hands touched the blade, Telarian's features seemed to warp and flow, becoming an iron mask calculating the ruin of all fleshy things, all emotion, and all light. Telarian announced in a voice shorn of empathy, "Your name . . . is Nis."

"Stop!" Delphe yelled. The mirrors went dark.

Her hands trembled. She had wondered where the diviner acquired his new blade. When she'd asked, he had shrugged, as if it were unimportant, a mere affectation. Now she wished she didn't know the truth.

"Delphe, he used that blade to strike down Brathtar," volunteered Cynosure.

"Strike down?"

"Knight Commander Brathtar is dead, slain by Telarian with the blade Nis. His body lies in a refuse pit of the under-dungeon, along with those of the Knights who witnessed his death."

"The Sign preserve us," she breathed. "He has betrayed us. Betrayed Stardeep . . . betrayed me!"

She nearly shrieked the last as a sudden blaze of anger briefly scorched mounting fear and dread. Her mouth was dry and a haze seemed to hang in the air. She wiped at her eyes. All the years they had worked together, shoulder to shoulder, seeing to Stardeep's needs, keeping safe their promise to the future—how many of those years had she blithely, unknowingly lived Telarian's lie?

The images showed a man seemingly in the grip of some sort of possession. But even that couldn't be true. During her recent conversation with Telarian, his wit, reason, and personality were undeniably that of the man she'd always known. No alien entity spoke through Telarian's shape. No, the man was responsible for his own actions. Damn him. How had he been corrupted?

"Where is Telarian now?" she demanded, her voice rough.

"I have been querying all nodes, but I cannot locate him."

"He's left Stardeep?"

"Possibly," replied the idol. "Though I note all my perception pools in the Knights' barracks are blacked out. He could be there."

Delphe stood, her face flushed with sudden decision. "We must confront him—neutralize him. By his own deeds he has shown himself to be Stardeep's enemy. Who knows what he'll do next, or what damage he's already done? At least now we know why the Traitor has been so active. Cynosure, activate a defender statue near the Knights' barracks, and transfer me there."

"I've already activated five," Cynosure said. "But Delphe, you are exhausted. I have tracked your activities, and I know how little rest you've taken. Do you think it wise to confront Nis's wielder now?"

Delphe swept her hand in a dismissive gesture. "We have to catch him before he suspects we know of his betrayal. If we wait, we may miss our best chance to move against him."

"Very well, Delphe," said Cynosure as the world blinked.

She then stood in the wide, high Parade Hall outside the Knights' barracks, where the Empyrean Legion often drilled and perfected its techniques. The many doors of the stables fronted the Parade Hall to the west, and to the south a high archway opened onto the main corridors of the Outer Bastion. To the east was another high archway, opening onto a steep, little-used ramp that led to Stardeep's underdungeon.

Flickering magical flames cast warm light down from the ceiling-mounted braziers, striking glints and gleams off the five humanoid constructs that shared the otherwise empty chamber. Each had thick metal plates bolted over a stone-sculpted body, reinforcing the granite strength with the protection only a magical forge could offer. Eight or nine feet tall, each defender's hands were curled into stone-and-iron fists as large as Delphe's entire body. Empowered soulsword or not, Telarian was about to meet the justice his perfidy had earned.

"Still no contact from within," uttered the lead construct. Cynosure equally inhabited all five mobile idols, while at the same time inhabiting all the rest of Stardeep. His power was vast. It frightened her to think Telarian had managed to insert his own twisted control over the powerful sentient artifact.

"In we go," she replied. As the lead construct moved to the barracks door, she quietly uttered words of hardening and strength, such that her own skin took on a hardness akin to stone.

A gasping, wide-eyed Knight's apprentice met them at the door. A young elf, not yet a month out of Sildëyuir, the apprentice had never seen one of Cynosure's statues walking about, let alone a group of five. All color drained from his face, and he tried but failed to produce any sound to greet Delphe.

"Where is Telarian? Is he within?" demanded Delphe.

The apprentice blinked and shook his head. He finally gained enough control over his voice to say, "He was, but he just rode out—he took most of the Knights with him, to counter the attack!"

"What attack?"

The apprentice stuttered. "Wha—you don't know? Telarian said—"

"Tell me what Telarian said, and where he has gone," she commanded.

He nodded. "Keeper Telarian perceived an attack against Stardeep launched from Sildëyuir itself, through the ancient tunnels of the underdungeon. Telarian led the Knights to oppose the Traitor's allies who seek to sneak in upon us all unawares."

"Which allies of the Traitor did Telarian indicate are moving against us—do they have a name?" she asked. Not that she expected anything but lies from the diviner's mouth. What was shockingly, horrifyingly apparent was that Telarian had emptied the barracks of an elite fighting force of more than two hundred Empyrean Knights. Two hundred Knights, whom he was apparently leading into the forlorn, unmapped tunnels whose existence predated the building of Stardeep, and Sildëyuir itself. For what purpose? Did he hope to sap Stardeep's strength by leading its defenders into an ambush?

One of the constructs stepped past the apprentice before the elf could answer Delphe, its metal footfalls echoing like a boulder-fall as it moved to investigate. The elf turned to watch the construct with wide eyes.

She repeated, "Apprentice—who attacks us, according to Telarian?"

"I . . . I am not privy to that information, Keeper. I suppose . . . it was nilshai who attacked—they are growing more aggressive all the time."

Delphe paused. Was that possible? Certainly it could be, but then the image of Telarian's face as he grasped Nis visited her. It was the face of a betrayer. All words that emerged from her fellow Keeper's mouth were now suspect.

She asked, "Did they go on horse?"

The apprentice shrugged. "Yes. He said the tunnels were wide enough to allow a mounted company swift passage for many miles."

Moments later, a construct different than the one that had rushed past the apprentice spoke with Cynosure's voice. "Only apprentices, smiths, and like support staff yet populate the barracks."

Delphe, already looking at the darkened archway leading into the underdungeon, was at a loss. Why had Telarian sent the Knights tearing off into the twisted tunnels beneath Stardeep on horse? The underdungeon tunnels connected, eventually, back into Sildëyuir, but that which lay between was unmapped, and worse, was demonstrably lethal. Threats lurked in those ancient warrens whose origins reached further back than Stardeep's delving. Traps fueled by ancient magic, and the restless spirits of those who had once lived there. The détente of a thousand years was based on the fact that no dwellers of those warrens ever wandered up to bedevil

Stardeep, and no organized force from Stardeep ever ventured into those narrow ways to discover the true nature of the presumed threats.

A stand-off now shattered by Telarian, because of some supposed attack.

"Cynosure, I am not sure what course is best."

"We could follow him, but it is clear he has the Knights' trust. With all ten defender statues, I could deal serious damage, but I would not want to unleash my strength against those whose duty compels them to answer to Telarian's orders."

"Of course. We must not oppose the Knights. They are our best strength, not our foes. It is against Telarian alone we must set ourselves. But first, I need to discover what Telarian truly intends. Does he dance on the strings of the Traitor's desire, or has he simply gone insane?"

Chapter Twenty

Sildëyuir, Moonveil Citadel

One by one, the glass towers softened, leaned, and fell into consuming fire. The burning citadel glowed so brightly the stars directly above the inferno were smeared out in the orange glare. The wide, fey plain had lost its innocence.

The scene affected her like a physical blow; Kiril's stomach twisted and her knees threatened to give way. She spit out a garbled curse, gasped, and took off running down the hill. Xet screeched and darted overhead in crazed, anxious patterns. She heard the sorcerer exclaim in surprise behind her. She cared not. Let the strangers follow her or stay back. Before her was Moonveil Citadel, one of the premier mansions of Sildëyuir. If Moonveil was in flames . . .

Raidon caught up, easily matching her stride for stride. He said, "I see figures sprawled in front of the fiery structure, unmoving. Better we approach cautiously. Whatever attacked this structure and set it ablaze may lurk nearby."

Kiril narrowed her eyes and scanned the periphery of the structure. She saw the bodies Raidon spoke of. The sight of what were likely injured or dead star elves sprawled like gruesome trophies in front of their home lent more speed to her stride. She yelled, "I hope the blood-flecked bastards responsible *are* still lurking. When I catch them . . ."

The monk kept pace, his breath inaudible, while her own grew louder and more ragged. Chain mail, even elven chain mail, was not designed to accommodate a runner. She heard another yelled protest from Adrik, this time more faint.

When she and Raidon reached the foot of the blaze, she was gasping. The heat from the fire drew beads of sweat instantly to her forehead and forearms. The figures they'd glimpsed silhouetted were indeed star elves. Twelve people were laid out in all, ranging in age from rickety elders to youths not yet into their first decade. She recognized Nandor, Avarin, and Nelandrion from visits to Moonveil when she was a child. Now they were dead. And . . . Kiril sucked in her breath. Each body lacked its eyes; bloody sockets stared in grisly parody of perception. Something had collected trophies.

"What Hells-spawned bastard did this?" she whispered. Were glass citadels all across Sildëyuir ablaze like Moonveil? Was the Traitor already free, and visiting his frustrated vengeance on his own people, those who had imprisoned him for so many centuries?

"Behind you!" came Adrik's warning, too late.

A flame had detached from the blackened, sagging mansion wall. It charged her and Raidon as they stared at the violated bodies. The flame raced across the ground, revealing in its bright core a humanoid conflagration. Surprised, her hand fumbled ineffectively for Angul's hilt even as the fiery creature collided with her.

Searing pain choked a strangely high-pitched gasp from her lips. The overheated air pulled the very breath from her lungs. The creature's burning limbs wrapped about her, pulling her close in a burning, elemental bear hug. Her hair smoldered and caught flame. She strained toward Angul, but her arms were caught within the encircling grasp. She couldn't reach Angul's hilt!

The monk drew his slender blade, and with masterful proficiency, laid into the burning creature's fiery core while deftly avoiding Kiril.

The fire elemental shuddered, and the elf renewed her effort to burst free. Success! She tumbled into the cool air, rolling to put some distance between herself and her foe and to put out the flames that burned her clothing. Beating out the flames in her hair, she stood, trailing a corona of dark smoke. The smell of burnt leather and hair pinched her nose.

Raidon danced back and forth with the living inferno, using his strangely shaped weapon in two hands, even though the blade was no longer than an ordinary long sword. The straight blade with its curved point danced like a needle, slashing, parrying, and plunging at the creature's fiery core. In turn, the dancing mote of heat and flame drew ever closer to the monk, pawing at Raidon with claws of flickering red and yellow. The fire consuming the citadel blazed steadily, and Kiril realized that fighting the elemental so close to the fire that spawned it was likely a waste of time. Every strike Raidon landed was burned away, revealing unblemished, sun-bright "flesh" moments later.

"Fall back, Raidon!" she ordered. "It shrugs off injury while it is so close to the great fire!" She hoped her surmise was true.

The monk danced away from Moonveil Citadel, as did she, now consciously avoiding Angul's lure. She had been true to her resolve regarding the whisky, and unless she needed to draw the blade to save her life, she didn't want to risk succumbing utterly to his control; without alcohol insulating her mind, she was far more vulnerable.

Adrik's voice broke over the roar of flames from the collapsing citadel. She glanced back soon enough to witness the sorcerer unleashing a blast of blizzard white, narrow where it issued from his hands, but wide enough to encompass the entire stalking flame. Raidon vaulted up and backward, gracefully avoiding the wintry spell. Within that chilly cone, the creature writhed, screaming a torrent of flame.

Raidon extended his blade as the miniature blizzard faded, using it almost like a spear, thrusting into the weakened creature. It shuddered one final time, then dissolved into so many fading flames.

The half-elf essayed a flourish with his blade, then sheathed it in the same elegant motion. He pointed upward and behind Kiril.

She turned. Four ugly silhouettes straddled the same ridge they'd topped a while earlier. Not the star elves she'd hoped to see. Instead, monsters. Each possessed three clawed legs supporting a body as sinuous as a snake. Their ropy arms were like tentacles, and at least three eyes sprouted from each squat, coiled head.

The creatures charged down the ridge as one. Three moved along the ground in an awkward but surprisingly swift gait. The fourth unfurled insectoid wings and took to the air, flying toward the dragonet that circled above the ridge.

Adrik shrieked as he dashed away from the newcomers. The three creatures on the ground bore down on the fleeing sorcerer. The flying creature pointed at Xet. A black spark easily jumped up to the crystal dragon. The tiny construct's color turned to red then black, and the dragonet dropped from the sky.

"Xet!" screamed Kiril. The little creature was more annoyance than companion, but . . .

Raidon tore forward, moving dozens of paces in the blink of an eye. As a creature wrapped a tearing, clawed tentacle around one of Adrik's flailing arms, the monk launched himself into the air. He delivered a snapping side kick directly into the attacking creature's knoblike head.

The other two monsters surged into the mix.

Kiril advanced, but she kept her eyes on the single creature that remained aloft. A nilshai. It must have been responsible for summoning the sentient flame from the burning citadel.

It chattered an obscene blend of music and syllables. With an audible crack, blue-green lightning suddenly connected the tips of its tentacles with Kiril's metallic armor. She screamed as the electric surge drew tight all her muscles into a single, full-body cramp.

She could put off the inevitable no longer.

Angul woke to blue fire in her hand.

The luminosity of the stars above tripled, and all shadows fled the field, or so it seemed to Kiril.

The swordswoman yelled again, her voice stripped of uncertainty and pain. It was the cry of a warrior certain of her eventual victory.

Kiril fell upon the creatures' flanks as they attempted to smother the monk, who in turn protected Adrik's prostrate form.

When her blade contacted the flesh of the first nilshai, she not only hewed through its tissue, but the cerulean flame from her blade immediately set it alight so robustly that its destruction was a small explosion. Flaming, white-hot bits were propelled in every direction. The nearest nilshai also caught fire, and a moment later, it too was consumed by Angul's cleansing influence.

Rarely was her blade so effective—only when Angul's true enemies were flushed from dark corners. These were aberrations! And Angul was forged for one purpose before all else: the eradication of all atrocities such as these whose mere existence so tainted the world.

The final, cowering nilshai uttered an ululation that Kiril understood as terror for its evil soul. She swept her blade through its abominable carcass, consuming flesh and spirit simultaneously with her unforgiving length of steel.

The last abomination continued to hover above the ridge. It spoke, and its voice was a synthesis of high-pitched squeals, grinding teeth, and tentacle flesh rasping across itself. Kiril heard it say, "I foresee my end. As I foresaw the deaths of my lesser sisters you've just slain. But I rejoice! For each death, even mine, is another stone in the path that leads ineluctably to Xxiphu's emergence! Even as I breathe my last—"

Kiril reversed her grip on Angul's hilt, then launched the burning blade as if he were a javelin. Angul punched through the air tip-forward, a series of ever-widening, flaming halos in his wake. The prophesying aberration's body was consumed in the cleansing inferno that followed contact.

Raidon Kane bent to one knee to support Adrik's head. The sorcerer shivered and gasped, "My arm! It . . . it hurt like fire, but now it's numb."

The monk examined the man's injured limb, easily visible through the shredded sleeve of his robe. Sucker marks made ugly circles across his flesh. At the center of each circle beaded a tiny drop of blood. The arm's color was fading toward a sickly green hue.

"Poison runs in your veins," declared Raidon. "Hold still." So saying, he tore away Adrik's shredded sleeve and used it to tie a tourniquet around the sorcerer's arm above the elbow. He cinched it tight, making the man wince. He hoped it was tight enough to slow the venom. Better the loss of a single arm than death.

The swordswoman walked up, her sword already tucked in her belt. Her blade had surprised Raidon with its incredible display. He wondered why the sword had been so ineffective when he'd first met Kiril at the Mere.

In her arms, Kiril carried the tiny creature she called Xet. Its iridescent color was slowly returning, and its wings flexed. The swordswoman cradled it with a tenderness Raidon hadn't guessed belonged to the elf.

He observed, "You said before that 'threats' wandered Sildëyuir. Are these what you spoke of?"

Kiril said, "Yes. The nilshai. Damned monsters that wield formidable sorcery. They are recent invaders, only becoming a nuisance in the last few years. Word of monsters in the lonelier stretches of the forest circulated, though most thought these 'nilshai' stories were jokes."

The swordswoman scowled at the burnt cinder that was once Moonveil Citadel. "Soon enough, we realized the nilshai were all too real. We discovered they were poisoning Sildëyuir for years."

"Poisoning?" asked the monk.

"They kill our children and steal away tracts of land that are never seen again."

Concern clutched Raidon's stomach. He had discovered his mother's home realm only to find it under attack by vicious invaders. Was she safe?

Adrik looked up from his ravaged, darkening arm. He asked, his teeth gritted against pain, "Where do they come from?"

Kiril gazed at the burning citadel. She said, "No one ever knew. Our sages said they hailed from a spectral reality that underpins our own. But Sildëyuir was disjoined from cosmology when it first took shape. It has always puzzled my folk why the nilshai exert so much effort to enter here, when Faerûn is far easier to reach."

Kiril paused, then continued. "But I know the truth, now. If any of my people were around to hear it, I would explain that the blood-flecking nilshai are agents of the Traitor, adherents who worship, as he does, the gods-damned aberrations of the primeval world. They are servants of the cursed Lords of Madness who seek to regain the realm denied them by the first gods."

Adrik grunted and said no more. Raidon took it as a warning, considering that the voluble sorcerer typically would have launched into a dozen questions. The monk tapped Kiril on the shoulder and said in a quiet voice, "This man requires a healer's craft."

Kiril frowned and hesitated, but she said, "Aid can be petitioned from a place near here."

Adrik smiled despite his pain.

They crested another ridge. Raidon supported the ailing sorcerer. Before them stood an elegant tower of pale white stone and glass. A sturdy granite wall ringed the structure. Blue lamps gleamed from the windows and the treetops surrounding the tower.

"Healing can be had in Tower Aerilpé," murmured Kiril. "Also, Lord Ilsevele has shown sympathy to the Keepers of the Cerulean Sign in the past. Now that the nilshai are unmasked as agents of the Traitor . . . everyone needs to know."

They followed the path down the silvered slopes of the grassy hillside, crossed a river on a bridge of luminous stone, and stood before the mithral gates piercing the wall surrounding the tower. The gates were closed, and in the high weeds that had sprung up around the entrance, they found the rotting bodies of the half-dozen elf guards, still in knee-length hauberks of white scaled armor. All were missing their eyes.

Kiril's hands tightened into fists as she looked at the slaughter. But all she said was, "I was wrong—we have no time."

Raidon said, "What about Adrik's arm?"

Kiril said, "We are days away from the next closest keep I know of in Sildëyuir. The sorcerer's best hope remains with us. One of the Cerulean Order keeps watch on the gate leading to Stardeep's forgotten underpassages. He knows healing arts."

Raidon replied, "Then let us make haste. Adrik wouldn't be here but for me."

He didn't give voice to his growing anxiety. How safe was his mother in a place that grew less sylvan and more like a war zone with every mile they traveled?

They went afoot for miles, heedless of the shining stars or the pearly gray glimmer that ringed the horizons. They halted for rest only when Adrik collapsed. After that, Raidon supported the sorcerer as they walked.

They passed over dry stream beds on crumbling bridges whose stones, once white, seemed discolored and bruised. They traversed empty crossroads, places where dim ways led to unknowable destinations beneath sagging silver trees. Now and then, murky windows of lonely spires fixed the travelers with blank, empty stares as they passed, unwelcoming and quiet. No lights burned from within those towers; all were dark and still, as if long abandoned.

"These seem as if they've been vacant longer than mere months or years," observed Raidon, who bore more and more of Adrik's weight as their journey wore on.

Kiril grunted, "The star elves have been in decline for the last millennia."

Raidon cocked his head, hoping for more explanation, but the swordswoman walked on. Further explanation would not alter the land's affliction, but understanding the situation might help stem his apprehension. The monk mentally took hold of his mind's reins and attempted to meditate on tranquility. What will be, will be.

With a day or more of travel behind them, they paused at the lip of a shallow dell. A silver-gray mist flowed sluggishly through the hollow and across the road, like a low fog. The stars above seemed strangely dull.

Kiril said, "We should go around."

Adrik detached himself from Raidon's help and mumbled a few arcane syllables, then said, "Good idea. The fog rebuffs my attempts to identify it. What is it?"

"A sign we draw close to Sildëyuir's edge, where the realm is not stable. Such intrusions have become prevalent since the nilshai's arrival."

The sorcerer said, "You're saying that the mist is . . . what? A crack in existence?"

"Perhaps. One you don't want to fall into." So saying, she turned and walked away from the road and up the side of a hill. Raidon supported the sorcerer, whose spell noticeably weakened him.

But the initial misty streamer, easily bypassed, was a herald of more sightings, occasionally in the distance, other times as barriers thrown across their path. Sometimes long misty arms twisted through the trees to their left or right, paralleling their path like a hungry predator. Other times they were forced to backtrack when their route was cut off by broad swaths of the gray miasma.

Finally the forest thinned and they moved into clear land. A barren, rocky plain sloped down to a flat expanse, as if to the sea. But what lay beyond the stagnant coast was not water. It was a shoreless ocean of gray mist, cold and perfect.

Alone on the beach stood a lean figure. They approached and saw it was a tall, lordly star elf dressed in black robes on which was emblazoned the symbol of a white tree on a field of blue. Raidon recognized a fellow initiate of focus and self-discipline in the man's ramrod straight posture, though he suspected the elf's mastery lay over magic instead of the physical arts. The elf had eyes of milk white, with no hint of an iris, and his graceful features were graven with the weight of long care. A platinum circlet clamped his shaved skull. Without hair, his elven ears seemed more sinister than fey.

A circle of dead nilshai lay about the elf's feet. Blood smudged his face and hands, and dirt stained his clothing. But he was unbowed. He watched calmly as they picked their way down the cruel slope. Raidon nearly carried Adrik when they joined the figure before the silent ocean where reality frayed to nothing.

"Edgewarden," said Kiril, her back straightening. Raidon understood she must hold great respect for this man. "I hoped you'd still be here, guarding Stardeep's flank."

He studied her without speaking for a moment, then he said, "It has been a long time since a Keeper last came to visit me here at the end of the world. But the Keepers of the Cerulean Sign are an old, dusty order, eh? I wondered if perhaps I were the last."

"Hells and blood! No aberration born or grown has yet been able to best me, and I wield the Blade Cerulean. I, at least, remain. There are Knights still in Stardeep—or there were several days ago. My companions and I must press into Stardeep to determine their fate, and the status of the Traitor."

The bald elf said, "These creatures"—he gestured at the dead nilshai—"who've thrice found me here at the edge as I walked the periphery—do their attacks have anything to do with your desire to enter Stardeep? I guess they must have sympathies for the conspirator who lingers in Stardeep's deepest dungeon."

Kiril swallowed. "You have the right of it. The gods-damned nilshai were agents of the aboleths all along. They and the Traitor serve the same abominable masters. I go to discover if the Traitor remains penned; I fear he's escaped, or is on the cusp of doing so. Angul and I will try to put things right."

The elf nodded, and Kiril continued. "Edgewarden, if I may—have you had any communication from Stardeep of late? Has news perchance reached you of a former Keeper named Nangulis?"

The man shrugged. "No one comes this way. Except for the nilshai, I haven't seen anyone before you in seven years."

Kiril dropped her eyes, glumly nodding.

The Edgewarden looked at Raidon and Adrik. "Are these Keepers I haven't yet met?" His eyes lingered on Adrik and he frowned. Raidon guessed Adrik would not normally be allowed entry to the hidden realm.

"No—"

The bald elf moved to Adrik, who lay glassy-eyed on the beach. "What ails him?"

Raidon looked up. "He was poisoned by a nilshai. Can you help?"

The Edgewarden bent and ran his fingers lightly over the sorcerer's arm, chest, and forehead. His eyes narrowed and he said, "I can provide relief, though my ministrations are only temporary."

So saying, he muttered liquid syllables that were like a cool, refreshing wind. When Raidon tried to recall the sounds a moment later, they were gone. The Edgewarden touched Adrik with fingers sparkling as if with stardust, and some color returned to the sorcerer's features.

The dark-robed elf stripped away the tourniquet and helped Adrik to his feet. The sorcerer was blinking and gazing around at the beach and misty sea in bemusement. He asked, "How did we get here?"

The Edgewarden patted the sorcerer's arm and asked Kiril,

"And your other companion?"

Kiril pointed at Raidon. "This one carries a relic of our order—his mother was a star elf, though as far as I know she never came to Stardeep. How she got an Amulet of the Sign is a mystery. She passed it to her son."

The Edgewarden squinted at Raidon, then said, "Such relics are few and far between in these waning days of Sildëyuir. What was your mother's name?"

The monk said, "Answering that question is the quest that brought me here. I do not know her name, only that she came from this realm."

"I see," responded the Edgewarden, shaking his head. "I apologize, but these lands are under threat of collapse . . ."

Surprising himself, Raidon broke the rules of proper discourse to interrupt. "But I just found this land! How can I protect my mother? What must I do to safeguard Sildëyuir?"

The old elf raised a placating palm. "If you and Kiril succeed in penning the Traitor, if he's truly free, then Sildëyuir may stabilize enough for me to continue my attempt to reinscribe its borders. If so, return and find me. I think I can help you find your mother. If not, nothing else will matter."

Uncertainty and hope strove in Raidon's chest. Aloud he said, "Then succeed we must. I will return to speak with you again, Edgewarden."

"In case you do not return, know this: I suspect your mother's name is Erunyauvë."

Raidon asked, "What, do you know her?"

"Many gifts are mine, including divination. When I look at you, I hear that name. And why not—would you be here right now if not for the amulet she left you? It is a name that is not without history of its own, though time is too short to relay it. If . . . *when* you return, I shall lend you my expertise in locating her. If she is anywhere within the realm of greater Yuireshanyaar, I can find her."

Raidon breathed a sigh and bowed his head.

Kiril broke in. "Edgewarden, please show us the path to Stardeep."

Ignoring the sorcerer, the Edgewarden said, "I shall, before another wave of nilshai descends. I sense them massing somewhere in this damnable flux."

So saying, he pointed up the grade they'd just descended. Raidon's eyes found a feature some twenty paces up the slope. What the monk had taken as just another boulder protruding from the sandy grit was revealed as something more: the rocky frame of a massive iron door. Had the Edgewarden dropped an illusion covering a doorway that had been there all along, or had he called the entrance into existence by mere desire?

Xet chimed and landed on top of the rocky frame holding the gate. The tiny construct slapped the door with its long tail. A dull gong tolled out across the misty expanse.

Kiril motioned Raidon forward. "Present your amulet to the doors. Angul would serve, but I prefer to keep him sheathed."

Raidon blinked, but he pulled forth the forget-me-not his mother—Erunyauvë—had given him. He displayed it before the sealed doorway. Nothing happened. He stepped forward another pace and touched the amulet to the lackluster iron.

Blue light sparked from amulet to gate. Stones danced and skittered down the slope as the entire beach shuddered. With an ear-splitting groan, the iron door swung wide, opening onto a shadowed, dusty stone stair descending into unguessed depths.

They entered Stardeep by a route rarely taken.

Chapter Twenty-One

Stardeep, Underdungeon

The tunnel split, and split again as the company plunged into the warren of sedimentary rock that underlay Stardeep. The walls were smooth and white, possibly composed of salt and gypsum, but here and there patterns reminiscent of shells, bones, and teeth were picked out in the Knights' lantern light.

"Shall I send exploratory teams into these side passages?" asked the Knight Commander riding at Telarian's side.

"Not necessary," replied Telarian. "They are a distraction from the main route. And the openings are too small for a mounted company. We shall continue along this broad way. We need to make good time in order to catch our opponents as far from Stardeep as possible." More accurately, as far from Delphe's influence as possible, he mentally added. He continued aloud, "Perhaps we'll make it through to the other end. If we can catch our quarry in Sildëyuir, all the better."

Thindhul, the Knight Commander, awkward in his new authority and betraying a nervous shiver unseemly for his station, said, "How far did you say?"

Telarian frowned. The Commander knew better than to repeat such an insipid question. The passages that perforated the ground below Stardeep were a mystery; they were not delved by Stardeep's architects, but were discovered only after foundations of the dungeon created to hold the Traitor were mostly complete. Their existence was a surprise, given that the land into which Stardeep was cut was assumed to be virginal, untouched earth called into existence at the same time as the rest of Sildëyuir. If the land beneath Stardeep was riddled with caverns, might the earth below Sildëyuir be as well? And what primeval race left those caverns behind?

Past exploration showed that at least two routes stretched between Stardeep's underdungeon and Sildëyuir's outermost edge. Every Keeper knew this much. Unfortunately, nothing more than a couple of incomplete maps remained from those original mapping expeditions. Plus a few oddly conflicting stories about the hazardous nature of the creatures who hunted the dim paths.

No one doubted that traveling the ancient tunnels was risky. Every so often, an enterprising Knight, eager to win a wager or make a name for herself among her squad, would venture into the enigmatic white-walled passages. Often enough, the foolish Knight was never seen again—for which reason the tunnels were forbidden. The restriction only heightened the allure among those already drawn to danger and derring-do. Expeditions of the foolish still launched into the tunnels every few years. Those lucky enough to return would tell tales more interesting than endless echoing tubes. These Knights would return bloodied and pale, babbling of haunting whispers echoing through smooth, endless galleries, great pyramids of living stone, and entities long dead when Sildëyuir was not yet conceived.

No one doubted that danger stalked the tunnels separating Sildëyuir from Stardeep. Great gates and a defender statue guarded Stardeep's flanks against intruders from the hoary past.

Against Angul, tunnel threats of the tunnels were likely to be less potent. Kiril might well decide to chance the passage, knowing few dangers could stand against her soul-forged steel.

Likewise, with Nis in hand, Telarian was confident he could win through to confront Kiril. Strictly speaking, he didn't need the entire mounted force of Empyrean Knights riding ahead of him. But that wasn't the only reason he'd commanded the Knights to accompany him.

You brought them in order to prevent Delphe from using them to hold Stardeep against you upon your return, should she learn of your hidden objectives, came Nis's emotionless voice directly into his mind.

True. It wouldn't do for the increasingly suspicious Delphe to sway credulous, virtuous Knights with her misunderstanding of Telarian's goals. This way, even if Delphe decided to thwart him, he commanded the stronger force. She'd have little chance to persuade their loyalties when they were already in the field. For all Cynosure's power, Delphe and the construct couldn't stand against the entire company of Empyrean Knights.

And if he gained Angul *and* Nis, even that wouldn't matter.

"Keeper!" spoke the Knight Commander, his tone terse.

A messenger afoot pressed along the line until she reached the side of the Knight Commander's horse.

The messenger was a Knight apprentice, a girl of no more than twenty, twenty-five years, he guessed. She said, "We've come upon a wide space ahead, filled with ruins. A sorcerous wall prevents the vanguard from advancing."

Telarian and the Knight Commander passed to the front of the column, a short journey in the narrow tunnel.

The Knight vanguard was arrayed before a flickering screen of green and gold, through which a wide cavern was visible. Past the distortion, Telarian glimpsed smooth-cut angles of black stone, broken arches, and the bases of columns whose heights were long crumbled.

From his saddle, he essayed a simple analytical spell. The screen was weak. And old. A wonder it still functioned. A barrier whose usefulness was concluded, except as a warning.

"Just push through," commanded Telarian. "It may feel unpleasant, but its ability to harm you is long spent."

When Telarian's turn came to breach the barrier, shrieking wind assaulted his ears. The lantern light flared, then settled to normal. The diviner stumbled over a ridge in the white floor—an exposed, fossilized spine of some larger-than-elf creature.

Beyond the exposed spine, the tunnel opened into a wide enclosure whose white walls showed compacted seams of eons-preserved bone, layer upon layer.

"Is this a graveyard?" he heard one of the Knights ask in wondering tones.

Near the cavern's center leaned a pile of broken stone. Telarian's eyes scanned the heap and then turned up to the cavern's ceiling. A dark hole, like a mouth agape in pain, punctured the otherwise smooth surface. The wind screamed through the aperture, howling and abrading the room and its contents with a haze of airborne grit.

The only other exit from the chamber was a tall set of double doors sheeted in hammered, coppery metal.

"Best ignore the ceiling breach—we'd never get the horses up there," yelled Telarian over the wind. He spurred his mount toward the doors. As he pulled up next to the exit, he was relieved to confirm they were sufficiently high and wide enough to permit two Knights to ride abreast. If he could open them. Rusty stains decorated the metallic surface of the doors where latches might have once protruded.

He reached out one hand and gave the left door an experimental push. Unyielding. He dismounted, grasped Nis with his off hand, and tried again.

Nis pulsed in his grip. Blade-sent geometries, dark and subtle, flared behind his eyes. A logic born of emotionless calculation bent his mind and suffused his body. Mere mortality was suppressed, and his musculature pulsed with certainty. He placed his hand again upon the door and stove it from its hinges. The other door fell as quickly.

Beyond was a natural bore through stone. The passage was basalt, but the walls were streaked with the same white stone as the previous tunnels. The same strata of ancient death lay compacted amid those pale veins.

Telarian surrendered his hold on the soul-forged blade, and the hint of recognition Nis felt toward the strata vanished. The knowledge of who might have been responsible for cutting these passages was again beyond his conjecture.

They made good time then, traveling straight and level, without any side passages to dilute their resolution to move forward. The wind's strength slackened as they moved farther from where it had first assaulted them, and finally failed altogether, so that only the sounds of clopping hooves rushed down the narrow corridor.

They camped once, strung out over several hundred horse spans, with Knight apprentices moving up and down the line with feed, food, and water for mounts and Knights alike.

When they rode next, they traversed not more than a few miles before they broke into an underground city.

Telarian found his steed traversing what had once been a street, its cobbles now buckled and misaligned. Squat tenements of white stone crowded along the road, mostly collapsed and shattered beneath the settling ceiling.

Flashing lantern beams picked out hundreds of bodies lying in the street, in positions of casual repose, as if they had settled for a midmorning nap from which none had ever risen again. The humanoid shapes were as hard and pale as the sedimentary rock in the tunnels. Telarian's first thought was that they were scattered, looted sculptures.

Telarian dismounted. He saw the forms were not posed in any way, like a statue might be. No, the remains were apparently people who fell to a disaster unrecorded. An image granted him earlier by Nis flashed before his eyes—a slender, white tower burning as it receded into the sky, leaving behind a plain of absolute black. The image dissolved. Telarian leaned in to get a closer look at one of the bodies.

Not elf, nor precisely human. Orc? The features were too gracile to be those of any modern orc. Some sages believed the farther one penetrated history, the more primitive one would find the inhabitants. Were these extinct people something related to goblins? Whatever they were, they hadn't survived into the current age in any realm or plane Telarian knew. Nor had he seen any such creatures in any of his visions of the future. Whatever civilization and achievements these humanoids may have once known, reality moved on without them.

Thindhul said, "Who knew Stardeep's underdungeon opened upon such"—the Knight Commander fluttered his hand at the scene—"such enigma."

"One that doesn't concern us," said Telarian, more to himself than Thindhul. Whatever the nature of the secrets and treasures hidden away in Stardeep's unexplored basements, they had no bearing on the reason they were there, or what he intended to accomplish.

"Very well. Which way do we go from here?" asked Thindhul, his tone sardonic.

Telarian rose and studied the wider streets and half-collapsed ceiling. A score more Knights issued from the tunnel out into the streets to set up a temporary perimeter. From the diviner's vantage, he counted at least five side streets, each as wide or wider than the street they'd emerged upon, though at least a couple were choked by shattered walls, collapsed ceiling sections, and fossilized bodies.

"We'll continue to follow the street we're on. Since it led to the tunnel, this was likely once a main thoroughfare. It should lead to the city's center. From there, we'll decide where to go next."

Thindhul nodded, and shouted orders for the Knights to form up behind the vanguard. With the streets so wide, the Knight Commander judged the space adequate for five Knights to easily ride abreast. Telarian left him to his duty and joined the vanguard as it picked its way forward, stepping around the twisted, stony corpses that littered the road.

As they progressed, the crushing weight of the fallen ceiling gradually lessened, revealing more of the city's architecture. Thick foundations gave way to arching white balusters, fluted columns, and slender balconies. The upward construction did little to draw the eyes away from the grisly, hardened remains of the city's former citizens, whose numbers increased the farther they moved.

By the time the vanguard entered the central city hub, the forms underfoot were as thick as cobbles. It was easier for the horses to trod those unfeeling backs than to pick their way through. Telarian was riding the vanguard, judging the Knights' confidence would be bolstered by his presence.

The ceiling arched up into a great dome, at the center of which a violet flame burned dimly, like the ghost of the sun. Beneath the flame rose a jumble of rock-hard bodies rising some forty paces from a broad base to a narrow tip. The cone-shaped cemetery mass was surmounted by a blood red throne of rough-cut crystal.

A lone, bone white figure sat upon that throne, unmoving and lifeless as the hundreds of fossilized forms who made up its court and supported its high seat.

Telarian called a halt. The vanguard paused some dozens of paces from the mound's lower edge. He waited for Thindhul to catch up as he continued to observe the panorama.

When Thindhul rode to Telarian's side, the Knight Commander asked, "Do you sense a threat?"

The diviner shrugged, "Perhaps we have stumbled upon the epicenter of some terrible genocidal ritual. However, that heap has the look of something assembled after the bodies were petrified."

"Either way, nothing to do with us, correct?"

The Keeper replied, "If that statue sitting on its pretty seat maintains any cognition whatsoever, perhaps it can provide us with directions."

Thindhul's mouth opened with a surprised gape. He said, "Is that wise?"

Telarian fixed the Commander with a wintry look, saying nothing.

Thindhul stuttered, shook his head, and finally declared, "I shall send someone to inquire."

The Knight Commander turned and gestured to one of the vanguard. "Knight Dilthari, ascend that heap and investigate."

An elf woman dismounted, gave the reins to a companion, and approached the heap.

She walked the periphery of the cone, looking for the best route to ascend the pile of rigid bodies.

The figure on the throne suddenly stood from its seat and looked down at Dilthari, just as the violet flame on the ceiling flared to three times its original luminosity. The figure, as naked and roughly preserved as all the other figures, absorbed that light across its hard surface in discrete patterns that resembled regalia and clothing. It was revealed as wearing a crown of light and a luminescent cape, and it brandished a long staff of streaming effulgence.

It coughed a plume of dust, then mumbled something to Dilthari in a language unknown to Telarian. The tone made it seem a question. The diviner quickly essayed a charm of language comprehension, as the figure spoke again.

This time, Telarian caught part of its question, ". . . more subjects whose salvaged essence can fuel my elaborate mechanisms?"

Dilthari continued to stare up, uncomprehending. Telarian shouted, "Stand away, Knight!"

The figure, despite its fossilized limbs, pointed down the slope with its intangible staff. Dilthari scrambled backward. The other Knights of the vanguard unlimbered crossbows and fumbled to fit bolts.

Dilthari gasped as if punched in the stomach and ceased moving. She half turned her gaze back to Telarian, surprise dawning across her features. To the diviner's eyes, it seemed as if the Knight exhaled a thin streamer of mist from her nose and mouth. The streamer flowed through the air toward the crowned one, who snared it with his blazing staff. Dilthari's flesh instantly cooled and paled to the color of salt. She toppled, becoming one more rigid carcass among the thousands of inert, fossilized bodies. As she struck the previously hardened corpses, her outstretched arm broke off at the shoulder with an unnerving report.

Even as Thindhul screamed, "Attack!" a volley of bolts battered the creature with such force it overbalanced and fell from sight off the back of the heap.

Telarian waited to hear the creature crash down, but several heartbeats of silence dashed his expectation. Instead, the dusty, dry voice mumbled from behind the heap. "Wake, wake, wake my sleepy ones! Open your dull eyes and stand—your prophet commands it! Dream no more in lonely exile!"

"By the Sign!" screamed Thindhul. The rubble on which the Knights rode began to shudder, heave, and crack. Every fossilized corpse scattered across the buried city's central hub, and all the way down the road along which the Knights were assembled began to twitch. Each became a terror of eon-hardened hunger.

A tsunami of screams scratched from a thousand rock throats. The noise slammed through the Knights, threatening to break even their renowned valor. The howls were of damned souls thrust suddenly back into bodies completely foreign to them. The hellish sound was one the survivors would hear echoing through their trances all the rest of their days.

Nis was in Telarian's hand a moment later, dashing his rising panic as water to a flame. Logic, cold and untethered to emotion, become his only companion. As Knights pulled their weapons and began to slash at the stoic undead that rose as a pale tide all around them, Telarian made for the throne. Clearly, even if a few Empyrean Knights were to survive the next twenty or thirty heartbeats, the puppeteer of this ghastly city had to be eradicated.

A dozen stony hands, blunt with erosion, pulled his screaming mount from under him. Telarian leaped free, his ebony blade pulling him up and away from the sounds of ripping horseflesh. Then he was on the central mound, dashing up the steep slope of solidified carrion, even as it began to shudder and separate. Each unit of the cone-shaped structure became a screaming zombie whose flesh was hard as bedrock.

He stepped on a writhing arm, a yowling head, and into a palm and out of it before the hand could clutch and hold him. He batted away a face whose gaping mouth threatened to bite him, turning the pallid stone into so much sand. Then he reached the apex, just as the perpetrator of the uprising surmounted the opposite side. Unlike his own uneven ascent, the energy-wreathed lich was raised securely in the hands of its newly animated followers.

Telarian and the relic lich faced each other from across the crystalline throne. The diviner looked into a countenance so weathered that only a shallow concavity faced him, incapable of displaying the least hint of feature.

The obscene crater that once housed a mouth worked, and it somehow spoke without tongue to shape its words. "The mechanism requires fresh infusion. Blood is too sticky and prone to clotting. Souls serve best." Telarian's spell of translation allowed him to understand the creature's supernatural utterances, but the lich's allusion to a mechanism escaped him. In any event, the context implied nothing pleasant for him and the Empyrean Knights.

Telarian swung Nis down and around from where it lightly rested on his shoulder, in a vicious cross-body swing. His foe easily blocked with its staff of blazing light. The contact jolted through the Keeper's arm, but Nis steadied him despite the flexing, heaving slope on which he stood.

My presence, or perhaps my twin's, Nis projected into his mind, *has awakened a thing that lay quiescent in Stardeep's basements since before Stardeep was delved. Splintered desires fuel this ancient shell, desires so potent they bleed out from the host and share animation with petrified remains of a murdered species.*

Chapter Twenty-Two

Stardeep, Underdungeon

The demon gauntlet snuffled and coughed, straining forward, following the fading scent of those who'd gone before. Gage was pulled along in the fiend's wake, his gloved hand held forward and down, slinking from tree to silvery tree. His quarry's path had steered wide of chill mist rivers that sliced through the nighted landscape. He was happy to avoid intersecting the impenetrable vapor—even his bound demon shuddered and bucked when he'd tried to insert it into the first standing bank he'd passed.

At length he came to the forest's edge. A margin of dead rock lay beyond, decorated with craggy boulders and narrow fissures. Beyond that lay a sea of colorless fog, chill and endless. He drew in a quick breath when he saw several corpses littering the beach, the decaying bodies matching those he'd dispatched earlier. One group of dead monsters lay near the edge of the fog, though several marked the perimeter of a large boulder about thirty paces from the mist's edge. The demon gauntlet bleated and tried to pull forward. Kiril and the other two had come this way. Had they entered the mist?

Gage studied the scene a moment longer, then moved.

The boulder was splashed with green and black ichor—the thief counted at least six of the loathsome creatures, battered, burnt, and . . .

An opening! A rectangular portal pierced the boulder's overhanging side that faced the fog sea. A massive iron gate lay torn from its hinges, scratched and partially crumpled. The lower portion of the cavity was choked with monsters, all dead, many showing signs of flashburn. Blasting magic had separated many of these from their putrid lives. He didn't see evidence of any bladework. Kiril had not drawn her Cerulean sword to defeat these beasts. Or was the slaughter the work of someone else? Impossible to say without a witness to describe what had occurred.

His demon glove strained toward the portal. Gage spent another ten heartbeats examining the doorway before darting forward, diving to clear the sprawled bodies at the last moment. He tucked his shoulder and rolled to absorb the impact of his quick entrance. The steep stairs beyond made this tricky feat even more difficult, but Gage executed the maneuver with panache.

At the stair's foot a tunnel led off, its downward slope noticeable. The tunnel's rock walls were streaked with deposits of white stone, but the light from the entrance topping the stairs didn't reach far. Gage produced a clear glass vessel and shook it vigorously. The chemicals within were inimical to each other, and given time, slowly separated. When mixed, the hostile essences fought, producing light.

His gauntlet yanked forward with surprising strength.

Gage grunted and resisted. His glove muttered, "Never forget, your soul is forfeit."

"I quaver in my boots," the thief replied. "Behave. Don't forget, acid burns. Remember what happened last time?"

The glove muttered something too quietly for Gage to hear. "Better. Now lead on. Quietly."

Gage advanced down the tunnel, surrounded by a dim sphere of light, his eyes wide for any evidence of his quarry.

Gage gave his light another vigorous shake to rejuvenate its intensity. How long had he walked these strangely smooth tunnels?

"More importantly," he muttered aloud, "how'd Kiril and her friends get so far ahead of me?" He gave his gauntlet a suspicious squint.

Ahead, a hole in the floor gaped nearly the entire diameter of the tunnel. His light picked out individual strands of thickly intertwined webs that obscured the hole's sides, but opened into a twisting funnel at the hole's center. A cold, dusty wind blew from the gap, as did a rushing, full-throated roar of moving water.

His eyes lit on a papery scrap that lay ensnared in the web about two body lengths down the funnel. Though stuck, its outer edge wavered in the chill breeze.

"I am on the right trail," he whispered, relief washing over him. The chance of the glove misleading him wasn't out of the question. It had grown more willful since the other glove, with the eye, was burnt to ash by Angul.

Gage stared into the webbing, wondering who had dropped the scrap of paper—Kiril, or one of the other two? Vellum was expensive. In fact . . .

The thief removed his pack. From it he produced an elven rope, a selection of iron spikes with eyeholes, and a battered mallet. He selected a point on the wall and sunk the spike with three strikes. The echoes of the malletfalls made him wince. Too late for second thoughts!

He threaded the rope in the anchored spike, tied one end into his belt, and let himself over the edge of the webbed hole. Hand over hand he lowered himself until he was close enough to snatch the lone vellum scrap from the sticky strands. It took a little careful tugging to extract his prize without ripping it. It was blank. Unpenned and already-spent spell scrolls possessed the same sense of limitless possibility in their clean expanse. They seemed eager for the next spell, the wilder and more potent, the better. Of course, they also represented a tidy sum of gold. He stowed his prize, worth a tenday's lodging in the finest festhall in Laothkund.

As Gage hauled himself out of the hole, he heard the unmistakable cry of a wailing infant below.

"What in Akadi's name . . . ?" He glanced down. A many-limbed white bulk filled the web tunnel beneath him. Dozens of pale, stone-hard eyes fixed on his own. From its mandibled mouth came the pitiful mewls of a crying baby.

Gage screamed. The gargantuan thing, its legs shaking off the dust of ages, rose beneath him. Its flesh was stone, as if a statue come to life.

The thief groped at his belt, his terror-numbed fingers finding the proper clasp more through luck than skill. He grasped a warm bulb—his most prized alchemical item, and worth considerably more than a tenday in a festhall.

The arachnid was too close, but dangling as he was, he had no other option. He dashed the bulb down, whipping it with as much strength as he could muster. The bulb detonated on the creature's face only a body length away.

The explosive fount punched up into his body. It reminded him of the time he'd leaped for a neighboring roof but missed and fell three stories. Except this time he was on fire. But, just like then, he blacked out a moment later.

Flickering light on a smooth white ceiling. Torchlight? A numbness slowly faded under a barrage of tingling—and pain. Gage blinked. Why would that be? He groaned as he sat up. His entire body was one contiguous bruise. Then he recalled the spider and the detonation.

The webbed hole lay several dozen paces away, its gooey coating ablaze. The explosion had propelled him past the gap. About halfway between him and the burning pit crouched a figure silhouetted by the flames. At first the thief took it for a detached portion of the spider, blown loose in the blast. Then he noticed the black scales, the horns, and as it slowly stood from its crouch, its flaring batlike wings.

Those black, finely grained scales looked familiar . . .

Gage dropped his gaze to his right hand. His gauntlet. Gone!

He jerked his eyes back to the figure. It stood now to its full height and beyond, reaching and stretching its long, clawed limbs as if waking from sleep. Or as if freed from an enchantment that bound its shape into something far smaller. Say, a glove?

The creature, clearly a demon, began to chuckle. One of its eyes fixed the thief with a sinister, gleeful glare. A mass of burned flesh and scars festered where its other eye should have been. Gage recalled again how Angul had burned his other gauntlet to a cinder, the one with the single, enchanted eye.

He scuttled backward on hands and legs. A sharp rock cut his palm.

The demon flared its wings. It interrupted its mirth to speak. "Recall the payment I've reminded you that you owe me, mortal, time and again. I'm afraid our acquaintanceship is over. The time has come for me to eat your soul!"

Fear tried to break his normally professional detachment, bringing an unfamiliar and unwelcome quiver to his limbs as he sprang upright. His voice, too, sounded weak and pitiful in his ears. "Demon! Uh . . . Hold, will you? Wait! I have more value to you alive than dead, if you hear me out. I offer a bargain!"

The scaled wings pulsed and the razor-sharp tail lashed, but the demon remained at the edge of the hole. Its single eye narrowed, and it growled, "Explain." Gage's wit failed him. He stammered then turned and ran.

The thief heard the demon laugh. Then, oddly enough, it screamed.

He glanced over his shoulder. The stone spider was back! Its upper body protruded from the burning hole at the demon's back, the pale stone of its carapace blackened and cracked with alchemical scorch marks. The wail of a baby burst anew from the insectoid maw like a little one hungry to suckle.

The spider's mandibles clamped the demon around its waist. The demon's wings burst into a fit of mad flapping, as a moth that is caught too near a flame. It bit, clawed, raked, and bucked with such ferocity the tunnel floor shook. All to little effect. With a chilling finality, the spider retracted its head and body back into its lair, dragging the hapless, howling demon with it.

The demon gave one final, soul-shattering scream, which ended abruptly.

Gage, without his gauntlets and unable to see, sprinted, whimpering, into the unrelenting darkness.

Chapter Twenty-Three

Stardeep, Underdungeon

A wind, bearing alien odors, brushed Raidon's face. He wondered by what dark, subterranean route the air had traveled, and for how long before caressing his face with its feathery, unseen hands. Black lakes, unlit mansions of stone, warrens of crystal, caverns housing forgotten secrets—who knew the depths of these passages whose extent was large enough to generate its own breezes, perhaps its own weather?

Raidon followed a conflicted woman. As they strode white-washed subterranean tunnels, Kiril muttered and mumbled as if possessed. More than once he saw her hand move toward the hilt of the blade she wore on her hip, only to flinch away before contact.

An obsession, certainly, perhaps something like the tie that bound him to his grandfather's daito? True, his fixation had given way to something less obviously lethal. The amulet bequeathed him by his mother had led him into a world beyond any he could have imagined. Was it not obsession that yet held him fast to Erunyauvë's legacy? This amulet of a Sign whose significance he didn't fully comprehend would point him toward his missing mother. With it, he could discover why she left him. If not obsession, something powerful, whatever its name, gripped him.

"Look at this!" came Adrik's startlingly loud call from behind. Raidon whirled, ready to defend the small group.

The sorcerer pointed to a greenish stripe of mold running along the wall of the tunnel, only a half-pace above the level of the floor. Raidon had earlier noticed the mold and discounted its appearance as unimportant. A sputtering light flamed and smoked from the coin Adrik clutched in his left hand. The illumination was born of a quick series of syllables the sorcerer uttered when they'd left Sildëyuir's light behind.

Kiril turned, one eyebrow raised in a question. Xet, riding her shoulder, belled a short, rising tone.

"Fungus wouldn't grow in such a uniform line unless this tunnel periodically floods," replied Adrik. "But then we'd see a parallel stripe on the other wall."

"What of it?"

"No matching stripe, no flooding. The only answer is that there must be a reservoir of water behind this wall. It must seep through, providing moisture enough for this growth!"

The swordswoman snorted, turned, and continued stalking forward.

The sorcerer swiveled to flash Raidon his eager expression. The monk said, "I missed that, Adrik—you have eyes for this sort of delving, it seems."

The sorcerer smiled at the compliment, at the same time raising a finger as if to make a further point. The monk turned and followed Kiril before the man could expound upon mold, moisture, their musty relationship, or some related topic likely to interest the monk not in the least. He appreciated Adrik's boundless enthusiasm for diverse topics—truly, he did—but in their present circumstance, he preferred to avoid such distractions.

Even as Raidon allowed introspection to sap his focus, he noticed the narrow tunnel through which they'd progressed was gradually widening. Far ahead, blue-green illumination seeped into the tunnel, staining its white walls with alien color.

"Kiril," Raidon said, "pause a moment. What does that glow ahead presage?"

The elf shook her head. She muttered, "How would I know what lies ahead? The only way to know is to move forward and look. One way or another, these tunnels lead into Stardeep's heart. Don't ask stupid questions, Telflammer."

Raidon cocked his head, wondering if she baited him purposefully. Now that they both knew his mother was native to Sildëyuir, referring to his Shou origin seemed a slap in the face. Or perhaps it was her implication that he had asked a frivolous question. Or perhaps he was merely losing his focus . . .

He pushed the irritation from his thoughts with an old mantra: Have no limitation as limitation. His thoughts couldn't be swayed by her words or attitude—only he could channel his mind—others' words imparted information only. They couldn't change the tracks of his knowledge or attitudes unless he allowed them to do so. He was free unto himself, not bound to limitations others tried to place upon him.

It was becoming clear, however, that Kiril Duskmourn would try even the serenity of Xiang Temple master.

The intensity of the light grew as they approached, and the tunnel fell away to reveal a wider space. One side of the tunnel fell away to become a ledge skirting the edge of a deeper cavern filled with strange growths.

Puff balls, fungal draperies, fronds, and toadstools grew in thick profusion within the wide depression, all glowing with varying shades of bioluminescence. Sprouting up through a layer of turgid black ooze were small, yellow protrusions, as wide and thick as fingers. A few toadstool caps grew so tall they towered above the level of the catwalk to brush the ceiling and spread flattened, mushroomlike canopies overhead. A smell like baking bread, citrus, and rotting flesh wrinkled Raidon's nose. A bluish glow hazed the air.

"Breathe carefully," advised Adrik, who placed a fold of his robe over his mouth. His muffled voice came again. "Spores."

Kiril grunted, "I wouldn't have guessed such a garden could survive in these darks. I wonder on what sort of rot this plot grows." The crystal dragonet belled unhelpfully.

She shrugged and walked onto the tunnel catwalk. Some hundreds of paces ahead, the ledge plunged into a smaller tunnel.

Raidon and Adrik followed her. Halfway across, the monk glimpsed a shape moving through the fungalscape. Turning his head, he saw some sort of . . . humanoid. It was a bulky, hunch-backed humanoid composed of mushroomy flesh partly covered in a bony black carapace. Its head was a puffball suffused with wavering filaments. The creature used daggerlike obsidian claws to slash its way through the fungal garden. Luckily, it was moving away from them. Raidon estimated its size equal to a giant.

The monk monitored the lumbering fungus hulk as they made their way along the ledge. Just as they reached the edge of the cavern, he saw the creature pause, then swivel its bulk. Before its polyp-sprouting face fully turned to regard the travelers, they ducked out of the wide cavern into the narrow confines of another tunnel.

Raidon doubted the creature could fit into the tunnel if it decided to follow. While the monk was confident of his prowess, he wondered if the techniques he favored against living foes might be useless on beasts composed of animate fungus. Could it even feel pain? Still, flying elbows crushed vegetable flesh as readily as animal.

Like before, the tunnel walls they traversed were smooth and white, except for the stain of fungus running in a widening stripe along the right wall. The blue, luminescent haze remained as thick as ever in the tunnel. Also . . .

"Adrik, bring your light closer, will you?" asked Raidon.

The sorcerer stepped over to Raidon with his lighted coin. Embedded in the wall were shells, bones, and teeth. More notable was a complete human figure, fully embedded in the wall and composed of the same white stone.

"What does this mean?" asked Raidon.

The sorcerer shook his head. "Magic, a massive concentration, once burned through here, but it is impossible to say how long ago."

"Did the elves do it when they created Stardeep? Or Sildëyuir?" asked Raidon.

Kiril, who'd paused at Raidon's first words, snorted. "This was here before Sildëyuir or the Traitor's dungeon were called out of the emptiness. Imagine the wizards' chagrin when they discovered the 'emptiness' was not so empty as everyone assumed. Races older than elves roam the worlds, and not all ancient events are recorded in history books."

Adrik brushed his right hand along the forehead of the encased figure.

The air cracked as a fossilized arm suddenly burst from the wall and snatched the sorcerer's wrist. Adrik screamed in concert with a wet grinding sound. The squeezing hand mashed the sorcerer's wrist like a piece of rotten fruit.

More loud cracks, and jagged lines appeared and lengthened on both walls. Pale limbs thrashed within widening fissures.

Raidon snatched the collapsing sorcerer and threw him over his shoulder. The hand gripping the sorcerer's wrist didn't relinquish its grasp but . . . there was little left for it to hold. Adrik was a familiar weight across the monk's back. Time to push concern from his mind and act in the moment.

"Go!" yelled Raidon as he dashed past Kiril. The swordswoman broke into a run, and Raidon led her down the empty but rapidly filling tunnel. The forms breaking free of the passage walls were—what? Undead? Undead whose flesh had so long rested beneath the earth that rotting skin, organs, and bone had become hard as stone. Or undead whose life was drained by some unspeakable ritual.

Within the featureless faces, Raidon perceived hunger, raw and unstoppable, multiplying with each new corpse that kicked its way out of the confining walls.

Adrik's heartbeat was thready, uncertain, but at least it persisted. It wouldn't for very long, though, if Raidon couldn't apply a tourniquet to the man's bleeding wrist.

The tunnel emptied to another cavern, smaller than the last one and roughly circular. Within this space the blue haze was thicker than ever. Broad black mushrooms sporting red pustules clustered at the room's hub. Looming among the ceiling-high toadstools was another ambulatory fungus hulk, like the shambling form Raidon had glimpsed in the previous cavern, but possibly bigger. Or perhaps it was the same one?

Limestone attackers flooded in from all sides, eroded and broken, possessed of an inarticulate fury. A wave of seven burst into the mushroom ring, intent on the towering creature within. The fungus hulk, its posture already hunched, lashed out a massive limb, batting all but two of the creatures across the chamber in arcing trajectories. The other two simply shattered.

"The hulk fights the undead!" exclaimed Raidon. An undead burst from the floor beneath him. He evaded a pale claw, barely maintaining the bleeding Adrik across his back. "Let's join it!"

Not waiting for confirmation from Kiril, Raidon plunged in amongst the woody stems, moving until he stood within ten paces of the native creature. The fungus hulk, possessing no eyes, nonetheless seemed to measure him in its regard. A heartbeat later Kiril joined them, her chest heaving as she fought for air after their mad dash.

The fungus hulk seemed to nod, a movement that involved most of its body, then it turned to stave off another wave of attackers.

Raidon let down Adrik, who moaned. "Hold on, friend," he told the sorcerer. Three more groups of stone-hard undead shuffled toward the mushroom cluster, plus five or six more lone shufflers. If he could snatch even an instant to care for his friend—

The monk dodged outside a white fist's trajectory. As the blow flashed past his head, he grasped it. Using the creature's own force, and assisting by twisting his hips, he swept the undead from its feet and into one of its advancing companions. The arm broke off the one he used as an improvised ballista, and the second toppled and fell.

Two more charged him, one straight on, the other advancing toward Raidon's right flank. The monk ran toward the closer one. Before it could wrap him in its rigid arms, he ran up its slablike front and poised on its head. His balance on the precarious perch was better than he'd imagined. The creature stumbled to a halt, confused. It batted at its own head, but Raidon evaded its grasp with well-timed hops. The other undead, intent on reaching him, careened full speed into the one upon which he stood.

The collision propelled Raidon into the air with double the force of a simple jump. He tucked his feet, accelerating himself into a midair spin. He drew his daito as he dived into a rolling landing, simultaneously sweeping the daito into the neck of another undead.

His blade, for all its provenance, became lodged in the fell thing's throat. Despite knowing better, he wasted a heartbeat vainly tugging at his grandfather's sword. He couldn't wrench it free! As he struggled, he was blindsided by an unseen slam.

Raidon staggered back, blinking stars from his eyes, his hand stinging where the daito's hilt had been torn away. A warm trickle began somewhere on his scalp. He was lucky the thing hadn't gotten a grip on him. If it had . . .

He looked for Adrik. Three undead obscured the sorcerer, battling Kiril, who'd apparently moved to guard the fallen man.

She'd drawn her sword! Argent flames raced along its length, threatening to mesmerize the monk. She sheared through one's arm, another's head, and cut the last in half. But five more jogged forward to take their place.

The fungus hulk remained standing, its head rising high above the scuffle. Its arms worked continually, battering, batting, and crushing the endless rush of undead. Heaps of broken stone were building all around it, piece by piece, and billows of powdery dust swirled in the blue haze. Wounds accumulated across its carapace, oozing bluish fluid.

The fungus hulk, Kiril, and the monk formed a rough triangle. Back to back, they were stemming the onslaught.

But for how long?

His skills had rarely been matched in his temple. But for all his expertise, his talent was better used against foes whose flesh was living, or at least supple. Of the many lessons he'd learned at Xiang, one was fundamental. In a fight, a defender either treated himself as the center and moved his foes around him, or he treated his foes as the center and moved around them. Raidon was a master of the former fighting style. Unfortunately, it was a style unsuited to fighting animated fossilized corpses.

He fell back, kicking, chopping, and evading until he stood only a few paces from Kiril. He yelled, "These creatures attack us without end! Are they truly undead, or is the earth itself forming and spewing them forth, mockeries of life meant to deprive us of ours?"

The ferocious but strangely vacant gaze of the swordswoman, as she methodically destroyed every monstrosity that strayed into her reach, gained some measure of animation. She muttered, "If they're being created as quickly as we can destroy them . . ."

"Then we are doomed if we make a stand here," finished Raidon, sidestepping the bull rush of a towering stone humanoid.

Kiril gritted her teeth and said, "Hear that, bastard? This fight is concluded already—you're just too dim-witted to recognize it." Raidon realized she spoke to her blade. "Ease up on me, and I can get us out of here. Should I die here, you'll be without a wielder. You'll have no vessel for your damned piety. We're close to Stardeep. Have you considered this uprising might be a ploy of the Traitor . . ."

She suddenly pirouetted in a full blazing circle, smashing half a dozen advancing figures to rubble. She continued, ". . . though these . . . undead or stoneborn . . . do not have the feel of something left behind by aberrations. They are something different. I doubt they are tethered to the Traitor's will."

"But they are no less a threat. We must flee someplace safer, somewhere we can tend Adrik. And, I tire," confessed Raidon. He didn't have a magic blade to feed him limitless strength, or to mend his bones and stitch his flesh when he miscalculated. The blood flowing from his scalp threatened to obscure vision in his left eye. Several cuts on his arms and chest threatened to spill blood, but were restrained from gushing only through his strict control and focus on his body. If one more stone fist penetrated his guard and smashed him, he might fall.

The animate stone with Raidon's daito embedded in its

neck trundled into Kiril, arms wide, undeterred by the length of steel. It knocked her back two paces. Her eyes lost their moment of coherence. She yelled in an oddly resonant voice, "Pretenders at life, feel the Cerulean Fire!" She lopped the arm, upper chest, and head from her attacker as if it were formed of clay, not stone.

The daito clattered free and Raidon retrieved it with an easy motion. He sheathed it immediately. He couldn't risk using it again, and more importantly, he did not want to view any damage upon the weapon from his brash attack.

Abruptly, a colossal hand reached down and plucked Adrik from the ground. Raidon yelled, but the fungus hulk turned and thundered clear of the mushroom grove. It ran toward an opening in a far wall, bowling over several stony attackers who failed to clear its path.

"Kiril, we must follow—that thing has Adrik!" The monk backed quickly toward the retreating fungus hulk. Had they been fooled by the hulk? Did it think the fallen sorcerer was food?

The swordswoman, with an obvious effort of will, also fell into a retreat. She called, "Follow it—the creature forges a path for us, knowingly or not!" Above her, the circling dragonet pealed an ongoing commentary on the battle raging below it.

As soon as Kiril committed to the withdrawal, Raidon turned and accelerated toward the hulk's broad back. Few things could hope to match the monk's unhindered speed. Dodging a few grasping arms, he caught up with the beast that clutched Adrik. He was right behind as it plunged into a wide tunnel.

The spore haze seemed to move with the creature. The light emitted by the haze gave everything an unearthly blue tint, a halo of sorts. By its illumination, Raidon saw the tunnel ahead was clear of stumbling fossils. So far.

The strange creature held the sorcerer securely in one arm, nestled against its chest like a mother might hold a babe. The pose lent Raidon sudden reassurance—for whatever reason, the fungus hulk was protecting Adrik. Intuition told him that as long as the creature lived, Adrik would be safe.

Raidon's shadow suddenly deepened and stretched ahead. Kiril and Angul must have entered the tunnel. He glanced back, saw the elf managing a pace quicker than he would have supposed, though her blade probably fed her speed. That sword, cursed though she proclaimed, was a relic of power unlike Raidon had ever seen.

In their wake, a flood of stone-clasped marauders followed.

Kiril held her sword like a standard. She marched beneath its haughty certainty. Angul burned like a brand, with a cerulean fire unique to it, illuminating the wide, high tunnel down which she coursed. The hard-edged light Angul shed fought with the softer, bioluminescent haze that clung to the fungus hulk, which bloomed along the same tunnel. The enigmatic creature yet gripped the sorcerer in a tender clutch. The beast bled ichor from scores of wounds. It had lost so much internal fluid without impairment Kiril wondered if the ichor was necessary for the creature's survival.

Such certainly wasn't the case for Adrik. A portion of the elf's mind, free of sword-influence, worried about the injured, too-quiet sorcerer. What did the great striding creature want with him? It didn't seem to wish any of them harm; rather, it had fallen in with them as if an old ally. Perhaps it was as concerned about the undead uprising in its quiet tunnels as they were. The horrors rumored to stalk Stardeep's under-dungeon had proved all too real. No wonder so few had ever managed to make the trek between Sildëyuir and the dungeon proper.

As she held Angul aloft, she noted on the back of her left hand the ugly burn scar she'd received more than half a decade ago, years after she'd set aside her duties as a Keeper. A too-close encounter with the magma heart of an active volcano. Nothing to do with Traitors, aberrations, ancient gods, undead, or fell sorceries. Seeing that scar pulled her more fully from Angul's mental grip. She took a deep breath. Gliding above, pacing her as it did so effortlessly these days, Xet chimed upon noticing her regard, as if to ask if she were returned to her right mind. She was, but she didn't sheathe the sword.

Behind them moved a cluster of ravenous fossils, and if her vigor evaporated, she'd fall behind into their remorseless clutch.

Then came a sound so hideous Kiril saw Raidon flinch. It was the sound of demons screaming torment, or the tortured cries of a thousand victims bawling out their last breath after days on the rack. It was a sound she hoped never to hear again.

The sound came from ahead. But no path was possible other than the direction of the hellborn screams. They continued their mad dash, and moments later, elf, half-elf, and fungus hulk emerged into a vast cavity.

The roof rose steadily upward and was crowned by a violet flame that stuttered and flared, one moment dim, one moment sun bright.

The light illuminated an army of hundreds, perhaps thousands of hard white figures in the midst of a terrible riot, all trying to crowd into a space beneath the light on narrow streets in the ruins of a blasted city.

Here and there, amidst the white backs and pale eroded heads, she saw the silhouettes of Knights. *By the Sign, how had they come here?* Many fought alone—isolated clashes surrounded by a sea of undead, each desperately swinging a weapon against a teeming mass that didn't register pain or loss. For each Knight she saw standing, she spied three more being ripped asunder by red-stained undead.

Despite the decimation of what must have been half an Empyrean company or more, the undead seemed more intent on reaching a central pyramid built of their stony brethren, which squirmed and buckled, but held its shape well enough to support a blood red throne of rough-cut crystal.

On one side of the throne a fossil, caped and crowned in violet luminescence, brandished a staff of deadly energy. Was it the Traitor, or some fell working created by the Traitor? No, Angul thought not. But yet . . .

On the other side of the ruby throne appeared a male star elf who wore the trappings of a Keeper! And in this man's hands, a blade whose outline was night's progenitor.

Something in Angul stuttered. It imparted to her, *That sword is somehow familiar . . .*

Kiril gasped. Angul had never before betrayed even a hint of uncertainty in the entire decade she'd wielded him.

At that moment, the fungus hulk gave voice to what sounded like a despairing moan. It crashed to the ground, turning its body as it buckled, protecting the man it held from its weighty fall. Kiril touched Angul's tip to the creature's lichen-covered carapace.

Dead, pronounced her blade. *A sacrifice for a righteous cause. Turn aside now, and go to that Keeper who yet holds faith with the Sign!*

Kiril winced. The blade's implication was that she, Kiril, did not hold such faith . . .

I will see us through this press, promised her sword. His fire fumed and grew, new strength rushed into her limbs, and surety of purpose infused her will. The last thing she saw as she plunged into the mob of animate neoliths was the monk bending to cradle Adrik's lolling head.

Chapter Twenty-Four

Stardeep, Underdungeon

Oppressive slumber relinquished its clotted hold, and Adrik opened his eyes. Tunnel walls rushed by on either side, bluish with luminescent haze. The hue seemed somehow familiar . . . such an effort to recall to mind why.

And what held him so snugly in arms overgrown with lichen and trailing tiny rootlets through the dank air?

He tried to voice his question, managing only to croak. The noise was enough to catch the attention of something above him—a great head swiveled forward and down to fix him with its . . . gaze? A lopsided, vegetable-like visage of wavering rhizomes and empty sensory pits. A vacant face, yet somehow, one that communicated intelligence.

Adrik was so far past exhaustion the face held little terror for him. He allowed his head to fall the other way, and saw that below, at the side of the great creature that clutched him, padded his friend from Telflamm, and the elf woman they'd met.

Unaccountably, sadness touched him. There were so many questions he had, like friends whose company he never tired of. But those friends were drifting away now. He sensed his curiosity dispersing to find a host whose life wasn't dripping away with each stuttering, slowing heartbeat.

What surprised him the most was the pain. The numbness began to give way to an agony unlike any he'd before imagined. Except for the pain right before the stern star elf guarding Stardeep's outer gate had healed him. Some lingering nilshai curse was released from the bonds that had temporarily held it. The taint began to bite into him anew.

He began to shriek. He tried to flail; the unrelenting grip of the fungus hulk held him fast. The tunnel walls continued to speed by, painted blue in the creature's spore halo.

He noted Raidon glancing anxiously up at him, but at that moment the tunnel disgorged into a ruin of arching white columns choked with thrashing fossils whose lives ended thousands of years, maybe hundreds of thousands of years ago. The blue light was drowned by a greater fire, the fury of which seemed to sear Adrik's eyes. The light reached him in shafts and rents obscured by crumbling spires and broken towers.

The swordswoman Kiril dashed forward. A hundred or more colliding stone figures turned from their rush down the too-narrow streets to fix their blind regard on the newcomers.

Adrik turned his face up, uncaring. For the pain was lifting, disappearing as suddenly as it had pounced upon his failing flesh. A calmness fell upon him, and into that pearly space came thoughts, wandering and unconcerned with the sprays of rock dust emerging from the cerulean whirlwind of Kiril as she moved into the ruined city chamber.

He saw a face, like his own, yet older. He recognized his brother Erik, fellow adventurer and wide wanderer in the world, who yet waited his return in Emmech. What plans they'd made! Once their fortune was secured, why, they'd disturb the councils of kings, confer with the elder mage of Shadowdale, and shake the foundations of the world! Ah, yes. He smiled to think on it. It saddened him, though, to imagine his brother waiting in vain. His heart could barely muster the strength to put one beat after the next. Then he envisioned his brother's grief when, long past Adrik's promised return date, Erik finally realized the truth.

The one he would see next, Adrik decided, would be the god whose domain was death. Would the great beast holding him transfer him directly into Kelemvor's hands? Memories, realizations, regrets—the time for all such activity was past. Accept it, Adrik, he chastened himself. Cease these mental acrobatics, compose yourself.

He thought then of a girl he'd once known. Her name . . . what was it? Chelsea, it was Chelsea, of course. A love cut down before its time when cruel disease had claimed her. His grief over her untimely demise was the final impetus that launched his adventures with his brother. With her end, nothing else could keep him home.

She awaits you now. And his childhood friend Macknar who'd drowned, and grandfather, too, most likely. Old friends, old loves. Would they greet him?

Suddenly Raidon was there before him, cradling his head. Was it real, or a vision? The monk's visage was scribed with compassion and regret.

Grieve not, he tried to say to the half-elf. Kelemvor comes, and shall deliver me to a place I do not fear to travel. Perhaps a place where I can continue to ask my questions.

His drifting thoughts persisted for one final heartbeat. Raidon's eyes, glassy with unwept tears, faded into a translucent mist, through which a golden light began to break, a celestial light whose brilliance washed Adrik Commorand away from the world.

Chapter Twenty-Five

Stardeep, Underdungeon

Bolts of consumptive fire leaped from the ancient one's immaterial staff. Telarian caught each blast on Nis's length, turning ravening flame to puffs of harmless ash.

More troubling was the Keeper's footing. Telarian's stance was a constant dance upon the biting heads and grasping hands of an imbecilic army of fossil zombies. Nis lent him an agility beyond the limits of mortal flesh, yet still he gasped and trembled on the cusp of failure. Cold calculation, another gift of his dark blade, revealed it was only a matter of time before a fatal blast or stony claw broke his defense. Then he would be pulled down by so many grasping hands his enhanced strength and blade-given healing would fail.

He attempted to close with the bolt-flinging lich, the creature both he and Nis agreed was responsible for the fossil uprising. Again, the undead creature was whisked away on its followers hands, while the elf's passage was thwarted by a frenzy of activity.

Had Telarian stood upon solid ground that wouldn't suck him down at its first opportunity, his own arsenal of prepared spells waiting patiently for release might have made the difference. *Waste no time on fantasies,* chastened Nis, *only on what is achievable.*

And so the unnamed lich and Telarian continued their erratic orbit around the throne, one vainly attempting to catch the other. And all the while, his insurance, the Empyrean Knights, died in the undead tide that surged around the central mound. He could hear their yells, their calls to each other, and their death screams.

His opponent suddenly darted its caved-in face away from Telarian. The diviner followed its gaze—and saw a blue flame outlining a sword twin in shape to his own. Angul! Wielded by Kiril, the blade flashed with an energy it had withheld when last Telarian beheld it, when he'd ordered a small troop of Knights to retrieve it.

Its power in Kiril's hands was nothing short of awe inspiring. She didn't attempt to bypass the massed petrified undead. She swept through them, reducing the creatures to so much dust within the vortex of Angul's flashing influence. He knew Nis could not equal what he now witnessed. Could it be, he wondered, that in Kiril's hands, lost love urges the soul fragment to greater heights?

Nis's failure to respond was answer enough.

The lich, too, recognized the greater threat that now approached. It redirected its bedeviling bolts toward Kiril. Telarian was tempted to yell out a warning, but was quelled by Nis: *Kill this creature while it is distracted.*

Telarian scrambled up onto the throne, and unlike his expectation, wasn't struck with some nameless curse. With a solid foundation underfoot, he was finally able to bring Nis to bear. Even as the lich realized its lapse, Nis's black length fell full upon its head.

The undead's crown of fire flared then failed beneath the stroke. But the fading crown provided Telarian's foe one last moment of salvation from Nis's penetrating blade. The lich countered with its staff, catching the diviner on the shoulder. Pain, quickly damped down by Nis, couldn't hide the smell of cooked meat.

The rending noise of stone being pulverized announced Kiril's arrival at the base of the pyramid of squirming bodies. She abandoned her sweep-and-smash technique in favor of agility. She ascended the active pile almost as nimbly as Telarian. He noted with interest that Angul's gifts to his wielder didn't include dexterity to the same degree that Nis did.

Kiril reached the summit and her eyes flitted across him, then Nis, but she turned her attention fully on the lich. She bellowed, "Suffer not abominations!" Her accompanying strike sheared the lich's staff into so many disintegrating tongues of flame. Even as it raised its fiery cape into great wings, as if to bear itself away, Kiril and Telarian simultaneously struck at it.

Angul stabbed low, into its abdomen, Nis swept high, at its head. The flaming wings collapsed and winked out. The unnamed king of fossils who'd sat alone beneath the violet flame for years uncounted tumbled down the mound, unsupported by its subjects. It struck the hard cobbles at the pile's base and shattered with a sound high and pure.

A wave of stillness was born in that instant, an expanding circle whose circumference quickly raced away in all directions, leaving in its wake hundreds of unmoving, eroded, cracked, broken, and blood-stained statues. Above, the violet flame guttered and winked out.

Here and there across the vast city, lantern light flickered to life as surviving Knights sought to coalesce back into a unified force.

Telarian wondered how many remained to service his greater scheme, but pushed such distractions from his head for the moment. Kiril demanded all his attention and wit as she stared coolly at him, her features highlighted by Angul's blue fire. He yet held Nis, whose length remained night's own domain.

Sheathe me, instructed Nis. As always, Telarian obeyed.

The diviner blinked, and sudden fear clawed at his guts. She'd cut him down! She—

Kiril sheathed Angul in one easy motion, plunging them into darkness. Into that absence of light, Kiril spoke, her tone strangely even. "What news of the Traitor, Keeper of Stardeep?"

Telarian called up a quick spell of radiance and set it to dance on the throne top. In that glow, he lowered himself from the throne to stand on equal, if uneven, footing with the swordswoman.

He replied, "The Traitor strains at its chains in a fashion never foreseen. It has assumed mental domination over my fellow Stardeep Keeper! Things have nearly fallen completely apart in Stardeep's Inner Bastion."

"The compromised Keeper," said Kiril, "that would be Telarian? I've heard his name from the lips of the blood-flecked spy he hired to steal Angul! Telarian, the one who tried to lure me to Stardeep with his promise that . . ." She gulped, and sudden moisture welled in Kiril's eyes.

The diviner frowned, swallowed his fear, and said, "You've been partly misled—it is Keeper Delphe, still ensconced in Stardeep, who has fallen wholly into the Traitor's grasp."

Kiril's eyes narrowed as she said, "Which means *you* are Telarian?"

He raised conciliatory hands. "I am—but forget what you think you know, and listen—"

The woman stepped forward and jabbed him in the chest with a pointing finger, asking, "And what of Nangulis? Was that your lie?"

"Hear me out, and you'll learn the truth."

"Out with it, then!"

He licked his lips. "Delphe, once under the Traitor's control, knew the one implement that could end her new master's escape was Angul. Thus she sought to steal him away from his wielder, and failing that, kill you and take Angul. To further confuse the matter, she used my name to shield her identity should her scheme ever fall apart. As it has!"

"So Nangulis . . ."

"Has not returned. I am so sorry," said Telarian. Though he couldn't produce Nangulis, he could offer her the next best thing.

"However, what was once Nangulis has stirred."

She looked back, hope and suspicion battling for control of her features.

"Just as Angul holds one half of Nangulis's fractured soul, Nis holds the remainder!" He drew forth Nis once more, the blade's cool touch returning his confidence threefold and quashing his fear beneath its black weight.

Kiril's eyes grew round. She murmured, "But how is that possible? When we forged Angul, we pulled from Nangulis all purity and zeal, discarding the rest . . ."

"Not discarded. Cynosure encapsulated all that remained of Nangulis, and preserved it against future need. A need that materialized when I realized Delphe had fallen into shadow."

"How?"

"I worked in secret, forging the blade beneath Delphe's very nose, until Nis was complete. At the last, she discovered my intent. I'm afraid that with Cynosure under her control, I was forced to flee Stardeep. But even with Stardeep's sentient construct set against me, with Nis in hand, I was able to escape. She'd closed the Causeway after sending out those few Knights she suborned to ravage the countryside. The only place I could flee with the remaining Knights still uncorrupted and loyal to the Cerulean Seal was down, into Stardeep's underdungeons."

Kiril gave a slow nod, her eyes still fixed to Nis's darkling span. *She believes,* imparted the blade to Telarian.

The diviner continued. "But Delphe's reach has grown long. With the Traitor's help, she roused the relic consciousness entombed here." Telarian made a wide gesture across the chamber. "If you hadn't come when you did, it is possible that I and the last of the Knights would have died, thus ensuring the Traitor's escape."

The swordswoman looked down at Angul, still sheathed at her side, then back up to Nis, and asked, "Can the two halves . . . ever be reunited? Can Nangulis live again?"

"It is more than mere possibility. In order to see Delphe destroyed and the Traitor's escape quashed, I believe that we must combine the blades at the edge of the Well—combine the two halves of Nangulis's sundered soul. The combined blade will possess the soul-forged traits of both weapons, and I suspect, possess more power than the sum of its parts."

Kiril smiled through sudden tears. Telarian returned her smile, but his thoughts were elsewhere. Like the Knights he'd already slain, and Delphe, whose death was now assured with Angul wielded against her. Kiril, too, would find herself a corpse, kicking out her last strength on Nis's cruel length. Only such sacrifices could avert the far greater disaster his vision foretold.

He gave a small sigh. Being the unacknowledged savior of Faerûn's mortal races was soul-trying work.

Chapter Twenty-Six

Stardeep, Underdungeon

Gage's third and last alchemical light was nearly exhausted. The thief gave the glass another shake anyway. A sickly yellow radiance seeped from the cold, egg-shaped vessel, less than a candle's glow. Light or dark, he was well and truly lost. He wandered caverns whose hollow ways didn't even run through the stones of the earth, but instead, through a metaphysical realm Gage did not and probably could not fully comprehend. Friendless, too, and likely hunted.

"Pity your poor adherent, Akadi." He grunted. Could the Lady of the Winds even hear his prayer? He doubted she who ruled the high places of Faerûn listened to the pleas of those who scurried through its subterranean tunnels, let alone through tunnels of an echo plane.

After another hundred or so steps down the smooth, white passage, the bulb's light noticeably weakened. Hardly bright enough for him to see more than a few paces ahead, but likely a perfect waypoint for giant stone spiders or demons nurturing a grudge . . .

When the radiance failed utterly, Gage returned the bulb to its pouch. He sighed, and hoped his anxiety over the light failing was worse than the reality.

He extended his left hand until his fingers brushed the cold, silky passage wall. In his right he clutched a dagger, ready to plunge it into whatever beast emerged from the unrelieved darkness that smothered his eyes. He could almost imagine the lightlessness was a whisper-thin blanket, covering him but not hindering his movement. If he could just rend it or wipe its sense-depriving swaddling from his eyes . . .

He shuffled along the tunnel, perhaps covering miles, perhaps far less. He chuckled, recalling how difficult it was to estimate time and space in the starry realm. He hadn't known how easy he'd had it then.

Ahead, a gleam not unlike a star's sparkle arrested his progress. He paused only a moment, then with his heart in his mouth, he doubled his pace, one hand yet sliding along the wall for guidance. The tiny light was moving. Throwing caution to the winds, he began to sprint. Perhaps the Lady of Winds was with him after all—despite his speed, he managed to catch himself when the tunnel ended suddenly in the side wall of a vast abyss.

He'd seen the reflected light of lanterns moving along the floor of the huge space. Lanterns! People moved far below on the floor of the cavern, wending between collapsed and disintegrating structures. He'd discovered a buried city. More importantly, he'd found people! A dozen of them, at least, by the number of lanterns.

Humanoids in shining armor, a few on horses . . . he sucked in his breath. A contingent of Knights, like those that attacked from across that misty Causeway!

Gage allowed himself a tight-lipped smile of satisfaction as he prepared to descend the slick walls to the level of the Knights. It was clear he'd nearly reached the edge of Stardeep proper, or at least those who could lead him to it. And ultimately, back to Kiril.

Perhaps she numbered among the milling figures below, who picked their way across a debris field composed of . . . broken and blood-stained statues?

Raidon Kane buried Adrik Commorand in the common grave the surviving Knights prepared for their fallen brethren.

Brief words of remembrance were uttered by the shocked and confused survivors, abrupt and unceremonious; Stardeep had fallen to the mad Keeper Delphe, and little time could be spared for ritual. Better to take vengeance against Delphe for her crimes than speak empty words at the edge of a grave. Time for proper grieving could wait until the dungeon stronghold was retaken.

The monk appreciated the sentiment. He placed his store of Long Jing, tea so fine it would be suitable for an emperor, upon the pale but peaceful chest of Adrik. Raidon murmured, "You were a friend to me, and I . . ." His throat constricted suddenly, but he continued, "I shall miss you. I . . . apologize for not being able to defend you. Your memory will follow me all the rest of my days." As he spoke, he wondered, for his sentiment rang with the force of prophecy.

Then white stones were placed to cover the shallow grave. More and more stones were positioned, one atop the next, until a high mound was formed marking the final resting place of star elves sworn to protect Stardeep, and one human sorcerer who had strayed into a realm fey and lethal.

Telarian intoned, "I christen this mound 'Cállambëa.' " The attending Knights murmured their appreciation.

Raidon whispered to Kiril, "Does that name have special meaning?"

She replied, "It could be translated as 'place of heroes' in a Sildëyuir dialect."

Finally the Knights quit the chamber of the buried city. Kiril rode behind the vanguard in the company of Keeper Telarian, on a steed that had lost its rider to the undead aggression. Raidon followed behind, on foot.

The monk observed the conversation between the estranged Keeper and the current. Both shared features Raidon realized must be common to star elves. He possessed similar features, diluted as those traits were by his Shou humanity. Mighty blades, too, each wore securely sheathed at their belts. Raidon mistrusted the darkness that blurred out from Telarian's sword, but Kiril seemed to accept it.

In fact, the swordswoman seemed overly eager to hear all Telarian had to say, so long as they touched on the possibility of Nis's and Angul's dissolution. This would somehow lead to Nangulis's miraculous return. Nangulis, the man whose soul had been wrenched into two pieces to forge a modern artifact. Raidon wasn't clear how Nangulis's dead body might be conjured up and revived in order to contain and stitch together the two sundered halves of his soul. Nor was Raidon confident of the sanity Nangulis might possess if such a thing came to pass—his experience with Angul didn't speak to mental stability.

Telarian glossed over such details, and Kiril allowed him to do so, aglow as she was in the possibility. The monk supposed she knew more of the metaphysics behind reversing the transformation than he did. After all, as his master used to mutter in Xiang, "From form to formless and from finite to infinite." He'd taken that mantra to mean that expectations should not be confined by the limitations of imagination.

Raidon was put off by Telarian's cold, emotionless tone and manner, especially when speaking of Nis, Angul, or Nangulis. Was the man devoid of emotion, or did he control his inner self so thoroughly? His voice wasn't that of a master of focus, whose timbre implied calm confidence. No, it was a voice devoid of the least hint of empathy.

The monk endeavored to watch Telarian with an especially sharp eye, despite the man wearing a uniform whose symbol was the duplicate of his forget-me-not. Kiril hadn't thought to mention it to the Keeper in her enthusiasm over Nangulis's imminent return, and Raidon decided to let the issue lie for the moment. If the man proved his worth, the time would come to reveal his mother's amulet.

The returning Knights traveled without incident. When they had almost reached the cusp of the Outer Bastion, Delphe unleashed her counterattack.

An elf of the vanguard, who Telarian had sent statues ahead, returned. He reported that free-running defender statues blocked further progress. The scout said the statues were willing to parley and would withhold their strength for the moment.

Kiril began, "Free running? Does that mean—"

"We're too far from Stardeep for Cynosure's intelligence to inhabit them. Free-running statues have only the intelligence of children, though apparently these bear a message from Delphe. Lies to slow us down," concluded Telarian.

"Still, I'd hear them, if only to gauge the deceit of the crazed Keeper."

Telarian frowned but nodded. He urged his mount forward. Kiril followed.

They passed the Knights of the vanguard and saw ahead a meeting of several tunnels, which created a space wide enough for five figures to stand shoulder to shoulder.

Iridescent sparks danced across the rigid forms of five humanoid constructs. Wearing thick metal plates bolted over their stone-sculpted bodies, their granite strength was obvious to any onlooker. Eight or nine feet tall, each of the defender's hands were curled into gargantuan mauls.

"Say your piece," instructed Kiril. She was ready to draw Angul at any hint of betrayal. She murmured to her blade, "Remember, these constructs are under the thumb of a Keeper who's betrayed her oath. Don't hold back like you did at the Causeway, or the aberrations win."

The central golem took a pace forward and spoke. "Telarian, I know what you seek. Rethink your choice and your life can be spared. Let us resolve this as the friends we've been for so long. Continue on the path you've set, and you'll find death your only reward."

Telarian glanced at Kiril and said, "Delphe is truly mad if she believes that such simple threats of bodily harm will persuade me to throw in with her and the Traitor!"

Kiril nodded. It seemed a sad ploy. Did some hidden ambush wait in the wings? Best not wait for it. She stood in her stirrups, but before she could draw Angul, she was distracted by Telarian.

His eyes were closed. One hand was out, the other resting on the hilt of his undrawn blade. From his mouth, words issued. He swayed in time to the words, now sounding like a chant. His pronunciation was deep and breathy, like the mournful cries of the wind through distant forest eaves. Tiny prickles needled across her scalp. The diviner was tapping strong magic.

She looked at the defenders. They seemed oblivious to Telarian's antics. Delphe had not overruled the constructs' inborn sympathies for Keepers. Thus, they held their power until the first blow was struck. Kiril refrained from drawing Angul. Perhaps the diviner could unleash a spell strong enough to impair the free-runners.

Still muttering arcane syllables, Telarian's enigmatic eyes

finally opened and a smile ghosted across his still-chanting lips.

Several heartbeats passed, then several more. All the while, the sound of distant wind grew louder, as if approaching, merging more and more fully with the diviner's cadence and pitch. The defenders repeated their offer, too dim-witted to understand that great forces gathered against them. Kiril wondered what Telarian was brewing.

"What—" began Kiril. A scream of tornadic wind drowned out the rest of her question, but also served as an answer.

All the fury of a summer storm was squeezed into a space that was orders of magnitude too small for it, pouring from the side tunnel to the golems' left. Sight and sound were instantly shrouded in electric streamers of white and gray. The roar was a physical thing, pushing back Kiril and Telarian. Their hair and the steeds' manes blew straight back, attempting to flee the lightning-laced vortex. Kiril backed her mount a few paces, though Telarian held his ground, his arms out, his words lost in the howl.

Finally, the storm issued out of the chamber through a tunnel on the opposite side.

The clearing air revealed eroded stone, blackened marks where lightning scoured the walls, and of the free-running defenders, no sign. The righthand passage echoed with the sound of fleeing winds, growing fainter and fainter in the distance.

Kiril worked her mouth, as if to relieve pressure felt when descending a mountain, and said, "A nice trick." She sat back in the saddle.

Telarian relinquished his grip on Nis's hilt, took a shaky breath, and nodded. "Lucky for the golems they are soulless artifacts."

"Why so?"

"Else it would have blown their spirits clear of the flesh."

Kiril's brow furrowed. "That smacks of necromancy."

"Kiril, as you know more than most, evildoers should not be spared their owed punishment."

"Where do souls taken go?"

"The wind bears the souls for eternity across all the planes of existence. When you hear the 'cries of the wind,' you may be hearing the voices of those who already enjoy such redemption."

The swordswoman's mouth hardened into a thin line. She'd killed innocents, to be sure, but those wrongly slain by Angul's too-swift judgment were free of further consequence. What Telarian described sounded too cruel for any but aberrations, whose souls were unclean. She hoped he would never use such a thing on a live creature. But as he said, the golems didn't suffer so.

Kiril asked, "Where did you learn such a bastardly curse? Such spells do not lie within the constraints of the Cerulean Sign."

"Are you then a spellcaster?" Telarian snapped back, his gaiety suddenly evaporated in cold venom.

She bit back the attack that teetered on her lips. Instead of calling him a vomit-stained cholera carrier who didn't know his arse from his face, she said, "We'll discuss this later, after I spit Delphe on Angul's unforgiving tip."

Chapter Twenty-Seven

Stardeep, Throat

The mirror revealed three of Cynosure's defenders in the spacious Parade Hall outside the Knights' Barracks. Each defender faced east, looking through the high archway that opened on the downward-plunging paths of the underdungeon. Delphe wondered what had become of the five free-runners she'd sent into the tunnels.

She glanced to the neighboring mirror, which showed an empty section of underdungeon tunnel immediately beyond the Parade Hall. If Telarian bested the five golems she'd earlier dispatched, he would return up this ramp. The moment she was able to scry him in the Throat was the moment she could begin to bring more substantial firepower to bear on the insane Keeper.

Delphe sat in her crystalline control chair facing the mirrored walls, few of which reflected the actual contents of the Throat. Waiting. Watching. The fires in the Well were muted, as if also waiting. That which the fires contained would know soon enough whether its external agent, Telarian, would fail or succeed in his lunatic plan.

"Something comes," noted Cynosure's voice from above.

Light grew in the tunnel, and into that light rode the vanguard of the Empyrean Knights. The free-running defenders had failed to hold Telarian from returning. She sighed.

The passage sloping up toward the Parade Hall grew wide, and the Knights took advantage of this feature to form up into a wedge.

Telarian next rode into view. Seeing him, now that she fully realized his twisted actions and ambitions, was difficult. To see that blade riding so nonchalantly upon his hip and understand its true origin . . . Delphe couldn't help breathing out a harsh, rasping breath. He looked so normal—how was it that his spirit had given in to darkness?

Next to Telarian rode a star elf woman not liveried as a Knight, though she rode a Knight's horse, and was herself armed and armored as a warrior.

"Cynosure, who is that woman?"

"Delphe, I know her, for I once served with her. She is Kiril Duskmourn," replied the sentient idol. "She was Keeper of the Outer Bastion before Telarian. I aided her as I aid you and Telarian now."

Delphe's eyes went round. "Kiril!" She had assumed the former Keeper long dead. What strange route had brought her to Telarian's conniving side?

The pitch of Cynosure's voice rose slightly as he added, "And the blade sheathed at her side is none other than Angul, the Blade Cerulean."

"By the Sign!" she gasped. "If she yet carries that relic, why hasn't she already sundered Telarian's head from his shoulders? Surely Angul can scent an agent of the Traitor!"

"They seem to have reached an accord."

"That makes no sense," Delphe snapped.

She saw Kiril speak, and Telarian nod in agreement. No

sound came through, but it seemed Cynosure was correct; the two were on friendly terms. Delphe blinked, groping unsuccessfully for some explanation of the relationship the mirrors displayed.

"Could it be," wondered Cynosure, "that the proximity of Nis confuses Angul's senses? The dark blade encompasses what was once a portion of itself. The dark, twisted portion, granted, but possibly enough to act as a mirror—Angul sees only itself in its amoral twin."

Delphe rubbed her chin, considering. Cynosure's conjecture was a real possibility. And if true . . . then Kiril wasn't truly in collusion with Telarian. Indeed, perhaps she rode with the diviner due to misinformation. Unless Kiril and Angul were now the Traitor's pawns—an unlikely event—they believed whatever lies Telarian fed them.

"Cynosure, I need to talk with Kiril. Immediately. Preferably without the Keeper of the Outer Bastion hearing our conversation. Is that possible?"

"I can try, Delphe."

"Telarian, ask the Knights to pause. An idea occured to me," said the former Keeper who rode at his side.

Telarian called a halt and warned the vanguard, "Do not advance until I give the word!" The Knights prepared themselves for a charge up the slope and into Stardeep proper via the Parade Hall.

"What idea?"

For answer, Kiril turned in her saddle and called back along the narrowing tunnel, "Raidon Kane, can we speak?"

The odd-looking half-elf who'd displayed amazing martial skill walked forward, his face the picture of calm acceptance, as always. Telarian frowned.

"Raidon, we're close enough to Stardeep's heart that you

might be able to use your mother's forget-me-not to bypass its defenses."

Raidon nodded, gave Telarian an appraising glance, and withdrew an amulet from beneath the collar of his silk jacket.

"A Cerulean Sign!" gasped Telarian. Alarm skittered through his mind. How had he missed that?

"Yes," agreed Kiril, "Raidon keeps a Sign, for him a family heirloom. In any case"—she waved away the questions forming on Telarian's lips—"with a Sign, we can wrench Stardeep's point-to-point transfer system from Cynosure long enough to deliver ourselves directly to Delphe."

"An excellent idea," exclaimed Telarian. "Let me see, and I shall attempt to do as you suggest." He held his hand out to the half-elf. Raidon looked askance at him, making no move to comply.

Kiril shook her head, said, "Raidon has held the Sign for years—it is firmly attuned to him, and him alone. You'd have no chance of using it without a lengthy bonding period, and we don't have time for that."

True, of course. He just wanted the Sign out of the hands of someone over whom he had no leverage. And the appearance of such a potent bane against the Traitor was, again, not something he had foreseen. Anxiety, his old friend, took his cold palm in its own unsettling grip.

Kiril continued. "Even without training, Raidon should be able to use it now that we're so close. Try it," she bid the half-elf. "Try to visualize the seams of arcane energy that infuse Stardeep. Try to . . . mentally pluck one and bring it to you."

Raidon's eyes unfocused slightly, and he said, "I sense something of what you say. And"—he looked up, pointing with his free hand—"a questing shaft of light even now reaches out to us. It . . . is here!"

Telarian choked.

A voice rang out—Delphe's voice. It said, "Kiril Duskmourn, gone from Stardeep these long years. Why have you thrown in with this deserter of the Cerulean Sign's ideals, he who even now plots to overthrow centuries of captivity and release the Traitor?"

Kiril started on hearing the voice. Delphe's voice, she supposed. So this was the woman who had defiled the oath and sought to aid the Traitor? She didn't sound insane. Of course, the truly mad rarely did, until you drew them out and exposed the foundations of their reasoning.

"Muddle-minded witch," declared Kiril, a sneer coming to her face, "don't insult me with your lunatic imprecations. What promise did the Traitor make that you'd join him in his defilement?" As she spoke, the swordswoman looked Raidon in the eyes and gestured sidewise with her head. She asked a question with her movement; could the monk figure out how to trigger a transfer? Perhaps she could keep Delphe distracted with meaningless babble. The demented enjoyed describing their aims, perhaps to justify a guilty conscience, or so stories suggested.

Raidon's brows furrowed in concentration as he gazed into the symbol on his amulet.

A disbelieving gasp came from thin air. Then Delphe said, "You believe I've thrown in with the Traitor while you stand with Telarian, whose mind is poison and whose hands are stained with the blood of Empyrean Knights?"

"Yes, I stand with him, but don't waste your breath with falsehoods and ravings. I know your mind has cracked. Your lies stain my ears, and the weak, craven cowardice I hear in your voice is near to making me vomit!"

Despite actual rancor, Kiril was more concerned with the

monk's progress. She watched as Raidon continued to stare into the Sign. A faint, bluish glow woke within the potent trinket. Raidon was accomplishing something!

Delphe's voice came back, heated but under control. "Has it occurred to you that perhaps—just perhaps—Telarian is the one who has become the agent of the Traitor? Perhaps he 'stains your ears.' What do you say to that?"

"Unlikely." Kiril snorted as she glanced at Telarian. The diviner rolled his eyes. Kiril continued. "Because he carries half of Nangulis's soul in a blade all his own. It was Nangulis, if you remember, whose sacrifice is the reason the Traitor doesn't already walk free." Kiril wanted to urge Raidon to hurry, but she didn't want to make Delphe suspicious. If Delphe knew what Raidon attempted, she could ask Cynosure to deactivate point-to-point transfers.

"Kiril," came the response, incredulity clear in the tone, "recall to mind the reason not all of Nangulis's soul was incorporated into Angul. Only those parts aligned with duty, purity, and self-sacrifice for a higher ideal were capable of empowering the Blade Cerulean—as you must remember. Think! It is not simply the 'unused' parts of Nangulis's soul that embodies Nis. Nis is composed of all the hidden, repressed, nihilistic portions of Nangulis, urges and neuroses all mortals share. When Telarian forged Nis, he drew from all those negative aspects and created a blade fit for a sociopath."

Kiril frowned and looked again at Telarian. The man shrugged at the ridiculousness of Delphe's claim. He whispered, "She merely seeks to sow uncertainty. We should advance." Despite his words, Kiril saw a tightening about the man's eyes.

"Think, Kiril—what would such a blade actually want?" exhorted the disembodied Keeper's voice. "Nis is Angul's opposite. Just as the Blade Cerulean seeks to destroy all abominations, the Blade Umbral seeks to release them!"

Kiril, ignoring Raidon to focus solely on Telarian, said, "The woman makes a point. When Nangulis and I discussed his—"

As the skin falls from a shedding snake, so did all expression slough from Telarian's face as he grasped Nis's hilt. He dragged forth its length and swept the blade around to decapitate Kiril. As he attacked, he said in an emotionless voice, "Delphe knows nothing."

Raidon watched with wonder as color returned to his amulet, filling in the gap so dark it seemed to encroach on the symbol of the white tree at its center. This was the color the forget-me-not possessed almost the whole time it had been in his possession. How many times had he pulled it out and thought of his missing parent? He rubbed his fingers across the tiny overlapping inscriptions, briefly wondering if his mother had known their meaning.

To his eyes, a wisp of luminous blue-white light flowed down the ramp, a languid rivulet that terminated in the air above him, Kiril, and Telarian. The strand was a connection!

Voices passed up and down the slender stream of radiance, but the Sign lent him certainty that far more than mere sound could be transferred via the magical circuit, if only it was properly tapped.

Kiril's voice and the voice of the female Keeper contended back and forth, but Raidon paid their meanings no heed. His focus obscured everything but the strand. The longer he stared into its light, the more he understood. Yes, he thought, I see . . .

Raidon grasped the end of the strand and mentally pulled.

The rearguard Knight fell into unconsciousness without alerting his compatriots who rode ahead. Gage guided the man's body down from his mount with one hand, holding the steed's reigns with his other so it wouldn't bolt.

In remarkably few breaths, Gage exchanged his dun-colored garments for the Knight's heavier, shiny raiment. He was frankly surprised at how light and flexible the armor was. As he mounted the huffing steed, he wondered if all elven chain was of such quality. Or, maybe the armor he'd just pilfered possessed a special quality known only to star elves. Perhaps he would keep the improvised disguise, if he survived. He mounted up.

He pushed forward through the trailing star elf ranks without difficulty—these Knights had lost too many of their company to adhere to usual protocol. They rode, but were barely cognizant of anything other than what they feared lay ahead. He smiled within his reflective helm. He was imagining the look on Kiril's face when he pushed up the visor and revealed his identity.

Ahead, the tunnel widened. A tangle of Knights gathered above on a sloping ramp, their gazes distracted by something behind them . . . it was Kiril! She was engrossed in an argument, perhaps with Raidon Kane, who stood to one side of Kiril's steed, or with the scowling elf who rode on her opposite side. Gage was close enough to hear passion in Kiril's voice, but not the words spoken.

Gage moved closer until he was only a few paces behind she who he'd tracked so far. Kiril turned to address the mounted elf. The man, apparently not liking what he heard, pulled forth a length of sword-shaped night. Gage thought he yelled, but all sound was eclipsed by a sudden, ear-piercing rumble that pulsed forth from the amulet the monk held high. Another heartbeat, and on the heels of the tumult came a flash that erased Gage's vision.

Gage yelled as his steed and saddle fell away beneath him. He fell into swirling, sky blue incandescence.

Kiril ducked under Telarian's treacherous attack, groping for Angul's hilt . . .

Empyreal dawn blossomed, brilliant and all-encompassing. She couldn't see a thing in the ubiquitous blaze. She felt herself pulled up and into a maw of light.

Despite being blind and off balance, her questing hand found and drew the Blade Cerulean. With Angul in hand, her eyes cleared. Her steel-shod feet found purchase on steady ground. The sweet kiss of Angul lent Kiril magnificent conviction.

She recognized that Raidon had successfully transferred her, himself, and all who had been near her directly into Stardeep's heart. Despite his lack of practice, the monk had managed to exclude steeds from the trip.

Kiril stood in the Inner Bastion, in the very Throat of the Well, where the Traitor's constricting fires reflected up the central shaft.

And not five paces from her stood Telarian, recovering from the rough transit as quickly as she, wielding Angul's dark echo. Telarian, whose surprise attack with Nis revealed him as the true agent of the hoary aboleths. She had unwittingly brought him into the dungeon's most protected chamber. Kiril realized Delphe had secured the inmost cell against entry not because Delphe was the Traitor's pawn, but to prevent Telarian from attempting whatever devious scheme he obviously intended. And like a bumbling fool, she'd asked Raidon to puncture those defenses.

Other figures blurred the edges of Kiril's perception, but her awareness, and Angul's, was reserved for the diviner.

Likewise, Telarian ignored the scrabbling forms of Knights who'd been pulled along with them into the Throat. Anyone not wielding a soul relic wasn't worth any attention at the moment.

Kiril yelled, "Prepare to be sundered from your sins!"

Telarian said nothing, nor did he move. The diviner stood with Nis drawn and held out before him in a relaxed, casual guard. His face was absent of the least hint of emotion. His posture was half-turned toward the Well. Indeed, the tip of his right boot overhung the shaft by a finger's length.

Kiril closed the five paces separating her from her target. She brought Angul around high and hard, intending to beat away the dark blade in a shearing swipe whose trajectory would ultimately end in Telarian's heart.

At the instant of contact, when Angul's fiery length struck Nis's sooty edge, Kiril lost her grip on the hilt.

She gasped, flailing after the blade that suddenly moved under its own power. Unexpectedly bereft of Angul's physical and mental scaffolding, she tumbled headlong across the floor, her body knocking Telarian down at the knees; he'd also lost hold of Nis.

Turning, Kiril saw the two blades hanging unsupported in the air, still crossed as they'd struck. Fire leached from Angul into Nis's lightless expanse, while darkness bled from the Blade Umber back to Angul. The crossed blades were like the wings of a hybrid angel, half-fallen from some celestial sphere, uncertain whether it would leap back up into the starry firmament, or dive down into the depths of the beckoning elemental chaos.

With a deliberate inevitability, the two blades scissored to form a single shaft of steel. Where there had been two, now one sword hung unsupported in the air, burning with a black-tinged fire, both darker than night and brighter than day.

Chapter Twenty-Eight

Stardeep, Throat

As Delphe blinked away the afterglow of the cerulean flash, half a dozen figures dropped out of the fading light.

Most of the intruders collapsed prone onto the hard floor of the Throat. Two retained their feet. Delphe recognized both. One was Telarian. The other, slim hipped and broad shouldered, was Kiril. Each bore a dire weapon, and each seemed eager to engage the other.

"Delphe," rang Cynosure's gravelly voice. "Containment breach in progress! Deploying physical safeguard."

The stone and crystal statue poised above the Well, unmoving in all the time Delphe had served Stardeep as a Keeper, suddenly fell free, plunging from the ceiling like a dropped anchor, flashing past the lip, its arms outstretched and its eyes trailing the light of Cynosure's focused consciousness.

From deep in the Well boiled a fount of racing purple fire. A sure sign the containment layer had collapsed, or was on the verge of doing so. The falling construct and rising plane of fire met in an explosion of white light.

Delphe leaped from her control chair, one hand grasping her Cerulean Sign, the other already essaying gestures that opened hidden arcane geometries. With a sick feeling clawing at her gut, she dropped a slab of invisible force flat across the lip of the Well, hoping it would buy Cynosure time to stem the breach below while she dealt with the situation above. How had Telarian and so many others penetrated Stardeep's very heart? Obviously, it was some sort of back door set up by Telarian—one more betrayal of his trust. However, this was not the time to contemplate failed security.

She returned her attention to the interlopers. Of the six or so intruders, many were Knights caught up in the transfer. Some few of these were groaning and blinking, beginning to rise.

"Oh, by the Sign," breathed Delphe as her eyes tracked back to Kiril, Angul blazing in her fists, and across from her Telarian, Nis darkening the chamber with only his presence. Kiril yelled a challenge; Telarian sneered. They were going to fight! In all Stardeep's history, had two Keepers ever come to blows?

Telarian and Kiril crossed swords.

The explosion of noise and light that followed knocked both wielders to the floor with the insensate Knights. Upon touching, the blades recognized the missing portions of the other. They merged, creating a new entity: a union of the soul-forged swords Angul and Nis. The new-minted weapon pulsed with fell energy, far outstripping its shape and mortal origins.

The Keeper of the Outer Bastion regained his feet. Next to him, Kiril raised herself to her knees. When her eyes found the linked weapons, she ceased all action except to stare at Angul-Nis as if entranced. Telarian moved past her, paying the swordswoman not the least bit of concern. Kiril's hands remained passively at her sides—she made no move to stop the diviner.

Delphe called out, "No!" as Telarian grasped for Angul-Nis's hilt.

A winged creature the size of a small dog dived at Telarian from somewhere behind Delphe's left shoulder. It must have arrived in the Throat with Kiril, Telarian, and the Knights. It screeched a strangely musical call and raked Telarian's hands with crystalline claws. The diviner snatched his hands back from the hilt. The tiny opalescent dragon took the opportunity to scratch at Telarian's eyes. He fell back from the hovering dragonet and the dangling blade, swatting and cursing.

The crystal beast belled a tiny cry of triumph as it stooped on the retreating diviner again. Then a thread of black flame extended from Angul-Nis, wavering and winding through the air like a worm in its hole. The dragonet didn't see the thread, so intent was it on Telarian. When the thread touched the tiny flying creature's shoulder, the dragonet squawked, then clattered to the ground, trailing dark smoke as it rolled.

The diviner laughed and advanced once more to stand before the free-hanging sword. Unimpeded, Telarian gripped Angul-Nis's hilt.

His eyes dissolved in night and his hair stood on end, each shaft seeming to project black-tinged fire. Telarian raised Angul-Nis above his head in a gesture of triumph. He began to laugh.

Delphe launched a silver mote trailing white sparks at the diviner, an enchantment of bone-binding. Telarian turned, still laughing, and deflected the spell right back at her on the flat of his blade!

She thrust her Sign amulet forward, intercepting the turned spell in a burst of crimson sparks. She blinked away the afterglow in time to see the diviner charging across the twenty paces that separated them.

Delphe screamed, still holding forth her Cerulean Sign, hoping to ward the diviner away with its potent symbology. If he was the Traitor's cat's-paw, the Sign should—

Telarian swept Angul-Nis through her hand. Color leached suddenly from the world as Delphe saw three fingers and half the Sign spin away from her palm.

Dawning shock replaced her strength, and she fell. Telarian chuckled and moved toward the lip of the Well, holding Angul-Nis high. Delphe tried to chant a spell, call on Cynosure to engage Telarian, or beseech one of the reeling Knights for aid. Desire collapsed to reality, and instead she clutched desperately at her maimed hand with the other, attempting to apply a tourniquet before her life bled out completely. Just a pace away, the light in her severed amulet dimmed and flickered out.

Telarian began to hack at the slab of force choking the Well, his laughter mounting in manic peals.

When she'd last seen Nangulis, tears rendered the world blurry and uncertain. As she perceived the human form stepping forward, as if out of the shadow of the conjoined blades, tears spilled anew from her wondering eyes, painting her surroundings in foggy striations of white, black, and red. Flashes of apocalyptic light, screams of pain, and a diabolical mirth echoing through the Throat faded from Kiril's perception. The concerns of the corporeal world were gone. She saw only the man to whom she'd once pledged her undying love. He who had just emerged from the conjoined sword.

Did she dream?

The figure turned his head and stammered, "Kiril, is that you? Where are we? I can't remember . . ."

Though her lips didn't move, she replied, joyfully, "Yes! I am here! Waiting for you. I've always waited for you. But after your sacrifice . . ." After his sacrifice, she'd known he was lost forever, a knowledge she drowned in alcohol. A knowledge which was now proved a lie!

Nangulis moved to her. He kneeled and took her hands in his. They were warm and vibrant. He asked, "What sacrifice?"

She squeezed, desperately returning the pressure of his grip. "Does it matter? You've returned to me, against all hope! Your sundered soul has finally been merged . . ." She frowned, briefly recalling the conjoined sword Angul-Nis. Why had Telarian gone to such elaborate trouble to bring the blades together? She doubted he wished merely to liberate Nangulis from the fractured pieces as a gift to her . . . she willfully pushed those thoughts away.

"My soul?" questioned Nangulis. "I recall pain, then nothing. I remember . . . coming to Stardeep. Yes! You were so beautiful in the starshine, so happy. We took up our duties. We served the Sign . . ."

"Remember how we used to laugh each night, after our duties, when we talked about the events of the day together?" asked Kiril, a blushing joy growing in her that she hadn't experienced in more than a decade. She was tempted to forget all else and drown within the moment. Nangulis was returned to her!

"How could I forget?" responded Nangulis. "You were my Bright Star, and I your Far Traveler." Tears streaked Kiril's cheeks as Nangulis recalled the pet names they'd used. They'd given each other the appellations after two lovelorn characters described in Sildëyuir myth. The story recounted the unbreakable bonds between two elder elves parted by events and even centuries, but who found a way to return to each other in the end. Two constellations in Sildëyuir's sky were called by the same names.

Kiril spoke, "You are my Far Traveler yet, Nangulis. You've

come farther than I ever imagined—you've come back from death itself to find me."

Nangulis released one of her hands to wipe away another streaking tear from her cheek. "Don't cry, Bright Star."

"I cry because I am happy," she explained.

"As am I . . . yet my recollection is blurred. You spoke of sacrifice and death . . ." He shook his head, confusion evident in his expression.

"Let us not speak of such dark things," urged Kiril. She had eyes only for the man before her. All around them, shapes moved, staggered, fought, and perhaps died. She ignored them as best she was able. Nangulis deserved her wholehearted attention.

Raidon Kane opened his eyes on chaos. He lay in a mirrored, many-walled chamber. Lying atop him was a faintly groaning Knight. He pushed the figure off and stood. He saw first Kiril, kneeling and apparently lost in some fell enchantment, for she seemed unconcerned that not ten paces from her, the Keeper Telarian wielded a blade of fire and darkness. With it he hacked at some invisible shape that overlay a central pit illuminated from beneath. His mother's forget-me-not, still clutched in Raidon's hand, twitched as if pained with Telarian's every blow.

He had triggered a transfer, but what had happened since?

He started toward Kiril, intending to shake her out of her odd daze. Running, his gaze took in another star elf female he didn't recognize. Was this Delphe, the betrayer Kiril and Telarian had spoken with? She lay on the floor not far from Telarian, clutching one mutilated hand with the other. Had the mad Keeper been dispatched so easily? Raidon's intuition was confused. His attention had been so focused on using his forget-me-not to effect a transfer into the Throat that he hadn't paid heed to Kiril and Delphe's conversation in the tunnel.

Telarian's unrestrained laughter and wild swings with a weapon whose every slash made Raidon's skin prickle was . . . worrisome. Had this Keeper also fallen to the Traitor's control?

He took another step and something stirred at his feet. He recoiled before he recognized the supine, smoking shape of Xet. The dragonet rotated its head to fix him with an entreating glance. Its mouth moved, and a single plaintive tone emerged.

Raidon reached down and stroked the creature's muzzle. Then he picked up the tiny thing. He carried Xet and set it down before the kneeling swordswoman. In Sildëyuir, the monk recalled how Kiril had revealed a strong affection for Xet—perhaps seeing it would snap her from her trance.

"Kiril, wake and see me," urged Raidon. "What transpired here? Should I oppose the remaining Keeper?"

A moment of quiet drew the monk's attention to the lip of the Well. The diviner stepped back just as something burst up from the cavity, dissolving whatever invisible cap Telarian had been working to destroy.

The figure emerged as if a ballista bolt, grazing the ceiling at the top of its arc. It came down hard on bent legs where Telarian had just stood. The entire floor shuddered under the impact. It was a statue, akin to those they'd seen in the tunnels, but larger, and splashed with ichor and gore, as if the construct were fresh from battle.

Telarian addressed the construct. "Cynosure, your time as Stardeep's warden is complete. Loose the bonds, so I can eradicate the Traitor."

A voice replied, coming not from the statue but from somewhere high on the ceiling. "Telarian, you've fallen to insanity.

Killing him will conclude his Final Pact of Apoapsis—a passage will be opened to the Abolethic Sovereignty! Xxiphu would rise!"

"Yes! It is destined to rise—the future is set!" screamed Telarian, nearly spitting with hysteria. "Unless I divert it here and now!"

If Raidon held any question whether Telarian had succumbed to lunacy, he had his answer.

"The future is ever changeable—each new day is a chance to alter fate. Don't mistake your false visions for reality," counseled Cynosure.

"To prevent atrocity, I must commit it," replied the diviner nonsensically. "You, more than anyone, must understand, Cynosure, you who helped me construct the Epoch Chamber. I do understand destiny can be altered—and since it was given to me and me alone to see so far into the future, fate is mine to shape! When a passage to Xxiphu forms over the Traitor's corpse, I shall travel it, ahead of the Traitor's spirit. With Angul-Nis in hand, I shall slay the Eldest, Xxiphu's sentinel who sits on all the abolethic city as if a throne!"

The construct shook its head. "You are deluded, Telarian—even if the combined power of Angul and Nis could slay the Eldest before he consumed you, the city would wake from the violence of your act. It would rise! What fell visions have so deceived you?"

The diviner sputtered then screamed, "I am the only one who can safeguard Sildëyuir, nay, all Faerûn, from the Sovereignty's return from its millennial sleep! I am not deceived, I am the lone true prophet of tomorrow!"

"No, Telarian. Your predictions are corrupted, likely by the Traitor himself, whose apocalyptic dreams insinuate every chamber of Stardeep. Even your Epoch Chamber. How can you be sure it was not the Traitor's aim that Nis be forged, not your own? How can you be sure that your current plan isn't the Traitor's plot, now guided by the nihilistic Blade Umbral?"

Raidon tried once more to rouse Kiril. The swordswoman remained absorbed in a private vision. He turned and prepared himself to charge the distracted diviner. Even as he did so, Telarian's head jerked to fix him with a rabid gaze, saying, "Angul-Nis sees you," before turning back to regard the construct.

Telarian, suddenly calm, said, "I've spilled too much blood following this course, construct. I shall not stop now. Step aside, or be destroyed."

Cynosure replied, "Lay down your weapon, or I shall wrest it from you." Even as Telarian composed a reply, the golem advanced a pace and punched with such speed even Raidon, for all his training, barely registered the blow. Telarian and Angul-Nis were equally unprepared. Elf and blade winged across the Throat, covering thirty paces without even skimming the floor. The diviner's form smashed into one of the great mirrors that tiled the many-walled chamber, shattering it into a thousand flashing shards.

Raidon expected the construct to follow up its advantage, but instead, it moved to the female Keeper's side in two large steps. Cynosure's voice from above said, "Delphe, we have but moments—accept this healing and ward the Well. I shall deal with Telarian." The construct touched the fallen woman's mutilated hand. There came a blue flash and a scream of agony from Delphe, but the construct was already moving toward the shattered mirror.

Not a moment too soon. Telarian retained his grip on Angul-Nis. As the man stood, a wave of ebon-tinged fire from the blade swept out, creating a wind of broken glass that left his wounds healed. The elf laughed as he advanced to join battle with the hulking construct.

A woman's voice came, "Aid me, Sign-bearer!" Raidon's

gaze jerked back to Delphe, who was standing, gesturing at him with a hand pink and uncallused like baby's flesh.

Raidon dashed to Delphe's side. He clutched his forget-me-not in his left hand. From it, a sky blue radiance leaked. She had called him the Sign-bearer . . .

Delphe pointed at two ebon-spiked tentacles scrabbling up and over the lip of the Well. She yelled, "The Traitor sends avatars to aid his pawn. Your Sign will provide some protection."

One spike plunged into the stone around the Well, while the other emitted a cloudy green beam aimed at Delphe. Following some unconscious instinct, Raidon intersected the beam's path with his amulet. His Sign flared and the beam guttered out.

Delphe said, "We must slay the avatar before it grows strong enough to summon the Traitor! Even as we speak, it fortifies itself . . ."

Raidon stepped toward the lip. He mentally plunged a questing tip of his focus into the amulet, seeking the inner core of power he'd discovered earlier. Fire woke in his hand then flowed up his arm and face, down his shoulders, chest, and opposite arm. His eyes sparkled like sapphires.

A silvery, sleek shape the size of a man pulled itself from the Well. Raidon stepped forward and connected with three solid cross-kicks, each as punishing a strike as he had ever delivered. With each hit, he heard the sound of breaking bones and bursting organs within the creature. It flinched, yet did not fall.

Behind him, Delphe chanted. Bolts of electricity singed the creature's flesh, releasing a burning, putrid odor that nearly stopped Raidon's breath.

Her bolts carved fist-sized pockets from the amorphous creature, yet it did not fall. Indeed, it seemed to swell after each burst. Raidon attempted to backhand it with the fist clutching the Sign, but an armlike appendage blocked. He slapped the appendage down with his free hand, and surfed his striking hand straight into the creature's torso. Gangrenous fluid burst forth, splashing the monk and burning his skin like acid.

"Recall when we found the bush in the snow, laden with spring berries?" asked Kiril. Another of her treasured moments shared with Nangulis. If she could reconnect with him, perhaps the sundered halves of his spirit would permanently merge . . .

"Yes. But other memories are beginning to resolve, of . . . being confined, unmoving sometimes, but other times unleashed to wreak retribution?"

"Let's not talk of that—"

"No, Kiril, we must talk of it, and you must help me. A great gulf of darkness stretches back from just prior to this moment. A gulf from which images I do not understand assail me."

"Nangulis . . ."

He squeezed her hand. "Please, Kiril. If you spare me whatever truth you're withholding, how can I ever be whole?"

The swordswoman wavered. She looked into Nangulis's eyes. How could she deny him anything? Perhaps, once the truth was revealed, they could leave this place and begin anew together.

"Listen, then. I have not the strength to repeat myself. The darkness that clouds your recollection is a ten-year gap during which a portion of your essence resided in the Blade Cerulean. The blade I wielded to beat back the Traitor whose escape was imminent." New tears seeped from her eyes. With her free hand, she scrubbed at them.

He cocked his head, his eyes narrowing. "Yes . . . yes!

The soul-forged blade! We had no choice. A purified soul to act as a lens that would focus the Cerulean Sign's duty like nothing else. I volunteered. And . . ." His eyes found hers. "Did we succeed?"

"Yes."

"Then why do you cry?"

"Because you were taken from me, and my life disintegrated!"

"Then how is this conversation possible?" wondered Nangulis. His eyes strayed from Kiril, but failed to focus on anything external. He said, "I see nothing but darkness—only you are lit. Where are we?"

"We are in the Throat, and the Blade Cerulean has joined with the unused portion of your soul! From that union, your spirit emerged, or its memory . . ." Kiril trailed off, confused. The image of Nangulis before her couldn't sense his surroundings, but she could, if she chose. Even with just her peripheral awareness, she knew the mad Keeper Telarian yet wielded the conjoined blade Angul-Nis. Which meant Nangulis's soul wasn't actually free of its soulblade confinement.

"You said we succeeded in stopping the Traitor."

"Ten years ago, but now—"

"And now . . . ?" Nangulis prodded.

"Now we are called again to defend Stardeep. The Traitor stirs, and his agent this time is nothing less than a deluded Keeper!"

"Then I must go back into that gulf of unknowing darkness?"

"I . . . perhaps if we . . ."

Nangulis said nothing, merely looked into her eyes, trusting her. It was her decision. She knew he'd accept whatever course of action she suggested. A hollow bloomed in her heart so vacuous she thought her chest would collapse. Her body knew; if she didn't relinquish Nangulis, ask his higher spirit to retreat to the blade physically housing it, Telarian's scheme would succeed.

"Nangulis, you know I love you, and I always—" Her voice broke, but she continued, "I always will. Know that. Know that if . . . when you leave me again . . ." She sobbed, unable to verbalize how she imagined her life would cease.

She said instead, "Cynosure's statue in the Throat just fell to Telarian."

"What must I do?"

"Return to the dark gulf. You must return to the sword. Find Angul! Find him, and yourself in him—pull away from all that is dark, undecided, and nihilistic. Be Angul again . . ." A sob escaped her, breaking her soliloquy.

The shade before her said, "I don't fear to return—the sacrifice was already made. I merely thank the guardians of Sildëyuir and the Sign that we were given this moment. Remember me, Kiril Duskmourn."

As Nangulis turned away, she murmured, "Until the day I die."

Telarian grasped a font of puissance, wondrous and overwhelming. He couldn't contain his joy as he wielded the conjoined blades. He'd never felt so free, so alive, so compelling. It was intoxicating!

He would have jumped and yelled in triumph if not for Cynosure. It had landed a strong initial blow, but Angul-Nis wiped away the damage before the crumpling pain could propagate through his flesh. His shredded clothing revealed fresh scars twining his forearms. He laughed—emblems of his coming triumph!

His eyes found the construct as it finished healing Delphe. He frowned. It charged him, one hand out as if to embrace him in a grasping palm. The idol moved swiftly for something that should have been slow and ponderous. But Angul-Nis revealed what Telarian must do. He thrust the blade forward cross-body, its tip down, deflecting the fist to the right and scoring it with flame.

The construct pulled its hand back, but not quickly enough to prevent Telarian from whipping Angul-Nis around and delivering a tremendous stroke to its wrist, severing the hand.

"Telarian, you are misled," came Cynosure's voice. "Can't you see it? The Traitor has you in its grip. You do not hinder him; you aid his greatest hope!"

Telarian suspected Stardeep's warden attempted to distract him. It knew it couldn't stand up to the wielder of Angul-Nis. He laughed, advancing. Delphe and Cynosure truly believed he was misled. Their lack of imagination and foresight was the reason he'd been forced to act alone. They were the ones responsible for aiding the Traitor by their opposition to his plan. Through their policies, if left unchecked, Xxiphu would eventually rise. They would never have allowed him to release the Traitor to his death—they would have argued that few alive could stand against him. True. But with Angul-Nis, few things were impossible.

He swung the conjoined blade in a scything whirlwind. Cynosure couldn't retreat quickly enough, and was caught in the blade-vortex. An explosion of blue-white flames and stone shrapnel heralded the statue's dissolution. So much for Stardeep's security.

To Telarian's right, the monk wielded an amulet of the Sign as if a cestus. With Delphe's aide, he was successfully staving off a Well-born avatar—a dream of the Traitor's hope of freedom. By the same token, the avatar, with its evolving form, firmly focused Delphe and the Sign-wielding monk away from him. Telarian's path to the Well was unimpeded. He walked to the edge and peered down.

All the previous times he'd glanced into the Well, he'd seen only empty space, and at the bottom, fire. With the conjoined blade in hand, he saw deeper, heard clearer, and understood more. Tentacular shadows streamed up the well, thick as sea grass. Abolethic melodies brooded and cajoled, swelling into a chaotic babble of sound that clawed at his certainty of purpose. Visibly containing and constraining the horror were the chains of Stardeep's bonds, those which kept the Traitor secure. Bonds that could be severed.

He saw where he must cut to end the Traitor's confinement. Even as understanding flooded him, Angul-Nis bucked and shuddered in his hand. He fumbled the blade and nearly dropped it down the Well.

Telarian swore, but retained his grasp on the blade. As his heartbeat stuttered in response to the slip that almost cost him everything, he appreciated what had just occurred. Fusing the two blades had also joined the two halves of Nangulis's spirit. The man, though formless, remained a Keeper of the Cerulean Sign. Somehow, despite having no physical shell in which to observe the world, Nangulis had learned what transpired in the Throat, and sought to oppose him in the only way he was able. Nangulis sought to rupture his own temporary existence by throwing himself back into dissolution. He was trying to break himself in two.

He would fail, decided Telarian. The conjoined blade enjoyed a power fueled by two soul halves, but the consciousness of the conjoined soul had little power over the blades. Nangulis's return was a surprising new element, certainly, but one with no ability to affect its physical shell, Angul-Nis. He was merely a ghost without form, a will without the ability to achieve an end.

The diviner laughed. While he wielded Angul-Nis, the blades would remain conjoined. Nis was more than a tool; it was also a trap. "Fight all you want," he whispered, "it'll do no good. I'll not let you go." Telarian tightened his grip and once more fixed his gaze into the swirling abyss before him.

The ethereal chains remained visible to him, five in all. The chains secured the Well, and the Traitor's ultimate prison. With Angul-Nis, he began to cut them. He sawed through the first one, and the swaying shadows choking the shaft increased the pace of their obscene undulation. The babble only his ears apprehended doubled in volume.

He sliced through the second phantom chain and paused. Something shrieked far down in the Well, something that had clawed at the boundary layer far past the limits of sanity.

The diviner smashed the third chain to shrapnel. A stroke like lightning leaped up the Well and shook all Stardeep. The light glared off the faces of Delphe, her mouth open in a hopeless shout, and the Sign-wielding monk, whose efforts were overcoming the avatar. Too late.

Something stirred in the Well's bowels, a shadow anticipating its release. A shadow that no longer retained elven shape, but instead pulsed with blasphemous abnormality. He was the High Priest of the Elder Ones, first servant of the vanished Abolethic Sovereignty, who had looked up the Well for a thousand years, who had tasted the blood of his betrayed kin, who sought to lead all star elves to extinction, and who was cast out of Sildëyuir for eternity. He sought to awaken the slumbering lords of Xxiphu from their lair in the nethermost craters of the deep earth. He was the Traitor. And in another few moments, Telarian would end the Traitor's life on the edge of—

"Remember me?" came a half-familiar voice behind Telarian as heart-stopping pain blossomed in the diviner's kidney. "Your spy returns for his payment!"

Angul-Nis slipped free from his spasming hands. "No!" Telarian lurched forward, windmilling for a grip on the sword spinning free above the Well.

The conjoined sword flared, emitting a burst of energy

black on one side, blue on the other. Then two blades fell away from each other. "No!" screamed Telarian, leaning forward.

Angul fell just three feet, tip downward, and knifed into the lip, and there remained quivering.

Nis tumbled free past the lip and down the Well. The diviner fell to his chest, extending half his body out over the lip as he made one final try to snare the Blade Umbral. But as he strained forward and down, someone kicked him savagely from behind. A terrible sensation of weightlessness sank into his stomach. Overbalanced, he slipped over the edge.

Nis and Telarian fell, Telarian screaming in dismay and mounting fear, Nis tracing a blur of darkness in its wake. Elf and sword flashed past the flickering shadow, past the burning boundary layer, and into the presence of the Traitor.

The High Priest of the Abolethic Sovereignty studied its mortal agent. It had expended so much energy molding and shaping the elf's mind. But the elf had failed, and with his fall into the Well, was rendered valueless. The sword Nis, whose creation was the culmination of a plan initiated with Angul's forging, stood embedded blade-first in the floor of the cell, smoldering . . . fading. Even as the Traitor attempted to bring his shackled hands near enough to the hilt to grasp it, to plunge it into his own heart . . . it smoked away, its half-soul finally and utterly extinguished. In this prison, there was no afterlife to accept it.

Only Telarian remained, now bound as the Traitor was bound, in chains of eldritch force. Unlike the Traitor, Telarian was subject to the needs of air and nutrition. Given enough pain, his heart would fail.

The Traitor concentrated on the blinking, confused diviner whose mind had proved so ripe for instruction. A mind still open to suggestion, capable of seeing a higher reality, a reality beyond the physical. Though the Traitor couldn't touch the diviner, he could influence the diviner's mind. What the Keeper believed to be real would be real. It was the malleable reality he had hoped to extend to all the world with the Abolethic Sovereignty's rise. For now, that reality was reserved for one.

The elf screamed as the Traitor extended a nest of writhing, tooth-rimmed appendages.

Failure demanded payment.

He began to extract his due.

Chapter Twenty-Nine

Stardeep, Throat

Gage was entranced by the fiery depths of the hollow cylinder. Empty but for an explosion of flaring, frustrated prominences. He turned and sheathed a blood-stained dagger. Backstabbing the insane elf and pushing him into the hole earned him a moment's respite. He removed his borrowed Knight's helmet. Kiril, apparently roused from whatever stupor had held her, appraised him with obvious surprise.

Her expression was every bit as bewildered and confused as he'd hoped. He grinned—priceless! You couldn't steal that kind of satisfaction.

"Gage of Laothkund—how?" asked Kiril. "I left you in the Yuirwood."

"Aye, but I didn't turn back as you instructed. I followed."

"Why?"

The thief grinned. "I was angry you sent me away, angry you wouldn't listen or accept my apology. I decided I would show my sincerity by helping you whether you wanted my aid or not."

"You followed us into Sildëyuir, and then into Stardeep's

outer tunnels? That must have been difficult."

"An understatement," replied Gage. He recalled again the stone spider, and he shuddered.

Kiril nodded, moved closer, and put a comradely hand on his shoulder. "Thank you . . ." Her attention shifted, and lit on the guttering blade Angul. Her eyes became glassy.

"Kiril Duskmourn!" came a glad hail. Gage and the swordswoman turned. The lone remaining Keeper approached, the monk Raidon at her side holding his lambent Sign.

The Keeper said, "I am Delphe. Thank the Cerulean Sign you listened to my plea."

Kiril shrugged. "Telarian's failure of patience revealed him. If he hadn't attacked me with Nis, I might have appeared in the Throat as his ally, not his enemy. He didn't know that, though, and your arguments made him doubt the strength of his own lies."

Delphe replied, "His lies . . . his subversion by the Traitor is Stardeep's most significant failure in all our order's history. And all along, he thought he was the one serving a higher purpose. An unbelievable tragedy." She sighed and ran a hand through her hair. Light from the Well blossomed orange and green, giving her skin a pallid cast.

Delphe moved closer and looked down. "I wonder what's going on down there . . . Cynosure?"

"Yes, Delphe?" The response emanated from the empty ceiling.

"The boundary layer is disturbed. How close did Telarian come to achieving his goal?"

"Too close. We must forge anew the constraints the diviner severed, else we risk the remaining bonds becoming unraveled."

Delphe looked at her newly healed hand and muttered, "A difficult task without my most potent tool—"

"You may borrow this, if you require its strength,"

interrupted Raidon, holding out his Sign. "It was my mother's, though now I begin to doubt she was ever a Keeper here. It may be she had it illicitly, and passed it to me without knowledge of your order."

Delphe smiled. "Whoever she was or is, I hold no grudge—if she hadn't possessed it to give to you, things would have concluded differently just now."

Raidon nodded.

"In any event," continued Delphe, "I am not attuned to it, but I can instruct you how to wield it in the manner required to refortify the Traitor's prison. You seem adept in its use, even without wizardly training, which is impressive and unusual."

"Thank you. I would enjoy learning more of the Sign. Perhaps through it, I can learn of my mother's fate."

The Keeper led Raidon around the curve of the lip toward the crystal command chair. She began to speak of visualizations, sigils, and interfaces. Gage stopped paying attention. His eyes lit on another fallen form.

"Your pet is hurt," he observed.

Kiril's head jerked around to scan the Throat. Concern tightened her eyes when she saw Xet's unmoving shape. She rushed to the dragonet's side and gently picked up the crystalline creature, now blackened and pitted.

"Xet?"

No movement.

"Gods damn you, you're not even really alive, so you can't die!"

The dragonet's tail suddenly wrapped about Kiril's cradling arm. A weak but audible bell tolled. The swordswoman looked up at Gage and let out a relieved breath.

Another bell-like tone sounded, stronger than the first.

"Where did you get the little guy?" wondered Gage, as he moved to rub the creature beneath the chin. The dragonet arched its neck upward like a cat.

"A geomancer employed me as his bodyguard for nearly a decade. When I left his service, Xet was his parting gift."

Gage nodded and asked, "Thormund, right? Too bad you left his employ. You wouldn't have had to go through all this . . ."

He regretted his remark the moment the last word was out of his mouth. Kiril's animation faded as her eyes riveted once more on the cooling sword plunged in the stone floor.

"Angul looks more peaceful than I ever recall seeing him," she murmured.

Cynosure's voice interrupted. "Angul is now as he was when first forged. Being split from Nis, the two halves of Nangulis's spirit are again divided. As before, Angul requires a wielder's touch to kindle his motivation."

Kiril said softly, "I remember now . . ."

Cynosure persisted. "Angul's life is only a half-life. Without a living wielder, the soul-forged blade will fail, releasing the soul to its final peace. All that will remain is a dead length of sword-shaped steel."

The swordswoman gasped, her hands tightening on Xet, who belled a small sound of displeasure. Yet she moved no closer to the grounded blade. The sword darkened further even as they watched. If Kiril didn't take Angul in hand soon, the Blade Cerulean would pass away.

Which would be a good outcome, Gage decided. Wielding a blade whose aspirations were too pure for real life had ruined the woman's life, destroyed her sense of self-worth, and driven her from the order to which she had once pledged undying loyalty. The world didn't work in black and white, and every time Angul forced Kiril down too narrow a moral path, she regretted it the very instant she sheathed the blade. It was a wonder, really, that Kiril hadn't ended her life long ago. Although such an act would have been judged unrighteous by the blade she bore. Perhaps she had not been allowed such an option. The thought chilled the thief, and he rubbed his hands together.

"I do not know . . ." said Kiril.

"Leave it," urged Gage.

"I should walk away," agreed the swordswoman. "I should relinquish Angul so Nangulis can discover, at long last, his final rest. With Nis beyond reach, no hope whatever remains that Nangulis can ever be returned to me—half his essence has fallen into the Well. From that separation, there can be no returning."

Unless the Traitor is finally freed, Gage thought, but didn't say.

Cynosure's voice came. "You have borne a burden past enduring for too many years. Let it go now. With Nis gone, the Traitor's best hope of freeing himself is also past. No one would think ill of you, least of all me, who aided you and Nangulis in forging the blade. Let it be. You deserve a life more urbane than fleeing deeds ill-done in the name of an unattainable standard of good."

Kiril watched Angul guttering and nodded, now freely but silently crying. She turned to Gage, handing him Xet. "Take him for a bit, won't you? I'll say my good-byes to Angul, and Nangulis, as I should have done ten years ago when the Traitor was first contained."

The thief nodded and accepted the slight burden of the dragonet.

Kiril moved to stand before the blade, her head down. Suddenly cognizant of her mumbled words addressed to the blade, Gage moved to join Delphe and Raidon by the crystal command chair.

Raidon listened as the star elf told him how to use his mother's forget-me-not, and was astounded. It possessed abilities deeper than he had imagined. Yet as she spoke, the larger part of him was more interested in Delphe than in her message.

For she was a star elf, and unlike Kiril, not hardened and molded by a decade of self-effacing hate. He imagined she might be something like his mother . . .

He imagined her then, someone not unlike Delphe, but with darker hair and moonlight shining on it, standing in a grove of sighing trees in Sildëyuir. From musicians unseen came elven songs, and wafting on the warm air the scent of sweet elven wine. She who the Edgewarden had named Erunyauvë. What was her story?

Delphe paused, said, "Are you listening, Raidon? To strengthen the boundary layer at the Well's bottom requires concentration and focus."

Raidon gave a slight smile, saying, "I was distracted, but please proceed. I have understood all you have so far explained. You were describing how, when imagining the three-dimensional likeness of the Sign, your mind can call forth the amulet's full powers."

"Yes, that's right," replied Delphe, somewhat mollified.

The image he'd constructed of Erunyauvë returned. On her chest lay the amulet she'd given Raidon. She smiled, and in that expression he saw a promise. She would explain her departure when their joyful reunion occurred, soon now. Having visited Sildëyuir, he wanted to return to where starry skies glistened and day's harsh light never burned. A place where he could discover the truth of his origin.

In Sildëyuir, he would learn Erunyauvë's true reason for leaving him, and her supernatural percipience in gifting him with the one object required to stem a primeval threat. To see so far into the future, she must command a considerable talent. But what a lonely power, too. If one saw the future so clearly, would destiny seem too rigid a road, a fate so certain that neither luck nor intervention could hope to alter fortune or misfortune alike? Perhaps such a choice faced Telarian . . .

Raidon swept speculation about Erunyauvë from his mind, and concentrated exclusively on Delphe's lilting voice.

Kiril watched Angul flickering, dimming with each heartbeat. Without her touch to enliven the half-soul, the Blade Cerulean's fires would fail. All her personal angst and troubles, tied directly to the blade, would cease, or at least no longer continue to grow. She could finally get on with her life. An image of her enchanted whisky flask appeared in her mind's eye. "No, I wouldn't . . ." She hoped she wouldn't.

Was Angul so much to give up? He was not Nangulis, after all—he was only a distorted image of Nangulis's overriding conviction, purpose, and duty as a Keeper. Angul, for all his power to destroy aberrations, was also a self-proclaimed justicar of all that was *right,* rather than a solver of problems. As Kiril had learned early in her career as Angul's wielder, such certitude can quickly lend itself to *right's* opposite. She'd cursed the blade enough, blaming Angul for her long exile from Stardeep and her lapse as a Keeper of the Cerulean Sign. The blade was anathema to her. Her chance to forget required only that she turn away.

The memory of Nangulis kneeling before her, his palm on her face, flashed before her. The warmth of his hand still haunted her cheek, he had touched her so recently; or his shade had. Did it matter? More importantly, could she truly live without him? Could she gainsay Angul, the last remnant of the love of someone who meant more to her than her own miserable life?

Leave him, she commanded herself. If she touched the guttering blade, she would be lost—the only opportunity she'd ever have to be shut of Angul's temerity was now before her. Who knows what future pain she might inflict upon herself and others as a thrall to the blade's righteousness?

No, better to walk away from the lip, bid him . . .

Good-bye.

"Farewell, Nangulis . . ." Her head fell as she imagined the rest of the day, the rest of the month, and the remainder of the year. She attempted to picture the rest of her life, however long it might stretch into the gray, lonely future.

A desolate cry broke from Kiril Duskmourn. She sprang forward, reaching for the Blade Cerulean's hilt. With a tug, the blade was free from the stone. Fire bloomed, sky blue and joyous. Angul burned anew and gladly in her loving grip. Angul's clarity of reason fell across her like a warm blanket. It was like . . . coming home.

"Angul," she whispered, her face transfigured. "I missed you."

FORGOTTEN REALMS®

THOMAS M. REID

The author of *Insurrection* and The Scions of Arrabar Trilogy rescues Aliisza and Kaanyr Vhok from the tattered remnants of their assault on Menzoberranzan, and sends them off on a quest across the multiverse that will leave FORGOTTEN REALMS® fans reeling!

THE EMPYREAN ODYSSEY

BOOK I

THE GOSSAMER PLAIN

Kaanyr Vhok, fresh from his defeat against the drow, turns to hated Sundabar for the victory his demonic forces demand, but there's more to his ambitions than just one human city. In his quest for arcane power, he sends the alu-fiend Aliisza on a mission that will challenge her in ways she never dreamed of.

BOOK II

THE FRACTURED SKY

A demon surrounded by angels in a universe of righteousness? How did that become Aliisza's life?

November 2008

BOOK III

THE CRYSTAL MOUNTAIN

What Aliisza has witnessed has changed her forever, but that's nothing compared to what has happened to the multiverse itself. The startling climax will change the nature of the cosmos forever.

Mid-2009

"Reid is proving himself to be one of the best up and coming authors in the FORGOTTEN REALMS universe."

—fantasy-fan.org

RICHARD A. KNAAK

THE OGRE TITANS

The Grand Lord Golgren has been savagely crushing all opposition to his control of the harsh ogre lands of Kern and Blöde, first sweeping away rival chieftains, then rebuilding the capital in his image. For this he has had to deal with the ogre titans, dark, sorcerous giants who have contempt for his leadership.

VOLUME ONE

THE BLACK TALON

Among the ogres, where every ritual demands blood and every ally can become a deadly foe, Golgren seeks whatever advantage he can obtain, even if it means a possible alliance with the Knights of Solamnia, a questionable pact with a mysterious wizard, and trusting an elven slave who might wish him dead.

December 2007

VOLUME TWO

THE FIRE ROSE

With his other enemies beginning to converge on him from all sides, Golgren, now Grand Khan of all his kind, must battle with the Ogre Titans for mastery of a mysterious artifact capable of ultimate transformation and power.

December 2008

VOLUME THREE

THE GARGOYLE KING

Forced from the throne he has so long coveted, Golgren makes a final stand for control of the ogre lands against the Titans . . . against an enemy as ancient and powerful as a god.

December 2009

EBERRON®

Land of intrigue.
Towering cities where murder is business.
Dark forests where hunters are hunted.
Ground where the dead never rest.

To find the truth takes a special breed of hero.

THE INQUSITIVES

BOUND BY IRON
Edward Bolme

Torn by oaths to king and country, one man must unravel a tapestry of murder and slavery.

NIGHT OF THE LONG SHADOWS
Paul Crilley

During the longest nights of the year, worshipers of the dark rise from the depths of the City of Towers to murder . . . and worse.

LEGACY OF WOLVES
Marsheila Rockwell

In the streets of Aruldusk, a series of grisly murders has rocked the small city. The gruesome nature of the murders spawns rumors of a lycanthrope in a land where the shapeshifters were thought to have been hunted to extinction.

THE DARKWOOD MASK
Jeff LaSala

A beautiful Inquisitive teams up with a wanted vigilante to take down a crimelord who hides behind a mask of deceit, savage cunning, and sorcery.

November 2008